DEADLY HOPE

ORDER OF THADDEUS
BOOK 10

J. A. BOUMA

PROLOGUE

MILL CREEK JUNCTION, MICHIGAN.
PRESENT DAY.

Summer had come early to Mill Creek Junction after a long, bitter freeze—bringing with it an unexpected surprise.

Spring had just begun to spring, and yet temperatures were already rising into the 70s, the warm air inviting flowering shrubs and trees to share their wares with the world and send out blooming scents of honeysuckle and jasmine, mingled with fresh-cut grass and the earthy spice of an awakening world from winter's slumber. The critters sure loved Mother Nature's gift, all manner of four-legged creatures scampering about with delight and birds singing their joyous songs of approval.

Not Peter Daniel Young. He was in a foul mood. Thanks to the new invasive species brought on by the promise of abundant-life blessing.

He slammed his hand down on top of his mug trying to stay the ringed perturbations rippling out in his mid-morning coffee from the quiet rumbles outside his office window, the heavenly scent of lightly roasted Rwandan beans riding on an updraft of air from the force of it all—but doing nothing to settle his own perturbations that had been rippling out in his head all morning.

It was a handcrafted clay thing painted a muddy green-brown with a raised Michigan mitten on the front. Something his café-owning girlfriend Lexi had given him when he started his new job last year at Mill Creek Baptist Church. Already had a crack running down its gullet after a misplaced legal pad sent it tumbling to the floor one morning on a day much like that one doing research for his Sunday morning sermon. Superglue did the trick, and it'd been his ministry companion the past year.

But those darn ripples had messed up that ministry thanks to a competitor who had set up shop at the other end of town.

Peeling back his hand, Peter checked for success, hoping he'd stayed the ripples and could get back to his work.

Warm yellow light from a banker's lamp peeking behind a stack of books hit the inside of his mug just so—throwing up a frown across Peter's face at the ongoing perturbations inside.

More from annoyance than anything, wanting to sip his brew in peace while prepping for the sermon coming due in a few short days. But if he was honest with himself, it was also from a bit of envy worming through his heart, given what those ripples meant.

It was like that moment in the movie *Jurassic Park*, when the thumpy bass flairs up the same rings of doom in the rainwater that's settled inside a massive T-Rex footprint—signaling the same doom from the massive resurrected theropod muscling itself through the jungle on its way to finding a tasty snack hiding out in a Ford Explorer stopped for no good reason right before a bloody goat leg comes flying at your moonroof!

Only this time, it was a massive charter bus muscling through Mill Creek Junction, the small Midwest town that had become Peter's home the past year after finishing graduate school training to be a minister. He'd taken up the post of lead pastor at the Junction's only Baptist church after its reverend retired—and his own version of T-Rex had been pushing through town all morning. Actually, a whole mess of them had been barreling off the interstate that sliced west across Michigan from Detroit, then rumbling down state Route 55 on toward the north-south main drag slicing through quintessential small-town America.

That wasn't the end of it.

Packed minivans and SUVs, compacts and sedans, even pickups had all joined the caravan of buses making their way down Main Street toward the fairgrounds at the north end of town. But it wasn't the county fair they were going to see, or a concert featuring the latest pimply faced one-hit wonder or geezer crooner well past retirement. Although, according to accounts flying around the WeShare social media platform, what was going on at the north end of the Junction was its own special kind of show.

The big tent revival kind.

With flashy lights and even flashier music, featuring a full-on rock band drawing in a crowd that defied demographics from across West Michigan to the spectacle and even beyond, featuring some traveling evangelists at the center. All of it in the name of the gospel, the good news of Jesus, regardless of the means.

Because why did those matter when the ends were justified, when souls were saved and the Holy Spirit himself had visited folks' paralyzed limbs and empty bank accounts?

Peter chanced another peek, frustration mounting at the gathering head of steam from the other end of town. Not to mention those rumbles messing with his morning coffee—brewed from beans roasted by his girlfriend, no less!

Same rippling perturbation thanks to those blasted coach buses barreling past his church up Main Street.

What's the saying? Insanity is doing the same thing over and over again and expecting different results.

Frowning, he mumbled, "I must be going crazy..." Then

promptly withdrew his hand and threw back a swig of brew, wincing at how lukewarm it had gotten. Jesus had chastised the Laodiceans for a lukewarm faith, and as far as Peter was concerned, the same chastisement held true for coffee.

But he leaned back and threw back another mouthful anyway, his taste buds bursting with the bright, citrusy, floral notes of the humble coffee bean from the Land of a Thousand Hills, his stomach churning with a disquiet dread at what the arrivals meant for him—for the Junction, even...

The door opened, interrupting his contemplation.

It was Katrina, a sweet-mannered woman in a pink flowery dress with gray curly hair and coke-bottle glasses, Peter's secretary. Reminded him more of his grandma than anyone who should be assisting a young buck in ministry like him. Not that he didn't need it; administration certainly wasn't his spiritual gift. He'd just felt weird when he started pastoring at Mill Creek Baptist bossing someone around who looked like the woman who slapped him around and set him straight his whole life. Wasn't fond of giving orders, but Katrina was more than willing to help out and put him on a good administrative footing. Even slapping him around a bit when he needed it—*especially* slapping him around a bit when he needed it!

"Hey, Kat," Peter said, the name he liked to call her. Usually made her giggle, because it made her sound forty years younger than she was.

Munching on a chocolate cupcake, Katrina threw up the giggle that usually set his mind at ease, her curls bouncing at her shoulders and her coke-bottle glasses sliding down her face. It helped, settling him some and reminding him he still had a flock of his own who needed his spiritual guidance—no matter what flashy new show had rolled into town.

"I'm going out for lunch," she said, pushing her glasses back up the bridge of her nose. "Want anything, dear?"

Peter waved her off, his mind drifting back up Main Street. "No, that's alright. Thanks, though."

Katrina frowned and put her hands on her hips. "Why so glum, Reverend? You look like death rolled over you!"

He almost corrected her, saying that *Peter* was just fine. Never could get used to the whole Reverend moniker. But he didn't. Knew that's what she knew, and that was fine.

Instead, he sighed and leaned forward, setting his mug back on his desk with a thud—and those darn ripples flaring up again.

He pointed at the thing and announced, "That. Right there."

Furrowing her brow, she took a hesitant step into his office, craning her neck over the piles of commentaries and stacks of folders full of scraps of paper.

"The Bible?" she exclaimed.

Peter startled, seeing the Good Book opened to the middle of Matthew's Gospel and his pen lying in its gutter. He took it and gestured outside before starting to chew the end of it.

Katrina glanced toward the shade-drawn window, a grunting rumble of something being thrown up on cue. "Are you talkin' about our visitors?"

He frowned, yanking the pen out of his mouth and throwing it back to his open Bible. "Do you know what those people are doing?"

Now she crossed her arms. "*Those* people? Last I heard, those people were *our* people. Good and godly brothers and sisters in the Lord."

He chuckled, then instantly regretted it. "Sorry, didn't mean to laugh. It's just...I'm not so sure what's going on up town is what I'd call good and godly. From what I hear, the ghosts of the 90s are calling for their pink-haired televangelists back!"

"Well, have you checked it out for yourself?"

Peter leaned back and frowned. No, he hadn't. Didn't need

to, as far as he was concerned. He'd heard this tune strummed before, and wanted nothing to do with it.

Katrina stood with folded arms, waiting for an answer.

"No," Peter conceded, cheeks warming some with embarrassment. "Not yet."

She shrugged. "Maybe you should instead of moping about it. And don't worry, dear. We ain't going anywhere! You're *our* pastor."

She tossed a half-eaten packet of her chocolate cupcakes on his desk, then threw him a wink and left. A familiar hum filtered back to him through his open office door as she left for lunch.

Peter reached for the cupcakes, but thought against it. Not hungry. He sat there listening to her leave, wondering if she might be right. Maybe he should go see for himself what the fuss was about. That way, at least he'd be able to have an educated discussion about what he thought might be happening with any of his congregants, or others in the Junction community for that matter.

Leaning forward, he muttered a complaint, "Always right, that one is..." Then he stood and followed her outside, wondering what was in store.

A cluster of cherry blossoms anchored to one side of the driveway stretching to Main Street were really starting to bloom now, their sweet scent helping him forget just a second why it was he was so irritated. The steady stream of cars reminded him, the line dwindling some from earlier, but still disconcerting—and disheartening. So he followed it, running through his head the events that led to Mill Creek hosting the blasted carnival that was sure to give him an aneurysm.

All of which led to the train of grunting, honking, shoving buses and cars making their way to the fairgrounds at the north end of the Junction. There was a new gig in town. A pair of twins, promising healing and hope for the desperate and downtrodden. Had rolled in and set up shop the past week, flattening the emerging weeds and grass from winter's slumber in the massive ground the size of three football fields and setting up a tent that would have rivaled P. T. Barnum.

Passing Millie's on Main diner, Peter chuckled to himself. Sounded about right, given what he figured would be going down inside the tent. And with how packed the favorite local joint was for lunch, looked like the circus had indeed come to town! Poor servers were dashing back and forth taking orders, and runners were balancing trays packed with food. The counter was just as packed with to-go orders as the main dining area. One thing's for certain, the carnival would be a cash cow for Mill Creek Junction, that's for sure.

"Pastorman!" a voice shouted at Peter from the alcove of a doorway.

Looking up, he smiled, catching sight of Max Blade dressed in what looked like a pirate costume. A wide-brimmed black hat stamped with a white scull-and-bones sat cockamamie on his head, and he was wearing a billowy white shirt with red-and-black striped pants. A stuffed bright-green parrot even sat on his shoulder.

Couldn't help but shake his head and laugh at the man.

"What in the world..."

Peter trotted toward Max standing outside his bar, Max's Place. A beat-up red Chevy pickup belched a bout of dark exhaust as it sped through the green light toward fairground destiny.

Max waved a hand in front of his scrunched-up face. "Sheesh! That'll shave half a decade off your life!"

Coughing, Peter gestured at the getup. "What the heck is this all about?"

He did a little jig and held out his hands. "Like it?"

"Sure, but I don't get it."

Max nodded toward the line of cars still snaking north. "If

people want to be plundered, parting with their hard-earned scratch to fill the coffers of some two-bit evangelists offering snake oil and holy water—figured, why not join the carnival barkers up the road in all the plundering fun!"

"When in Rome..."

Petting his stuffed parrot, Max grinned proudly. "Exactly."

Peter chuckled and slapped his back. "Ah, Max. Ever the thespian."

"Thespian?" Max exclaimed, spinning toward him with a scowl. "I'm as straight as they come, partner. Anywho, so what do you think of all this Christian fun?"

"First, it ain't Christian. Second—" Peter stopped himself before he said something he'd regret. Folded his arms, he went with, "—you don't wanna know what I think."

"Ahh, jealous, are we?"

"Am not!"

Max raised a brow. "Mmm-hmm. Whatever, pal. I know coveting eyes when I see 'em."

Peter went to raise another protest, but shut his mouth. Was it that obvious?

Envy and coveting had always been two sides to the same fatal-flaw coin for him. Especially when it came to professional accomplishments. As they say, numbers don't lie. And with the upstart prophets or apostles, the evangelists or whatever the heck they were calling themselves—they put his little bitty Baptist church to shame.

"Well, whatever's got your pastorman gander up in a tizzy," Max went on, stroking that parrot head of his again, "don't matter to me what those holy rollers do. So long as they come for a burger and a pint or four afterwards. Ordered up a slew of extra kegs to quench their Holy Ghost thirst."

Peter shook his head. "Sorry to break it to you, Max, but not sure these folks are the drinking type."

A squawking gasp escaped the man, even as his fake pirate

bird fell from his shoulders. He scrambled after it, questioning, "Are you sure about that, pastorman? Thought holy rollers were the drinkin' type."

"Yeah, pretty sure no."

Fetching his parrot, he let a curse slip. "Then what am I gonna do with all these kegs I just bought?"

Peter shrugged. "Don't know, Max, but I've gotta go."

Heading back up Main Street, he felt a little bad leaving the man to figure out a plan for his beer. Figured as the Junction's only bar, Max would work something out. Maybe Peter would take a keg or two off his hands after he saw for himself whatever was going on north of town.

The walk was several more blocks to the fairground, but it did Peter's legs and lungs good to get out into the sunshine and warm air—and his soul.

Max was right: He was jealous. Of the crowds of people flocking to the upstart church, the energy and Broadway-style show, of the young people, of the news it had been making around the area and reports of hope and healing on WeShare posts.

It was basically everything he had envisioned for himself while studying to be a pastor half an hour away at Grand River Theological Seminary. Yet all he had to show for himself was a small-town church of a hundred people, an out-of-tune piano and guitar, and a leaky roof that was in desperate need of repair. Farthest thing from the show attracting the line of cars belching more of that exhaust Max said would cut his life an eighth.

Nearing the edge of town, and end of the line, he took a breath and shook his head. None of that mattered. What did was getting to the bottom of what was happening in his town— what was happening *to* his town.

Lord, set my heart right; keep my eyes fixed on you, Jesus!

Peter heard it before he saw it. Felt it, even, before he heard it—the bass of the sound system pumping through the Junction air, joined with the cheering cries and singing of hundreds, even thousands of people packed under the big-top tent.

There it was.

Reaching the edge of town now, he spotted a sea of cars of all variety packing the fairgrounds with a massive tan canvas structure anchored at the center. Reminded him of the circus he visited as a kid. A cheer rose up along with the hook of a familiar worship chorus he'd heard on the radio by the band accompanying the evangelists. A maw of darkness stood at one end of the tent, people crowding inside and flickering with red and blue and green lighting. Music sounded like it had ended and someone was speaking now.

Heart picking up pace, Peter made for the entrance, wondering what he would find inside.

"...the dawning of a new wave of the Holy Spirit's descent upon the world!" a voice echoed throughout the vast hall from a stage at the center in a Southern twang.

From what Peter could tell, a man was speaking. Tall and fit, with broad shoulders and blond hair, wearing skinny dark jeans and a sloping V-neck shirt, a hand wearing a single white glove—one half of the act, apparently.

Another voice joined him, a woman: "So come, all y'all who are burdened by debt and disease, and find a new anointing in the Spirit—a blessing straight from the glory realm that is yours by right of the shed blood of Jesus Christ!"

Peter's stomach clenched with a mixture of dread and anger, the familiar verse from Matthew's Gospel being twisted by the man's partner as catnip to the desperate who had gathered under their big top for a blessing.

A chorus of ecstatic utterances erupted from the eager crowd primed for their message, a train of believers stretching down from the stage now and snaking around the perimeter of the tent. People on crutches, people in wheelchairs. Others looking frail and gaunt and held upright by attendants in flashy, silver sequined jackets. They were being paraded across the stage as a coterie of aides, along with the unknown twins themselves, laid their hands on the faithful after handing them something—some falling backward to the stage, slain in the Spirit as it was called; others rising from their wheelchairs and casting them aside.

And the crowd was going ecstatic—literally, cheering and dancing, shouting with indecipherable languages and weeping with joy.

Peter was familiar with the brand of Christianity that was on display. Pentecostalism and the more charismatic varieties of many Christian denominations had been something he'd studied in graduate school but never paid much attention to. From the charismatics he knew, and other churches he had studied, they were usually pretty orthodox, having committed themselves to the fundamentals of the faith while believing signs and wonders and miracles were still active in the life of the Church. Never spoke in tongues himself, nor had he dabbled in the sorts of faith healings that marked the Christian brand. He also didn't think they were too outside the bounds of historic Christianity, and the stagecraft wasn't the issue.

But what he saw now...

Something about it all seemed off to Peter. That disquiet dread began filling his belly again, accompanied by a deep sense that something sinister had visited his town.

Before he could process it all, he felt something fall on his face. Light, airy, fluffy.

It slid down his nose and into his open hand.

A feather.

White and barely registering against his skin, the fluffy thing no bigger than a quarter and as light as the air around him humming with an ecstasy that sent up goose pimples skittering across his skin.

Another one joined it, then another, Peter holding out both hands now and brain freezing with a mixture of indecision and intrigue as they filled his palms.

"What the..."

He snapped his head toward the top of the tent, eyes widening with a mixture of confusion and horror.

His vision was clouded by a blizzard of white fluffy feathers, hovering and whirling and dancing above.

"This isn't right..." he muttered to himself, more people going down around him and the stage really filling up now as more sought the hope of healing.

A sudden scream, high and heady, sliced through the vast space. It was joined by a cackling laugh, followed by a rush of ecstatic cries and laughter and delighted cheers.

"Manna from heaven!" the woman exclaimed before launching into an indecipherable cry.

Joined by her twin: "The angels of the Lord himself have visited us this day, y'all! There is healing in his wings, which we believe will manifest itself this day!"

Peter stood still, hands held open and piling with more feathers, skin barely registering the white fluff—whether from how light they were or from the sheer shock of it all, he wasn't certain.

What he was sure about was that something strange had visited Mill Creek Junction. Something sinister, even.

And Peter didn't know what to do about it. Not in the slightest!

But he did know who to call.

Just hoped he would have some answers.

For him. For his people.

CHAPTER 1

WASHINGTON, DC.

Silas Grey stalked his target just as he had back in the good old days with America's finest, the Army Rangers.

In silence, with careful aim, and with the intent to kill.

Well, in this case not exactly kill. But definitely score. Because he was already down one, and he needed the win.

It came more naturally than he thought it would after being holed up in his office for most of the past year. Not that he necessarily minded. Being Master of the Order of Thaddeus, ancient defender of the Christian faith stretching back to the founding of the Church, had its perks. Not least of which was access to a bazillion-book library and more resources than he could imagine, thanks to the Vatican—which he certainly put to good use for his own pet research projects. After all, he was an academic at heart, even though he cut his teeth on sand and steel after college joining the Army Rangers when Dad died in the Pentagon on 9/11.

But now, back in the saddle pursuing an enemy for a good cause felt like sliding back into a pair of skis he hadn't used since childhood. And boy, did it feel good!

Sweat was beading at his temple now, his shirt sticking to

his back thanks to an early heatwave that ushered in a taste of summer. The sun was high, the skies were clear, the air crisp and fresh. The coppery taste of fight-or-flight adrenaline was thick in his mouth from the morning's pursuit. Tall grace whispered in his ears as a gentle breeze blew past, carrying with it the earthy scents of the emerging spring, flowery yet spicy. And the cold, hard steel felt familiar in his hands, like the hand of an old lover.

Carefully, quietly, Silas cocked his weapon into firing position, steadying his aim and adjusting his crouch, one end of his mouth slowly curling upward.

Now I've got you...

He'd finally caught up with the target after a mad dash through the wooded lot after his partner had taken one in the leg. No use crying over it, given the rules of the engagement. So off he went to take his revenge and win the battle. The knucklehead who'd scored against his teammate had made more noise than an elephant, he was so loud—the guy barreling through the thick foliage without a care to be heard.

But then the target went silent, seemingly disappearing on the other side of a shallow riverbed and up a steep embankment. By the time Silas caught up with him, he was nowhere in sight.

Except for a few telltale signs.

The first one was the paw prints left behind on that embankment of a massive man scrambling for his life. Mud clumpy, leaves cast aside, rocks and sand tumbled loose down at the base.

The second sign was the candy bar wrapper. Snickers. Freshly opened and still smelling of chocolate and peanuts and caramel. Silas chuckled to himself when he found it at the top after scrambling up the embankment, having a good idea who it belonged to.

Then there were the broken twigs and trampled weeds and

flowers jutting off the main path leading to a field of tall grass a klick west of his position. Perfect hiding place, but looked a bit off the reservation—which would cost the target in more ways than one.

Crouching through the switchgrass still tan from winter, Silas moved with that silent, careful, intentional gait Uncle Sam had hammered and honed over two decades ago now through his service with the Rangers. And boy, did it feel good!

Had been half that long since he'd been in the service employing those skills, having received an honorable discharge from the military after his time was up to pursue the academy, ending up at Princeton University as a professor of religion. Truth be told, he sort of missed the thrill of it all—stalking and taking down his prey, heart beating a mile-a-minute, lungs screaming for air, head filling with the Nirvana that comes from riding an adrenaline high on toward destiny.

And now, lying low with his target sighted down the end of his barrel, and none the wiser, he was having a blast.

Not that he didn't get his Rangers fix every now and again since leaving the Army. God's providential intervention that fateful spring morning had taken care of that when he was rescued by his now employer after getting nearly blown to smithereens at an event keynoting a conference on his pet project, the Shroud of Turin. The Order of Thaddeus had offered him more than his fair share of opportunities to stalk a new kind of prey and fight a new kind of good fight the past few years.

From searching for the lost Ark of the Covenant to battling a risen Knights Templar; from wresting the Christian faith from the clutches of political maneuvering to wrestling with the demonic (which weren't all that mutually exclusive!); from the latest challenges defending the Bible and the Church's foundational Creed—and that wasn't even touching on what he had to deal with keeping a dueling resurgent threat against the

Church at bay that had risen from the shadows of history to finally destroy the Christian faith, Nous and the latest Theoti threat from the new kid on the block. All of it had offered him more than enough to whet his Ranger-honed appetite.

The last year, though, had been a completely different story —where the battles had been fought less with cold, hard steel against the Church's enemies and with the firing synapses of his brain working out the troubling mysteries seeking to destroy the faith, and more with email and his cell phone against the bureaucratic machinations of the Order. It all started at the turn of the year.

Questions were being raised from the Vatican about the amount of money being spent, which apparently still controlled the purse of the ecumenical Christian order—who knew? Silas certainly hadn't, still only a year or so into his new gig as Order Master. He was still busy saving the Church from no uncertain doom, much more than worrying about the balance sheet, which apparently was running into the red. And a number of cardinals back in Rome were throwing up a stink about it.

Victor Zarruq, the former Archbishop of Libya and with the Order's Board of Directors, had reassured Silas that all would be well. He had revealed the questions were less about the Order than the internecine struggles between factions within the Vatican, not to mention the broader Church, where said factions insisted the Protestant and Orthodox wings of Christianity should bear more of the financial burden. Regardless, all the administrative, bureaucratic bull had been one big headache. But that wasn't even the worst of it.

Some had even started targeting SEPIO, the Order project the late Master Rowen Radcliffe had established half a century ago to be a more muscular, deliberate outworking of the Order's mission from the founding apostle himself, Jude Thaddeus. *'Contend for the faith that was once for all entrusted to the saints,'* he had written in his letter to the churches of Asia Minor, a clarion call that had become the core mission of the religious order he established. All that contending the past few years had a cost; defending the faith usually does. There were some, however, who were balking at the costs—financial, yes, but also *optical,* the fallout from various missions over the years not playing all that well in the press.

Again, Zarruq counseled all would be well. That it was more about conflicting camps within the Church vying for power, political and theological struggles taking up their cause with the Order. But Silas wasn't so sure. His experience with the Army and the academy told him these sorts of struggles have a way of spinning out of control—and blowing things to kingdom come!

And that wasn't even touching on the fact Silas was in the middle of planning a wedding with the woman who happened to be his top lieutenant, Celeste Bourne. They'd been engaged for over a year now, and they were both getting restless to get officially hitched, their plans getting sidetracked with the demands of their job. He'd wanted to march down to a District of Columbia courthouse and let a justice of the peace take care of it all. One look from the bride-to-be shot that one down right quick! Which made sense, given Celeste wanted a grand, fairy-tale affair back home with her Mum and Daddy in a quaint English countryside church. And he wanted to give it to her.

Crouching in the high grass, the cares of the world pressing in against him on top of the high-noon sun beating down upon his back, Silas heaved a breath and sighed it quietly through pursed lips. Always something, as his partner Matt Gapinski would say.

Speaking of which...

Time to end this thing.

Adjusting his grip, he took careful aim and adjusted his posture—

Just as a twig snapped under his weight.

Sending the target sailing up ahead to his feet looking like a gorilla doing a pirouette—the bald, burly guy jumping up and spinning around to meet Silas barrel for barrel.

But the man didn't even have a chance to pop off a shot.

Pew-pew-pew Silas's gun sounded in three rapid-fire puffs, his finger triggering three pellets sailing from his barrel against his target's chest in bright splats.

"Sonofa—"

"Silas, Gapinski?" a voice shouted from behind, intercepting the man's curses.

Gapinski looked down at his chest. Three globs of fluorescent pink and yellow and blue paint were splattered across his fatigues and dripping down his generous gut. He dropped his own weapon, an air-powered paintball gun, looking up at Silas in shock.

Silas stood grinning widely. "Gotcha."

"No fair!" he complained. "You've got the skills of a cobra kai!"

"Army Rangers, more like it."

"Even worse! My tax dollars at work, I tell ya." Rubbing his chest, Gapinski winced. "Hurts like a mother, too. Did you have to aim for my ticker?"

Silas shrugged. "It's the Rangers way, my friend. Besides, it was game over anyway."

"Huh?" said Gapinski, retrieving his gun.

"Yeah, you left the game." He pointed to a set of bright orange posts marking the edge of the course. "Which means you forfeited when you wandered off course."

Now Gapinski frowned. "So you're saying you didn't really have to shoot me then, because you'd already won?"

"Like I said, the Rangers way," he said with a wink.

To which Gapinski responded with a wink of his own.

Sending three *pew-pew-pew* shots splattering against Silas's own chest.

He looked down to find the same fluorescent paint patterned across his chest.

"What'd you do that for?"

Gapinski blew the barrel of his paintball gun. "That's the *Gapinski* way."

"Shooting the winner?"

"Suppose that's what you get for showing off, love," a voice in perfectly polished British English called from behind.

Silas spun around to find Celeste Bourne wading through the grass toward their position, along with Abraham Patel, his partner who'd taken one in the leg.

"Hey, darling!" Silas went to her and placed a peck on her cheek. "How did you find us, and what are you doing here?"

"Yeah. This was a no-girls-allowed affair," Gapinski said.

"Don't know the meaning of the word," Celeste said.

"Three words, actually."

She frowned; he backed off. Turning to Silas, she answered, "And you're forgetting I'm former MI6. So there's nothing I can't find out when I want to."

"Don't I know it..." he mumbled.

Celeste raised a brow. "Excuse me?"

Silas cleared his throat. "Yes, dear."

"Good lad."

Leaning toward Silas, Gapinski said, "Boy, does she have you pistol-whipped!"

Receiving dueling glares from the couple-to-be.

"Uh, sorry," he said with a chuckle, rubbing the back of his neck. "So what's the deal? And where's Torres? You two are usually a pair."

Flashing him a wry grin, Celeste answered, "She had something to take care of. An appointment with a physician, I believe. Unfortunately for you lads, playtime is over. Something has come up."

"Always something..." Gapinski cursed.

Silas's face fell, agreeing with the man. He wanted just one day where the future of the Church wasn't riding on his shoulders. But he nodded, leading the other three down a well-worn trail through the woods that led back toward the start of the paintball course.

Slinging his paintball gun around his shoulder, he asked, "What's happened that couldn't wait?"

"There's been another incident, reported half an hour ago from our field office in Mumbai."

Silas startled. "Mumbai?"

She nodded. "The agent had been hearing rumors of the arrival of a large stage erected under the cover of darkness in a massive field outside the city, with invites sent out through a dark-web node on WeNet to taste and see the goodness of old-time religion sometime soon."

Gapinski smirked. "The Braun brothers strike again..."

Silas frowned, the memory surfacing from last year when Markus Braun used his massive social media platform to try to subvert the Church. The man had turned a million lines of code into a \$16.2 billion tech start up called WeNet that rivaled the major social media networks—a constellation of platforms from video to publishing to newsfeeds, the most popular of which was WeShare. And then used it to con his brother Hartwin into disproving the Bible before going full Dan Brown on the Christian faith itself by throwing shade on its central creed.

Shaking himself from the memory, he asked, "I assume that old-time religious experience included the promise to make people healthy and wealthy?"

Celeste nodded. "Indeed, and more."

"How so?"

"Apparently, there had been some strange diseases afflicting a pocket of Dalits in a neighborhood outside the capitol city, with rumors of healing."

"Da-whatchamacallit?" Gapinski asked.

Silas explained, "A member of the lower rung in India's caste system, characterized as untouchables. So what happened?"

Celeste explained, "Large numbers of these cast-asides, people struck blind and deaf, paralyzed even, were visited by a pair of roving evangelists. A white couple, man and woman. Twins by the account received from the field operative, who brought a full recovery through some mystical means."

"Sounds a little too familiar..."

Abraham ran off ahead and handled checking them out from the paintball course. Reaching Gapinski's car parked at the staging area, Silas slung his gun off from his shoulder and set it on the ground, recalling the other bits of intel that had come in from other field offices around the world.

Similar large tents had been erected in cities from Sãu Paulo, Brazil, to San Pedro, Belize; from Nairobi, Kenya, to Kaduna, Nigeria—all bringing revival-style healing services. East Asia was new, but each intel report coming into the Order's DC headquarters at the Washington National Cathedral all reported the same healing phenomenons, and by a pair of evangelist white knights.

Celeste nodded. "Indeed, it does. But with a twist."

Gapinski snorted a laugh. "What could be twistier than a Majority World faith-healing service performed by two white evangelists? Admittedly cliché, but twisted, nonetheless."

"Agreed. This time gold flakes started falling from the ceiling of the small neighborhood chapel they had rented."

Silas twisted up his face in confusion. "Gold flakes? I don't understand."

"You mean, like, manna from heaven?" Gapinski asked.

"Something like that," Celeste answered. "And here's the thing. Apparently, the bloke in the Order field office got his hands on a sample of the substance—and get this."

"Don't tell me it tested as real gold," Silas said, leaning against the passenger's side door.

"It did. The bloomin' gold dust was genuine gold! Which led to a stampede amongst the poor Dalits, leading to several deaths."

"That's awful."

Gapinski quipped, "Gives a whole new meaning to gold rush."

Silas and Celeste flashed him disapproving frowns.

"Sorry..."

Celeste continued, "What's worse, is that the—miracle, if you can call it that, was called down by the two white Western-ers, on command. Which apparently inspired others, apart from the Dalits who had shown up, to throw money at the trav-eling evangelists, hoping for another bout of the abundant life raining down upon them."

Silas scoffed. "Nothing more than some Vegas-level parlor trick. And guarantee those healed were rounded up and paid. We've seen this sort of thing throughout the last century from these health-and-wealth types."

"Yes, but that's the thing," Celeste went on. "Our other oper-ative in Nigeria, reporting on the healings, confirms that at least four of the men and women she spoke to received their full sight back."

"They were blind, but now they see?" Silas asked.

"How positively biblical," Gapinski quipped again.

Celeste said, "The agent is still working to track down more, but it appears there were genuine healings through these upstart evangelical tent meetings."

"Along with a healthy haul of scratch, I'd imagine..."

Silas crossed his arms. He imagined they did make bank.

Such was the hallmark of them types, those mostly American evangelists. Offering the hope of healing and wealth to desperate people. Feeding on that desperation that hauls in tens of millions of dollars to buy jets and feed their lavish lifestyles—all the while their victims fall deeper into poverty and despair.

A noise caught his attention, rising just above the din of late-afternoon chirps and buzzes from the surrounding forest. A different kind of buzzing, tingy and muffled but near.

Glancing around, he caught sight of his phone buzzing in Gapinski's car, from a number he didn't recognize with an area code that looked odd. Could see it lit up and rattling around on the passenger-seat floor.

He opened the door, climbing in to retrieve it when it went silent. He retrieved it and slid out of the car, swiping it to life and noticing he had three missed calls from the same number.

Gapinski leaned over his shoulder. "616? Where's that?"

Silas shook his head. *Better yet, who is that? And why the persistence?*

There was a voicemail message from the unknown number. He played it, putting the phone on speaker and raising it between him and his teammates.

"Hello, Dr. Grey, it's Calvin VanDyke from Grand River Theological Seminary here in Michigan."

"Grand River whatchamacallit?" Gapinski asked.

Silas put out a quieting hand, knowing immediately who it was. Someone who had partnered with him early in his academic career to foster an ecumenical consensus around the Shroud of Turin.

"Sorry to bother you, and you're probably wondering how I got your number. I could tell you, but then I'd have to kill you," VanDyke said with a chuckle.

"Cheeky fellow," Celeste said.

Silas nodded, wondering why the professor had called.

"Anyway, a former student of mine, Peter Daniel Young, contacted me with a—shall we say, troubling occurrence in his town. Some strange healings, something about feathers falling from the ceiling of a massive tent set up on the outskirts of town."

"Feathers falling from the sky?" Gapinski said with a start.

Silas's wide eyes met Celeste's own. Sounded way too on the mark, like the falling gold dust.

"Anyway, he contacted me to ask if I knew of anyone who could help give guidance. I wished I could help myself, but I'm neck-deep in my class work. I'm sure you remember how it is. And since you're the illustrious Master of the Order of Thaddeus now—"

Gapinski snorted a laugh. "Illustrious..."

Silas threw him a frown; he threw up his hands in surrender.

"I thought you'd like to know about—whatever it is, but also could offer some help. Figured you'd run into something similar and could give guidance. Anyway, sorry to bother you, but if you can help, give me a call back for the details."

The message ended, and Silas put the phone back in his pocket. "Strange healings, massive tent. Sound familiar?"

"And don't forget the falling feathers!" Gapinski added.

"Eleven of such sites have popped up in the last few months," Celeste said. "Now this one stateside in some backwoods town in Michigan?"

"Don't forget the newly uncovered one in India."

"Right, so thirteen."

Gapinski shivered. "Bad, bad juju number."

"But what does it mean?" Silas asked.

Celeste said, "Perhaps we should get back to the farm, Master Grey, and have a think about it."

Silas frowned. So much for a day off...

CHAPTER 2

Couldn't give me one day, could you, Lord? Just one day without the vocational crazy?

Had been the perfect Silas sort of day, with a clear blue sky and full sun, and a day full of possibilities that didn't include anything to do with the Order of Thaddeus.

No saving the faith. No bombs exploding—real or metaphorical. No Church at the mercy of the villainous Nous or Theoti or whatever. No reports or spreadsheets, no trainings or defenses to prepare. Just him sleeping in until the cows came home. Then gorging on an over-sized slice of quiche Lorraine with applewood bacon and Gruyere cheese at one of his favorite spots in Georgetown, Dean & DeLuca, with an even larger cup of dark-roast coffee and a paper copy of *The New York Times*. Then on to the National Mall, where he had walked without a plan or a purpose, ending up at the Tidal Basin amidst a grove of cherry blossom trees and falling asleep perched against one of their trunks, the sweet and tangy scent of the budding flowers sailing high on a light warm breeze lulling him to dreamland. Would have probably slept the day away, too, had Gapinski not phoned him up for a spontaneous paintball war.

And then the worm had turned. Again. Something about a rise in faith healings in the Majority World that smacked of something familiar. Combined with VanDyke's call, it all told him to buckle up—for what, who knew...

Silas sat strewing in the passenger's seat of Gapinski's Nissan Altima smelling of fried fish and french fries, a yellow wrapper from the Golden Arches telling him it was the leftovers of a Filet-O-Fish sandwich. How anyone could eat that stuff was beyond him. Made his stomach churn at the sight on top of the smell, and on top of the man's crazy driving.

Staring out the window, Silas caught himself. Caught not only his judgment of his partner's eating habits—though he still maintained anything from Mickey Ds deserved a bit of finger-wagging, especially Filet-O-Fishes. But also caught his complaint against the Almighty himself. Which definitely didn't deserve even a pinkie's worth of finger-wagging! Not only be he was God, but his complaint against the Order was garbage.

He had the best job in the world, and he knew it, helping preserve and defend and promote the Christian faith and all. Had access to all the scholarly resources and primary documents to his heart's content, though not as much time as he'd like. Had more than his fair share of adventures globetrotting for the sake of the Church, though he could do without the threat of no uncertain doom and death.

He just needed a break. A breather. A bit of R&R after so much whiplash-change the past few years and the break-neck pace he'd been running ever since his life had been upended after Nous tried to take him out and then Princeton finally did, sacking him and ending his career. Add to that the mawing rift between him and his brother Sebastian, to the point they were literal rivals and enemies now—all of it had caught up with him.

Probably didn't help matters that he was forty now. Not to mention engaged and closing in on marriage.

Gapinski slurped the leftovers of some soft drink. Silas startled at the sound, shaken from his stewing and contemplating.

"Want some DP?" he asked, gesturing his super-sized drink cup toward him.

"DP?" Silas asked with a raised brow.

"Yeah. Dr Pepper."

He waved a dismissive hand and returned outside. "No thanks. Gave up soda twenty-five years ago."

"Really? Like totally and completely?"

"Pretty much. Around fifteen."

Silas shifted in his seat, uncomfortable with the personal chit-chat but also welcoming it. Got his mind off from what he feared lay ahead.

But he pressed on, adding, "Growing up, I'd been sort of the chunky one of us twins, between me and Sebastian. Was mocked mercilessly for it, so I decided to do something about it. Lost forty or fifty pounds and got in shape."

"You, a chunkster? Who would have thunk it!" Gapinski exclaimed with marvel. "And now look at you. You're fit as a fiddle. Not that I've got a thing for ya or anything, pal," he said with a wink before returning to his drink with a slurp.

"Gee, thanks. I think. How about you hop to it and get us back to HQ?"

"Yes, sir."

Gapinski floored it, weaving in and out of the late-afternoon DC traffic, making Silas regret his command. Soon, he was taking a side street through a tree-lined neighborhood of red-brick and wood-painted houses stretching back to the 19th century. He sped past an elementary school with a weathered wooden swing set and a soccer field, then blew through a stop sign before taking a sharp left into a drive entrance near the base of the north transept of the Cathedral Church of Saint Peter and Saint Paul.

The sight still caught Silas's breath, the sacred structure known as the Washington National Cathedral looming large in a brilliant golden hue, the home to the Order of Thaddeus. It almost had been reduced to rubble two years ago now, coming under attack from a suicide bomber bent on bringing the American symbol of Christianity to its knees in a series of coordinated attacks designed to wipe the Church from the face of the earth. Had it not been for a resurgent Knights Templar, the plan might have worked—one of the more remarkable adventures Silas had been on in his three-year career with the Order. Had taken the better part of two years piecing the ancient structure back together, but they had gotten their old headquarters back—with a few modifications thanks to Silas's leadership.

Gapinski disappeared through the black maw of a parking entrance, Celeste and Abraham close behind in her car. Taking a dip, they moved swiftly underneath the national Christian architectural icon. The edge of the narrow drivable passage was lined with LED lighting, showing the way forward down under the massive building. Old stonework still standing from the terrorizing destruction shone in the faint light before curving into a spiral that revealed newer masonry. They turned ever downward beneath the stately structure before reaching the bottom, which was vastly different from either the stone-lined passageway or the stone-built building above it.

The light had noticeably brightened into a dim white, shining off the large car park of gray cement. Several cars, all black, were docked in parking spots and waiting to be used for covert operations. Gapinski parked next to one of them and the pair got out of the vehicle.

Silas still remembered the first time he had been brought down into the bowels of the Order's operation center after being rescued from the first in a series of renewed terrorist attacks perpetrated by Nous. Gapinski, Celeste, and Greer, another operative, had saved him from what was basically an assassination attempt. When they had arrived back then, the glass doors they were now nearing had opened with a *whoosh*, and greeting them had been a tall, portly man with graying, thinning hair wearing a black cassock, neck ringed by a white clerical collar.

Rowen Radcliffe, former Master of the Order of Thaddeus until he was killed protecting one of his own, Celeste.

Silas still remembered that tired, if not determined look he wore when he greeted them. As if the future of the Church rested on his shoulders. He could still hear his long cassock whispering and still see the carport light glinting off his golden buttons as he rushed to meet the arriving agents.

Only now it was Zoe Corbino meeting them through the gently swooshing glass doors.

The scent of sanitized air flooded Silas's senses as he and Gapinski, Celeste and Abraham shuffled into a familiar slate-gray hallway washed in the same dim, white light as the garage. Men and women swarmed about the halls ahead, doing their duty to protect and guard the Church.

"Celeste rang ahead and said you'd arrived," Zoe said, eyes wider than normal behind those baby-blue glasses of hers. "So I thought I would meet you first. Before..."

She trailed off, biting her lower lip with averting eyes.

Silas took a step forward. "Before...what?"

"Before Zarruq found you."

A whistle was thrown up from behind. "Looks like someone is in the doghouse."

He glanced back to find a grinning Gapinski. Whose face quickly fell before he averted his own eyes.

"I'll be in my study. Give me a minute to catch my breath, then send Victor over, if you find him."

Zoe nodded and trotted off.

"When you're finished," Celeste said, "we'll be awaiting your arrival in the bunker."

Silas took a breath, then nodded, wondering what the representative from the board of directors wanted.

"Good luck," she whispered as she passed. Gapinski trailed her and turned around to make a slicing motion at his throat with his finger.

Silas offered him one of his own fingers with a wry grin before heading to his study, his little slice of heaven with floor-to-ceiling bookcases lining the walls and brimming with modern and vintage tomes weighing down their shelves. Their heavenly, sweet-and-musky papery scent was a balm for the former professor. At one end was a large stone fireplace, the kind a person could walk into if they desired, usually with a fire crackling and popping away. At the other end was a large wooden desk, ornately designed with pillar legs and wooden sides with a series of monitors standing behind. The center of the room was commanded by a sizable Persian-style rug with two burgundy leather couches facing each other, complemented by two well-worn, overstuffed burgundy leather chairs at either end. Further on stood a mini bar nestled between two bookcases. Silas would make for that first thing.

Except when he arrived, someone else had already beaten him to it.

Victor Zarruq, the tall and widely girthed man, skin bronzed a lighter shade of ebony. He was shrouded in billowing light brown vestments, an interweaving pattern of green and black and blue running down the center. Resting on his bald head was a matching hat embroidered with the same pattern.

He spun around, drink in hand, a wide smile stretching underneath a salt-and-pepper bushy beard—heavy on the salt. Polished white teeth gleamed beneath deep-set eyes through a smile widening into delight.

"Master Grey! Just the man I was hoping to be seeing. Figured I would find you here after your paintball outing."

Heading for the bar himself, Silas offered a nervous chuckle. "You heard about that."

The man took a sip of his drink, scotch on ice, by the look of it, and smacked his lips together. "I hear all, my friend. I hear all."

"I'll keep that in mind..." Silas poured himself his own glass of whiskey, neat, then promptly took a swig. The oaky, spicy caramel liquid sent his senses firing on all cylinders; the alcohol hit his stomach hard, but was welcomed.

"Just tell me this," the former Archbishop of Libya said, "Did you win?"

Silas smiled. "You bet I did."

Zarruq laughed, a boisterous baritone sound erupting from his generous belly. "I would be expecting nothing less from a former Army Ranger. However, playtime is over. Time to get down to business."

Silas took in a worried breath and nodded, then led them to the cluster of couches and chairs at the center of the room. They sat and settled into the plush, well-worn burgundy leather chairs arranged across from one another. At first, the pair sipped their drinks in silence, the crackling of fire their only soundtrack.

Until Zarruq chimed, "So, how are you getting along, Master Grey? I believe you've come upon your one-year anniversary recently, isn't that right?"

Silas threw back a swig, wondering why the throat-clearing from a man whom he had known to be more forthright. But he swallowed hard, stepping up to bat at whatever game the man was playing.

"Actually, it's around a year and a half."

"Really? My, my, how time flies when you're fighting to

preserve Christ's bride!" He offered a chuckle; Silas said nothing.

Zarruq sipped at his scotch again, setting it down and continuing, "So you like your new role? You're feeling like you've found your footing, that you've found your wings for flight?"

"I do..."

"Because you know that if you ever need anything from me, any help navigating the role, I am here for you. You know that, Silas, don't you?"

A heat flashed up Silas's neck straight to his ears, making them burn with the memory of his commanding officer from Iraq, Major Peppers. Man would pussyfoot around like Zarruq was doing then, being all coy and indirect about whatever the heck he was trying to get to.

Irritated him then; irritated him now.

So Silas took a breath and threw back the rest of his whiskey, smiling and praying to the good Lord above to stay his tongue. He knew Zarruq meant well, having been sent to lend a helping hand when Silas had thought he meant to spy on him. Hadn't been the case at all, so what was going on now?

"You seem troubled, Victor," he said. "Like you're saying something without saying something. So, what aren't you telling me?"

Now he took a breath, his generous gut inflating like a balloon before the former Archbishop set down his drink and rested his hands on his belly—then settled in for what came next.

"I'll get right to it, then," Zarruq said. "There appears to have been a...development."

"Development? What kind?"

"An imminent no-contest vote."

"No-contest vote..." Silas said, brow furrowed and head swimming with possibilities. "What do you mean by that?"

Zarruq fell silent, his eyes going to the floor as Silas's brain caught up to the meaning of his words.

"Wait...you mean for me? A no-contest vote on my role as Order Master?"

He nodded. "I am sorry, Silas. It has taken me by surprise as well."

"Surprise isn't exactly what I would call it." He needed another drink, so he stood and hustled back to the bar.

"You must know that I have reported nothing but good things to the board. I believe you're doing a smashing job, executing the original vision of Saint Jude Thaddeus to contend for the once-for-all faith and that Rowen built upon in recent years—"

"But?" Silas snapped from the other side of the room as he sloshed three fingers of scotch back into his glass. He clenched his jaw in regret, but let the question hang without apology.

"But...well, some have wondered if someone a bit more seasoned in the Order was a better choice."

Silas returned and slumped into his chair, taking a mouthful of the oaky, spicy liquid and holding it a beat—his tongue tingling with the strong alcohol that was an antiseptic cleanser for the mouthful of words he wanted to give Zarruq from what he was feeling.

His heart was racing now, head feeling light, wobbly. This felt like Princeton all over again, him being dragged in front of a finger-wagging dean who wasn't pleased with who he was and how he lived his role. Only this time, he hadn't even signed up for the job! Rowen had named him his successor before he suddenly passed. Even before that, no way would he have chosen this life had the Lord himself not fingered him for the job after all that had happened.

"I didn't ask for this," Silas finally said, taking a more measured sip of scotch now. No need to push the alcohol; he needed his wits about him.

Zarruq leaned forward, face having fallen and creased with pain. "I completely understand, knowing that Rowen himself appointed you his heir, which was his rightful duty under the Order's charter, and then even further knowing how you came to the employ of the Order in the first place. And please know that plenty more members share my sentiment, believing you to be the right person for the job. The exact person for the job. Rowen Radcliffe knew what he was doing, and we respect him for it."

"But?" Silas asked again, though with less bite and more trepidation, not really wanting to know the answer.

"But, there are some, one or two really, who would rather focus on more...shall we say, 21st-century issues than previous-century ones."

Now Silas raised a brow, throwing back the rest of his scotch. "Such as?"

"Such as issues of justice and equity and inclusion. The more social elements of the gospel."

"As if contending for Christ's once-for-all faith doesn't also cover contending for those issues?"

"That's what I have said, although some of these voices are louder than my own."

Silas set his empty tumbler on a glass end table next to him, saying nothing and wondering what it all meant. For the Order, for him...

"It's too early to tell where this will go, as it is all so recent."

"How recent?"

Zarruq looked away again, to the floor, before replying, "Since the complaints from the Vatican."

"About funding and exposure."

"That's right."

"And these—who did you say it was bringing these charges?"

The man took in a measured breath, revealing, "Father Eckhard Weiss, and a few others."

"The German?"

"That's right."

"It's always them type..." Silas growled, growing impatient now and wanting to be finished.

The archbishop laughed. "Tis true, I'm afraid."

"So Weiss and his cronies are using the heat from the Vatican and other ecumenical denominations to pull the levers of their political machinations?"

Zarruq leaned back and frowned. "Sounds that way, but you needn't worry. I am going to monitor the situation and report back as soon as I hear anything more. The vote isn't scheduled for another few weeks, so there's time."

"Time? For what?"

Now he grinned, those white teeth returning. "To work my magic."

Before Silas could respond, the phone resting on the end table buzzed with attention.

"Excuse me," he said, answering it. "Hello?"

"Silas, it's Celeste. There's been a development."

Development...

Seemed to be the word on the street that day.

CHAPTER 3

Silas was joined by Victor Zarruq zigzagging through the light gray corridors toward the newly built command center down the hall from his study. Dimmed recess lighting above fell on them and other personnel hustling past. LED lights along the floor led the way as the dueling scents of plaster and fresh paint from the rebuild effort competed for attention.

Overseeing the cathedral rebuild project, Silas had the foresight to upgrade and enhance the original bunker, as they called it, into a center of operations fit for the 21st century. Celeste had joined him in the effort, leveraging her experience with MI6 in foreign intelligence to create a much more robust nerve center to assess and coordinate the various threats coming against the Church across the world.

Winding their way toward the command center, he couldn't help but think about his conversation with Zarruq. No-contest vote? The thought unsettled his stomach, the churning waves of disbelief rising into a torrent of anger just below the surface. How could they go after him like that, after all he had done for the Order—after all he had done for the Church? Not only preserving and contending for the once-for-all faith, taking more enemy fire and gut punches than he had as a Ranger. But also as a leader who neither wanted the title and responsibility nor sought it out for himself, offering a steady hand when Radcliffe passed suddenly.

The whole thing was riling him up with every step. But rounding the final bend on toward a pair of double doors, he knew it didn't matter. What did was whatever development lay beyond those doors.

So on approach, he took a breath and started counting backward from a thousand, a ritual he had developed in the Middle East to deal with rising anxiety in the heat of battle.

999, 998, 997, 996...

A pair of biometric scanners greeted Silas at the doors: one for his eyes, the other for his palm. Slapping his hand against the one, he put his face near the other, then waited.

985, 984, 983, 982...

A *blurp* sounded as the scanners performed their duty, though he imagined it was more an aural indicator for the user than anything that worked the gears that would open the doors.

969, 968, 967, 966...

A few seconds later, there was a click, and one of the doors retracted inside the bunker.

Silas took a breath and stepped inside. Time to get to work.

The opened door revealed a space that was similar in size to Silas's study, but altogether different. Dimmed recess lighting around the perimeter shone down upon narrow tables lining the dark walls commanded by workstations manned by agents dutifully executing on SEPIO orders. Where a fireplace had stood crackling and popping away at one end, a massive screen tracked critical mission updates and news footage from the world's major outlets reporting on items of interest to the Church. At the center of the room, where a set of leather couches and chairs anchored Silas's personal command center, a raised platform with a conference table mounted with small screens, chairs, and direct-line phones to operation centers around the world was awaiting his control.

The workroom looked more like a CIA black-site warehouse that he had spent a time or two in service of Uncle Sam, stretching the length of a modest basketball court and nearly another story in height. And all the chocolate marble walls and creamy brown tiles from the main level of the restored Washington National Cathedral above were replaced by the utilitarian white walls and charcoal carpet he'd grown to loathe from his Ranger days. A black cage stood in one corner, wires coming out the top with tiny blinking red and blue and white lights behind a mesh fence. Looked like a sophisticated server, powering several workstations silently arranged in a neat row on one wall.

The whole environment was patterned after a similar room hidden beneath the Vatican Secret Archives he and his SEPIO teammates had visited a year ago. Barnabas, the curator they had worked with to bring an end to the threat concerning the Nicene Creed, mentioned Rowen Radcliffe had helped them build out their own command center. He figured leaning on the former Master's insights, combined with his and Celeste's, was a good way to bring SEPIO into the twenty-first century.

"Alright, talk to me," Silas said, making for the raised platform at the center, Gapinski and Celeste already seated at a U-shaped table angled toward the massive screen.

Celeste went to answer when the doors opened again. Naomi Torres hustled into the room behind him, face drawn and creased by what looked like worry. Mascara smeared the edges of her eyes as well, as if she had been crying.

Silas took a seat at the head of the U, with Celeste at his right hand and Gapinski slouched next to her. Zarruq sat on his left, and Torres pulled up a seat next to him. He almost pushed forward, ignoring her condition, but thought against it.

He turned to her, saying gently, "Sorry to put you on the spot, Naomi, but...are you alright?"

She stiffened and took in a measured breath. Her eyes fell to the table before answering, "I got some bad news, that's all."

"Bad news?" Gapinski said, sitting up himself now and scooting to the table. "What bad news?"

Celeste asked, "Does this have anything to do with the physician's appointment?"

Torres swallowed and nodded. "A few weeks ago, I felt a lump in my—" She stopped herself, reddening as she glanced around the table. Face falling, she made a circular motion with a hand above her chest.

A cold dread spread through Silas. No...

Clearing her throat, she continued, "Given *mi mama* had a run-in with breast cancer, before she passed in the car accident that took both my parents, I figured it was worth getting my headlights checked out."

Apart from the distant clattering of keyboards at the perimeter workstations and the low HVAC hum, silence permeated the table. They all knew where she was going.

"One test led to another, and it looks like I am my mother's daughter."

Celeste moaned a sigh, reaching across the table with an extended hand of solidarity. Torres's face flushed red and eyes glistened, her mouth struggling to smile as she grasped her hand.

"Cancer?" Gapinski simply said, throat choked and eyes brimming with the same emotion under a furrowed brow.

"I am so sorry..." Silas said, not knowing what to say. Never was any good at those sorts of moments, his brain freezing with indecision at the right words to offer.

Gapinski did it for him: "You'll kick cancer's ass. No doubt about it, She-Ra Turner!"

"Absolutely!" Celeste said. "I haven't any doubt about it."

Torres giggled and wiped her eyes. "*Gracias.* And, yes, that's the plan."

"What is that plan, if I may ask?" Silas said. "How long will you be out of commission?"

Celeste flashed him a sideways glance, and he knew his all-business sense of things got in the way of being sensitive to the moment. What a jerk!

"Sorry, I didn't mean to come across as being insensitive. Of course, whatever you need to get better, we're one-hundred percent behind you."

"Yeah, a bazillion percent!" Gapinski added.

"Are you OK to continue?"

"Absolutely!" Torres said.

"Because if—"

"No, it's fine. *I'm* fine!" she said even more resolutely. She sniffed and daubed her eyes. "Plan is surgery and then to start chemo after that. Thankfully, we caught it in time. But I carry the genetic marker of *mi mama*, and hers spread quickly before —" She again took a halting break, then quickly added, "But thankfully modern medicine is far more advanced than what she had. And we caught it in time. And I know God has my back. I trust it'll all work out."

Torres left it at that, folding her hands on the table and offering a smile to Silas.

He said, "We'll certainly trust and *pray* toward that same end."

"Amen," Celeste said.

"Here, here," Gapinski echoed.

"I will light a candle for you this evening," Zarruq said, "and keep it lit until you are cancer free. And let us all join with the psalmist in believing what he himself wrote about in Psalm 27: *I believe that I shall see the goodness of the Lord in the land of the living. Wait for the Lord; be strong, and let your heart take courage; wait for the Lord!*"

"Amen," Silas said, joined by Gapinski and Celeste again.

Torres wiped her nose and waved a hand. "Alright, alright, enough about me. What's with this text I got about some virus?"

Silas nodded and turned to Celeste. "Virus? Is that the development you indicated?"

"Indeed," she said with a nod, turning to a small screen anchored to the table. "As you know, we have been monitoring the upstart evangelistic revival tent meetings popping up across the globe. First and mostly in Africa, then on toward Latin America. The latest seems to have appeared State-side in a small town in Michigan, according to a voicemail message we received a few hours ago, though it is yet unconfirmed. Then an hour ago, something curious came across the wire from a medical mission the Order sponsors."

"Medical mission?" Silas asked with surprise, before adding with a mutter: "And here Weiss is complaining about not enough emphasis on social justice..."

Zarruq made a *tsk*ing sound and flashed him a look that told him it was neither the time nor the place to litigate that one.

Heat ran up his neck in embarrassment. He nodded and said, "Sorry, continue."

"Can I just ask," Gapinski said, sitting up and eying the table. "It's not, *the* virus, is it? Resurrected from the pit of hell the collective humanity sent it to after science did its thing?"

Celeste shrugged. "Not entirely sure at the moment, given the scant reports coming from Africa at this point. However, it does appear different from other respiratory ones over the past decade that have spread like wildfire and resulted in widespread death, shuttering the world for spells at a time."

"Phew," he said, swiping his brow. "Because if I have to endure another lockdown stuck in my apartment without going to the latest big-budget action flick and stuffing my face with a bucket of heart-stopping popcorn, I think I'll pop!"

Torres smirked. "Not seeing some bro-culture flick on the big screen seems like a small price to pay for saving lives and getting the world back to normal, Hoss. Don't you think?"

"Maybe..." he muttered, his cheeks flushing red.

Silas cleared his throat, throwing the pair a sideways glance. "Continue, Celeste. If it isn't some respiratory virus, what is it? And it doesn't seem to be widespread, does it?"

"So far it is mostly concentrated in pockets throughout Africa, affecting people in ways far different from what the world has seen from recent pandemics, and even localized epidemics."

"How so?"

"Our medical missions have gotten reports of mass blinding and sudden paralyses. Others have lapsed into schizophrenic fits. But none of them have resulted in death—yet."

Silas leaned back in his chair. "But with the way the world was wrecked from previous viruses, and the fallout from it all still affecting the global economy, the world isn't going to be taking any chances if this becomes a bigger thing."

"I see two-week quarantines in our future," Torres quipped.

He frowned, the memory of the last go around still fresh.

At the start of it all, arriving passengers from affected continents were quarantined. Then air travel was cut off altogether. Didn't matter, though. The recent virus still got through, first into Europe and Asia, then into North America. It was more concentrated this time in urban pockets, but eventually spread to more rural parts.

Celeste turned to Torres. "You're probably right about that, Naomi. The governments of the world have wised up with their containment measures since the last go of it—swiping a page or twelve from the playbook of more authoritarian regimes, with digital passports and containment camps."

"No way are the people of the world giving up their movie theaters again," Gapinski said.

"You really think it will come to that?" Silas asked. "This new—virus, or whatever it is, spreading across the world and ravaging it again?"

Celeste shrugged again. "Like I said, too hard to tell. What our agents have reported thus far is that no one has been exempt from what they are seeing. Young, old; healthy, not; male, female; rich, poor—doesn't matter. The virus is attacking without discrimination, leading to permanent disability, which will surely lead to permanent loss of income and livelihood."

Torres brought her arms to her shoulders, as if chilled. "Could be the Big One epidemiologists have been fearing."

Silas looked at her and frowned. Could be…

He sat up and scooted to the table, bringing it back around to the Order. "I appreciate what this all means, given recent events. But what does any of this have to do with the Order of Thaddeus—aside from what our medical missions are witnessing?"

Celeste scooted to the table as well. "Right. Well, as I mentioned back at the paintball encampment, we have also witnessed a blossoming of revivals, big-tent style. All coinciding with these outbreaks. At least in Africa so far."

"And what is the nature," said Victor Zarruq, joining the discussion, "of these so-called revivals you make mention of?"

"Actually, we have been provided some footage from one of our agents in Nigeria."

Tapping on the tablet anchored to the table, she brought to the massive screen ahead a video that looked as though it was shot with a smartphone. The picture was fairly clear, if not a bit dark, looking across a sea of black faces all bouncing up and down, heads thrown back and excited utterances being thrown up in an unintelligible chorus.

A pair of white speakers were on a stage in the midst of the sea of black bodies. A man and woman by the look of it. People were streaming across the stage in front of the woman, who seemed to be offering them something. After the administration, people in wheelchairs shot to their feet, others cast aside crutches, still more who had been led by the arm startled and stared around the stage, as if they couldn't believe what they were seeing.

The man, blond, was saying, "If you believe in your heart and confess with your mouth that Jesus is Lord, you will be saved! You will find the greatest anointing you have ever imagined. Your body will be saved through healing. Your bank account will be saved through a flush blessing, pressed down to overflowing. Your businesses will be saved—" The rest was lost, the recording having cut out.

The footage ended, and Zarruq mumbled something under his breath with a grunt, shaking his head and flaring his nostrils, cheeks flushing pink. He seemed to know something, and he wasn't happy.

Silas said, "I couldn't help but notice, Victor, that you seemed to have an opinion about what we witnessed." Raising one end of his mouth wryly, he added, "Care to share?"

Zarruq swung a massive arm toward the screen. "Stuff and nonsense is what that was."

"Care to be more specific?" Celeste asked.

"He means prosperity gospel stuff and nonsense," Torres said. "Don't you?"

Zarruq nodded with a grin of his own. "That is exactly right, my lady. Keen eye. Impressive."

"Well, having those jokers on TV for much of my 90s childhood helped hone the eye, not to mention firsthand experience."

"Really?" Gapinski said, spinning her way. "I thought you were raised Catholic."

"I was, until..." she trailed off, face falling before she recovered. She cleared her throat and explained, "Until my parents died in a car accident. My Tío Juan took me in and raised me. And he had quite the appetite for this flavor of Christianity, believing that God would bless him if he sowed his seeds right. *Mi Papá* dabbled as well..."

"And what is this Christian flavor?"

"The prosperity gospel," Zarruq said, propping his elbows on the table, "makes the very bold promise that God wants you to prosper. That God wants to reward you if you have the right faith. If you're good and faithful, God will give you endless goodness and happiness and blessing."

"In other words, a boomerang effect," Celeste said. "Good things will always come back to you."

He nodded. "That is correct, and an apt way of framing it. If you sow goodness, you will reap goodness. Think positive thoughts and you'll live a positive life. Nothing is impossible if you exercise the right kind of faith."

"Sounds thoroughly American," Silas said, not having been familiar with the flavor of Christianity Zarruq was describing. He recalled what it was rooted in, Pentecostalism and charismatic forms of the Church, but hadn't paid much attention to it during grad school. Far more interested in relics and ancient Church history than the manifestations of Christianity in the modern world.

Zarruq crossed his arms with a scowl. "Indeed, it is a thoroughly American religion. It has become the great civil religion, really, offering a transcendent account of the core of the American Dream with a creedal account encapsulated inside. It worships Americans, deifies them. And it has been exported more times than I care to consider to my African continent—to my very own Libyan country! The worst export, beyond pornography, even!"

"Tell us how you really feel, chief..." Gapinski quipped.

He turned to him. "Oh, believe me, I will! The teachings

have brought nothing but destruction to my homeland of Africa."

Poor guy's eyes got big as saucers, and that pinkish hue returned. Zarruq looked like he was about to share a piece of his mind about this flavor of Christianity. Silas didn't doubt he had seen a thing or two, knowing how preachers had used desperate Africans seeking simple relief from poverty and disease to finance their lavish lifestyles. But all that would have to wait, because something from it all was stirring in him now.

So he intervened: "Let's pull this back and consider what we're dealing with."

Nodding, the archbishop backed off, leaning back in his chair.

"What we know is, we've got some sort of viral outbreak on our hands, a contagion that's disabling people—something we are not in any way equipped to handle and should probably coordinate with the World Health Organization."

Celeste nodded. "Jolly good idea. I will make preparations to send along all we know on that front."

"Thanks. Now the other side of it we are equipped to handle—these upstart revival meetings and charismatic services that seem a bit troubling. With the invitation from my professional contact to services in the Midwest that bear echoes of what we've seen overseas. I think you know what this is adding up to."

"Road trip!" Gapinski said with a grin. "I'll bring the Ding Dongs and Cheetos. Oh, and a case of Dr Pepper should do it."

Celeste threw him a frown. "Brilliant. A Yank in charge of sorting our food supplies for an excursion across America..."

"Hey! I'll have you know, I earned my Boy Scout merit badge in backpacking, so if there's anyone among us who knows how to pack—"

"Ding Dongs and Cheetos, it's you. Yes, we know, dear."

"Nobody's sorting anything," Silas said with intervention. "A day trip to Mill Creek Junction is probably a good idea. Seems like a longshot, but worth checking into. Again, for a day, on one of the Gulfstreams. Me, Gapinski, and Celeste. Torres, you stay here and—"

"No, I'm coming along!" Torres said emphatically.

Silas took a breath, knowing he needed to tread gingerly. "But, your diagnosis..."

"I'm not dead, Silas!" she snapped. "At least, not yet."

Silas nodded, going silent.

She sighed and looked at the floor. "I'm sorry. I didn't mean to bite your head off. It's just, the last thing I want to do is to be stuck inside here while you're traipsing across the country on another mission."

Gapinski snorted a chuckle. "It's some Podunk town in Michigan. I'd gladly swap and get stuck inside here while you're traipsing across the country on another mission." She flashed him a look that said too far; he dipped his head and cleared his throat. "Sorry..."

"Are you sure about this?" Silas said, worried not only about pushing his agent too far during such a diagnosis, but also the liability she might pose during such a mission.

She clenched her jaw and nodded resolutely. "Absolutely. I can do the mission. No worries from my end. I'm coming along."

That was good enough for him. He nodded in reply. "Alright, then. No worries from my end, either."

Mill Creek Junction, here we come...

CHAPTER 4

MILL CREEK JUNCTION.

*W*hat a day...

Climbing out of his Honda hatchback, the driver's side door throwing up a wicked, embarrassing yelp, Peter Young slung his messenger bag around his back. The trusty companion through his previous life on Capitol Hill in Washington, DC, and then through three years of graduate school studying to be a pastor, was bearing a notebook and well-worn Bible, pages edged by crimson and stained by a decade of scrawled inky thoughts.

He trudged to the door of his favorite Mill Creek Junction place, Max's Place. After what he'd been dealing with all day, the local watering hole offering greasy food and hoppy beer was just what the doctor ordered.

Sounded like it was what the doc ordered for the whole town, too—the noise and light and smells reaching him a good ten paces away.

Opening the door, the force of the place smacked him in the face.

First it was the crowd, the noise and jumble of conversations fighting for a hearing above the din of Marvin and the Gang jamming it up on stage. Every table was filled and then some, with men and women packed in the aisles, milling about and roaming from table to table, conversations drowning and joy-filled.

Then it was the smell. The air was thick with the staples of American cuisine: fried potatoes and grilled meat; lots of fries and hamburgers, some fish thrown in for good measure; the tang of garlic and pepper, onion and cabbage. Riding alongside it all was a hefty dose of barley and hops and wheat. Which meant lots of booze was flowing that night.

"Preacherman!" a voice shouted above the din, recognizable because of the nickname the man had given Peter last year when he arrived at Mill Creek.

Max Blade, owner of the bar, mouth wide with a giddy grin. "Nice of you to join the party!"

"What party?"

"Haven't a clue! But business is booming anyway with those holy rollers having rolled up into the Junction. Apparently all that jumpin' and jivin' across town gave 'em a workout in need of a bite to eat—and a bit of libation, which was unexpected. I mean, just look at the place!"

Peter smiled and glanced around. He was right. It was hopping. Recognized many Junction folk, some from his congregation, most not. The others must have been from out of town. The holy rollers, as Max called them, coming for the circus across the tracks.

Max slapped Peter on the back and guided him to the bar, where he eased into a chair and slumped against the polished dark wood smelling of lemon polish.

"Surprised to see you here, preacherman," Max said, pulling Peter's usual from the draughts. An India Pale Ale, locally grown.

Peter raised his head. "Why is that?"

He shrugged. "You being a holy roller yourself and all, figured you'd be headlining the circus."

"I am *not* a holy roller!" Peter said with more bite than he intended.

Max finished pulling his drink and backed away with a raised hand. "Sorry to have hit a nerve, pastorman. Didn't mean no offense."

"No, I'm sorry. Shouldn't have bit your head off. Just having a bad day, that's all."

"Sorry to hear, partner. Maybe this will help..." he set his drink down and told him to holler if he needed anything.

Peter thanked him and promptly took a sip, the citrus notes combining nicely with the hoppiness. He turned toward the room as Max sauntered off to attend to some tables.

The band was striking up another tune now. Marvin was working a number on the ivory of the old, boxy, honey-stained Hammond B3 organ. The drums kept up a nice *rat-a-tat-tat* rhythm, too, while a young man with long hair strummed his electric guitar with a twisted-up face that said he was feeling what the organ was putting down.

Sighing with relaxation now, Peter took another mouthful of the hoppy goodness. The beer and jazz acted as the balm he needed for the day's troubles.

Started with the nonsense he'd seen under the big top—the ecstatic utterances from the gathered, the message from the two mystery speakers, the freakin' falling feathers! But it got worse from there.

Several people in his congregation had called asking for prayer. One had some sort of visual episode that knocked out their sight. Another was having a biopsy done on a lump they'd discovered the past few days. Then some folks were losing their hearing, and others had random paralysis episodes—even one chronic marathon runner! That didn't include others he'd heard about who had gotten sick across the area. Seemed fishy, but he knew from experience that sometimes these things came in waves.

The day ended with a phone call to his former academic mentor Calvin VanDyke from seminary. He listened with care and said he knew just who could help. Some religious order from DC. Said he'd put in a call and see what he could do, and apparently they'd agreed to come out. Wasn't holding his breath, though.

Peter spun around back to the bar, reaching for his bag and pulling out his Bible. The Apostle Paul had it right in Romans 8: '*We know that the whole creation has been groaning in labor pains until now...*' All thanks to Mama Eve and Papa Adam for rebelling against God, plunging all of creation into chaos. All the sickness and disease, disabilities and death was enough to make one give up on it all. Especially one in ministry, who had an up-close-and-personal viewing of the brokenness of creation nearly every day.

Just a few months ago, he had presided over the funeral of a guy a little younger than him who had died of cancer. Left behind a young wife and twin boys. Came out of nowhere, and now he's six feet under while his family struggled to string together a life without him.

Taking a swig of beer, he opened his Bible. He'd always maintained the two went well together. As Benjamin Franklin was rumored to have written, "Beer is proof that God loves us and wants us to be happy."

Amen. He'd drink to that.

And he did, throwing back another mouthful as he began flipping through the Gospels, beginning with the book of Matthew. Seemed like a good place to start reviewing some of the biblical evidence for healing in Jesus' ministry.

There were those he healed of leprosy, that horrible condition that killed off skin and limbs. Then the deaf and mute. The paralyzed and the blind man—or *men*, rather, having healed lots of them type. Seemed like everywhere he turned Jesus was healing somebody—healing as much as teaching!

So why didn't he do it now?

He looked up, taking in a measured breath and looking toward the door leading back out into the night where the circus was still going on.

Maybe he still is...

He returned to his Bible and flipped a few pages forward when he landed on a familiar passage. One end of his mouth curled upward. Now there was a good story.

Taking a swig of beer, he read about how Jesus heard that his friend Lazarus was sick and dying from a message sent by the man's sisters, found in John's Gospel, chapter 11:

But when Jesus heard it, he said, "This illness does not lead to death; rather it is for God's glory, so that the Son of God may be glorified through it." Accordingly, though Jesus loved Martha and her sister and Lazarus, after having heard that Lazarus was ill, he stayed two days longer in the place where he was.

Peter always found this story fascinating. Not only did it give the reader a glimpse into Jesus' own personal life, humanizing him by cluing us into the fact he had friends he cared about. But it was just a weird story!

Here's Jesus, who had healed lots of people up to this point —blind people, the deaf and mute, people paralyzed, others sick with other ailments, like Lazarus—yet he doesn't rush to his bedside to bring the healing one of his good friends needed! The kind of rescue and re-creation he had literally come to bring and bear in this broken, busted world.

But the story went on. He picked up where Jesus explained something interesting to his disciples:

"Our friend Lazarus has fallen asleep, but I am going there to awaken him." The disciples said to him, "Lord, if he has fallen asleep, he will be all right." Jesus, however, had been speaking about his death, but they thought that he was referring merely to sleep. Then Jesus told them plainly, "Lazarus is dead. For your sake, I am glad I was not there, so that you may believe. But let us go to him."

Peter took a swig of beer and sat with the reality of what he had read: Jesus knew Lazarus had died and seemed to *let* him die—for a bigger, divine purpose. That his followers would believe, in him.

He raised his head, looking at the bottles of whiskey and rum and vodka that lined the back wall, considering how this illness and this death fit within Jesus' bigger plans—how it fit within God's sovereign purposes for the world.

Returning to the passage, Peter read that Lazarus had already been dead for days by the time Jesus and the disciples arrived. Then the dead man's sister had a few choice words:

Martha said to Jesus, "Lord, if you had been here, my brother would not have died. But even now I know that God will give you whatever you ask of him." Jesus said to her, "Your brother will rise again." Martha said to him, "I know that he will rise again in the resurrection on the last day." Jesus said to her, "I am the resurrection and the life. Those who believe in me, even though they die, will live, and everyone who lives and believes in me will never die. Do you believe this?" She said to him, "Yes, Lord, I believe that you are the

Messiah, the Son of God, the one coming into the world."

Peter had to smile. Martha was obviously pissed that Jesus didn't come rushing to save the day. Made total sense. Who wouldn't lay into him after all they had seen him do for total strangers—giving back their sight and hearing, their limbs and lives? Yet when one of his best friends gets sick, Jesus can't muster up the time and energy to come and heal him, to keep him from dying?

Had to have been what Martha was getting at, the subtext of it all. In fact, who *hasn't* gotten pissed that God didn't jump to heal some cancer or save someone they loved from death—healed their own cancer or sickness even?

Peter's face fell, recalling his own anger at his own cancer diagnosis a few years ago. There he was, having spent time working as a minister on a college campus, he was training to be a pastor to continue serving God in that way—and he gets cancer? Where was God in *that*? And then going through the motions seeking healing and restoration...he was as pissed as Martha was!

Downing another mouthful of beer, he returned to the story, Jesus arriving to a house in mourning—and the other sister:

When Mary came where Jesus was and saw him, she knelt at his feet and said to him, "Lord, if you had been here, my brother would not have died." When Jesus saw her weeping, and the Jews who came with her also weeping, he was greatly disturbed in spirit and deeply moved. He said, "Where have you laid him?" They said to him, "Lord, come and see." Jesus began to weep. So the Jews said, "See how he loved him!" But some of them said, "Could not he who opened the eyes of the blind man have kept this man from dying?"

What an accusation! What an indictment, even.

Peter considered all the people in his own life who had died from various illnesses—good people, godly people who were pillars of the churches he'd grown up in and served. Then there were his own people, going blind and deaf, losing use of their limbs, losing their lives...

It was enough to lose faith sometimes in the goodness of God, not to mention the *power* of God with so much sickness and disease and brokenness in the world. Where is he when life goes off the rails like that?

But then there was the truth of the matter.

Jesus was still all-powerful and all-wise, for he was not only fully capable of resurrecting Lazarus—he was fully *willing*. He cried over Lazarus' death, and then did something about it.

But not according to Mary's or Martha's or even Lazarus' own timing. He moved according to his sovereign, providential plan. To bring himself glory and honor. Which the story was ultimately about.

Peter drained his beer and read the moment Jesus raised his friend from the dead:

Jesus said to her, "Did I not tell you that if you believed, you would see the glory of God?" So they took away the stone. And Jesus looked upward and said, "Father, I thank you for having heard me. I knew that you always hear me, but I have said this for the sake of the crowd standing here, so that they may believe that you sent me." When he had said this, he cried with a loud voice,

"Lazarus, come out!" The dead man came out, his hands and feet bound with strips of cloth, and his face wrapped in a cloth. Jesus said to them, "Unbind him, and let him go."

There it was: the purpose of the entire episode of sickness and death.

Peter leaned back on his stool and looked off at those bottles of alcohol again, considering the meaning of it all.

'Did I not tell you that if you believed, you would see the glory of God? ... I knew that you always hear me, but I have said this for the sake of the crowd standing here, so that they may believe that you sent me.'

The manifestation of God's glory, for the sake of belief...

He went back to his Bible.

But it was missing.

What the...

Furrowing his brow, Peter searched the floor, thinking it had dropped.

Nothing.

He looked around at the couples sitting on either side, but both were locked into deep conversations.

Then he looked up to find Max Blade holding the Good Book.

"Looking for this?" Max said with a grin.

Peter frowned. "Come on, man, give it back."

He reached for it, but Max yanked it from his reach.

"Uh, uh, uh. No siree. I have a strict no-Bibles allowed policy."

"You can't ban the Bible! That's against the law. Not to mention bigoted."

"Yeah, I suppose so. Just jerkin' yer chain anyway, pastorman." Max set the Bible back on the bar in front of Peter, then grabbed his empty glass. "This one's on the house."

"Gee, thanks."

Pulling his beer, Max nodded toward the Bible. "What were you reading anyhow?"

Peter set a hand on its worn black cover. "Just studying up on Jesus' healings. What it meant for his followers then. What it means now..."

Max snorted a laugh and plopped down his drink. "Why don't you ask your holy-roller friends up the road! They seem to think they're modern incarnations of the Big Guy Upstairs."

Peter's phone buzzed and danced with interruption on the bar next to his Bible.

"Saved by the bell, I guess, eh pastorman?"

He chuckled. "Hold that thought." Then he answered the phone, the number not familiar. "Hello, this is Peter."

There was a silent pause on the other end, followed by a sniffle and some muffled voices and beeping in the background.

"Hello..." he tried again.

"Ye—Yes, hello, Reverend."

Peter's pulse suddenly spiked, his chest feeling heavy and head swimming with recognition.

Sounded like Katrina, his assistant.

He checked the number again. "Is this Katrina?"

She laughed. "It is."

"Where are you calling from? I didn't recognize the number."

"Mill Creek General."

"The hospital?" Peter exclaimed, standing up now. Max crossed his arms and moved toward him, mouthing a question he ignored. "Is everything alright? Are you hurt?"

"Well...I'm not hurt. But all isn't right, that's for sure."

"What happened?"

"Doctors aren't entirely certain, but it appears I'm paralyzed."

The word hung in the ether between Peter's ears and his brain.

Paralyzed.

Kat?

Did not compute...

"Sudden onset paralysis, the doctors are calling it," Katrina continued, as Peter stood in stunned silence. "I was having dinner with a friend and there it came, all of a sudden. Thankfully, she was with me, otherwise I wouldn't have known what to do!"

"I bet..." was all he could offer. Katrina was single, in her sixties. He thanked God for his provision and protection.

But...still.

Sudden onset paralysis—what the heck, Lord?

"I'm so scared, Peter," she whispered before bursting into muffled cries. "Would you pray for me?"

He did, while his mind reeled at the turn.

What's happening to my town?

Hadn't a clue.

But he hoped VanDyke's religious order did.

CHAPTER 5

The Order jet landed half an hour outside Mill Creek Junction the next morning with a bounce before skidding to a shuddering stop at the end of the runway at Grand Rapids International Airport.

Silas gripped the supple armrest of the Gulfstream G650 as it recovered from its halting landing, the sweet scent of leather rising at his tightening grip.

"Breathe, Silas, breathe," Gapinski said with a chuckle across from him.

Exhaling through pursed lips, he threw him a glare that told his partner all he needed to know. Back off. Gapinski did, the man looking outside as the jet taxied to their private hangar.

Hated flying. Always had. Was the reason Silas signed up with the Army instead of going Air Force. But when he was tapped for the Rangers, which required jumping headlong out of helicopters, he had to suck it up, put on his big-boy pants, and get over his fear of flying. He did, mostly, but the anxiety of it all still carried with him every time his feet left God's green earth.

Speaking of which...

As the jet continued onward, Silas glanced outside to take in the lay of the land—which wasn't much. It was flatter than a flapjack out there, the airport a plainspoken concrete monstrosity without any character that was surrounded by low-slung office buildings and warehouses. Definitely nowhere near the kinds of places he and SEPIO had ventured the past few years. Perhaps that was a good thing! Little chance of Nous or the Church of the Theotites or any other enemy of Christianity pitching a tent in these parts.

So he hoped.

But Silas knew better. Given the shades of similarity to what had been reported in far-flung regions of the world, he wouldn't put it past the Church's enemies to set up shop in such a place. But how it all fit together, and whether the Order's enemies had anything to do with what was surfacing was anyone's guess. Seemed unlikely, but again, Silas knew better.

Regardless, the pastor sure was happy they were coming. Peter Daniel Young was his name, a former student of Calvin VanDyke at Grand River Theological Seminary. When Silas returned his call, the professor spoke highly of the young man about Silas's age. VanDyke didn't know what to make of what had come to his neck of the woods, but given Silas's new role at the Order, he figured he might be interested in taking a peek.

Silas didn't know what to make of it all either, but hopefully the picture would become clearer sooner than later—whatever it was.

A black Cadillac Escalade was waiting for them when the Gulfstream parked inside the darkened hangar. Wasn't Gapinski's car of choice, but the oversized chrome wheels and supple tan leather and SiriusXM hook-up seemed to make up for the fact it wasn't a Mercedes.

Silas rolled his eyes at the excess, having to constantly corral the spending habits of his assistant director of operations. And with the board of directors now putting SEPIO under the microscope, making hay of such expenses, he almost did again. But he didn't. Let it go and hoped the expense got lost in some line on some budgetary spreadsheet. Because not only did he learn keeping his people happy was important—and Gapinski's rides were important to him—he also learned not to skimp on vehicles during missions, however inconsequential they may seem.

The drive to Mill Creek Junction wasn't much better than the airport, the highway cutting east through farmland being tilled by bright-green John Deeres for the upcoming planting season and suburban sprawl composed of cookie-cutter plastic houses that made his skin scrawl.

Not that he expected anything more. After all, it was the Midwest; it was Michigan. Life as an Army brat certainly clued him into that kind of bland life of comfortable sameness. But given his globetrotting father had shown him what urban life can really look like, and given he'd spent most of his adult life on the East Coast in cities, big and small, with more character than these Walmart specials could muster—it all felt so foreign to him.

Silas smiled to himself, knowing the deeper truth of it. He was a bit of a pretentious sonofagun when it came to culture and architecture and cuisine, even religion. He wasn't like many east and west coasters who turned their noses up at the Midwest as fly-over country, looking down on their conservative values and way of life. More that he didn't understand the life, given his own experiences. And perhaps not a bit reflective of Dad, who instilled those more urbane values in his sons.

Perhaps that attitude would change with this visit.

Gapinski pulled off the interstate and made for Mill Creek. After a quick stop at a Shell for gas and snacks—mostly for snacks, Gapinski's stomach already grumbling—they jumped onto a state route that headed toward their target.

"Do we know anything of the town?" Silas asked, marveling at the flat, barren terrain. "Is this big tent revival typical?"

"Not sure of the religious aspect," Celeste said, swiping through her phone. "But I did find something on the town's website, a bit of their history."

"Mill Creek Junction has a website? Can't be too backwoods, I suppose."

She hit him in the shoulder. "You're pretentious little git, aren't you. At any rate, listen to this."

She cleared her throat and read:

A hundred and forty-four years ago, our ancestors saw fit to start a new town along the mighty Grand River that would also be a new way of life. A life built on working the land and feeding the world, the windmill at the north end of town still standing as a monument to that vision. A life built on gumption and ingenuity, where anyone could make something of themselves if they put their mind to it. A life of morals and ethics and religious conviction. A life of learning and working and building and marrying and raising a family. A life of giving and sharing and communing and supporting one another. We are Mill Creek Junction. Welcome!

"Sounds homey," Gapinski noted. "Like a good place to raise a family."

"Looks like it, too." Torres pointed forward, the Escalade firmly riding on Main Street now.

They were leaving the flat farmland for something a bit more interesting. Oaks and maples and sycamores towered above the road ahead on either side, followed by neat rows of turn-of-the-century homes telling a story that plucked at Silas's heartstrings.

There were inexpensive bungalows painted brown and beige and white, along with red and brown brick, tree swings hanging from those large, old trees. Then more modest craftsman-style homes—some last century, some this century; two-stories and split levels; some all bright and others painted with contrasting trim; all with generous porches that bespoke an era long gone in America. Down a wide side street overhanging with more of the same towering trees, generous two and three-story colonial revival houses, smoke curling from chimneys, bespoke of a wealthier side of town Silas wouldn't have expected.

More traffic too, their Escalade coming to a stop half a mile outside the main downtown according to their GPS, if you could call it that. Maybe an accident, or construction. Unless it was because of the show north of town. If that was the case, this might be more than they bargained for.

Waiting for the traffic to get going, Silas caught sight of the license plate in front of them: Ohio. Glancing behind in the rearview mirror, he caught sight of another, a front plate from Illinois. Both states were a hundred miles from there.

Maybe they were for sure getting more than they bargained for if people were coming from far and wide!

"Where's this church of ours?" Silas asked, the traffic picking up pace again. "Mill Creek Baptist, isn't that right?"

"Shouldn't be far, if this damn traffic would get a move on," Gapinski grumbled.

"Monitoring WeShare posts for the area," Torres said, staring down at her phone, "looks like quite the carnival north of here. There's a massive tent, a rock band strumming up the latest worship tunes, complete with fog machine and light show."

"Fog machine?" Gapinski said, twisting up his face.

Celeste responded, "It's what all the Christian kids are into these days."

"And adults," Torres said, holding up a WeShare profile of some middle-aged couple with raised hands. "There's a video, as well, of the pair speaking gibberish."

"In tongues, you mean?"

"I suppose. They sounded like they were from New Jersey."

Gapinski snorted a laugh. "Sounds about right..."

"Apparently, the small town has become an overnight travel destination."

"Apparently," Silas said. "I've seen license plates from the surrounding states. But let's not draw too many conclusions yet until we see for ourselves."

Took another twenty minutes, but soon they arrived at Mill Creek Baptist Church. Cracked blacktop led to a modest lot of the same, with faded yellow parking lines empty but for two cars anchored next to the handicap spots in front of a rather sad looking structure. A one level building, sided with beige plastic siding, jutted off toward the left from a large hall with a sharply peaked roof. Silas figured that was the sanctuary, as a tall cross was anchored to the roof at the far end. Looked like a whale with a spout of holy water spraying from the top.

As someone who grew up Catholic, with all the architectural accoutrements of high church leftover from the pre-Vatican II era, Silas could never understand why his Protestant brothers and sisters, especially the Evangelical type, were more content to worship in spaces decked out in metal chairs and stage lighting than the glories of stained glass and crucifixes, with ceilings that soared high with buttresses and walls decorated with bright saintly icons. Not that he cared much, but he found the jettisoning of the sacred for the slick depressing.

Gapinski parked the Escalade in the visitor parking spot and the crew got out.

Silas led them into a darkly lit lobby smelling not much different than the church he grew up in. Mold and mildew, old wood and stale Folgers. Funny how churches smelled the same, no matter the denomination.

Gapinski breathed in deep and grinned. "Ahh. Home sweet home."

"Are you of Baptist origin, Matthew?" Celeste asked.

"Oh, yeah. Grandpappy was a Southern Baptist minister."

"I forgot about that," Silas said, looking through wide windows peering into the main hall he correctly pegged as the sanctuary. Honey wood pews with crimson cushions arrayed in neat rows dutifully faced a large wood cross emptied of Christ's body anchored to the wall behind a large wood pulpit—a typical-looking Protestant sanctuary.

Celeste said, "So same family of Protestants, eh?"

"Naw," Gapinski said. "Same flavor, different family. Believe I saw this one's an Independent Regular Baptist church."

"As opposed to irregular Baptists," Silas said.

He laughed. "Good one! I'll have to use that someday."

"Hello?" a voice called out behind.

Appearing from a darkened hallway was a man of modest height wearing a flannel shirt and skinny dark jeans. Hair was cropped short on the side, the rest of it long and slicked back. Looked late thirties, around Silas's age.

He said, "Sorry to bother you, but we're looking for the pastor. Reverend Young."

The man smiled and shook his head. "Reverend. Never can get used to that one. Just call me Peter."

Silas threw Celeste a raised brow, communicating: *He's the pastor?* Not only were the buildings different between Catholics and Protestants, so were their ministers!

Celeste offered her hand with a smile. "Celeste Bourne, director of operations with the Order of Thaddeus. We're the lot Professor VanDyke said were coming to call on you."

"Ahh, yes. But Bourne...as in that Ludlum character?"

Gapinski explained, "She was a Bourne before Bourne was a Bourne."

Silas suppressed a grin, recalling when he wondered the same thing and got the same curt answer from his fiancé. Celeste smiled curtly and nodded, saying nothing more.

"Good to know," Peter said. "And thanks for coming. Really appreciate it! I've been super unsettled the past few days with all that's been going on north of town that I really haven't known what to think of it all. Or what to do about it."

Silas crossed his arms and asked, "And what exactly is *it* that you've been dealing with?"

"Why don't you follow me to my office, I can lay it all out there."

After Silas introduced himself and the rest of SEPIO, Peter led them through the darkened hallway that looked like a set of offices, that stale coffee more pronounced now, along with the scent of copier ink and some sort of pine candle.

The pastor headed left at a T-juncture and asked, "Silas Grey...did I see you on some WeShare video defending the Bible sometime last year?"

Silas chuckled, the memory of the crazy, harrowing Gospel zero adventure rising back to the surface.

Gapinski ribbed him with a chuckle. "You're famous, chief!"

"I guess so. And, yeah, that would be me. One of our many missions to contend for the Christian faith."

Peter pushed through a windowed door into a cramped space lit by fluorescent lighting. A few bookshelves lined one wall behind a CEO-style desk with two brown herringbone wingback chairs in front and a complementary tan couch along one wall.

Silas recalled a priest friend of his from the UK telling him the difference between them sorts of ministers and pastors. As he put it, pastors have offices, priests have studies. He was bemoaning the style of mostly American ministries compared to those overseas. Looked about right, though he felt a bit guilty for his judgmental eye.

Taking a seat behind his desk, Peter asked, "So what are you guys, anyway? VanDyke was pretty coy about your identity."

"Well, we could tell you," Torres said, taking a seat on the couch, Gapinski joining her, "but then we'd have to kill you."

Peter laughed. "Duly noted."

"Ordo Thaddeum," Silas said, sitting in one of the wingback chairs.

Peter tilted his head and furrowed his brow. "Order of Thaddeus?"

Celeste took the other seat. "You know Latin, pastor. Impressive."

He smiled. "Peter, please. And yes, I took two semesters in seminary, but know just enough to be dangerous."

"With this Calvin VanDyke character?"

"That's right. And quite the character he is. Sorry, but I've never heard of your Order."

"I wouldn't have expected you to," Silas said, recalling a similar conversation with Radcliffe those few years ago. "We've sort of been working in the shadows, protecting and preserving the memory of the Church from nearly the very beginning of her existence."

"Thaddeus..." Peter said, leaning back now. "He was the disciple known as Jude. He wrote the letter to the churches in Asia Minor that bears his name."

"Exactly. And he was the founder of the order."

Peter scoffed. "Seriously? I wasn't aware that religious orders were around then. Now, I'm more of the low-church, Evangelical variety—clearly, as a Baptist pastor!" They all shared a laugh. "But I had always thought the first ones didn't start until the early Middle Ages. The Order of Saint Benedict, one of the earliest and most enduring, wasn't it?"

"Officially, you are right," Celeste acknowledged. "Unofficially, Thaddeus, or Saint Jude as he is also known, the patron saint of lost causes, was acutely aware of the forces already pressing in against the Church and the teachings of the faith. Just look at his letter! Jude told the Asia Minor Christians that he wanted to write to them about their wonderful salvation in Jesus, but there was a more urgent matter."

"*Contend for the faith that was once and for all entrusted to God's holy people,*'" Peter mumbled to himself.

"Jude 3," Silas said. "Our founding mission statement, if you will."

"I'd memorized the verse after experiencing a sort of crisis of faith years back. Formed the foundation to my own passion to reclaim and retrieve the vintage Christian faith. Something Calvin VanDyke turned me onto."

Vintage Christian faith. Silas liked that, and liked this pastor more for using that language. His own language. Maybe he wasn't so bad after all. Even if he looked like one of those hipster pastors than any priest he'd grown up with.

"That's right, Peter," he went on. "Contend. Fight for. Preserve and protect. Not only the faith itself, but the shared, collective memory of the faith. Within years of the Jesus movement, Jude Thaddeus was already concerned about people who wanted to pervert the message of God's grace into a license for immorality and to deny Jesus Christ our only Sovereign and Lord, as he wrote."

"Sounds like my kind of Christian Order." Peter took a breath and sat up at his desk, fiddling with a pen. "And sounds like just the sort of thing the Junction needs..."

Silas threw Celeste a sideways glance. "Why don't you take it from the top. VanDyke said something about feathers falling from the sky?"

He nodded. "From the ceiling, actually, of the massive tent out at the Junction fairgrounds."

"What, like some stage gimmick, released from sheets suspended in the air?"

"Not according to the dude headlining the whole thing. Claimed God said he'd cover you with his feathers."

"But that isn't in any way meant to be literal," Celeste said, brows wrinkled with confusion.

"That's what he said! Or what he said others say. But then

he said there's healing in the Lord's wings, which led to this healing service."

"Healing service?" Torres said with expectation from the couch, eyes wide and hopeful.

Silas's stomach sank at the sight. Could only imagine what she was going through, facing down the barrel of the dreaded 'C' word. And now we're walking headlong into some sort of faith-healing situation? He didn't like it, didn't like having Torres along with this one in particular. But what could he do?

"That's right, but I didn't catch much of it," Peter went on. "Left before I saw anything happen on that front. Lost my appetite."

He shifted in his chair, then leaned back, taking that pen with him and clicking it and looking off in thought.

Silas said, "Was that all? Feathers from heaven and a faith-healing service?"

The pastor took in a breath and looked at him, as if contemplating whether to go there.

Then he did, saying, "There's another thing about it that doesn't sit right."

"What's that, pas—" Celeste stopped herself, then smiled. "I mean, Peter?"

He chuckled, then sat up. "Well, there's been this rash of sickness descending on Mill Creek."

"Sickness?"

"I'm sure it's unrelated. More correlation than causation." He took a breath and raked a hand through his slick hair. "I'm probably more sensitive to it all after getting a call about my dear executive assistant. She had this random episode of sudden onset paralysis that's really thrown me for a loop."

That sent Silas sitting up straight and giving Celeste a sideways glance. She registered the same intrigue. Not quite panic, given the reports they had heard, but certainly taking more interest now.

"Did you say she was paralyzed?"

Peter looked at Silas, then to Celeste, seeming to register something between the two. "What aren't you telling me?"

Celeste glanced at Silas, who nodded her onward. "For the past few weeks, we have had agents in the field keeping us apprised of various goings-on with a cluster of revival meetings that sound very similar to the one here in Mill Creek Junction."

He chuckled. "Agents in the field? What are you, Navy SEALs for Jesus?"

"We get that a lot," Gapinski said.

"Point is," Silas said, ignoring the man, "those reports sound similar to what you've experienced here. And then we got word of a—how should I put it..."

"You should know," Celeste interjected, "that this intel is highly confidential. Not even the Western media has gotten hold of it. I'd wager whether the WHO or CDC, even CIA or MI6 is aware."

Peter sat up straight now, eyes widening and mouth opening in a question.

"What Silas was going to share is there appears to be some sort of contagion making its way around the globe. First in Africa, then in Latin America."

"Contagion?" he exclaimed.

"Manifesting in blindness and deafness, skin conditions and...well, paralysis."

The pastor sat still, eyes locked on Celeste and mouth groping for words.

Finding them, he asked, "And you think what's happened elsewhere is happening here?"

Silas put up a cautioning hand. "That, we don't know. What we do know is that what's happened elsewhere, with the revival tent meetings, sounds similar to what happened here in Mill Creek."

"Happening," Peter corrected.

"What do you mean?"

"Happening. It's still going on. In fact, the next....well, show, which seems about right—the next service is starting at noon. So you can go see for yourself, if you'd like."

Silas looked at Celeste, who nodded her agreement. Did seem worth checking out, considering what they'd known was happening across the globe. And to hear about the same in small-town America...perhaps seeing for themselves was a good idea. Get boots on the ground and scope out the terrain.

So he stood. "Lead the way, Pastor Young."

CHAPTER 6

A warm breeze tinged by the dueling spring scents of jasmine and lilac gusted up from behind as Silas joined the rest of the gang piling into the rented Cadillac Escalade. Inside was hot, the sun having crested toward high-noon now and the smell of leather overwhelming the welcomed springtime goodness.

Slamming the door closed, he could feel himself growing irritable, wishing to be back out in that springtime air and back at another round of paintball, not stuffed inside a rental SUV in some Podunk Michigan town.

No matter. Suppose that was his lot, wasn't it? Dropping everything at the drop of a hat to come to the Church's aid. After all, he had wed himself to her—for a time, at least.

But man...sometimes she was a demanding mistress!

Gapinski roared the SUV to life and drove the SEPIO crew and Pastor Peter back out onto Main Street—ending real quick in a sea of cars and trucks and SUVs, presumably all heading to the same show north of town. Which gave him time to wrap his mind around the mission.

Stop whining and get to it, Grey...

Taking a breath, Silas started to get his head in the game,

reviewing what he knew—from the initial reports from Order medical missions across the globe, to the upstart revivals, to the contagion.

But he didn't know what to make of any of it!

Not the claims of healing and miracles by preachers; not the thirst for a connection to the tangible experiences of God's power by parishioners. Definitely not the rumors of another threatening contagion that could send the world spinning back into yet another dystopian lockdown nightmare and economic depression of our own making!

The Escalade picked up pace somewhat, and Silas rolled down his window, that lilac-jasmine laced breeze a gentle kiss against his face.

None of it was adding up, and none of it seemed to be any business of the Order of Thaddeus, anyway. Certainly not SEPIO's, which was more used to fighting against threats from outside the Church, not something coming from the inside, and more adept at more muscular defenses of the faith than— whatever they were signing up to investigate.

And besides, for Silas, this sort of faith-healing and miracles business had never been part of his own religious experience growing up. There was a charismatic Catholic church across town in Arlington, Virginia. Even visited their youth group a few times with some friends from high school, more for a girl he was chasing on the cheerleading team, but still. Was a bit to woo-woo for him, preferring the quiet, dependable rhythm of the weekly liturgy and Mass and Father Rafferty's homilies to the tongue-speaking and dancing around. That is, when he wasn't throwing spit wads at his brother Sebastian.

And then his own professional life had been much more about combating theological liberalism and its threat to vintage Christianity, leveraging the insights of relics and alike to retrieve and preserve the Church's collective, ancestral memory. Which translated perfectly to the Order of Thaddeus when he was brought on board, leveraging his twin experiences with the Army Rangers and Princeton University to continue that preservation and retrieval effort.

But this...

He was a fish out of water on this one. They all were, it seemed.

Which never boded well.

Traffic continued to trundle along, but soon the homes and trees that greeted them on the outskirts of town before arriving at the Baptist church gave way to the heart of Mill Creek Junction. Single and double-story shops and restaurants and other businesses lined both sides of Main Street. Colorful and budding trees lining the sidewalk, with moms pushing strollers and old men milling about. Looked about like you would expect from small-town America.

"Would you look at that," marveled Gapinski. "Mayberry, USA."

"Suppose it's gotta be somewhere," Torres joined in from the passenger's seat, staring out the windshield.

"Yeah, but never thought I'd see one up close and personal."

Silas didn't either. And a sort of envy suddenly rose up as he spied people coming and going in and out of banks and jewelry shops, what looked like a diner and the town's only bar—all without care, free of worries.

Free of *his* worries, more like it. What lies within small towns lies within all towns, city-size or not. Plenty of divorce and abuse, plenty of unemployment and paycheck-to-paycheck living, plenty of crime and poverty, plenty of people living lives of quiet desperation.

And yet...

There was something about the quiet life of a Mayberry, as Gapinski put it, that beckoned him. Not sure it suited him, but it did hold some appeal. He glanced at Celeste staring outside, one end of her mouth curling upward. Perhaps it suited *them*. One day...

Enough daydreaming. Time to get to it.

Soon enough, they would.

A Starbucks and law office sharing the same strip of commercial real estate at the far end of town flashed by. The wooden sails of the town's original windmill peeked above the treeline in the distance. Rumbling across a set of railroad tracks, they passed the final cluster of towering trees, opening up into flat farmland as far as the eye could see.

And the fairgrounds—which were quite the sight to behold.

A tent, larger than any Silas had ever seen since maybe the childhood circus, was erected at the center of a massive plot of flat land. Cars of every kind, new and old, were arrayed around it. People of every kind—age, ethnicity, income-level, you name it—were flocking inside through parted flaps. Thumping base and the whine of an electric guitar, followed by the *rat-a-tat-tat* of a rock star drummer floated toward them as Gapinski parked in the last row, shouts and whistles and claps joining the chorus floated their way. It sounded unlike any Christian event he'd ever experienced.

Climbing out, Silas muttered, "Sounds like the last Bruce Springsteen concert I went to."

Following him, Peter said, "Just wait till you get inside."

The grass lot was already emptied of people, the visitors having already gone into the tent for the revival meeting—or wherever it was. The few stragglers they'd followed into the fairgrounds were dashing toward the entrance, the SEPIO crew close behind.

"Hey, check this out!" Torres exclaimed, smirking and shaking her head as she pointed at a vanity plate slapped on the backside of a Chevy compact.

It read: *100 GRND*.

Gapinski squinted and craned forward. "A hundred...grind? I don't get it."

"It's a hundred *grand* dingleberry!"

"On a Chevy Cruze? Boy, oh boy, they must be prayin' themselves into a lather for that one!"

"And right next to a 100 FOLD," Silas quipped, pointing to another sedan from out of state, a Lincoln MKZ sedan this time.

Celeste leaned toward it for a look. "Uncertain what that stands for."

"It's the hundredfold blessing," Torres explained.

"The whatchamacallit?" Gapinski asked.

"A common refrain within prosperity gospel that takes Jesus' teachings about blessing literally, from Mark chapter 10: *'Truly I tell you, there is no one who has left house or brothers or sisters or mother or father or children or fields, for my sake and for the sake of the good news, who will not receive a hundredfold now in this age...'*"

"Sort of a money-back guarantee for following Jesus?"

"Something like that."

"With that kind of guarantee, who needs Vegas?"

"Come on," Silas said, getting impatient at the music ramping up now. "We should get to it. Don't want to miss all the fun."

Weaving through the cars, they made it to the opening, tent flaps suspended back and letting in a view of a large crowd singing and dancing inside, lit by pink and blue and yellow flashing lights—along with letting out a clearer hearing of the chorus blaring from the song revving up the audience:

> *Breakthrough, breakthrough, breakthrough-oo-oo.*
> *Breakthrough, breakthrough, breakthrough-oo-oo.*
> *Breakthrough, breakthrough, breakthrough-oo-oo.*

"Catchy," Gapinski said, head bobbing back and forth.

"It's something alright..." Silas grumbled, arms folded and frowning. "Let's try and get a closer look."

Pushing through the clumps of people standing at the back, they made it to an aisle stretching down the center. Five seats stood empty several rows up at the aisle near the middle. Silas and his teammates made for them as the next verse started:

> *It's your breakthrough-day*
> *God's showing the way.*
> *Health and wealth by right they're yours.*
> *It's your breakthrough-day.*

Silas took a deep breath as the chorus struck up again, the place smelling of dirt and straw, sweet and salty bodies, surveying the place that was unlike anything Christian he had seen.

The space was vast, like the circus he had been to as a child, or that Springsteen concert back in Princeton. A stage was set at the center, those pink and blue and yellow lights flashing down on a band leading the audience in the song. Then they panned around the vast space, flashing on the audience standing and swaying and waving their arms. Chairs were arrayed around the center, stretching the length and width of the space, all filled with those standing worshippers. Speaking of which...

It was striking who was there: men and women, young and middle-aged and sun-setters, black people and white people, Latinos and Asians—a real diverse measure of the spectrum. While he couldn't tell the income or education status, based on the cars in the parking lot and the clothes on those bouncing up and down, it looked like the revival meeting wasn't catering to the barefoot bumpkins, but middle-classers and even those on the upper end.

But then something else caught his attention up the way.

A full row of people in wheelchairs. Again, some older and younger, middle and late-agers and others looking in their twenties and thirties. Heads were raised and hands were lifted high. He thought he caught a reflecting glint of tears streaming down the face of one woman at the edge.

As the bandleader belted out that blasted chorus again, Silas wondered what they were thinking. What was going through their head as they sat listening to the proclamation of health being their right, of God promising healing? Hope, expectation, faith—all of the above? Even more important: What would they find that afternoon?

Looked like they might find out…

The song ended and bounding up on stage was a pair, blond and tall and stylish. A man and a woman, each wearing skinny jeans and flannel shirts and ironically oversized glasses.

The man's hair was shaved at the sides and his long hair swept to the right with a daub of grease to keep it in place; the woman's was full and long at the shoulders. Gold jewelry clung to their necks and wrists and fingers, and the man oddly wore a single white glove. Even from that distance Silas could glimpse gleaming straight white teeth—sort of putting an exclamation point on the end that these two were the embodiment of their prosperity-gospel promise.

But who they were—now that was the question…

"Y'all ready for your own breakthrough day!" the man said as the gathered took their seats, voice lilting with a Southern twang.

"Looks like your pals from the South are headlining the affair," Torres said, ribbing Gapinski.

He frowned, narrowing his eyes and crossing his arms. "Looks that way."

"God wants the abundant life for y'all," the woman said, sounding like her twin. "He created you for success! He created you for victory, for breakthrough! And we are here today to declare that this day is *your* day!"

Gapinski snorted a laugh above the din of rising adulation. "Holy exclamation points, Batman! This chick must be on seven triple-shot venti lattes from up the road."

Silas smirked and folded his arms. "She's on something alright…"

"That's right, Paulina," the man said. At least they had a name to one of the faces; that was a start. "Maybe God has been whispering something to the very core of your inner being, something that seems completely impossible. Maybe it seems like y'all will never be healthy again. Or that it's impossible for y'all to clear your debts and get y'all bank accounts back in the black—can I get an *amen* to that one!"

The crowd echoed a hearty *'Amen!'* on cue.

"Maybe it seems like y'all will never get married," Paulina said, picking up the baton, "or lose weight or to execute on that business dream tucked away in that heart of yours. My brother Dexter and I declare what Jesus himself declared in the Gospel of John, chapter 10: *'The thief comes only to steal and kill and destroy. I came that they may have life, and have it abundantly!'*"

And now they had the name of the second wackadoodle. Except according to the raucous applause thundering through the tent, neither of them were viewed as such.

Which would make for an interesting mission, convincing the convinced in the hollowness of the promises. Except nothing was happening that was mission-worthy of the Order of Thaddeus.

"Now, in the natural realm—the physical realm," Dexter went on, "it may seem that deck is stacked against y'all. You've got no idea how any of this will come about. No idea how y'all are gonna lose the weight or gain that promotion, how you'll recover from cancer, or get pregnant and get married—well, perhaps not in that order!"

He chuckled at his funny, flashing those pearly whites. The audience ate it up.

"Regardless, it seems like the odds of winning are less than zero! But here's the thing: if y'all have any hope of realizing those dreams, of that vision for your life coming to pass —then y'all have got to get your mind moving in the right direction. You've got to speak your truth, use your words to bring into existence what you know God already wants for your life. One that's fully healed and brimming with goodness!"

"That's right, brother!" Paulina said now, as if it was a tag-team effort. "Don't just describe your situation; change it! Because, as we say—"

Both Paulina and Dexter held out their mics, summoning from the audience the line that would finish their thought.

Which they gave on cue: '*What you say, you shall have!*'

"Exactly!" Dexter exclaimed. "We know what the abundant, prosperous life that God has always wanted means for people like all y'all! Welfare and well-being and wealth. Success and good fortune—no, a *wheel* of fortune spinning round and round in y'alls favor!"

Crowd seemed to like that nifty metaphor. Lots of '*Amens!*' and hoots and hollers and declarations of '*Victory, hallelujah!*'

Silas glanced at Torres down the row, thinking about her cancer diagnosis and wondering what she was thinking about it all. The promise of abundance, the promise of health and healing by speaking her truth in faith.

He knew that's not how faith worked, not how God and his sovereign providence worked in the world. Yes, he healed. But the norm seemed to be more suffering and sickness than healing and help. And even when it came, it was through God's common grace thanks to medicine and science, more natural and mundane methods rather than supernatural, miraculous, *flashy* ones.

Would probably be the case for Torres as well, however she navigated her diagnosis.

"Blessings and abundance from here to high heaven!" Paulina said, taking over. "Don't forget what Jesus Christ himself said, what Dexter just quoted: *'I come that you would have abundant life, that you would enjoy life.'* What he most certainly didn't say is that y'all have got to wait to die and get to heaven before you will be blessed. No, no, no! God came to give you and me and the rest of the world—y'all right here in Mill Creek Junction, an abundant life!"

The woman held the audience's gaze with a toothy grin, many standing now, reaching their hands out toward the pair, as if they were deities themselves ready to dispense the goods, then and there.

Paulina launched into another leg of her self-help speech when Peter leaned toward Silas. "What do you think of all this?"

"What I *think*...you don't want to know," Silas said. "But what I make of it, that's another matter."

He chuckled. "What do you mean by that?"

Silas shifted toward Peter, Dexter taking over from his sister now and the Order Master not giving one lick what he had to say.

"What I mean is that I don't know enough about the theology of it all to know what I think yet."

"And here I thought you were some theological ninja master!"

"And here I thought you were some pastoral ninja master, yet here we are."

Peter laughed now. "Fair enough."

"I mean, yeah, God cares about whether or not his people, or any people, for that matter, are thriving—spiritually, economically, socially. He heard the oppressive cries of his people in Egypt and sent them Moses. He provided food from heaven when they were wandering in the desert. Jesus himself taught in his sermon to not worry about what we will eat or drink or wear, because *'indeed your heavenly Father knows that you need all these things.'* And he continues to promise in Matthew chapter 6 that if we *'first for the kingdom of God and his righteousness, and all these things will be given to you as well.'* So that's all true. But that doesn't mean God is some genie in a bottle we can summon at every financial and professional whim."

"I get that. Then what do you make of it all?"

Silas looked back to the row of wheelchair-bound people, each and every one of them entranced by the promises being made up on stage.

"What I make of it all, is that you've got two Southern hicks preying on the hopes of the financially and physically desperate, committing spiritual malpractice along the way. Grifters who probably got snake oil and anointed prayer beads for sale on some merch table at the back and will bleed these people dry of their money, and whatever hope they've got left."

"Tell me what you really think!" Peter exclaimed.

Silas went to continue when a voice interrupted—

"Pastor Young? Is that you?"

From the row in front, down a few chairs.

Peter looked up first, then startled before Silas saw a sweet-faced woman with gray curly hair and coke-bottle glasses sitting stiffly.

The pastor audibly gasped, face twisting up as if his brain was not computing what he was seeing.

Who was this mystery woman?

CHAPTER 7

The band returned along with the lights, strumming up a familiar worship tune that sent people back to their feet even as it sent some others into the aisles desperate for health and wealth. The thumping bass and *rat-a-tat-tat*ing drums and flashing glow combined with an adrenaline ping from the turn sent Peter's head feeling light and stomach feeling wobbly.

Could hardly believe his eyes. His personal assistant, from their Baptist church, at a charismatic faith-healing service? Couldn't make sense of it.

On the one hand, Peter certainly could. He understood she was suffering, and rightfully scared of what had happened to her body. He'd been through his own bout of tragedy when he had his cancer diagnosis a few years ago, so he understood the fear and the helplessness and anxiety over the future.

Even though it was the good kind of cancer, he'd had some complications with it and dealt with his own level of suffering and all the questions it accompanied about the goodness of God and his sovereign will for our lives and the world. Couldn't imagine being paralyzed like Katrina, single and all alone and having to find help to do basic things like eat and bathe.

So he got it. At the personal level, and at the intellectual level, seeing her all stiff and searching for healing and all. But still...

On the other hand, Peter would have thought the woman had been grounded better in the faith. Grounded in an understanding of God's providence and sovereignty, and all that means for our trials and tribulations. Grounded in the promises of the gospel for forgiveness and eternal life, not as a ticket to the American Dream. He'd only been pastor of the church for less than a year now, but even his sermons would have hopefully given her a groundedness in historic Christianity that opposed the hollow promises made from the stage.

So seeing her seated in that row at that revival concert...

It did not compute!

A jab at his side brought Peter back to the moment. He felt his cheeks flush at having lost all words for a beat or two, so he didn't glance at Silas after the helping hand.

Clearing his throat, he asked, "Katrina, what are you doing here?"

She gave a nervous chuckle, the poor woman looking stiff and statue-like in her chair, her neck the only thing that was craning toward them. "Oh, you know, just listening to the encouraging words of the preachers!"

"Now, let me tell y'all something!" Paulina boomed as the band dropped back to just a handful of chords and cymbals, bringing their attention back to the front. "Have we got something special in store for all y'all fine folks this day."

Katrina cooed with anticipation. "Chat after the service, pastor," she said, waving Peter off.

Peter's stomach sank at it all, wondering what was going through her head, wondering what she was being dragged into.

"Who's that?" Silas asked lowly.

"My assistant. The one I told you about."

"The paralytic?"

He nodded. "Spontaneous paralysis. Looks like she's still in that state, too."

"And looks like she's come for the same reason as all the rest."

He nodded again, saying nothing. If someone like Katrina could be roped into such a service, clinging to the promises and riding its false hope into the sunset, then was anyone from his church safe from the allure of the prosperity gospel?

Paulina stepped back from the edge of the stage and looked at her brother, the twins exchanging a glance and a nod, which seemed to shift things to a different level.

A beat later, a pair of stagehands in black with headsets crowning their heads carefully dragged on stage a long gilded table, legs ornately decorated with a white linen runner draped down the center.

Peter couldn't see what was on top, but they looked curiously like—

"What the heck?" he muttered as Dexter launched into the next phase of the afternoon.

The evangelist said, "We know that Jesus gave us a powerful way of remembering what he accomplished on the cross for the world." He reached for something at the center of the gilded table.

A loaf of bread.

Holding it high, he said, "*'This is my body, broken for you,'* Jesus said, *'do this in remembrance of me.'* What we believe—no, what we *declare* is that prosperity in all realms of life flows from this fruit of Jesus' suffering."

At this, many cheered.

Then his sister took a goblet, gilded like the table and shimmering in the light from jewels encrusted on its face.

Raising the cup, Paulina declared, "*'This cup is the new covenant in my blood,'* Jesus declared, *'Do this, as often as you drink it, in remembrance of me!'* This is the blood of Christ, shed for y'all. He was pierced for our transgressions, he was bruised for our iniquities, the punishment that brought us peace was upon him."

As if on cue, the crowd roared: *'And by his wounds we are healed!'*

Shouts of triumph rippled through the tent, as if believing the cross itself had destroyed sickness and disease. As if believing the reason Jesus had come was to heal our physical wounds—rather than our spiritual ones, our sin and rebellion against God through his death on the cross.

The crowd was clapping and dancing and moaning with abandon now. Even Katrina seemed into it, her face beaming with a wide smile, crow's feet at the edges of her eyes signaling her jubilation where her hands and feet could not.

First the prosperity gospel nonsense, and now a thoroughly orthodox experience of the central Christian rite, the Lord's Supper? Didn't make sense in the slightest. Dread began churning in Peter's stomach now, wondering what was coming.

"We know that Jesus took our infirmities," Dexter said. "He bore my sickness. By his wounds I am healed."

'By his wounds I am healed,' the audience declared in agreement.

"We partake in the Lord's Supper to remember what Christ has already accomplished for us on the cross. Our prosperity, our health, is guaranteed by his broken body and shed blood! We partake of these elements, saying, 'Thank you, Jesus, by your shed blood my sins are washed away. By your body, I am healed!'"

'By his body I am healed,' the audience said as one.

"The bread and wine—or juice, for some of us non-drinkers." Dexter chuckled, and a ripple of laughter echoed him through the tent. "These elements are much more than mere symbols. They are spirit! Both the body and the blood are spirit. Infused with the power of the Spirit to change our circumstances. Thus, we take these elements into our bodies as spirit."

Paulina said, "And we declare that y'all who take them will be healed." She paused a beat, bending toward the audience before adding with a shout: "Today!"

Now the audience was on their feet. Those who could manage it, anyway. More shouting and amening, dancing and you name whatever else signaled worship and joyous expectation—the crowd was doing it.

"Any and all who wish to receive Christ's abundant life, bought and paid for and *guaranteed* by his shed blood on the cross—come forth as y'all are to receive what is rightfully yours!"

A number of other stagehands, this time in suits, made their way to the stage bearing baskets.

"What the heck is this?" Peter asked, turning to Silas.

"I was wondering the same myself!"

The Brit, Celeste if Peter recalled, leaned in now. "Do you suppose those baskets contain the elements?"

Didn't register at first. And then it did.

Wide-eyed and mouth feeling dry as sandpaper at the realization, Peter said, "You don't mean the *communion* elements, do you?"

She nodded. "Or Eucharistic, as some would say, but yes. That is precisely what I am meaning."

Peter looked to Silas for confirmation, his heart hammering in his head now at the thought that the elements of the Lord's Table would be used in some pagan voodoo service like this.

But Silas only shook his head. "Who knows, all I know—"

"Oh, please, pastor!" someone said with interruption. "Please, will you take me to the front?"

It was Katrina again, head spun around with pleading eyes, face twisted up with the same pained expression of hope and anticipation.

Peter's eyes went wide, and his mouth gawped for words.

Is she asking what I think she's asking?

Before he could respond, Silas filled in the blanks for him. "We would be happy to, Katrina. Wouldn't we, Peter?"

He snapped his head toward Silas, drilling him with questioning eyes under a furrowed brow that weren't the least bit happy at his proposal.

But Silas drilled back with his own pair of insisting eyes, widening them and tilting his head, motioning toward the stage as the aisle filled up. Perhaps the Order Master had a plan, and perhaps he should trust him.

Turning back to Katrina, Peter swallowed and smiled. "Yes, Kat. We would be honored."

That wide grin and those crow's feet returned, the woman crying out, "Oh, goodie! Thank you, Jesus, for your healing. Thank you, pastor, for your help!"

He could only smile, not sure he could join her in her thanksgiving, knowing the letdown she would get at the stage. If nothing else, maybe it could serve as a teaching moment for his parishioner, as gut-wrenching as it would be.

Since he was seated at the end, Silas stood and went into the aisle, motioning for three others sitting in the row in front to move. They did while Peter joined the man. Once cleared, the pair carefully went into the row to retrieve Katrina.

"Sorry for the trouble," she said as the men carried her out. "Hate aisle seats, and my neighbors and their boy were kind enough to bring me and help me get situated."

A wheelchair stood folded at the end of the aisle. Her neighbor's son unfolded it for them, and they set her in its seat.

"This is so exciting!" Katrina said, facing forward. "The Lord is gonna send a healing blessing straight into my bones, I just know it!"

Peter's stomach went watery as he grabbed hold of the cold plastic handles and stared down the barrel of the aisle leading toward the ceremony up front. He glanced back at Silas, who nodded him forward, people streaming around them now in a scramble toward the front searching for the same hope that Katrina was.

He nodded in return, sighing with resignation and pushing the wheelchair forward.

Lord, I hope you know what you're doing...

There was a real crowd at the base of the platform, bodies cresting toward a ramp leading up to the top. The music was louder now, speakers stacked on top of one another blaring the worship music they had heard on their first arrival.

Breakthrough, breakthrough, breakthrough-oo-oo.
Breakthrough, breakthrough, breakthrough-oo-oo.
Breakthrough, breakthrough, breakthrough-oo-oo.

Peter rolled his eyes. He wanted to puke. He just might, especially after the verse started up:

It's your breakthrough-day
God's showing the way.
Health and wealth by right they're yours.
It's your breakthrough-day.

It wasn't that he was sickened by the lyrics; they angered him. Not only the flat-out demeaning false teaching that put God on puppet strings to do our bidding, but also the false hope it offered to those crowded in front—people like his dear Katrina. He wanted to run up on the stage and just blow the whole thing up!

Not literally, of course. Maybe preach a sermon that reminded people of the goodness of God despite our suffering and pain and—he glanced down at Kat—paralysis. Because no way was Katrina walking off that stage. A thought that burrowed deep into his gut like lead.

And yet there they were. Reaching the stage and beginning to ascend a ramp to the main-stage platform, along with the rest who were looking for the same hope and healing.

Looking around now at those who had joined the parade of desperation, Peter saw people who were being led by the arm or waving walking sticks around, clearly blind. Others were in similar wheelchairs as Katrina, stiff or slumped over, being wheeled or wheeling themselves toward the light of those two blond-haired charlatans. Still others had indiscernible illnesses, that perhaps weren't illnesses at all. Perhaps they needed to get out of a mountain of debt, or were looking for a promotion, or longed for the American Dream out in the suburbs.

And there they all were, thinking their payday or healing was found under a big-top tent on a fairground in Mill Creek Junction, with those twin bozos as the ringleaders.

Greeting Peter and Katrina and Silas were those ushers and their baskets. It wasn't until they got closer that he saw what they bore.

Prepackaged communion cups. The kind with the little unleavened wafer underneath a clear plastic seal, resting on top a foil one with grape juice hiding underneath.

There was a scoffing from behind at the sight, and the mutter of "Sacrilegious abomination...."

Peter chuckled. "Amen, brother!" Then he glanced back at Silas. "Tell me what you really think."

While they waited, Silas explained, "Perhaps it's my Catholic past rearing its head, experiencing the broken Body and shed Blood of Christ more communally, more purely that's got me hot under the collar."

"Oh, I don't know," Peter said, pushing Kat forward and trying not to be too loud about his own complaints. "Whether you're Catholic or not, I think the principle remains: How do you transform the memory markers of the world's most consequential event—the sacrificial death of God's Son for the forgiveness of sins—into something resembling a late-night Stouffer's TV dinner?"

Silas grunted. "Exactly. Why don't they serve Twinkies and Kool-Aid while they're at it. At least it would taste better!"

Peter laughed to himself and pushed forward, starting to take a liking to the mystery man from the Order of Thaddeus.

A mild-mannered looking fellow, stout with trimmed gray hair, handed Peter one of the sacrilegious packets.

Had to chuckle to himself as he held it in his hand, this "experience" of the Lord's Supper, something he himself experienced during childhood. Like the TV dinner staple of American consumerism, this prepackaged Jesus meal lacked substance, meaning, and community. A few years ago, he got into a heated argument with his mother about it all when he returned home for seminary, complaining about how it shrink-wrapped the Eucharist into some prepackaged pseudo-spiritual thingamabob that was borderline heresy.

Yet there he was, holding the heretical thingamabob for one of his parishioners. How far he had fallen...

Looking up at her pastor, Katrina said, "Now be a good dear and help me out with the Lord's Supper, would you?"

Peter took a breath and looked to Silas, whose face seemed to register the same irritation, brow wrinkled into a scowl and jaw clenched into a frown. At least they were on the same page on that one!

Didn't want to, but Peter complied. Popping the top to the TV dinner, he took the little wafer cracker and set it in Katrina's open mouth—asking Jesus to forgive his participation in the sacrilege even as he thanked Jesus for breaking his body for him and for the world. Then peeling back the foil seal, he placed the tiny plastic cup of grape juice up to her mouth and tipped it until it emptied, thanking Jesus for pouring out his blood for him and Katrina and for the world.

He also prayed for the American Church, asking Jesus to forgive Christianity for reducing the majesty and grandeur of his sacrifice to the equivalence of a Stouffer's frozen entrée. Wanted to do what he did last time that happened: Walk right out of the tent, leaving the band and lights and fog machine in his dust.

But he didn't. Instead, he waited for the line to move forward, glancing down at Katrina, whose eyes were closed and lips were moving in a silent, muttering prayer.

One of the ushers tapped Peter on the arm and motioned them onward.

Peter complied, pushing Katrina toward the pair of evangelists who seemed larger than life now.

They were deep in prayer themselves, arms draped over people seeking the same kind of supernatural miracle Katrina herself was. On closer approach, Peter nearly lost it at who he saw between the pair.

A young man with a crown of dirty-blond hair stuffed under a navy knit cap, gauges the size of nickels in his ears, and tattoos of Chinese characters along his forearm. It was Cameron, his favorite small-town barista with whom he'd been having discussions over C. S. Lewis's *Mere Christianity*. Discussions had been going well, him opening up about his deep questions about faith and life. But Peter could hardly believe his eyes!

What was Cameron doing praying with these two faith healers?

Peter pushed Katrina along, trying to get closer to make sense of it.

When Cameron suddenly began yelling, "I can see again! I can see!"

Then he began jumping up and down, face wide with

delight and eyes wet with emotive joy. Had never seen the kid like this before, yet there he was: jumping and lifting his hands up in adulation toward the heavens, fist-bumping Dexter and Paulina who were crowing about the miracle from heaven.

Which was interrupted by still more people crying out with claims of healing: blind people regaining their sight; deaf and mute regaining their hearing! Some who had been hobbling along were casting aside their crutches, and empty wheelchairs littered the stage now.

"This is bizarre," Silas said lowly from behind.

Slowing to a stop again in all the euphoric pandemonium, Peter turned to face him. "That's one way of putting it. And I'd have completely written it off as the hysterical cries of crazy people caught up in the moment, or actors paid to bolster the claims. But with Cameron..."

Peter looked back at the young man kneeling on the floor now, crying with abandon and still yelling, "I can see!"

"You know that guy?" asked Silas.

"Yeah, he's my barista."

"No way..."

"And we're in a book club together, reading Lewis."

"As in C. S. Lewis?"

"You know of any other Lewises?" scoffed Peter. He took a breath and shook his head. "Anyway, no way he's faking it."

"Zero chance?"

"Less than zero."

A piercing scream suddenly split the atmosphere, cutting them off.

In front—and down in front.

It was Katrina!

She was muttering something incoherent under a torrent of blubbering cries, her arms rising from the wheelchair's arms and hands shaking, fingers flexing even. And now her legs were out straight ahead!

"I'm healed! Lord, Almighty, I can move!"

She let loose the kind of giggling laughter you hear from people on rollercoaster rides, the sheer adrenaline rush pushing the inner child out into the wild.

"Lord, Almighty, I've been healed! I can move my legs!"

And she did, jumping up from the wheelchair and skipping across the stage to join Cameron and the others who had been touched by something miraculous.

Leaving Peter in her wake with a million questions.

CHAPTER 8

Silas shut his passenger's side door with more slam than he intended. Couldn't help it after what they'd just witnessed, his mind spinning with possibilities and heart jumpy with the adrenaline rush. Something strange was going on. And he didn't have the slightest clue what to make of it.

He settled back into the soft black leather Escalade seat even as his stomach was unsettled from what had happened. Gapinski joined him at the front, yapping about the crazy while the others piled in the back, muttering to each other about it all.

Putting a foot on the dashboard and rubbing his chin, he wondered: What *had* they just witnessed? What had just happened—in front of his very own eyes?

"What the hey-ho-day was that?" Gapinski said, reaching into his coat.

"That was most unnerving," Celeste said. "And I mean all of it. From the showtime spectacle and music to the message and then the...well, I suppose I should call it healings."

"Yeah, that was definitely cuckoo for Cocoa Puffs!"

"*Muy loco,*" Torres agreed. "*Muy loco...*"

Peter was silent, eyes wide and staring out his window in the back row.

Silas turned around, drilling the pastor with questioning eyes. "What the heck have you gotten us into?"

The pastor looked toward the front, meeting Silas's gaze, brow furrowing with confusion. "What are you talking about?"

"When we signed up to this gig, we didn't think it was to join the circus. And to take part in the circus by aiding in some voodoo magic ceremony! Not to mention getting some poor paralyzed woman's hopes up with the promise of healing."

"Hey, I didn't know that was going to go down! And besides, I told you strange things were going on here. The kind of nonsense all of us just witnessed. I'm just glad you got to see it up close so you would believe I wasn't just overreacting. Sounds like that was exactly what you thought."

"Boys!" Celeste shouted, putting out a staying hand. "Let's put away the swords, shall we? I understand emotions might be running a bit ragged from the...shall we say, unexpected occurrences inside the tent. But let's not bite each other's bloomin' heads off. We still have work to do."

She particularly drilled Silas with a glare that drove home the point. He felt his cheeks flush. Not only with embarrassment from being called out, but also from biting the poor pastor's head off. He didn't need that. None of them did. The whole thing had unnerved him, and he'd acted like a jerk in response.

He took a calming breath and nodded. "You're right, Celeste. And sorry about that, Peter. Biting your head off. Just unnerved by it all, I guess. But no excuse, regardless."

Peter nodded in reply, offering an acknowledging smile.

"So now what?"

Celeste offered, "If there is anyone who can sort this for us and bring clarity, Victor Zarruq back at HQ should be a world of help."

"You're right. Probably time to phone home and give an update, anyway."

Gapinski finished unwrapping something, then added, "And figure out what the hey-ho-day is going on here!" He chewed into a chocolate cupcake filled with white frosting and hummed with pleasure.

"And what, pray tell, are you eating?" Celeste asked, arms folded.

His eyes went big, and he hung his mouth open dumbly. "Uh, a cupcake?"

"Where'd you get that?" Silas asked, slightly annoyed the man was gorging on desserts during the heat of a mission.

Gapinski swallowed and wiped his mouth. "The Shell station, when we rolled into town."

"You got enough to go around, Hoss?" Torres said, crossing her arms as well.

"There's one more. Want it?"

She snorted a laugh. "Yeah, right. But didn't your mama ever teach you about eating in front of people?"

He sighed and rolled his eyes. "I'm famished, alright! And big boned."

"Haven't we heard that before…"

"And the peanuts on the flight over did jack squat. Wouldn't fill a famished monkey!"

"And you think a cupcake will?"

He hung his head before snatching another bite. "Maybe…"

Silas smirked and shook his head. Gapinski and his regular eating patterns. To each his own, he supposed.

He placed a video call to Victor back at the farm. Celeste was right. If anyone could help them make sense of this, it was him.

Soon the man was on the screen, a wide grin playing behind a bushy salt-and-pepper beard. Looked like he was in the new operations center. Probably keeping tabs on the developments around the world with the contagion and the other mystery revivals.

Holding the phone out for all to see, Silas said, "Hi, Victor. Got the rest of the SEPIO crew here and Peter Young, the pastor we connected with."

"Ahh, there are my intrepid ecclesial explorers. Find anything interesting in the hinterlands?"

Silas shifted, glancing over his shoulder at the rest. "You could say that."

"Victor," Celeste said, "we ventured out into the charismatic revival service here in Mill Creek Junction and had a bit of a controversial experience. We hoped you could shed some light on it."

Zarruq tilted his head and hummed. "Really? Do tell."

She did, explaining what they had witnessed, including the inspirational message and the purported healing of Peter's executive assistant.

The man groaned, slouching back in his chair. "Sounds like a stock prosperity gospel service to me," he complained, shaking his head and mumbling something under his breath in his native Libyan tongue.

"That's what we'd like more help with," Silas said. "As we're confronting—whatever it is we're confronting, we had hoped you might shed some more historical light on what we are up against."

"What do you want to know?"

"How about you start from the top. Where did it start, what's it rooted in, who were the main proponents?"

The large man shifted, leaning back and bringing his hands to his belly.

"The prosperity gospel," Zarruq started, "is rooted theologically in a thoroughly pagan system of thought called New Thought, a metaphysical healing cult of the 19th century that taught the mind empowers you to unlock your true reality. Phineas Quimby, the father of New Thought, did not claim to be teaching historic Christianity or the Bible. Remarkably, his teachings invaded the Church like a virus, staying with us for two centuries!"

"And what did he teach?" Celeste asked.

"That all sickness and disease have their origins in the mind. That we can heal ourselves through right thinking, believing hypnotism was such a key to unlocking these powers. He insisted that he himself had discovered the secret healing methods of Jesus embedded in his teachings. Not only that, he taught that Christ was simply a man like you and me who used mind-control to bring healing to his subjects—from the blind man to the deaf, the leper to the paralytic."

Silas frowned. All sicknesses they had witnessed "healed" at the charismatic service.

"All of these teachings spread like wildfire during his day and have carried through to this day. Mostly because prosperity preachers leveraged Quimby's theology and teachings, beginning with Norman Vincent Peale."

"*The Power of Positive Thinking* guy?" Gapinski asked.

"Correct. That book is probably credited with single-handedly helping spread New Thought beliefs farther than they might have spread. But earlier, a chap by the name of Smith Wigglesworth took Quimby's teachings to a new level, focusing on signs and wonders. Healings, miracles, tongues—those were core."

Silas glanced at Celeste. That sure sounded familiar.

Zarruq went on, "He taught that believers should not take any sort of medical treatment for any illness. Instead, they should speak their healing into existence and believe in faith that it would be so. Of course, if people weren't healed of their illness, they were to blame. Sick people were responsible for their sickness, as well as healing, blaming it on their own unconfessed sin and lack of faith. He had no regard for biblical teaching on praying and trusting God's will or God's purposes through physical trials and sanctification from unhealed sickness. As you can imagine, Wigglesworth brought massive spiritual confusion and toxic abuse to those who were sick and desperate."

"*Dios mío...*" Torres said, folding her arms against herself, as if in an embrace. "Imagine telling sick people that they were the problem."

"And then," Zarruq added, "putting the blame on hurting people when he failed to heal them! Both are still part and parcel with contemporary prosperity gospel teachings."

Silas shook his head. What tragic heresy. He glanced at Torres, whose face was drawn and eyes cast to the floor, arms still crossing her chest and rubbing her arms. How must she feel in the face of all of this with the burden of cancer? That it was her fault, that she didn't have enough faith?

"Then there is the granddaddy of them all," Zarruq continued, "Kenneth Hagin. Who you could call the father of the Word of Faith movement."

"The Word of Faith movement?" Gapinski asked.

"I'm unfamiliar with that as well," Celeste said.

"The Word of Faith belief system," Zarruq explained, "is a popular kind of Christian theology that's entirely out of step with historic Christian orthodoxy. It tells people they can get healing from illness, money in their bank accounts, jobs and promotions, babies and automobiles—you name it. But the trick is that they must speak these things into existence by faith, through the spoken word."

Gapinski scoffed. "What, like abracadabra I want a Lamborghini Diablo?"

"Precisely!"

He smirked. "I gotta learn that trick."

"Not the kind of teaching you want to take part in, Matthew. For the man's services were characterized by demonic-like behavior and false teaching. In one wild tale, Hagin paused a sermon he was preaching and began to laugh wickedly, acting demon possessed. Leaving the platform and his sermon behind, he walked through the throngs of people and flicked his tongue like a snake. More disturbingly, he shouted, 'Drunk again!' whilst people convulsed on the floor and screamed hysterically, falling over in ecstatic states."

"Disturbing is right," Celeste said.

"And creepy!" Gapinski said.

"And that is not the most disturbing part of Hagin!" Zarruq said.

"What could be more disturbing than flicking your tongue around like a snake?"

"Sick..." Silas said, becoming increasingly unsettled, angry even, at the theological foundation that seemed to sit below what they had witnessed.

He was also itching to do something about.

"It doesn't stop there! What Hagin taught that was more openly blasphemous still was 'little god' theology—which was not even hiding his heresy at that point!"

"Little god?" Silas said, the language striking something familiar in him.

Zarruq nodded. "That's right."

Celeste scooted to the edge of her seat and leaned toward the phone. "Now that has a familiar ring to it. Like the new upstart pseudo-religious entity we encountered a year ago. The one giving challenge to Nous."

Silas snapped his fingers. "That's right. The Church of the Theotites, or deities."

"By that wackadoodle Sha character," Gapinski said.

"Theoti, little deities."

Celeste said, "Are you thinking that perhaps they might be the ones behind this new—whatever it is?"

Running a hand through his hair, Silas shrugged. "Not sure. But we should keep a lookout for their involvement anyhow."

"And our other fine, furry friends," Gapinski added.

He frowned, knowing the truth that if this circus was somehow about the Church's demise and bringing spiritual confusion to the Christian faith, then Nous and his brother Sebastian were sure to be involved.

"Victor," Celeste asked, "what is this little god theology you were going on about?"

He replied, "It teaches that a Christian believer is as much an incarnation of God as Jesus of Nazareth himself was, created on the same terms of equality with God and given the same standing in God's presence. Hagin said that God made us as much like himself as possible. The same class of being, even, that he is himself! That everything that can be said of Jesus can be said of us."

Silas twisted up his face. "Everything? In what way?"

"Everything that Jesus did, we can do. Healing, creating abundance, what have you. Benny Hinn is another one of these popular prosperity preachers who took this little-god theology to the stratosphere, including calling himself Benny Jehovah!"

"Wait a hot second," Gapinski said, sitting up. "Isn't Jehovah another Hebrew name for the God of Israel?"

"That's right," Silas said.

He whistled. "That takes some mighty big cajones to put yourself on the same level as God!"

Zarruq cleared his throat. "As right as you are, I might put it a bit less colorfully..."

Gapinski blushed, popping the rest of his cupcake in his mouth and sinking in his seat. "Sorry…"

"Then there's Oral Roberts," Zarruq went on, "which brings us closest to our own day. He didn't mince words when it came to his idealized version of Jesus and the gospel, teaching with a fiery boldness that Jesus' highest wish for everyone was that they would prosper materially and have physical health in this life equal to Jesus' peace and power in the soul. Perhaps that's because he woefully got Jesus' teachings wrong on the subject!"

"How so, Victor?" Celeste asked.

The man chuckled, which rolled into a belly laugh. "He believed that Jesus said, *'Beloved, I wish above all things that thou mayest prosper and be in health, even as thy soul prospereth,'* when actually it was the Apostle John who said it in his third letter, offering a loving greeting to his readers."

"So you're telling us that he built part of his theology on a faulty reading of Scripture?"

"Precisely!" Zarruq shook his head and muttered something again in his native tongue.

"Just goes to show," Silas said, "how important a solid foundation is to one's beliefs."

"Well put, Silas. Roberts stood at the headwaters of the explosion of televangelism and rock-star prosperity preachers who claimed to bring healing to the sick and open up the storehouses of blessing from heaven. Remarkably, he claimed to have raised dozens from the dead, including a baby in the middle of a service."

The archbishop closed his eyes and shook his head, muttering something under his breath.

"So all of these people," Silas said, trying to bring it all home, "became household names for the so-called 'name it and claim it' theology, the prosperity gospel."

"Precisely," Zarruq said. "They perpetuated, and in many ways produced, the teachings that say God is required to respond to our faith and the words of confession we utter in faith to bring about the abundant life. In my view, all prosperity gospel roads are paved with bars of gold—leading one straight into the bosom of the Devil himself."

"Tell us what you really think..." Gapinski muttered.

Silas asked, "What do you propose we do about it then?"

"Expose it and outlaw it!" Zarruq thundered through the phone.

"Outlaw it?" Torres asked. "A little extreme. Sounds like the Taliban!"

"Well, not literally. But it can no longer be tolerated in conservative evangelical circles as merely a sideshow of tongue-speaking, miracle-believing, well-intentioned Christians and leaders. It must be called out, exposed, and stripped naked for what it is: a false gospel, led by false teachers, peddling false teaching that is a disease, not the cure, leveraging the hopes and dreams of desperate people using cheap parlor tricks and David Copperfield illusions."

Celeste said, "Then how exactly do you propose we expose it? What you're suggesting seems like a bit of a tall order, considering how entrenched it is, how widespread."

Zarruq shrugged. "I am not sure how to answer that one. I suppose that's why they pay you the big bucks, as they say."

Gapinski laughed. "What line of work are you talking about, and how can I get in on it?"

He chuckled. "But if you were to ask me, I suppose we should be looking at their motivation."

Silas said, "How do you think we should go about figuring that out?"

"You remember that Jerry Maguire quote," Gapinski said.

"Which one?"

"Come on, Silas. Only the most quotable of quotes!"

"Show me the money," Torres said.

Gapinski nodded. "Exactamundo."

She patted him on the leg. "That ain't Spanish, Hoss."

"It ain't? Huh…"

Celeste looked to Silas. "Now what do you propose we do?"

He glanced at her, Silas mulling something that was turning into a possibility that just might work to expose it all as the sham it is.

"I've got an idea," he said. "Thanks for the background on what we've stepped into, Victor. We'll be in touch."

CHAPTER 9

Saying their goodbyes, Silas threw open his door and climbed out. Then he started across the field of flattened, browned grass serving as a parking lot for the religious carnival that was boiling his blood.

Hoping to the good Lord above that he knew what he was doing!

"Love, what are you on about?" Celeste asked, chasing after Silas.

The others following now, he glanced back and said, "I'd say it's about time we get to it and start peeling back the layers to this onion—SEPIO style."

"With a scalpel or hacksaw?"

He threw her a grin. "Prefer the former but will settle for the latter."

"Oh, I like the sound of that!" Gapinski said.

"And what does that mean?" Torres shouted, Silas pulling away from his teammates in his eager hustle. "What do you have in mind?"

Heat rose at the back of his neck. Not only from the high-noon sun beating down on them now. But also from a sudden shot of embarrassment. Because honestly, he didn't really know exactly what he had in mind.

All he knew was that sitting around inside that pimped-out SUV while the revival service continued its spectacle, with its thumping music and magical-thinking messages and strange blessings seemingly falling from the heavens—in the face of all that, doing nothing wasn't an option anymore. He'd seen enough to know something wasn't right about any of it. And it wasn't just about the healing, either.

It was the tone and tenor of it all. The hyped music and flashing lights and fog rolling off the stage. The people standing and waving, singing and shouting, expecting to be hit over the head with an abundant-life blessing—by God, that day, to cure some ailment or fill some bank account. All promised by the Bobbsey Twins that put the best prosperity gospel preachers he'd heard to shame—with their designer skinny jeans and V-neck shirts and stylish haircuts, those words that sounded like honey to the ears yet were vinegar to the stomach. Putting God on the puppet strings of our every American middle-class whim.

And that wasn't even touching on the Eucharistic element that Silas didn't even want to touch with a ten-foot pole! Turned his belly something fierce just thinking about it, the sour tang of bile rising at the back of his throat an apt description of the whole blasted thing! It was presented as an add-on at the end of the revival event, a religious ritual complementing the rest of the Christian service. But it also seemed more than that—whatever *that* was.

No, sir, sitting time was over.

It was go time.

At least he had a sense of where to go. After that...

It was up to the leading of the Holy Spirit!

"Oy, Silas, love!" Celeste shouted from behind with irritation. "Slow down!"

"Yeah, bro," Gapinski added. "Where's the four-alarm fire?"

Silas stopped at an old Chrysler LeBaron the color of ground beef to let the others catch up, a memory of his very first car brightening his sour mood some.

"Still waiting on my reply, chief," Torres muttered, coming up with the others out of breath.

"To what question?"

"To what the heck is the plan?"

"Good question, Silas," Peter asked, wiping sweat from his brow. "I'm beginning to wonder myself."

Silas replied, "We're done sitting on our hands. Time to get some answers. Inside."

"Inside?"

He started back for the tent. Weaving between a navy Ford Fiesta and a silver Toyota Camry, he gestured toward the imposing structure. "Looked like there was another entrance, at the back. Glimpsed it on our way in, several people coming in and out. Figured we slip in and have ourselves a look around while the show goes on."

"Not a bad idea," Celeste said. "SEPIO is pretty adept at shoving a camel through the eye of the needle when it needs to."

Silas threw her a grin. "There's the spirit!"

Gapinski snorted a laugh. "Just glad we ain't the rich men Jesus was talking about in that little ditty of his, or we're all in deep doo doo!"

"I don't know, Hoss," Torres said. "If you believe it's your breakthrough day, then you might fulfill Jesus' teachings!"

"Luckily for us, I'm quite content with my SEPIO salary and vow of poverty."

Hustling to Silas's side, Peter asked, "And how are we going to do that, slip inside and look around?"

The pastor's voice betrayed a reticence Silas had no time for. So he ignored him, picking up the pace as they came up to a towering canvas wall arcing toward the back where he had spied the opening.

"Petey—can I call you Petey?" Gapinski said to the pastor as they hustled past thick rope anchoring the tent to iron loops cemented into the ground.

Peter sighed, but nodded. "People do."

"Excellent! Anyway, gotta remember SEPIO rule numero uno, Petey, if you're gonna join our crew."

"I hate to ask, but what's that?"

"Fake it till you make it."

"Sounds like fortune-cookie wisdom."

"Don't know where it came from. All I know is it works."

"So pragmatism's king, is that it?"

Gapinski shrugged. "When you've got a Heckler & Koch G36 assault rifle slinging 750 rounds a minute at your ass, you tend to go for pragmatism."

"Thanks. I'll keep that in mind."

Coming up to the back entrance, Silas slowed, putting out a staying hand. He could hear their whispered steps across the grass, the bunch crouching low behind parked cars. A piece of canvas waved at them on a gentle breeze across the way, the music ratcheting back up now and coming at them all muffled.

But no guard. Singular or plural. No one, in fact. Seemed empty.

So Silas swallowed and straightened, picking up his pace into a deliberate gait toward the maw of darkness like they owned the joint.

Didn't take long before he slipped inside, the rest close behind.

That blasted chorus was struck up again, with people naming and claiming their breakthrough day. The back portion was wide and dim, stretching the length of the football field-size space behind bleachers packed with the shouting, singing faithful. Through their feet, Silas could see a line of people still stretching through the parted crowd on the floor snaking toward the stage.

Some were pushing wheelchairs, others hobbling along on crutches. Still more were being led by the arm and others with upraised hands—all waiting to ascend the stairs to receive their blessing from the mystery twins.

Scratch that.

To receive their strange blessing from a strange mystery pair that made not a lick of sense—all hoping to be touched by the same strange power, or whatever the heck it was, that had given Katrina back use of her limbs.

Couldn't blame them, with what Silas had seen up close. Even he couldn't deny the truth of it. Whatever *it* was—which was what drove him to trespass the back parts of the carnival. A minor violation in a long line of them with SEPIO that sometimes needled his conscience. He told himself it was for a good cause—and it was, fighting for the faith. But sometimes he wondered about the lengths they would go, the lengths he himself would go to guard and protect it.

Tables lined the back of those bleachers with what looked like sound equipment and computers controlling the red, blue, and green lights flashing now. A pair of young men with headphones were hunched over the mess, oblivious to their entrance with backs turned to SEPIO.

Along the back canvas wall, pinewood crates were stacked along with cardboard boxes stuffed with bubble wrap.

Silas headed there first, silently gesturing for the others to spread out.

Time for answers.

The bassy thump and trebly twang of the worship music, combined with the dimness of the backstage and undulating lights drowned out all sense of things. Eyes had started to adjust to his surroundings from stepping in from the sunny outdoors, but his ears couldn't hear much more than the racket.

Not much time, so they'd have to make quick work of things before anyone started asking questions.

Or a more common SEPIO outcome: the lead started flying.

Coming up to the crates, Silas instinctively reached around with his right hand under his coat, checking that his Beretta was safe and sound.

Hope for the best, prepare for the worst.

Ready, willing, and able.

Nothing special about the crates. Pine wood, beat up pretty good from use, no shipping manifests he could see or any other identifying marks.

"Find anything interesting?" Celeste said, coming to his side.

He shook his head, turning one of the crates on wheels around for a closer viewing.

Empty. Except for black foam packing material in long thick sheets.

"For the sound system, perhaps?" she said.

"Probably right."

He checked a few more of the crates. Two tall, long ones on wheels; a few other fat and squat ones resting on pallets. Same empty result.

Turning his attention to the boxes, he could see several smaller boxes resting beneath the bubble wrap. Dark purple things with an image on the face obscured by the packing material.

But Silas instantly recognized what it was picturing.

A silver platter with a complementary silver chalice filled with crimson liquid and a loaf of bread.

The bread and the cup.

The memory markers of Christ's Body and Blood.

Prepackaged like a Stouffer's TV dinner and given out like candy on Halloween to Cameron and Katrina and everyone else waiting for their strange blessing.

Silas's mouth curled upward with success.

Bingo.

Casting aside the bubble wrap, the bass and treble giving him a headache now, he took one of the boxes the size of a cigar box and turned it around, looking for an opening.

Sealed shut with cellophane.

Turning it over, he searched for the manufacturer.

When a strong hand clamped down on his shoulder with purpose.

Right before it spun him around to face the music. And the box was ripped from his hands.

He was facing a large man. Tanned and all neck, with arms bulging through a black suit that looked far from a Macy's off-the-rack special. Something more from 5th Avenue or Beverly Hills Boulevard.

"Whatcha you doin', partner?" the goon growled in a Southern twang, sausage and onions riding high on a hot breath.

Before he could answer, Gapinski stepped up to Silas's side. "Sorry about that—*partner.* But we were just looking for our breakthrough-day blessing."

Silas stifled a laugh.

Took the man a minute, but he narrowed his eyes and clenched his jaw with irritation.

Now another man stepped up to the plate. Same tan, same neck, same arms bulging through a fine suit. Maybe Zegna or Armani.

"Who are you?" he said with the same growly Southern twang.

If SEPIO's first rule of engagement was fake it till you make it, the second one was don't be afraid to flash your creds at the drop of a hat.

In this case, their Vatican creds. Especially to avoid the lead-flying outcome that was all-too common in SEPIO missions.

Sure, the Order of Thaddeus was no longer a strictly Catholic entity, having spun out into an ecumenical one with involvement across the Church's denominational spectrum. Still, there were enough ties to the Eternal City and its official entities to not make it a lie.

Silas took a step forward, drilling the first man's dark eyes. "We're operatives with the Vatican on a fact-finding mission." He could read instant confusion on his face before his eyes flashed recognition.

Worked every time.

"What does the Vatican want with our worship service?"

"You tell me? What reason would the Holy See have for sending us to investigate a charismatic religious service? Perhaps the purported healings, or the promise of abundant-life prosperity, or leveraging the hopes and dreams of the desperate and dying to fill your own coffers?"

Silas knew he was sowing confusion with his rapid-fire questions. He also knew he was getting too prickly right off the bat. Couldn't risk offending the prospects just yet. Still, it looked like it was working.

Goon One turned to his partner, who shrugged, then narrowed his eyes. "I asked you first. Who are you and what are you doing here?"

"We asked you second," Celeste said, stepping into the ring now. "There have been rumors of multiple strange goings-on in these parts. So what reason would the Holy See have to be concerned, if in fact it was all on the up-and-up?"

"I have no idea! You're the one claiming to be investigating on their behalf."

"Ahh, but that's the trick, isn't it. What are we investigating?"

That face stood frozen, though now growing a shade more crimson. "That's what I asked you!"

"You tell us," Torres said, joining in now to make the SEPIO circle complete.

Then Gapinski again at her side: "Yeah, Bub, what's the deal?"

Silas could tell the one fella was growing irritated, and they were losing him. Goon Two just shifted on his feet, dumb with speech and probably dumber than a sack of chicken feed. If they weren't careful, the pair might call in reinforcements—or worse, think that getting the local police involved was the best route to go. Figured Peter could work his local minister magic if it came to it. But that definitely wasn't something he wanted to risk.

Not yet, anyway.

So he said, "What my partners are trying to get at is, there have been these rumors of healings and other strange things happening inside."

"Not rumors," the man said.

The other goon started, "It's the wonder-working power of the blood—"

Before being cut off by his partner: "This is a restricted area, partner. I'm going to have to ask you to leave now."

"Ask away," Gapinski said, folding his arms and staying put.

No one moved, Silas glancing around the place as another song started blaring, those crates along the back calling out for his attention again, along with binders he could see resting on those tables piled with equipment and the computers those geeks were manning.

What secrets did they hold?

He knew it was pointless to press it further. But they'd be back, if it came to it.

So Silas said with a smile, "Alright, we're leaving. Thanks for cooperating. I'll put in a good word with the Pontiff for you."

Then he turned and left, the others following close behind.

Didn't take a parting glance on their way out, though Silas could sense Goon One and Goon Two guarding the entrance with folded arms. Probably were jibber-jabbering into wrist mics, too, styling themselves as Secret Service agents ready to go to the mat for their bosses—whoever they were.

"See anything of interest?" Celeste said, coming up to him as they weaved back through the Ford and Toyota from earlier.

"Not really. Just that box of prepackaged Eucharistic elements."

"Oy. Makes my stomach churn with positive annoyance at transforming the bread and cup in that way."

"Hear you there. But other than that, didn't get much. You?"

She shook her head. "Nothing on my end either."

"Or ours," Torres said, gesturing to Gapinski as the pair hustled up from behind.

"Roger that," Silas said. "Let's get back to the car and debrief from the afternoon's events."

"Over food?" Gapinski asked with eager eyes. "Saw a bangin' bar and grill on Main Street that looked promising."

Torres smirked. "Told ya that chocolate cupcake wouldn't be enough."

"Can we go check on Katrina first?" Peter asked. "I'd like to make sure she's alright."

Silas went to object, mind focused on the mission at hand. But he realized it was the right thing to do. Not only for Katrina's sake, her pastor checking in on her, but also for Peter's.

"Sure thing. Then afterwards we'll debrief, over food."

"Yes! I'm famished," Gapinski said, the group returning to their Escalade and piling inside.

Silas echoed his sentiment. Hungry for food, yes, but more.

To figure out what the heck was going on in Mill Creek Junction.

And whether the Order should care.

CHAPTER 10

The place called Max's Place was packed with patrons, buzzing with conversations, and smelling of greasy food and hoppy beer.

Just Silas's kind of place, especially one that served bison burgers piled high with all the fixings and sweet potato fries along with an India Pale Ale with backbone. Although, it seemed a bit too packed for the mid-afternoon. Perhaps it was always happy hour in small-town America, what did he know?

What he did know was that he was famished, stomach growling and head growing faint from hunger. He chuckled to himself as he scoped the place, thinking he was sounding like Gapinski now from want of food. Thanks to his clockwork metabolism, they got an excuse to grab some grub and debrief on the noon-time festivities. And what a festival it was.

The trip to what Silas thought would be to Nowheresville, a favor for an old professional acquaintance, had taken a turn toward the strange in no time flat.

It wasn't just that a bunch of people seemed to get healed—although that was yet to be determined—it was the whole kit and caboodle! The pageantry of it all and the trappings of the worship service—with the concert-level lighting and band; the

Tony Robbins-style preaching, the promise of health and wealth taking center stage; the Eucharistic elements, the bread and cup memory markers of Christ's broken body and shed blood, used as props for the circus. All of it was whacked out. Whatever blessing had manifested itself at the hands of those two mystery evangelists was strange, no doubt about it.

Silas didn't know what to make of it all. And he sure as heck didn't know if it had anything to do with the Order.

He stretched out in his chair at a scuffed wood table tucked next to a stage in the corner of the local watering hole, a pocketful of questions burning his legs and no answers to be found for miles. Figured one or two might turn up in a pint of beer, maybe even a glass of whiskey. At that hour, mid-afternoon, such things usually did. But with the way the day had just turned, he wasn't sure.

"Man, this joint sure is hopping," Gapinski said, eyeing the place.

"Max is a popular character," Peter answered, "and he makes a mean bison burger."

"Can't wait to sink my teeth into that one!"

"Hoss eat a bison burger? How original," Torres quipped.

"Hey! Silas is getting in on the bison burger action. Speaking of which..."

His head followed a pair of servers with trays piled high heading toward the table. But then it fell when they bypassed them to another.

"Don't worry," Silas said. "It'll get here when it gets here."

Gapinski crossed his arms in a huff. "I only hope I'm still alive when they do..."

Packed to the gills and surely breaking fire code, the place was humming with what you'd expect after a long day of work, but in the middle of the afternoon. Every table was full plus the bar, with servers running drinks and plates stacked with those popular burgers and fries from the back kitchen out to the floor at a regular pace. Stage was empty next door, and Silas wondered what it was like later in the evening when work was out and people needed to unwind if it was that crowded that early. Perhaps Mill Creek had the same idea as him, finding answers to their questions about what the heck had gone on up the road in a pitcher of brew.

Running through the numbers again from the noon-time service, Silas tried making sense of it all but came up empty. What the heck was going on? What were they going to do about it, if they even should, considering someone had been healed right before their eyes?

After Peter's assistant, Katrina, had her...episode—Silas couldn't quite bring himself to call it a miracle, not yet anyway, even though it seemed just that. Afterward, he and Peter had brought the woman back to her seat, where a whole new round of cheers of amening and thanksgiving erupted from the neighbors that had brought her to the service, and then those surrounding her. Became a mild celebrity from it all, people wanting to praise the miracle and get the inside scoop—touch Katrina even, perhaps believing some of the power that had restored the use of her arms and legs would rub off on them.

Worried that the older lady might have some psychological reaction to the whole event or that it was all a mistake, they had returned to confirm Katrina was not only healed but also well. The pastor had first insisted they take her to the local hospital straight away, wanting to make sure nothing odd was happening to her body—in a natural way beyond what had happened to her in a seemingly supernatural way—but she wasn't having any of it. Insisted she was fine and the Lord Jesus Christ healed her! Why would she need some hospital doc poking and prodding her when the Great Physician himself had visited her with his healing power?

The two went back and forth until finally they settled on her making a follow-up appointment in the next day or two after recovering from it all back at home. Getting Katrina settled, Peter suggested they all grab a bite to eat and debrief about the whole affair. Silas and the SEPIO gang quickly agreed.

A middle-aged woman with shoulder-length curls sidled up to the table with a tray of drinks. Sheila, her name tag read. Another large man with an apron and eight-ball head slick with sweat came bearing five platters of bison burgers piled high with fries. The table sang their praises then quickly got to work.

Silas's first stop was his beer, taking a long swig of the decent IPA Peter said was homegrown. The hoppy citrusy brew already started working its magic at first sip, sending his taste buds standing at attention and the synapses of his brain firing now.

It was go time.

Taking another swig, Silas asked, "So what do you all make of what happened up the road?" Then he promptly chewed into the greasy bison meat stacked with tomatoes and pickles and lettuce, the mayonnaise and ketchup and mustard running together in a tangy, orangey hue.

Pure Nirvana!

Everyone else around the table settled in with the same, popping fries and taking bites and throwing back swigs of brew with quiet contemplation, whether from hunger or from confusion at how to answer the question.

What did happen up the road?

"All I have to say—" Gapinski said, mouth full of fries. He paused to throw back a swig of dark beer, then continued, "—is that this whole thing is cuckoo for Cocoa Puffs!"

"Not sure I'd put it that way," Torres said, raising her glass, "but I'll drink to that."

"Cuckoo, maybe," Silas said, looking to Peter for guidance, but finding none. The pastor was picking at the worn wood with a fingernail and not engaged, burger and drink left untouched. He went on, "But we can't deny what we saw. The woman was stiff as a board in that chair, unable to move or walk. Then…"

He trailed off, throwing back a swig of the hoppy, citrusy goodness, not able to wrap his mind around what he had witnessed. He popped a few fries, waiting for someone else to put the pieces together.

"I wonder, though…" Celeste said, trailing off herself before settling back in her chair with her drink.

Silas swallowed. "Wonder what?"

"Whether we're certain the woman was ill to begin with."

At that, Peter raised his head. "Absolutely."

"So there's no possible way she was faking it?" Celeste asked, taking a swig of her raspberry beer.

"None."

"Pretty definitive, don't you think?" Silas asked. "Because from my understanding, these sorts of ecstatic religious experiences can get people carried away. Like they need to prove the genuineness of the experience."

"Got that right!" Torres snorted a laugh in her glass. "I've seen people do *muy loco* things to make sure the party line was maintained, even faking being slain in the spirit and speaking in tongues."

Peter threw back a swig of beer and frowned, his brow going with it. "Are you seriously calling Kat a liar?"

Silas put up a hand. "We're not calling your assistant anything. We're just wondering how she could be seemingly paralyzed one minute, then dancing and jumping up and down the next—as if she had been healed or something!"

"That's because she *was* healed." Peter tore into his burger now, chomping as Silas eyed his teammates while the seconds ticked by. He swallowed and chased it with a swig of beer, then added, "Has to be."

Silas waited a beat to respond, shifting in his chair at the claim. "Why is that? Or why do you think that's the case?"

Draining half the glass now, the pastor explained, "Because after Kat called me from her hospital room, I went to see her with my own eyes. Got chatting with the doc that diagnosed her too, and he laid it all out. Sudden onset paralysis, that's what he confirmed."

Celeste said, "So the woman was genuinely paralyzed then?"

"More than genuine. Definitive. And besides, this whole charismatic faith-healing stuff is so far outside Katrina's orbit, I about fell over when I saw her at the service! Never would have expected her at something like that. I mean, she's a Baptist for goodness' sake!"

"If there's anything I can confirm," Gapinski said, mouth full of fries, "it's that what happened an hour ago is definitely not the Baptist norm! Grandpappy would turn over in his grave if he knew I was at such a thing myself."

Peter nodded. "Exactly. And same goes for Cameron."

"Who?" Torres asked, her own mouth full of fries.

Silas answered, "The other man we saw healed of blindness, isn't that right?"

Peter nodded. "Exactly."

"Who's this bloke?" Celeste asked. "And blindness, you say?"

"So he claims..." Silas replied, leaning back with a mixture of skepticism and dread—didn't know which emotion to pay attention to.

Peter rolled his eyes. "Cameron's my Starbucks barista. A young man who's spiritually interested in Jesus but the farthest thing from a holy roller who'd show up at a charismatic revival meeting."

Celeste frowned with consideration. "Unless, of course, he was desperate for healing."

"Exactly. Except he wasn't blind a few days ago when he was making my latte!" The pastor threw back a swig of beer and shook his head. "No, if he's claiming blindness, I believe the kid. No doubt. Same as Kat."

"So two spontaneous illnesses," Torres said, "both healed by some itinerant charismatic faith healers at a revival meeting rolling through some backwoods small town?" She chuckled and took a swig of beer herself. "No offense or anything."

Peter smiled. "None taken. But, yeah, that seems about right."

"That's nutso to the maxo!" Gapinski said, draining his drink now.

"But let's be clear, the one isn't verified," Celeste said with caution. "Your friend, Cameron, is it? We don't know he was truly blind, not like Katrina's paralysis, as far as verification goes. Medically, I mean."

Peter nodded. "You are right about that, not in the same medical sense. Not like I had a chat with Cameron's ophthalmologist or anything. But there is nothing about this kid that would tell me he was faking blindness only to later claim some sort of miraculous healing by some itinerant charismatic faith healers."

Silas drained his beer and sat back. None of this was adding up. Although perhaps it was adding up to something he didn't care to admit.

These people really were healed at some itinerant charismatic faith healers' revival tent meeting rolling through Small Town, America!

"Hold the phone, peeps," Gapinski said, "Are we saying that a pair of David Copperfields just healed a blind man and paralytic, along with however many other yahoos jumpin' and jivin' to the Holy Spirit's beat?"

The group went silent, the truth of what he said settling around the table.

Several seconds later, Peter finally broke the silence: "Seems to be the case."

"Then what about the rest of it all?" Celeste asked. "All the Oprah woo-woo nonsense about your breakthrough day and God's guaranteed abundant life?"

"That's a whole other ball of ugly," Silas said, sitting up to the table and wishing for another beer but settling for a handful of fries. "But it's not like we haven't seen this sort of thing before."

"We haven't?" Gapinski asked. "I mean, we have?"

"Well, not we per se, aside from the exportation of the prosperity gospel across the globe the past century. I mean the Church, historically."

"Do tell, professor," Celeste said, mouth raised wryly. "Or perhaps I should say, Master Grey."

"You mean Montanus, don't you?" Peter said.

Silas nodded. "That's right. And nice thousand-dollar Jeopardy answer there."

The pastor chuckled. "Not really. I had a tough Church history professor in seminary."

"Guessing Calvin Van Dyke?"

"The one and only."

"Hold up," Gapinski said. "Montezuma, who?"

Peter frowned. "Not the Mayan warrior king. Silas is talking about the 2nd-century false teacher."

"Dating back to AD 156," Silas explained, "he was perhaps the Church's first bona fide charlatan, coming from Asia Minor along with two 'prophetesses' named Prisca and Maximilla, promising new revelation that tapped into greater depths of God's love and plan."

Gapinski snorted a laugh. "Sounds like Tweedledum and Tweedledumber up on that stage in that big-top bonanza."

"Something like that."

"But it wasn't just Montanus," Torres said.

Silas turned to her, one end of his mouth raised with curiosity. "Do tell, *professor* Torres…"

She giggled and pushed her chestnut hair behind an ear. "Yeah, yeah, yeah. I had some training in the prosperity gospel when I was younger. With my uncle, but also before my parents passed." Torres frowned and took a breath at the memory. "Anyway, when they got caught up in it all when it was making its way through Mexico, I remember doing a bunch of research about the Renaissance Church leader Erasmus speaking strongly against what he termed was ecclesiastical trickery of his day."

"Interesting. Go on."

Shifting in her chair, she said, "Well, he described nuns of a convent frightening new members with the appearance of an evil spirit, going so far as to call in a priest to exorcise this spirit that wasn't even real! He was speaking out against charlatans, their lies and staged wonders, who held people captive to their spiritual power."

"And you suppose that is what is happening here," Celeste said, "in Mill Creek Junction with the twins?"

"I can certainly attest to the staging wonders part," Peter said. "I mean, are falling feathers the sign of God's in-breaking or offering tangible proof of angels fluttering about?"

Silas said, "That's right, I'd forgotten about that. Then again, you can't discount the miracle we witnessed."

"What it comes down to," Celeste said, "is knowing and understanding a biblical definition of what a miracle is in the first place to counteract these charlatans and frauds, I'd imagine."

"And what is this definition?" Gapinski asked.

"Well, biblically," Silas answered, "a miracle is a witnessed phenomenon in our world that's delivered powerfully by God through an anointed, authorized agent—whether directly or indirectly. Their extraordinary character captures the attention of those witnessing this miracle, and it points to a power beyond the phenomenon—the source can only be attributed to God, given how grand and *extra*-ordinary it is."

"Yeah, you lost me."

"In other words," Peter tried, "a miracle is the moment when God suspends or works to transcend or even subvert natural laws—where he personally steps into the ordinary moments of life to rearrange what is happening inside someone's story, to change their circumstances according to his mighty will and purpose."

"Uh, guys," Gapinski said, "I'd say someone getting their sight back and regaining use of their limbs is pretty much right on the money!"

Torres nodded. "Have to agree with Hoss on that one."

Silas frowned, then added a nod of his own. Had to, given what they'd witnessed. Yet the ending wasn't written on that script yet. Not by a long shot.

He scooted to the table and popped a fry into his mouth. "Setting aside what we all witnessed, because we'll get to that—but with this talk of miracles, it doesn't mean that miracles themselves have ceased, or that we believe they have. Rather, we want to be careful about what qualifies as a biblical miracle. It's far deeper than what charismatic teachers and prosperity preachers suggest. Again, not discounting the supernatural, not at all."

"And if I hear you right," Peter said, "it's also not about questioning God's sovereign working in the world. It's about having a proper respect for what he accomplishes in the world through his mighty power. If we finger everything as a miracle, then nothing is miraculous and we can't recognize when God's mighty power does break into our lives."

Silas nodded. "The problem is that most of the so-called miracles performed by so-called modern faith-healers or people styling themselves as modern-day prophets is that they just aren't miracles. They're not stopping the earth's movement around the sun or walking on water or turning water into wine. They aren't even offering instant healing—of cancer or other chronic illnesses. And even when they do heal, it's really more a matter of God's providential, prayer-based timing."

"Be that as it may," Celeste interjected, gesturing to Gapinski. "Again, to Matthew's point, if a man did in fact regain his sight, and a woman did in fact regain use of her limbs after medically verified paralysis, then where does this leave us?"

Slouching in his chair, Silas took a breath and shook his head. "Not sure. But we're going to find out. One way or another, we'll get to the bottom of what these kooks are up to."

"And what is it you're getting to the bottom of?" a voice interrupted from behind. "And who's getting to the bottom of it?"

A tall blond woman approached, mid-thirties and dressed to impress, wearing a string of pearls set against a pink blouse and black skirt that rode above the knees.

Peter startled, face suddenly draining of color. "Oh, hey Tracy."

He turned to Silas with wide eyes, mouthing something he didn't understand.

"And you are?" asked Celeste, always the no-nonsense one of the group. Silas had learned it was her British way.

The woman eyed her before striking out her hand. "Tracy Nolland, with the *Mill Creek Junction Guardian*."

Eyeing it as if it were an alien specimen, she shook it with a plastered smile. "Celeste Bourne. A pleasure. But did I hear you correctly? Did you say *Mill Creek Junction Guardian*? As in—"

"The editor-in-chief of the town newspaper," Peter quickly explained.

Now Celeste twisted up her face in confusion. "I'm sorry, but did you say *Guardian*? As in *The* Guardian?"

Silas cleared his throat and stood. "You'll have to excuse her.

She's British, and they've got their own similarly named newspaper and all."

"A pretentious lot, aren't they?" she muttered.

Tracy locked her jaw into a grin, then pressed forward. "At any rate, I couldn't help overhearing your little round-table discussion on the goings-on up the road at the fairground. The healings and whatnot."

The table instantly shifted at the mention of their conversation. And from a member of the press, no less!

Not good...

"I believe I heard Katrina DeGraw was part of the spectacle. Healed of some sudden paralysis, isn't that right? And isn't she part of your congregation, Pastor Young?"

"Where did you hear that?" Peter said in a rush.

Tracy smiled curtly. "A source, who also saw you with her during the event, as well as some other GI Joe-looking fellow."

Gapinski snickered at that line, glancing at Silas while Celeste and Torres suppressed their own grins.

Silas crossed his arms. "He's got no comment."

She regarded him with similarly crossed arms. "Really? And you are?"

"The GI Joe-looking fellow," Gapinski whispered.

"Matthew..." Celeste *tsk*ed.

"Really? And you are?"

Torres smirked. "Got any new material, sister?"

Peter cleared his throat. "They're just some...well, people I got connected with to help understand what's going on here."

"And what is going on here?" Tracy asked.

Silas rolled his eyes now, getting irritated at the interruption. Nosy piece of work, isn't she? Never had liked the press, especially after the hatchet job they'd given to their work in Iraq. And his opinion of them was diminishing by the second.

He went to give her the second brush-off when a voice

yelled out above the din of barroom conversation, interrupting the interrogation.

"Howdy, pastorman! Who ya pallin' 'round with today? Oh, hey Tracy."

She smiled and threw the man a wink. "Hey, yourself."

A tall, lanky man in a flannel shirt and dirty jeans with long hair poking out from a black cowboy hat walked up behind Peter and slapped a hand on his shoulder.

Peter looked up and reached out a hand; the man shook it. Then he addressed the group: "This is Max Blade. Owner of the bar and a good friend."

Max scoffed. "'Parently you ain't all that discerning with who you're friendly with!"

"Whatever, Max." He pointed around the table, introducing the SEPIO group by name. "A friend of mine connected us after the religious service started up."

He crossed his arms and grinned. "Ahh, yes. The holy rollers up town. Hey, I heard they had themselves a genuine healing or two!"

Peter shifted in his chair and threw Silas a look. This just kept getting better and better.

A commotion suddenly split through the din of barroom conversation. Several people were standing now and moving toward the bar. Others were pointing at a television up above the back lined with bottles.

Silas himself now stood. "Looks like something's happening."

Gapinski crossed his arms and huffed. "Always something…"

He hustled over to the crowd, where a news anchor was reporting from Atlanta, Georgia, in front of a several-story building of glass and brown brick.

"It's happening elsewhere!" someone shouted, pointing at the screen.

The chyron named the reporter as Mara Mitchell, and the sign was a large blue dot with some line-drawn bird mid-flight next to white CDC letters set against the same blue backdrop.

"It's another pandemic!" another cried.

Silas knew exactly what those letters meant, especially given the early reports they had from the field of a contagion blooming in certain parts of the world.

Centers for Disease Control.

Not good...

CHAPTER 11

Silas's belly began rumbling with a ping of dread, a familiar tightness gripping his gut and a coldness spreading through his veins when he knew deep down that things were about to get real.

Sometimes it was from instinct thanks to his service with the Rangers and then the past few years with the Order. All the crazy he'd experienced had certainly hammered and honed his sixth sense foretelling when stuff was about to hit the fan. More often yet his foresight was thanks to the Holy Spirit, the Third Person of the Trinity gearing him up for whatever was coming down the pike, like when the Apostle Paul was warned no uncertain doom awaited him in every city to come.

Yet still Paul went, and still Silas went hustling over to the television blaring the breaking news alert, the suspicion growing that things were coming to a head that would drag SEPIO further into a mission still undefined.

"Turn it up, would ya!" Max shouted. The woman who had brought them their food told him to shut his pie hole, but obliged.

The rest of the room was crowding toward the bar now,

necks craning toward the television as a pair of talking heads went back and forth with serious faces and panicked tones.

Silas joined them, along with the rest of his SEPIO teammates and Peter, pushing closer toward the bar for a better viewing and hearing.

When there was a buzzing at his leg.

He pulled out his phone. It was a text from Zoe.

'It's happening! Worldwide contagion! SEPIO agents confirm ground-zero sites!'

He chuckled to himself, the triple exclamation points from his normally reserved director of ops support highlighting the urgency of the matter.

Then he frowned. Looked like they might be in it more than Silas realized. Guess his gut instincts or the Holy Spirit or both were right. But the *what* of the matter was still a mystery.

And he guessed the breaking news alert would muddy the waters even further.

Stuffing the phone in his pants pocket, he turned back to the television to get the low-down.

When his phone buzzed with another interruption.

He huffed and dragged out the dang thing again. Another text from Zoe: *'Zarruq needs to talk! ASAP!'*

Silas texted back: *'Alright! But can't talk now. Will call soon.'* Then he swiped on *'Do Not Disturb'* and turned his attention to the display above the bar.

Celeste sidled up to him with crossed arms. "The mother ship, I presume?"

He nodded. "Victor wants a chat, and Zoe seems more frantic than usual. She texted with what I imagine we're about to find out from CNN." Then he leaned in and whispered, "Worldwide contagion, spreading possibly from the ground-zero sites our SEPIO agents in the field reported on earlier."

"The mysterious revival tent meetings?"

Silas nodded.

She sighed but didn't startle, not revealing anything to anyone around. Like the good former-MI6 agent and director of operations she was.

"Speaking of which…" Silas gestured toward the TV, where the picture was returning to a familiar perky, well-makeuped blond, Mara Mitchell.

"…just joining us, we are reporting an exclusive story that is about to unfold shortly from inside the building behind me. The Centers for Disease Control will confirm a contagion is quickly spreading across the globe that threatens the health of every person on the planet, potentially leading to the deaths of millions."

Gapinski snorted a laugh from behind. "Oh, is that all…"

"Put a cork in it, would ya?" Torres complained.

Stiff and serious, Mara continued, "Originating in Africa and spreading across the world as far as South America, we have confirmation that a viral contagion is taking hold of people without mercy and without discrimination. It appears to affect the central nervous system in wide-ranging ways. Anything from blindness and deafness to sudden onset paralysis."

Silas and Celeste snapped their heads at one another in sync, eyes wide with knowing dread.

Peter leaned in-between them and whispered, "Did she just say what I think she said?"

Silas answered, "Sounds like what we witnessed north of town."

"I'd say! Blindness and paralysis? I mean, come on!"

He turned toward the pastor and frowned, the freighted weight of the truth of the matter sending up another flair of cold dread through his veins.

Peter continued, "Sounds like the rest of the world is going through the same medical nonsense as Mill Creek Junction.

And now to know it started overseas....what the heck is going on? What's my town in the middle of here?"

"Hold on, reverend," Celeste said, patting his arm.

"Unlike recent pandemics," Mara continued, "where a single virus was responsible for a collection of related immune responses, mainly spiking temperatures with shortness of breath and difficulty breathing, combined with loss of taste and smell, this particular contagion seems to bear no rhyme or reason across the globe. From São Paulo, Brazil, to San Pedro, Belize; from Nairobi, Kenya, to Kaduna, Nigeria—men, women, and children have all come under a dizzying array of symptoms that have no obvious connection."

The cities sent an immediate ping of recognition flaring up in Silas's brain. Leaning toward Celeste, he said in a hushed rush, "Weren't those the sites you mentioned back in DC that were flagged by our SEPIO agent for the recent revival meetings?"

She sucked in a breath and ran a hand through her chestnut hair, "You're bloomin' right!"

"What are you talking about?" Peter asked in the same hushed rush.

Silas put up a hand and pointed back at the TV.

The camera panned to another correspondent sitting in the plush comforts of a studio. "If you're just joining us," a well-makuped anchor named Kai Renolds began, hair slicked back and glistening under too many klieg lights to count, a camera swooping in for a view, "this is a CNN breaking news report with Mara Mitchell standing by at the CDC for what we anticipate to be a rather ominous announcement from the government on an emerging pandemic. Now Mara, is there any indication whether the contagion, as you put it, has reached our own shores?"

Mara frowned, the equally well-makuped woman, hair blond and blown, lips glistening maroon, appearing on an 80-

inch screen mounted next to the CNN anchor. She replied, "As of yet, there have been no confirmed cases in America or Europe, for that matter. Although, as in pandemics of recent years, it is too soon to tell whether we can expect to hold back the inevitable, given the interconnectedness of the world."

Now Silas frowned, knowing better. The freighted sighs from Peter and his SEPIO teammates behind told him they knew better too. He glanced around the bar and out the front door of frosted glass gleaming from the mid-afternoon sun. Oh, it was in America, alright.

The male anchor Kai turned toward the camera. "I want to stress that we have scant details as of yet. So no need to panic. Don't start hoarding toilet paper, for goodness' sake!"

"No time to panic?" Max Blade shouted a row back, face creased with pained lines, the man placing a finger in an ear and shaking his head. "Why the hell not?"

A few chuckled nervously around him, the room shifting suddenly at the emerging news.

Mara nodded, face seemingly paler now and more serious. "That is right, Kai. We are still awaiting word from the CDC on that front and—"

"I'm sorry to have to cut you off, Mara," Kai said with interruption, the picture fading back to the glossy studio taking back the reins of the broadcast, "but we have just received word of a hastily organized press conference at the White House with President Santos himself. Let's listen in."

The picture faded to a middle-aged Latino man walking to the dais of the White House press room, President Robert Santos. His dark hair streaked by sophisticated silver was trimmed neatly and slicked to one side. He wore a well-fitted navy suit with a matching navy and red polka dot tie set against a pink shirt, carrying on his trademark flare for fashion that had made him a darling of the media during the presidential campaign a few years ago and early years of his administration.

Silas couldn't help but smile, knowing he had a hand in helping bring Santos to power after he exposed the political conspiracy surrounding his closest contender, Amos Young. Though he hadn't voted for him, preferring the independent Matthew Reed, Santos had run a fairly moderate administration so far, hewing closely to his Catholic convictions in everything from abortion and the death penalty to poverty and social justice. His poll numbers showed it as well, garnering a high 60s approval rating across the political spectrum.

And there he was, about to brief the American public on a crisis that had all the markings of a made-for-Netflix limited television spectacle.

The white flashes and clicking of camera shutters quieted once the president took his position. Santos stood stiffly, somberly and looked straight into the camera positioned at the back of the room, delivering it straight to the American people as he had the past few years since taking office.

Max's Place went dead quiet. No one moved, no one drank their beer or ate their burgers. It felt like the day when those two planes slammed into the World Trade Center. Life had stopped.

President Santos began, "Throughout my administration, I have made it a priority to be open and transparent. To give it to you straight and not sugar-coat the truth. Today is one of those days."

Gapinski snorted a laugh. "That sounds sufficiently ominous."

Silas turned toward him and threw him a frown. Sure did.

"My fellow Americans, I want to speak with you about an unprecedented contagion outbreak that we believe started in Africa and is now spreading throughout the world, with cases confirmed in Brazil and Belize and stretching north now toward our southern border. It is identified as a neurological viral contagion, being called *nervirus*—coined from the Latin *nervi* for 'nerve.' Later today, the World Health Organization will officially announce that we are in a global pandemic."

The bar gasped as one before splintering into a multitude of panicked conversations.

"Shut your yappers!" Max yelled, gesturing to the television with an angry hand while the other was pressed against his ear.

Silas furrowed his brow. Odd fella.

President Santos continued, "We have been in frequent contact with our allies to determine the best course of coordinated action. And let me reassure you that we are marshaling the full power of the federal government and the private sector to protect the American people."

He stopped, drawing in a breath and grabbing hold of the presidential lectern. "I must tell you that we are in for a rough road ahead if we do not take the steps that my administration is taking today. Already, there are reports of blindness and deafness, paralysis and even death afflicting those who have come under this contagion. From every indication, *nervirus* is an aggressive contagion, and if we do not institute the necessary protocols for containing this emerging threat, thousands of people will be afflicted and the same will die."

"Always something..." complained Gapinski.

"Young and old, healthy and not, male and female, rich and poor—*nervirus* does not appear to matter to this particular contagion, which we are learning more about by the minute. We have the best doctors in the world, all of them, really, in our beloved country, working around the clock to analyze and understand the contagion, here and on the ground. What we know so far is that it attacks without discrimination, leading to permanent disability, which will surely lead to permanent loss of income and livelihood."

Another rumble of mumbly panic rippled through the bar, people talking in quiet whispers and others beginning to hold one another now at the news. Silas guessed the scene was playing out across the country, whether small town or big town, the same panic and anxiety about the future would be gripping the country, the world.

"But rest assured," President Santos went on, "this is the most aggressive and comprehensive effort to confront a foreign contagion in modern history. I am confident that by taking these tough measures, we will significantly reduce *nervirus's* threat to our citizens and we will ultimately and expeditiously defeat this contagion.

"After consulting with our top government health professionals, I have decided to take several strong but necessary actions to protect the health and wellbeing of all Americans. To keep new cases from entering our shores, we will be suspending all travel from Africa and South America to the United States for the next thirty days."

"*Lo siento, presidente,*" Torres said. "But I'm pretty sure that ship sailed a few hours ago, *amigo.*"

"I am also instituting a mask mandate across all federal buildings and properties and encouraging all state governments to join in the effort to curb the spread of infection."

Gapinski moaned. "Not the masks again!"

"I am also instructing the Department of Education to institute a nationwide closure of schools for the next thirty days. The last thing we want is to put our beautiful children and their teachers in harm's way. And invoking the Commerce Clause of the constitution, I am requiring a full lockdown from any exchange of goods and services for monetary value, other than essential services, such as hospitals, grocery stores, and pharmacies." The president leaned in now, adding, "in other words, do not go to work and do not buy and sell. Stay home! Smart action today will prevent the spread of *nervirus* tomorrow."

"Can he do that?" Silas muttered to himself.

"Sounds like the bloke just did," Celeste said.

Peter added, "The Commerce Clause does give wide latitude to the federal government to regulate interstate commerce, but I'm not sure about intrastate commerce."

The pair looked at the pastor with raised brows.

He chuckled. "I was a government major and worked on Capitol Hill for a stint. Politics is sort of a side hobby. Don't know how this will pass legal muster, and I have to assume states will challenge it in court."

Silas said, "Either way, things just got real."

"And with SEPIO quite possibly in the middle of it..." Celeste added.

He nodded, saying nothing.

"Huh?" Peter asked, brow furrowed with confusion.

"Never mind."

"No, what does that mean? Who's SEPIO and what are they in the middle of?"

She threw Silas a glance. He simply said, "Later." Then nodded toward the television again.

"From the beginning of time," President Santos continued, "nations and people have faced unforeseen challenges, including large-scale and very dangerous health threats. This is the way it always was and always will be. It only matters how you respond, and we are responding with great speed and professionalism. My administration is coordinating directly with communities with the largest outbreaks across the world to both offer aid, as America does in these situations, but also monitor the situation for our own sake."

"How generous..." Gapinski muttered.

The president shifted, folding his hands on the lectern and taking a breath. "If we are vigilant against *nervirus*—and we can prevent the chance of infection, which we will—we will significantly impede the transmission of the virus within this country, if not stop it in its tracks. This *nervirus* contagion will not have a chance against us! No nation is more prepared or more resilient than the United States. We have the best economy, the most advanced health care, and the most talented doctors, scientists and researchers anywhere in the world.

"We are all in this together. We must put politics aside, stop the partisanship and unify together as one nation and one family. As history has proven time and time again, Americans always rise to the challenge and overcome adversity. Our future remains brighter than anyone can imagine. Acting with compassion and love, we will heal the sick, care for those in need, help our fellow citizens and emerge from this challenge stronger and more unified than ever before."

Pausing, he nodded toward the camera and ended with: "God bless you, and God bless America. Thank you."

Then the president strode off without taking questions. His press secretary began fielding them instead and explaining more how the protocols would work.

No one in Max's Place was interested in any of it. The crowd dispersed with muttering grumbles and silent shock. Whether from the contagion itself or the mitigation efforts, it wasn't clear. A virtual lockdown was the last thing anyone wanted, but with such a contagion spreading through the world, and now seemingly showing up in Small Town, America, it might be the only thing that stopped it from wreaking havoc.

"What's our next move, chief?" Gapinski asked Silas, the SEPIO crew huddling together along with Peter. "Can't be a coinkydink that the same areas that saw those looney-toons revival tent meetings around the world are also seeing the contagion spread."

Torres smirked. "Yeah, what are the odds, right?"

"Vegas odds, I tell ya."

"What's he talking about?" Peter said to Silas. "Sounds like what you and Celeste were chit-chatting about earlier. And what's this SEPIO business, anyway?"

Gapinski snorted a laugh. "We could tell ya, Petey, but then we'd have to kill ya."

Silas went to answer the pastor when someone threw up a yelp.

It was from behind, at the bar.

The Max Blade character. He had both hands against his ears, face pinched and pained.

"What the..."

"Max, honey," Sheila, their server, said with her hand on his back, face drawn and lower lip quivering with concern. "What's the matter?"

Peter gestured with his head toward Max and walked over. Silas and the SEPIO gang followed.

"My ears..." he yelled, far louder than he needed to.

"What about them?" Peter asked.

"There's this tuning-fork ting to 'em, and I can hardly hear nothin'. Like sitting at the bottom of a pool, the sound all—"

Max stopped short and looked up, eyes going wide and mouth hanging open as if in a question. He shook his head then slapped his hands against his ears, his mouth moving up and down but nothing coming out.

Peter threw Silas a worried look. Before either of them could ask what was what, Max yelled, "I can't hear nothin'!"

The pastor gasped, eyes going wide and pleading with Silas for answers.

Silas went to get them, stepping over to the bar now. He raised his voice: "What do you mean you can't hear?"

The man's face was panicked now. Like a piece of meat had gotten stuck in his windpipe and he couldn't fetch a breath, that mouth of his trying to work again but nothing coming out.

Until it did.

"I said, I can't hear nothin'!" he shouted, his voice giving out in a high-pitched squeak before voicing the truth of the matter: "I've done gone deaf!"

Silas spun around to his teammates and Peter, every one of their faces confirming what he knew in his gut to be true.

Nervirus had indeed come to Mill Creek Junction.

Officially.

They were standing at contagion ground zero in America.

CHAPTER 12

What a trip...

An ache began needling Silas's forehead between the eyes an hour ago. Now it was blooming into something he worried would be more a migraine than a mere headache. He closed his eyes, pressed two fingers together, and rubbed his left temple, then settled back into the black leather passenger's seat and let out a sigh.

All he'd wanted was a day—just one day to himself. A day where the worries of the Order and cares of the Church didn't weigh on him or demand his attention. Where the only decisions he had to make were between Die Hard and Top Gun, between takeout Chinese or pizza, between beer and wine.

That wish went out the window the moment they'd touched down in Michigan, and the final nail to its coffin was nailed in Max's Place.

Now all Silas wanted was nothing more than a hot shower and soft bed, maybe a nightcap to set things right after all the crazy turned sour—and then some. Maybe curl up with a good action-adventure conspiracy thriller, some yarn from James Rollins or Steve Berry. Even a bargain-bin Kindle ebook would do. Anything to let him escape from this emerging lockdown nightmare of his world and instead plop him into someone else's crazy-ass plot requiring the suspension of disbelief. Let *them* solve the world's problems for a few weeks.

But that would have to wait. All of it would. Especially the nightcap, and probably sleep. SEPIO had work to do, at least Silas thought they did.

Though what it all amounted to was about as clear as goose crap. Because life was becoming increasingly stranger than fiction these days.

The sun was slipping beneath the horizon as SEPIO and their tagalong rolled up in their Escalade to Mill Creek Baptist, the sky inflamed with tendrils of orange and red clouds stretching toward the emerging inky darkness above. Stars were out in force in these parts now, diamond specs of starlight having burned out millennia ago making their way to the Junction's slice of Earth.

Climbing out of the luxury SUV, Silas stretched his back and took in a deep breath, his senses filling with the sweet smell of flowers and smoke riding high in the emerging night-time air still surprisingly warm for that time of year. He gave himself permission to take in the view, that sea of diamonds entrancing him now, enticing him with small-town life, even. Never caught sight of that on the East Coast, that's for sure, the big-city lights drowning out God's handiwork. Perhaps he could be won over yet.

Fishing for his keys, Peter led the group to the church door. He fiddled with the lock, dropping the keys with a clangy clatter in the waning light before finally sliding the key into the lock and clicking it open.

Following Peter inside, the competing scents of copier ink and stale cardboard-tasting coffee and old wood nearly forced Silas back outside for fresher air. But they had work to do. Figured the pastor's office would be as good a place as any as a home base for the moment—to debrief, to plan, to start adding all the pieces up of what had been unleashed on the world, and on Mill Creek Junction.

Silas was never any good at math. But he did know that 2 + 2 equaling 5 was more than some Orwellian trope. When the world threw up that equation at you, there was sure to be a whole bunch of crazy at work behind the scenes.

Because two verified medical events plus two verified healings was adding up to a whole lot of crazy by Silas's and the Order's standards. Which was saying something!

Before heading to the church, they had spent time with Max Blade. The bar owner was understandably distraught after his hearing-loss episode. Peter sat with the man to settle him down. Wasn't part of the pastor's congregation; apparently not in the slightest. Just the way Peter was, helping where he could.

Taking the reins himself, Silas asked Max questions about the symptoms and the potential causes. Took some doing, but he managed to get some answers through scraps of paper he'd managed to rustle up in the man's second-story apartment above the bar. The story Max told was interesting.

Apparently, Max had been having weird symptoms the past few days. Started with a ringing in his ears that came and went, until it didn't. Sound would go in and out too, but it wasn't until around noon that day when it really took a nose-dive. The bartender just thought it was waxy build-up or seasonal allergies messing with his senses; sometimes both did that to him.

But then all of a sudden, pain bloomed in his inner head, right behind his ears. Then poof. Nothing. No sound. Not even a low-grade hum, just all of a sudden vanished!

Poor guy wavered between being good-humored about it all, trying to put on a brave face, to being distraught and borderline whimpering from the tragic turn, not knowing how he'd cope without his hearing. Especially not knowing if it was permanent or temporary, if there was a cure or he was left to fend for himself in a soundless world now through sign language and scraps of paper.

Silas didn't think he would've handled things any better. When he asked Max if he'd been overseas at all, to Africa or South America, the guy nearly laughed them both out of his apartment! Hadn't traveled out of Michigan in a decade.

That detail of the story confirmed it: Mill Creek Junction was a new epicenter of the emerging worldwide contagion. The who, what, where, why, and how was the mystery.

Which brought Silas and the gang and the pastor back to Peter's church office for a late-night pow-wow.

SEPIO style.

Flipping on the lights to his office, Peter asked, "Can I get anyone any coffee?"

"Got anything stronger, bub?" Gapinski asked, slouching into the couch.

Torres joined him. "Yeah, maybe a bottle of Jack or Jameson?"

Peter laughed, shuffling to go behind his desk. "We're a Baptist church. You think I've got Jack Daniels stashed away in my bottom desk drawer, or something?"

Gapinski shrugged. "Didn't stop my grandpappy Southern Baptist pastor from having his own stash..."

"Got Folgers and maybe a few tea bags lying around."

"If you don't mind," said Celeste, "I'd quite like a cuppa. Perhaps a spot of PG Tips or Twinings tea?"

"Uh, I think it's Lipton," he said, logging into his computer.

She slumped into one of the wingback chairs at the desk with a sigh. "Bullocks."

"Again, we're a Baptist church."

"Suppose it'll have to do."

"If it makes you feel any better," Silas said, "we'll be suffering together."

"The things we do for the Church..."

Peter laughed and left to get the late-night fuel for the crew.

Using Peter's desktop computer, Silas logged into a secure node at the Order's HQ network to bring up a video conference. Didn't take long and soon he was staring at the profile of Zoe clattering away at her keyboard, those baby blue glasses of hers perched at the edge of her nose.

"Nice of you to drop in, chief," she said, pushing her glasses back up to her face.

"And nice to see you too," Silas muttered. "Anything else you can report beyond what we already know from President Santos's address?"

Zoe put up a finger, continuing to clatter away before the screen changed to a view of the horseshoe table on deck in the middle of the main operations center.

No one was there yet, but Silas assumed they'd have company soon. So he leaned back in the chair to wait. A few minutes later, the door opened and Peter returned with a tray of five mugs and a large silver carafe.

Setting the tray down on his desk, the pastor handed the one mug of hot water with a tea bag draped across the corner to Celeste, then promptly poured the fresh brew into the other mugs. Surprisingly, didn't smell half bad, the rising steam spreading the earthy notes throughout the office.

Silas grabbed one and took a sip, humming with pleasure but confused. "This isn't Folgers, is it?"

Peter took a swig himself and shook his head. "Nope. Found a stash of Seattle's Best in a back cupboard." He turned to Celeste and shrugged. "Sorry, but you're still stuck with Lipton."

She took a sip of her own and frowned. "Not fair."

Static and clangy noises filled the room, coming from the computer. Victor Zarruq and Zoe, joined by the tech wizard Abraham Patel, were taking their seats at the backend of the table now.

Silas scooted back to the computer and turned it toward the room, getting everyone involved on screen for HQ.

"Hello, SEPIO," Zarruq said, eyes looking more tired than usual set against his dark round face, his salt and pepper beard not managing a usual smile either. He still looked regal as ever in his creme-colored vestments with embroidered cuffs bearing a pattern of his Libyan homeland, but his eight-ball head was missing a cap of the same green, black, and red embroidery.

"Victor, I must say," Celeste answered, "you're not looking at all well."

The archbishop managed a deep chuckle. "Well, we've been having a go of it at our end trying to make sense of the disaster unfolding across the world. So sleep has been hard to come by."

Gapinski leaned back on the couch with a loud yawn. "You're telling me."

Silas threw him a frown. "The contagion has thrown us all for a loop, I'd wager."

"The contagion?" Zarruq snapped, which wasn't like him. "That's not what I'm speaking about, although it certainly is a dastardly affair. Yet another worldwide outbreak splintering the world apart. Feels like the end is nigh some days..."

Celeste threw Silas a glance before saying, "Then what have you had a go about?"

"The charismatic tent revivals?" Silas asked. "Is that it?"

"Of course that's it!" Zarruq's face fell, a fearful dread etching it with worrying lines.

"What charismatic tent revivals?" Peter asked from the other wingback chair next to Celeste.

Silas gestured to the pastor. "Victor, this is Peter Young, the Baptist minister who we were connected to through my long-time professional contact. He's been showing us around Mill Creek Junction. We've been having a go of it ourselves."

He updated the archbishop on the latest happenings, from

the healing of Peter's assistant on stage at the charismatic revival meeting in town to Max's sudden onset of deafness, as well as the other sicknesses around town. Victor sucked in a worried breath through pursed lips at the news, then *tsked* loudly and shook his head, muttering something under his breath in a foreign tongue.

Silas said, "Sounds like you've got some news to share of your own."

Zarruq nodded. "Indeed. SEPIO agents in the field have been offering us a clearer picture of what has gone on inside the revival services, and it isn't pretty."

"Sorry to interrupt," Peter said, clearing his throat. "But can I just ask a basic, knuckle-headed question?"

Silas turned to him and nodded. "Shoot."

"You've told me something of the Order of Thaddeus, but this sepia—"

"SEPIO," Celeste corrected.

"Rhymes with rapido," Gapinski added. To which Torres smacked him on the knee. "Ouch! Why d'ya do that?"

"Because I'm the only one who's allowed to speak *español* in our group," Torres said. "And believe me, Peter, I hear ya. Took me awhile to wrap my head around it all myself."

Peter smirked. "I'm still not sure what I'm wrapping my head around."

"A decade ago," Silas explained, "the Order realized it needed to make a more deliberate effort in contending for and preserving the memory of the faith. In the face of a number of threats, both inside and outside the Church, our former boss, Rowen Radcliffe, realized the faith was quickly coming to a precipice unless the Order took measures to deliberately preserve and protect the Church's once-for-all faith and teaching tradition. Project SEPIO was launched to spearhead that movement. An acronym for *Sepio, Erudio, Pugno, Inviglio, Observo.*"

"I don't…"

"Protect, Instruct, Fight For, Watch Over, Heed. That's the Latin translation."

"And the full meaning of the Latin word *sepio* itself," Celeste added, "captures the project's mission perfectly: 'to surround with a hedge.' In the case of our stated project mission, surround the memory of the Christian faith with a hedge of protection. Not only the dogma and doctrine of the faith, but also the Church's objects and relics containing the memory of the faith, exploiting them to inform and nourish the faith of God's children—and keeping their faith safe."

"As I explained earlier," Silas went on, "The Order of Thaddeus was originally a Catholic religious order and Vatican-run initiative. Same for SEPIO. But now it's an ecumenical effort at protecting the Church and preserving Christian faith."

Peter chuckled, shifting in his chair. "I'm sorry, but *protect*? From what?" His face was twisted up with skepticism now, glancing from Silas to Celeste. "And you mentioned something about keeping the faith safe. Again, from what?"

Gapinski snorted an interrupting laugh. "Annnd here's where you might want to grab your tin-foil hat, amigo."

Torres smacked his knee again.

"What? I can't say amigo?"

"That was for the tin-foil hat comment."

"As I was going to explain…" Silas said, drilling Gapinski with a look. "Nous."

"Nous?" Peter said.

He nodded, a reminder of the personal stakes he had pinging his gut, given his brother Sebastian had taken over as head of the organization. Last time he'd seen him, the man was fleeing the shattered husk of some sort of temple headquarters for the newest threat to the Order and the Church. Never did find out what happened to him, whether or not he survived, where he'd gotten off to. Didn't much care, given his betrayals over the past few years and levels he'd sunk to destroy his faith —to destroy him even.

"And don't forget the newest kids on the block," Gapinski added.

"Oh, yeah," Torres said. "The Church of the Theotites."

Silas nodded, leaving his personal feelings at bay and refocusing on the moment. "Nous and Theoti have been a real pain the last few years. Genuine threats to the Church that are bent on destroying it, destroying the Christian faith itself."

"Nous and Theoit..." Peter said again with an edge to his voice now that reminded Silas of what people sounded like when someone said they were abducted by aliens or saw Bigfoot.

He let it go and nodded. "I know what it sounds like, but Nous is a very real entity that has been waging war against the Church for centuries."

Peter settled back in his chair, going quiet.

"In the past, they struck at the heart of Christian ideas by propagating heresy and seeking to undermine the essence of the Christian faith by destroying her teachings. Its power and influence has waxed and waned over the centuries and manifested in various ways. But in recent years, they have stepped up their game big time—and with violent results. Remember the attacks against churches across the world a few years ago?"

Peter nodded. "Sure."

"We were running security ops," Celeste answered, "to determine the nature of the threat across the world." She nodded toward Silas and then to Torres and Gapinski. "Us four, with the Order under the auspices of SEPIO."

The pastor whistled, saying nothing more.

Silas continued, "Theoti is a threat that manifested last year. Both as a competitor to Nous to claim for itself the mantle of the Church's greatest threat, but also with ambitions of their own to create an alternative spirituality. So, yeah, I know how it sounds, but we're swimming at the deep end of the pool, here. Are you up to speed?"

Peter nodded, taking in a measured breath and sitting up at attention.

Turning back to the computer, Silas said, "Sorry for the rabbit trail, Victor."

"Quite alright," the archbishop said. "Only proper we bring the newest member to the party up to speed."

"Speaking of which, you were about to bring us up to speed. Something about a clearer picture with what's been going on overseas."

Zarruq shifted and nodded. "Indeed. It appears that a brother-sister pair have been headlining these so-called charismatic revival meetings across the Majority World the past few weeks."

That got the room's attention.

"Brother-sister pair?" Celeste said, sitting up and tossing Silas a knowing glance.

"That's right. SEPIO agents have assembled video footage from inside the meetings, and the pair are consistent."

"What are the odds," Gapinski said, "our own Tweedledee and Tweedledum from up town are the same pair?"

Torres smirked. "How many brother-sister pairs are headlining so-called charismatic revival meetings across the Majority World?"

"That's the point I'm making!"

Peter leaned against the desk toward the computer, asking, "Do we have a name to go along with the faces?"

"Let's see..." Victor put on a pair of glasses and began shuffling through a folder of notes. "Ahh! Here it is. Dexter and Paulina Bucks."

Torres startled. "Did you say Bucks?"

He nodded. "That is right, my dear. Why?"

"No reason..." she muttered before slumping back.

Silas wondered what that was about, but let it go. He leaned back toward the computer, asking, "Do you have any photos of the pair?"

"On it," said Zoe, pushing those baby blue glasses back up her nose and clattering away.

A few beats later, the video changed to a set of photos from inside similar canvas tents, a pair of evangelists on a stage under spotlights in dimmed darkness. Grainy and a bit hard to make out the pair entirely, but it was close enough.

"Are you kidding me..." Silas said, slumping back into his chair, tossing a knowing glance to Celeste.

She frowned and nodded. "That confirms it then."

"Our twins," Peter said, nodding with a frown of his own and taking in a breath through pursed lips.

Silas had to chuckle to himself at the sight. Clearly this was the guy's first rodeo solving a mystery of such epic, global proportions saving the Church from no uncertain doom.

There they were. The blonde who had been introduced as Paulina, and then the fella she named as her brother Dexter.

"Looks about right," Celeste said. "The hair, the features, the pair working the stage together inside a canvas tent."

"Paulina and Dexter Bucks..." Silas said, narrowing his eyes as their antagonists came into sharper focus. But of what, exactly, they were their enemies—now that part was as clear as goose crap.

Gapinski snorted a laugh. "Bucks..." He shook his head and laughed again.

"What of it?" Torres asked.

"Seems a bit on the nose, doesn't it? Evangelists preaching the good life, the abundant life, with all their health and wealth nonsense—last names *Bucks*?"

Man had a point. But Silas moved on: "What do we know about these characters?"

Victor answered, "They are related to the infamous prosperity preacher Benjamin Bucks, who built an empire of franchised ministry centers, called Abundant Life Victory Center."

"Catchy," Gapinski said.

"And dastardly."

"How so?" Silas asked.

Victor huffed and crossed his arms. "Because the prosperity theology espoused by the likes of Benjamin Bucks and his heirs has no connection to Christian theology. It isn't good news; it is fake news, a fake gospel. Its message has zero connection to the Bible and what it promises ultimately fails. God never assures his people that they will be healthy and wealthy—in this life, anyway."

"Tell us what you really think, chief..." Gapinski quipped from the couch.

Silas threw him a frown as Victor continued: "Our hope, the Lord's promise, is Christ's riches. A personal, intimate relationship with our Creator and the gift of life eternal with fully resurrected bodies in the new earth, living in God's presence for all eternity. Ultimately, the largest problem with the prosperity gospel isn't that it offers too much, but that it promises too little. Salvation from the consequences of our sins—hell, ultimate death—is what the Church's gospel promises, not a house with a white picket fence full of junk!"

Celeste said, "And that is what these Bucks characters have been promising?"

"Exactly. From the original church, if you can call it that, planted in Northern Virginia to Vancouver, where Benjamin made his permanent home, and all across the world with their crusades."

"And his son and daughter joined the family business, eh?" Torres said.

Victor answered, "Niece and nephew, actually. Adopted."

"For what reason were they adopted?" asked Celeste.

"Some family tragedy or something or other," Victor

replied. "Not entirely sure, but what we do know is that the pair, twins actually, did join the family business, as Naomi suggested. However, their uncle hasn't been seen of late."

"Why not?" Silas asked.

Victor glanced at Zoe, who answered, "Still working on that front of things. What we do know is that the brother-sister pair have been globetrotting the past few weeks, going from Kenya to Brazil to—"

"Let me guess, West Michigan, USA?"

"It appears that way," Victor said. "And now with the latest contagion raging throughout the world, these healing sites have become a sort of Mecca for the desperate."

"Wait, what?" Silas sat up straighter at that bit of news.

"That's right. These revival sites have taken on new meaning across the globe with news of the pandemic. Tell them what you've been seeing on the internet, Zoe."

She cleared her throat and shared, "It appears Westerners are flocking to these sites in the global South now, seeking healing with reports of the miraculous intervention in people's illness making their way across WeShare."

Silas scoffed. "Miraculous intervention..."

"I wouldn't scoff too easily, dear," Celeste said. "You know what you and Peter witnessed, first with that bloke Cameron and then with that dear woman Katrina. In fact, wasn't it you, Peter, who were positively surprised at both of their appearances at the revival meeting?"

Peter shifted and cleared his throat. "That's right. A spiritual-but-not-religious college kid and a Baptist church secretary—"

"And a former-Catholic religious order walk into a charismatic revival..." Gapinski muttered with interruption.

Torres snorted a laugh. "Sounds like the beginning of a good joke."

"That's what I was thinking! Slap me some skin, sister." He held up his hand; she gave it a slap.

Silas cleared his throat loudly, not amused. The pair slouched in their couch, sufficiently chided.

He said, "Anyway, I see your point. People desperate for hope and healing go to desperate lengths. Even showing up at religious services they wouldn't normally set foot in."

Celeste nodded. "Right. And by all accounts, it appears to have worked. Miraculous cures visited at least these two individuals."

"That's debatable."

"Is it?"

Silas went to answer but didn't have one. Such things never really had a place in his spirituality, being much more interested in the theology of the faith than the mystical side of it.

"Uh, oh…" Peter said, face frowning at his phone.

"What now?" Silas asked.

"Apparently, the twins are slated to have another healing service."

"When?"

"Tomorrow. Noon. It's all over WeShare."

"Always something…" Gapinski said.

Silas had to agree. "And with news of the contagion raging across the world, and it breaking into the US, I'd imagine news will be flying across WeShare."

"Which means Mill Creek will be positively bedlam tomorrow!" Celeste said.

"And SEPIO with a front-row seat to it all."

"I've got two extra rooms and a fold-out couch at my place next door," Peter offered. "You're welcome to crash at my parsonage."

"You're a charm, Peter," Celeste said. "Thank you."

Silas stood. "It's settled, then. Sleep, then another visit to the carnival for more answers."

Torres joined him. "Sounds like your run-of-the-mill SEPIO mission."

Gapinski yawned. "Yeah, except without the car chases and gunfights."

Peter twisted up his face. "Car chases and gunfights? Who are you people?"

The line Radcliffe used when asked the same question popped into Silas's head.

"The good guys, Peter. Come on, let's hit the sack."

CHAPTER 13

A restful sleep on the sofa couch and a venti dark roast coffee was just what Peter needed after a crazy few days. Especially since a thick canopy of charcoal clouds promised rain. April showers bring May flowers, they say. He also hoped it brought answers.

Because between what had happened to Kat, and then Cameron, along with how unsettled he was from the big-top bonanza charismatic service—they needed the Lord to throw them a bone!

The wind whipped Peter's hair in his face as the Escalade raced along a single-lane road running along the western edge of Mill Creek Junction. He hoped they weren't too late, because they needed to get to the bottom of what had come to his small town. And that second showing of the charismatic revival was just the ticket to finally getting to the bottom of all the crazy.

At least that's what he hoped.

Because the plan Silas had outlined that morning seemed as crazy as what was going on a mile away.

He closed his eyes and breathed in deep, the morning air still crisp yet satisfying. Could do without the smell of manure though, the black stuff scattered across the fields of celery and onions that had been the bread and butter of Mill Creek stretching back a few generations and starting to work their magic. He eyed the shoots of green dotting the black landscape glistening with dew from morning sunshine struggling to break through. In some ways, he wished for the kind of life that only had to worry about the care of crops, rather than the care of souls—or in his case now, with all the crazy and the Order of Thaddeus, care for Christianity itself.

Ever since he was a boy, Peter had seemed destined for pastoral care. When other boys played cops and robbers or pretended to fight fires, Peter was preaching to a congregation of stuffed animals perched on his bed. And while his adolescent peers had dreams of joining the army or becoming doctors and lawyers, he had wanted to be a pastor. That changed in college, where he studied government at Freedom University before getting a job on Capitol Hill. God changed his life course in a winding path that sometimes gave him whiplash, but the Lord had been faithful.

And now he was racing through backcountry roads to try and save not just the people of his church, Mill Creek Baptist, but the Church itself from no uncertain doom—whatever that doom was, which wasn't yet clear.

What was clear was that he wished this plague hadn't visited the Junction. Hadn't visited his Mill Creek Baptist people, his Junction friends. He wished things were back to the way they were before the contagion had visited his town, before the twins showed up with their magic show, before the Navy SEALs for Jesus came barreling in to save the Christian faith.

A quote sprang to memory. From his favorite childhood book, *The Lord of the Rings*.

'I wish the Ring had never come to me,' Frodo said. *'I wish none of this had happened.'* To which Gandalf replied, *'So do all who live to see such times, but that is not for them to decide. All we have to decide is what to do with the time that is given to us.'*

Peter sighed. Exactly. On both counts.

He just wasn't sure yet what he was deciding to do with this time the Lord had plopped in his lap...

The shrilly sound of a cellphone cut off his memory.

From behind.

Spinning back, he caught Silas pressing his phone to his ear.

"Hey, Victor," he said, listening while the African archbishop spoke about something on the other end.

His eyes suddenly flitted from the back of Gapinski's seat to the pastor. And they didn't move as the SEPIO head nodded and *yeah*ed and *mmm-hmm*ed the man on the other end.

Something had happened. No doubt about it. And it looked like Peter was the "something" being talked about on the other end of that dang phone.

Silas nodded. "Alright, thanks for the call. We'll standby for more and call in with anything else we discover on that end of things, as well as any plans we make for dealing with all the crazy—here and overseas."

He said goodbye and shoved the phone into his pants pocket.

Celeste said, "All quiet on the Western Front, I hope."

Gapinski snorted a laugh. "Fat chance of that!"

Silas frowned. "Not sure about the Western Front, but *our* front just got more interesting."

"What's your meaning?" Celeste asked.

"As in Mill Creek Junction."

Peter sucked in a stabilizing breath. "What's happened?"

"Sounds like word's gotten out about the healings. Cars lining up for miles on both sides of the interstate trying to get in for the service."

Celeste said, "Well, the twins are putting on another show of things."

"And there's news now that the contagion is in the United

States, affecting people in the same way it affected some of the folks in Mill Creek Junction, and elsewhere overseas."

"I would imagine the panic about the contagion will be driving scores of people to check out a purported hub of healing."

"Exactly. Which could make things interesting at the fairground."

"Violent even, if space is limited."

Silas nodded, saying nothing more.

Peter ran a frustrated hand through his hair. Another show with another line of people desperate for hope and healing? It was like a bad dream in the middle of Groundhog Day!

"Should be an interesting day," was all he said.

"How are you feeling about all this?" Silas said, addressing Torres.

Peter leaned around from the passenger's seat, wondering the same thing.

She shrugged. "How does a monkey feel before getting injected with an experimental drug that could end in his death?"

"Like a guinea pig?" Gapinski said, eyeing her in the rear-view mirror with a grin.

She frowned, clearly not appreciating the humor. He mumbled a '*Sorry*' and got back to driving.

Couldn't blame her. Silas's brilliant plan was to use Torres as just that, a guinea pig. Thought the crazy religious organization SEPIO, or whatever it was, could use Torres's cancer diagnosis to test the assumption that the twins were actually healing people. And the head of it all wanted to visit the afternoon revival service again, sending the woman up on stage to receive the blessing of divine healing that the Bucks were dishing out.

Everyone seemed skeptical of it all, that anything would come of it and it was a needless wild goose chase. And frankly,

Peter was aghast at the request, using the woman's tragedy as an operational tactic to get to the bottom of the mystery.

Torres seemed to take it in strides, not showing how Silas's idea made her feel. But with his experience as a pastor, Peter could read her: There seemed to be a mixture of skepticism and hope in her mannerisms, something he had seen before in others he had sat with through personal tragedy, especially the health-scare variety.

But the SEPIO head honcho pressed on, insisting it would be the perfect way to test the mystery, with a verified health problem—and a doozy of one to boot—while disbelieving anything would come of it.

Except to Peter, Kat had been clearly healed. Saw it with his own two eyes, both before and after. Throw in the fact it looked like Cameron had been healed of his blindness as well, and Peter wasn't as convinced the healings were fake.

Something strange was going on in the Junction alright. But perhaps the Lord was using these traveling evangelists to bring healing to people who had been afflicted. Perhaps he was making his name known among the skeptics and doubters right there in Mill Creek Junction. Perhaps there'd even be some sort of revival in the area, in America, with the Junction at the center of it all—like the Azusa Street Revival over a century ago in Los Angeles. Wouldn't that be something!

Peter leaned his back against the dashboard and took in another measured breath of outside air, that coolness and manure slapping him in the face again.

Perhaps...

"Are you sure you want to go on with this?" Celeste asked, resting a hand on the woman's shoulder from behind. "I am not one to challenge authority, and far be it from me to go against our venerable Order Master..."

Silas chuckled. "I feel a 'but' coming on."

"But..." she said, one end of her mouth curling upward.

"This is one of the more cockamamie plans spun up from SEPIO yet!"

"Gee, thanks..."

"I mean no offense in that, but do we really want to put a woman who has just learned of a cancer diagnosis through this sort of wringer—the emotional and spiritual, not to mention the physical side of it with going through the motions of hopping up on that stage and ingesting the Eucharistic elements in that sort of way?"

Silas shifted, his face falling and jaw clenching, the back of his neck reddening some before rushing to his cheeks. He was getting irritated or embarrassed, or perhaps both. Either way, the woman had him back on his heels, which Peter wasn't necessarily sad about.

Clearing his throat, Peter added, "I agree with Celeste, here. As someone who's had cancer himself, using it as some mission tactic just doesn't seem right. No matter what ends it might justify."

Silas went to answer when Torres put a hand on his leg. "How about I take this one, chief?"

Opening his mouth, Silas shut it then nodded for her to answer.

"I appreciate the concern, *amiga y amigo*. I do. But this is my choice. I want to help. Want to use my—" She stopped short, taking a breath and swallowing. As if the next word tasted sour in her mouth, or it was lodged in her throat.

Clearing her throat, Torres went on, "I want to use my cancer to get to the bottom of this mystery. Whatever it is. When I got word of my diagnosis, I picked up a book called *Don't Waste Your Cancer*, by this Protestant pastor John Piper. Figure this is one way not to waste what God has seen fit to put on my plate. And who knows, maybe I'll get healed through it all!"

She gave a half-hearted chuckle, the rest of them smiling with her in solidarity.

Silas put a hand on her leg. "Sorry I wasn't more sensitive in my ask. Sometimes my head overrules my heart, or just flat stops it from registering what folks like Celeste and Peter here intuitively knew. This is a big physical, emotional, and spiritual ask. I know that, asking you to put all three on the line to get some answers, looking for a healing miracle in this way. So I'll ask again—and I really do mean it: Are you sure about this?"

Didn't even bat an eye. "Definitely."

"Because if not, we can scrap it and—"

"Without a doubt."

He nodded, glancing out the front windshield. "Good. Because it looks like we're here."

Coming south now toward town, the SUV groaned as one at the packed lot and queue of cars stretching along Main Street back into town. Place was even more packed than the first time, and the sound of it all coming from the massive canvas tent anchored at the center reminded Peter of a Rolling Stones concert, the deep bass and high ting of drums and guitars and singing thumping toward them already.

He said, "Looks like we'll have to hoof it from here."

"Looks like it," Silas said.

"Yeah, but how?" Gapinski asked, slowing now and craning his head around.

Peter clasped a hand on his shoulder. "You're in the country now, pal. Doesn't matter where you park, as long as you're not on private property and not blocking traffic. Just pull over to the shoulder and throw on the parking brake, you should be fine."

"If you say so..."

They found a spot along the road and parked. Gapinski nearly sent the thing headlong into a rain gutter running along the side, the tall green grass obscuring the view. Cattails should have been a dead giveaway, but these were clearly city folk who were out of their element.

People were pouring out from the entrance when they finally waded through the sea of parked cars. Looked like a dead end.

"Maybe we can push our way in," Silas said. "Make like we're on official business, because we sort of are."

"Just not with Bucks Incorporated," Gapinski said.

"Will the Vatican card work again?" Peter asked.

"Not with them…" Celeste pointed at the entrance, where the two goons from earlier were making their presence known.

Gapinski snorted a laugh. "Tweedledum and Tweedledee."

"Looks like they're scoping out the crowd," Torres said.

"Probably for us, after what happened last time!"

"Which leaves the side door wide open," Silas said.

"Are you sure about that?" Peter asked. "Surely they'll have others looking for a group of five interlopers trying to sneak inside."

"Interlopers?" Gapinski said. "Speak for yourself, pal."

Ignoring him, Silas asked, "What do you have in mind then?"

Peter pulled out a pocketknife, then flipped up a blade.

"Usually we go in with Sig Sauers and Berettas blazing," Gapinski said, "but I'm always up for a good knife fight."

Peter frowned. "No, not a fight. We cut our way in."

"How positively vandalous of you, Peter," Celeste said with a grin. "I quite like the sound of that."

"Me too," Silas said, leading the crew around the backside of the tent for the second time.

"Better watch out, pastorman," Torres said, "or you'll end up one of us in no time flat."

Peter laughed. "Yeah, right…"

The group neared the side entrance they had slipped into last time, ducking behind a row of parked middle-class sedans, snouts facing the tent. Two replicas of the other two goons were indeed standing guard in the shadows, but they slipped by with ease, giving the big top a wide berth now before circling around for the kill.

Silas reached it first, pulling out his own blade from his boot. Larger and thicker than Peter's. Felt foolish now with his Walmart special, but the Order head honcho told him to help him cut one side while he cut the other.

So he did, flipping the blade back into place and thrusting it into the canvas. It gave easily, but the act made him uneasy. He sliced down just enough for a peek inside, then parted the canvas for a look.

Place was filled to the brim with worshipers, more this time. All facing toward the stage with arms raised and voices carrying high and wide.

With zero clue he and SEPIO were breaking inside.

Silas had already finished slicing down one side of the portal into the tent, so Peter got to it, standing and thrusting the blade back into the canvas and slicing straight to the bottom before cutting toward the center.

Soon Silas was stepping inside with the others close behind.

Looking around for accusing eyes and finding none, Peter folded the blade inside the knife and shoved it in his pants pocket. Then plunged into the darkness with the rest.

What the heck was he doing...

Getting answers. For Katrina as much as SEPIO.

And the Church.

He just prayed to the Lord above there were some waiting on the other side.

CHAPTER 14

Another one of those moments Silas felt a little slimy, tearing into the tent like that. He rationalized it to himself that it was a free event open to the public. They were just creating their own entrance.

Such was life with SEPIO...

Not wasting time for someone to discover their subterfuge, Silas led the group along the tent's backside. His mind jumped to the problems waiting for him back home. The board of directors who'd gotten their knickers all knotted up, as Celeste would say, at the recent events that had put the Order of Thaddeus on the map under his leadership—and not in a good way. From deaths by assassination to destroyed historic buildings to car chases that ended badly.

Not that any of it was his fault. But he knew from his experience with Uncle Sam that didn't matter. The buck stops at the chief's desk, thanks to President Truman for that well-worn aphorism. Only Silas didn't know what that meant when he returned, what the board had in mind. Probably end up the same way his last career had ended up.

Sacked. Kicked to the curb. Left professionally dead.

Just his luck.

But he couldn't worry about that now. And he trusted the Lord for his future—come what may.

What mattered was the mission at hand. The cheering, singing, shouting Christian faithful and religiously curious who were all looking for a blessing from above with desperate, upraised hands from a pair of carnival barkers. While the world was launched headlong into a contagion that most likely had spread from Africa to South America and somehow ended up on the front stoop of Mill Creek Junction. Where not only were people coming down with the seemingly disconnected afflictions associated with the mystery contagion. But people were being healed from the symptoms—the blindness, the deafness, the paralysis.

All thanks to the Bobbsey Twins, whose motives were far from clear and whose methods were even more opaque. Who had seemed to come out of nowhere promising health and wealth just when the world needed it.

So, no. Silas knew his problems back at HQ mattered jack squat compared to what was going on in this small town.

Time to get his head in the game.

It was go time.

On the double.

Another tune was struck up now from the band doing its thing at the center of the tent. Less rocky, more downtempo. And familiar. He slowed to a stop and listened behind a group of farmers swaying to the tune.

> *Amazing grace, how sweet the sound*
> *That saved a wretch like me*
> *I once as lost but now I'm found*
> *Was blind but now I see.*

A ping of emotion began seizing Silas's throat, working up

into his head and down into his gut from the memory the tune conjured.

It was the one he'd heard way back when on that military base in Iraq, Camp Liberty. The sound of men singing it had caught his attention sauntering along a dirt road dealing with the emotional fallout from the sudden, grizzly death of his best friend thanks to a roadside IED.

The song wouldn't let him go. Dragged him kicking and screaming into that tent. A similar one to what he was standing in now set up at one end of Camp Liberty that held the on-base chapel services.

But that service was far different from this one.

There, a minister had shared about the crazy love of God. That no matter what we've done, no matter where we've been, the invitation of new life, of forgiveness, of salvation and rescue from sin and death was waiting for every single person on the planet.

It wasn't something we could earn through performing religious rituals or knowing the Bible backward or forward. Wasn't given to the person from the right family or country or even religious background. It was offered purely at the invitation of a God who came back time and time again to pursue wayward sheep, to rescue lost sinners.

Like himself.

Tears pricked his eyes now at the singing of another verse:

> *Through many dangers, toils and snares*
> *We have already come*
> *'Twas grace has brought us safe thus far*
> *And grace will lead us home.*

That song had changed his life. Literally, having given it to the Lord in the chapel service thanks to that song. Really it was more a rededication of his life to Christ, given he had been catechized in the Church as a Catholic child and been raised to understand his salvation as a grace gift.

But still...Silas had truly given his life to Christ that day, alongside someone else who would become a friend and then an enemy. Now look at things. He was the head of a religious order fighting to protect the Christian faith and retrieve the Church's memory.

He chuckled to himself and shook his head. The Lord sure works in mysterious ways...

Silas went to continue walking around the tent's periphery, when another verse was struck up.

And stopped him flat.

"Wait a minute..." he muttered in confusion at what he heard blaring across the cavernous tent.

Abundant life, open to me
Because My Savior died
Restored to health
And given wealth
In Christ it all is mine!

"That's not right!" Silas exclaimed, drawing the attention of a pair of those farmers.

But he didn't care. Now anger suddenly seized him in a way that the joyous emotion of his sweet memory had at the start of the song.

A hand rested on his shoulder. He startled. It was Celeste.

"You alright, love?"

Silas gestured toward the stage. "Those bozos co-opted a song about the crazy love of God and our salvation—and they turned it into an abracadabra formula genie bottle rub for God to grant us our ever-livin' wish!"

"I know, I caught the *Amazing Grace* switch myself. But we

can't worry about that now. We've got to keep our gaze fixed ahead, blinders fully up."

He knew she was right. But he burned with righteous indignation at the way the gospel had been transformed into an entirely self-serving measure.

Now it really was go time!

Turning to his crew, Silas motioned toward an aisle overflowing with worshipers. Would be tight, but they needed to get an up-close look at what they were dealing with.

"Come on!" he said above the din of another song carrying the tent to new heights of self-centered religious fervor.

They set off for an opening between a set of bleachers that led into the main area alighted with flashing red and blue and green lights, fog pouring off the stage and into the crowd of hopeful, expectant worshipers.

Boy, was there a crowd! Really packed in now, mostly standing room only. The very front was filled with several rows of chairs and a smattering of people in wheelchairs. Smelled different, too. Like what Silas remembered from growing up as a kid at his Falls Church, Virginia, parish, with all the smells and bells. Was surprised by the incense and candle wax flooding the place at such a non-traditional service. But he figured the charismatic preachers were priming the ecstatic pump with ritualistic intent.

Peter pointed toward the stage. "Wonder if those chairs are reserved at the front."

"Good call," Silas said.

"Fake it till you make it?"

He smiled and nodded. "You catch on quick, kid." Turning to the others, he said, "Let's head straight to the front. I want a literal front-row seat to the party this time. Torres is our calling card. You still up for this?"

"*Absolutamente!*" Torres said with a nod above the din of singing.

"Come on then."

Silas led the group squeezing through the shoulder-to-shoulder crowd down a narrow walkway to the front. Could see now that it was cordoned off. Reserved. Probably an invite-only affair, requiring a wink and a nod from the supposed sick so the Boppsey Twins could showcase their magical powers that bestowed God's abundant life.

Then again, last time it was a free-for-all, and they had a verified healing on their hands. So maybe it was more a holding area for those who wanted a healing touch or the provision of a job. Who knew.

Making it through the gauntlet of ecstatic faithful, they reached the section.

And right on cue, a pair of stocky men in suits put up a pair of hands. Different from the other two the day before, but same cardboard cutout. Tall and bulky and all neck, shoved into dark shirts inside expensive suits.

"Hold up, partner," the man said in the same Southern twang as Tweedledum and Tweedledee from yesterday. What's the deal with that? Must be a job requirement. "This here is a restricted zone."

"Getting a lot of that the last few days..." he muttered.

The other man strained for a hearing, but Silas shook his head. Instead, he gestured to Torres. "It's my friend. She's got cancer. She's hoping for a breakthrough day."

"Cancer, you say?" the first man startled, glancing at his partner.

"That's right. We heard through social media there would be another healing service, like before. And I need to help her to the stage."

"But what about the others?"

"I'm praying for a new job," Gapinski said.

Silas rolled his eyes before explaining, "We're all together. All hoping for a breakthrough day."

Tweedledee shook his head. "Sorry. Limited space."

"Don't you have some sort of BOGO program going on?" Gapinski quipped.

Silas threw him a look that told him all he needed to know. The man dipped his head and took a step back. He explained to the others they'd meet up afterwards.

"Alright, show us to our spots," he said, nodding to Torres who nodded back with confirmation.

"Sure thing," Tweedledum said, leading them down a wheelchair accessible aisle. "And remember about the freewill offering."

"The what?"

He handed Silas an envelope. A cream-colored thing of heavy, expensive cotton-fiber paper, instructions printed in gold metallic ink. It read: *Enclosed is the firstfruits from my bountiful blessing from the Lord, in the amount of $ _________ . ____ '*

A not-so-subtle hint that this time it was a pay-to-play healing service.

Heat rose up the back of Silas's neck. Reminded him of the abuses of the Catholic Church during the years running up to the Reformation, when political and religious overlords used the indulgence system to milk desperate people of their hard-earned money for the prospect of escaping the flaming fires of hell.

Grifters gonna grift, he supposed. Whether Medieval Catholic ones or modern charismatic Protestant ones.

Silas raised the envelope with a forced smile, taking one of the two seats left open at the end of the aisle. They had a decent view of the stage, sitting eight or nine rows back. The rest of the chairs were filled with all manner of people.

Some with canes and some others with white walking sticks used by the blind; some with bald heads, the fallout from rounds of chemo; many more were hunched over or propped up in wheelchairs, their gazes transfixed on the stage with arms raised, some with visibly wet cheeks. All were expecting a blessing, a touch from God above. To bring healing, to keep them alive, to provide for their needs.

Still others looked like Silas. Healthy enough, but perhaps seeking a different kind of blessing. To find a job or get a different job. To pay off debt or move into a safer neighborhood. To rise above whatever circumstances they found themselves in that were not as agreeable as those greener grasses on the other side of the fence.

All of it made Silas's blood pulse hot and stomach churn with a mixture of disgust and dread.

Lord Jesus Christ, Son of God, help us figure out what the heck's going on here...

The music wound down now, and the stylish pair Silas had grown to loathe were skipping across the stage from some green room in the back, hair looking as expensive as ever along with their ripped skinny jeans and low-hanging V-neck shirts and gleaming jewelry.

"Mill Creek...hello y'all!" the blonde woman said, Paulina.

A half-hearted cheer rose up in an echoey greeting.

"Hello, *Church!*" her brother Dexter added, bending over with a knowing grin, as if trying to pull a more enthusiastic response.

Which he got, the crowd raising more of a joyous raucous now, some rising to their feet and clapping and calling out with an enthusiastic greeting of their own.

Sure knew how to work a crowd.

"I love that last song y'all sang," Paulina said, walking toward the stage's edge with mic grasped between both hands, "and the promise it holds! *Abundant life, open to me because my Savior died. Restored to health, and given wealth. In Christ it all is mine!*"

The place erupted in another boisterous, ecstatic agreement.

Silas felt his hand close into a fist, his nails biting into his skin.

Clenching his jaw to keep from bolting to the stage, he closed his eyes and eased a breath in through his nostrils.

Steady, Grey...

"How do we live and lean into that?" the woman went on. "Well, Jesus taught us the way, didn't he? What you sow, you shall reap! You cannot expect a blessing if you withhold. You cannot expect a harvest of wheat if you sow a sack of stones! Non-tithers are non-breakthroughers!"

Clapping rippled across the tent. Silas knew where this was going.

"Some of y'all," Dexter said, taking over, "are believing and trusting in God for the salvation of y'alls children, whether spiritually or physically lost with some affliction. Some of y'all are burdened by babies with severe sickness and loved ones who are dying painful deaths."

"There are others," Paulina took over, as if it was a tag-team effort, "who've been trying to have children, and y'all have been believing that God will show up in y'alls life in this way for years. Others need a job. Or y'all are in debt up to your ears. Or y'all have been trusting God will bring financial breakthrough your way. Well, I stand before y'all this day to declare this is y'alls breakthrough day!"

The crowd roared at this. Some around them began chanting *Breakthrough day! Breakthrough day!*

The chant built into a crescendo, the brother-sister pair looking at each other with delight and raising their fists, pumping to the beat.

Dexter exclaimed, "That is right! This is your breakthrough day! There is a special anointing here today for y'all to grab hold of your own breakthrough this day. And Lord knows we need one, given the contagion that has been ravaging the world. But also in the individual contagions that have been ravaging our own individual worlds for years—decades even."

"Low expectations and listless careers," Paulina said, taking over again. "Fear of men and disordered households. Bodies that are out of shape and overworked."

Torres leaned over and whispered, "What the heck does any of this have to do with the Lord or Jesus' good news?"

"Jack squat," Silas growled. "It's like Brené Brown and Tony Robbins had a baby!"

"*Exactamente!*" Torres said. "If I wanted this nonsense, I'd flop down on my sofa with a box of chocolates and a bottle of Malbec and flip to the Oprah Winfrey Network."

"Tell me about it."

Paulina continued, "We want y'all to sow a seed of faith into God's work in this world so that he can bring a bountiful blessing in y'alls life. Don't skimp out on the Lord Almighty, either! Give your best seed-gift and he will breakthrough with whatever y'all are asking him for this day."

"That's right, sister," Dexter said. "After this service, we are going to anoint every single envelope that is put forward—but here's the thing."

He stopped, stepping to the edge of the stage, keeping the audience firmly in his gaze and holding up a familiar cream-colored envelope.

"Put your best seed inside of it. The ushers are passing around the envelopes. Sow your seed, then in a few moments come down the aisles to the platform. When we open the way for those who need a true breakthrough day, we're gonna lay hands on y'all and anoint y'all after y'all place your offering in the buckets here on stage."

There was a stir around the tent as men came streaming through the aisles bearing stacks of those envelopes the goon had already given Silas. As they passed out their goods, Dexter and Paulina stepped to the center, a spotlight falling on a table with the familiar elements.

Bread and cup. Body and blood.

The Lord's Supper.

The Eucharist.

"We believe," Paulina said, "that healing and the celebration of the Lord's supper are linked. There is a harmony here between the Christian ritual and the abundant life Jesus Christ paid in full for y'all! It is the most powerful signifier of the resurrection power that is available to y'all straight from heaven. For those who believe in Jesus' abundant life, his power is applied personally to y'alls circumstances. By receiving the bread and cup this day, y'all are personalizing Jesus' agony on the cross as your own."

"That's right, sis," Dexter said. "I don't know about y'all, but I feel the celebration of the Lord's Supper should be some of the biggest healing rallies around the world, every single day!"

"Amen, brother!" Paulina smiled at Dexter then returned to the gathered faithful. "Now, say it with us: Thank you, Jesus, by your shed blood my sins are washed away."

The crowd intoned: *'Thank you, Jesus, by your shed blood my sins are washed away!'*

"By your broken body, I'm healed."

Now it shouted: *'By your broken body, I'm healed!'*

Dexter continued, "We offer you these elements as a divine vehicle for transmitting God's divine healing power. The bread and wine are much more than symbols. They are spirit! The body is spirit. The blood is spirit. We take it into our bodies as spirit."

Holding the bread high, he proclaimed the familiar refrain: *"'This is my body, broken for you,'* Jesus said, *'do this in remembrance of me.'* What we believe—no what we *declare* is that prosperity in all realms of life flows from this fruit of Jesus' suffering."

Paulina took a goblet for the second time, gilded like the table and shimmering in the light from jewels encrusted on its face. She declared, *"'This cup is the new covenant in my blood,'* Jesus declared, *'Do this, as often as you drink it, in remembrance of me!'* This is the blood of Christ, shed for y'all. He was pierced for our transgressions, he was bruised for our iniquities, the punishment that brought us peace was upon him."

Right on cue, the crowd roared: *'And by his wounds we are healed!'*

"We know that Jesus took our infirmities," Dexter said now. "He bore my sickness. By his wounds I am healed."

'By his wounds I am healed,' the audience declared in agreement.

"These elements are much more than mere symbols. These elements literally pass along the benefits of the cross to impute to us divine health! They are infused with the power of the Spirit to change our circumstances."

Paulina said, "And we declare that any and all who take them will be healed." She paused a beat, bending toward the audience before adding with a shout: "Today!"

The audience seemed to leap to their feet as one. Those who could manage it, anyway. Then more shouting and amening and dancing.

"Any who wish to receive Christ's abundant life, bought and paid for and *guaranteed* by his shed blood on the cross—come forth as y'all are to receive what is rightfully yours!"

More ushers appeared near the stage from off-side, bearing the same baskets holding those Stouffer's prepackaged Eucharists.

"I suppose that's our cue," Torres said, standing as others around them poured into the aisles.

Silas joined her. "Suppose so. Still want to go through with it?"

"Definitely. Not that I'm expecting anything. But..."

She trailed off, face falling some and giving Silas a dose of regret for dragging her into his scheme to test whether the healing was genuine.

Lord Jesus Christ, Son of God, I hope I know what I'm doing!

They joined the group of people desperate for a blessing.

He added for good measure: *And why don't you heal Torres while you're at it!*

Reaching the stage, there was a real crowd cresting toward the familiar ramp leading up to the top. The music was louder now, speakers stacked on top of another blaring that pathetic, if not catchy tune:

> *Breakthrough, breakthrough, breakthrough-oo-oo.*
> *Breakthrough, breakthrough, breakthrough-oo-oo.*
> *Breakthrough, breakthrough, breakthrough-oo-oo.*

Silas rolled his eyes at the song, wanting to puke. He just might, especially after the verse started up:

> *It's your breakthrough-day*
> *God's showing the way.*
> *Health and wealth by right they're yours.*
> *It's your breakthrough-day.*

Soon, a pair of ushers and their baskets greeted Silas and Torres. He craned his head down for a look. There they were.

A little unleavened wafer underneath a clear plastic lid, resting on top a foil seal with grape juice hiding underneath.

Had to be a thousand of them inside. Like little prizes at the kiddie carnival he and his brother had gone to with Dad.

Suppose it fit the bill!

A mild-mannered looking fellow, stout with trimmed gray hair, handed Torres one of the sacrilegious packets.

She smiled and bowed her head. "*Gracias.*" Then she shuffled forward as the line advanced.

Silas went to go with her when he held up the basket to him. He went to object, saying he was just along for support, but thought against it. Might as well take one for the road.

Nodding, he cupped it in his hand before slipping it in his jacket.

He went to join her when the other usher held up his basket and nodded toward its mouth.

Inside were those blasted cream-colored envelopes. Some looking little more than filled with a bill or two. Others, sadly, looking like a deck of cards.

Clenching his jaw, Silas strained out a smile at the usher and pulled out his wallet, fishing out a few bucks hanging around inside. Seemed appropriate.

Slipping them inside and licking the flap closed, he held it up to the man and dropped it in the basket. The usher blessed Silas on his way to meet Torres.

Who was already at the front.

And hanging with the twins!

The woman had her hand on Torres's shoulder. Silas slid to her side as she started some sort of ritual.

"Repeat after me." Paulina intoned: "As I partake of this bread, heal my body."

Without missing a beat, Torres said, "As I partake of this bread, heal my body."

Then she popped the top and placed the tiny wafer on her tongue, closing her eyes and swallowing.

Now Dexter placed a hand on Torres's other shoulder, the one gloved in white. He seemed to hesitate but followed his sister's lead: "As I partake of this cup, make my body whole."

Torres said, "As I partake of this cup, make my body whole." Then she threw back the grape juice.

The pair started muttering some incoherent mumbo-jumbo

under their breaths, faces pinched and bodies rocking back and forth, hands still planted on Torres's shoulders. Paulina was intense, with eyes closed and a halting manner to her praying. Dexter not so much, like he was going through the motions, praying the same thing he'd prayed hundreds of times over.

Torres glanced at Silas, who shrugged. Her look told him all he needed to know about what she thought of it.

Muy loco, is right!

Then they were finished, an usher taking Torres by the hand and sending them down the stairs. They scurried through the crowd toward the back where the rest of SEPIO was waiting.

"Well?" Gapinski asked, face wide with a grin.

"How was it?" Celeste asked, a bit more reserved. "Was it positively frightening?"

"Wouldn't say frightening," Torres replied, arms wrapped around her chest in a hug. "More weird than anything."

"Do you feel anything?" Silas asked with a bit too much eagerness.

Right before his eyes widened and face flushed red. What Torres was dealing with wasn't like Katrina's paralysis or Max's deafness. Wouldn't know if it worked without 'feeling' around, which Silas clearly understood.

"And by feeling anything," he said, "I mean do you feel any different?"

"Gee, let me check, chief," Torres said, "Hold that thought while I feel around."

His face drained to white as she turned around, shielding her teammates from her examination.

Gapinski clasped Silas's shoulder. "The old OMIF routine."

He turned to him with a confused, furrowed brow.

"You know. Open mouth, insert foot. It suits you."

Silas frowned, but before he could come back with a retort, Torres turned around. Her face was grim and head bowed.

No one asked her the result; no one had to.

A voice suddenly rang out above the din of music from behind.

The group turned around to find a familiar face running down the aisle, jumping and skipping and fisting the air.

"I'm cured!"

"Isn't that the bloke from the town pub?" Celeste said.

"Yeah, Max Blade..." Peter said.

Right before Max spotted them and beelined it for the pastor, throwing his arms around Peter and hugging him to death.

"I can hear again, pastorman. I can hear!" More jumping, more hugging. "Those other preacherpeeps worked a mighty miracle!"

Silas threw Celeste a wide-eyed look. Another bona fide healing.

Just not Naomi Torres's. At least as far as she could tell.

What the heck was going on in Mill Creek Junction?

What the heck was going on with those Bucks twins?

CHAPTER 15

The helicopter purred with all the affection of a lover after a night of bliss, though Paulina Bucks wouldn't know from personal experience.

Her line of work had not only forbidden such extracurricular activities outside the bounds of marriage. It had also stood in the way of discovering it for herself *inside* of marriage, which even her guilty pleasure reading Christian romance novels—bonnet books, as Dex called them—didn't afford.

She was married to Christ, and blissfully so. But not in the traditional, nunnery sense of it, with those pesky vows of poverty and renunciations of the trappings of the modern world. Instead, she was a modern apostle to the masses, spreading the hope of Christ. She was a prophetess of the abundant life, sharing the gospel of Jesus' prosperity guaranteed to all his children.

And loving every minute of it.

The outside world blurred by in a palette of green and brown earth tones, punctuated by the still-life tones of modern life—houses painted white, barns painted red; blue, silver, and black cars of various makes and models; azure swimming pools and silver roofs crowning public schools educating the next generation—all of it flashed by underneath the belly of the luxury helicopter.

Why drive when you could fly? And in style.

Featuring a generous cabin of polished mahogany wood accented by 14-karat gold gilding and creamy leather seats still smelling as sweet as the day those poor goats were slaughtered, it was the standard in luxurious flight for anyone who was anyone. Including two charismatic twins escaping the back-breaking work of evangelizing the faithful and unfaithful alike, giving them inspiration and insight into tapping God's abundant life.

If only for a day. For the real work was just beginning.

And yet, as Paulina stared out the window in the seat opposite her twin brother, she did so with a peculiar sense of longing.

It had been awhile since the flat farmland and single-family dwellings and mom-and-pop storefronts of Middle America flashing by in still-life hues had been part of her world. The creams and golds and mahoganies were the palette of her life from childhood after her uncle Benjamin Bucks adopted her and her brother from no uncertain ruin. Not that she minded.

From a young age, she had worn designer clothes from the best brands, twirling in dresses from Burberry and Gucci and Dior, before driving her first Mercedes off the car lot when she turned sixteen. She had always had her own bedroom with adjoining bath, complete with a walk-in closet larger than most kids' bedrooms her age filled with those designer clothes and shoes she wore once or twice before moving on. Trips to Paris and Cairo and Shanghai were commonplace, staying in five-star hotels with rooms that took up entire floors decked out with the finest accoutrements—silk bedding, gilded bathtubs and toilets, in-room snack bars chock-full of more candy and cookies and ice cream than her childhood heart and stomach could hope for. That wasn't even touching on life as a young adult quickly approaching middle age, and all the luxuries she drank deeply from her everyday life...

But the day's event anchored at one end of Small Town, America, half a decade on the other side of that middle-age crest had given her a glimpse into a world that was simpler, that seemed truer and more genuine than the one of her family's construct.

Paulina took in a measured breath through pursed lips and swallowed away the sentimental feelings of a girl who had died three decades ago. Not sure why she was clawing at her from beyond the grave, but she couldn't stand for it. Not now.

Not when they were so close to having it all...

She took in another breath as the helicopter sped toward home, relieved to have a moment to catch her breath after a whirlwind tour across the globe the past few days. Well, one of their homes anyway.

The others were scattered around the world in hubs for the ministry empire. There was the castle in Bath, England, bought on the cheap and renovated to meet the Bucks's exacting standards. Then the estate in Nairobi, Kenya, that had been a wild game preserve until the NGO ran out of money; her uncle had fun turning that into a sprawling complex of imported wood and local cut stone. And the mansion in São Paulo, Brazil, left over from the colonial aspirations of the Portuguese empire. Another was still being built in Mumbai, the second largest English-speaking population in the world with a burgeoning middle class primed for the abundant-life message the Bucks had been exporting for a generation.

Their primary home was in Vancouver, British Columbia, Canada, where their adoptive uncle had built his ministry empire. It was a sprawling compound with two guest bungalows sitting behind the main mansion built on a hundred-twenty acres of rolling green hills flanked by forests and streams and a large lake. Whirling across flat West Michigan, she missed the home that had seen her through childhood. But where they were heading was the next best thing: a house on the bluff along Lake Michigan, their three-level home-away-from-home where she had spent every summer since childhood.

Paulina stared out below in contemplation, watching the shadow of their bird pass the world below. Replacing her sentimentality from earlier, a deep pity rose high at the sight of so many living such quiet lives of desperation, at the majority of the world eking out mere existence when they should be thriving and flying as high as she and her brother were!

Did they not know what was available to them? The health and wealth, the faith and victory? After all, Jesus himself said he came to preach good news to the poor and give sight to the blind, coming that we might have an abundant life. Life to its fullest. Our bestest life, right now!

Her ear suddenly tingled, as if the skin and cartilage of this aural appendage along with the skin and hair surrounding it rippled with memory from the fire that nearly ended that life. Her life.

And her brothers...

Catching her breath, Paulina turned to Dex, asleep in the chair across the aisle. She reached for his hand, finding it cold and clammy resting on the creamy leather armrest, the rivulets running through his skin and up his arm like melted wax jolting her heart a beat. Rarely was it ungloved, the requirements of their profession more than the consequences of Dexter's vanity. She was fortunate to have long, thick hair to hide her own imperfections, though the skilled hands of a plastic surgeon had done wonders.

Still, they had been marked by tragedy. Literally bearing the marks of their suffering, which ran counter to their messaging. As miserable of comforters as they were, Job's friends were right when they exclaimed in chapter 8, '*See, God will not reject a blameless person, nor take the hand of evildoers.'* Their father had not been blameless; he was blameworthy. And she and Dex had paid the price.

Shifting at the memory swirling in her now, Paulina squeezed his hand, once then twice then a third time.

I. Love. You.

Dexter didn't stir, having become used to her grabbing him so. The pair were inseparable after their parents and siblings died in the fire that nearly brought them and their good name to ruin. Had it not been for the kindness of their Uncle Benjamin coming to their aid, they would have been consigned to the trash heap of history, eking out a life in foster homes much like the ones racing by below.

A shiver ran up her spine at the thought.

Stirring next to her now, Dex arched his back and stretched his neck. She frowned, worried the stress of the day was too much at the end of so many similar trips. First Kenya then Nigeria before a week in Brazil and Belize. The small West Michigan town was a stopover until the big show in Mumbai. But an important stop, nonetheless. A fork in the road that would set their course for the days ahead.

Decades even.

"Hello, sleepyhead," Paulina cooed, squeezing his hand before letting go. "How was your catnap?"

"Too short. I could use another hundred of them strung together. I reckon my body has forgotten what time zone we're in."

"I know the feeling." She yawned, stretching her arms out and chuckling. "Clearly!"

Dexter smiled and grabbed her hand, squeezing it three times before adding one more with a widened grin.

I. Love. You. Toooo!

She matched it. But then he did something unexpected. His hand wandered up her arm to her shoulder and then her neck, his fingers combing through her thickened blond hair to push it behind her reconstructed ear still bearing the signs of what their father had done.

The twins held one another's gaze, the Yin to each other's Yang since that fateful night-time terror.

Taking her ear between his thumb and forefinger, he began rubbing it gently, massaging what the surgeon had carefully reconstructed. At his touch, her blood skated through her veins along her quickening pulse. An ache rose within her belly now, too. Neither pagan nor obscene. Rather, it was of recognition—that her brother was her other half, the stronger part of her who had survived and was leading them forward.

The crackle of the intercom and the voice of the pilot announcing their arrival in short order interrupted their quiet moment.

The pair startled as one at the noise, a learned behavior from the memory of the crackling wood consumed in the inferno all around them in their bedroom those many years ago.

They shared a laugh, and Paulina said, "You'd best buckle up, baby brother."

"Who's calling who baby?" Dexter said with a smirk as he reached for the buckles stuffed behind his back. "We're twins, sissy!"

"I am, Bubba! And you know it to be true."

"By a few minutes."

"I'll take however many minutes I can claim if it means telling you what to do."

He laughed now, reaching a hand across the aisle again with a grin. "To changing the world, together."

She eyed it, noting he had slipped his white glove back on, before grasping it.

"Together."

They held steady as the helicopter hovered in for a landing

with a careful sigh, as if relieved to be standing with two feet on solid ground. They didn't let go even as they stepped out on the airstairs leading to the helipad of bricks formed in a concentric circle not far from Mill Creek Junction.

Paulina was equally relieved to have landed at their vacation home along the lakeshore. Less afraid of flying, more relieved to be out of that backwoods hole in the ground and eager to get on with the final preparations for the days ahead.

"There they are!" shouted a short, slim man with a mane of pewter hair above the din of the chopper blades winding down to nothing. He was walking down a red-brick walkway from the backside of the mansion of similar red bricks soaring three stories against the clear-blue sky, the crashing waves of Lake Michigan sounding with a gentle welcome from beyond the mansion.

"Unky Benji!" Paulina squealed, her mouth turning upward at the unexpected surprise. Letting go of Dex's hand, she dashed across the walkway toward the man's outstretched arms tanned from his latest trip to their Caribbean hideaway in Cuba.

He wasn't supposed to be back in the country for another week, handing over the reins to her while away. Looked like he lost weight, Unky's cheekbones jutting up at wicked angles and clothes dripping from his slight, frail frame. She choked back tears at his appearance, at all he had been through. But the surprise visit was welcomed, if not a bit curious.

Benjamin Bucks had taught Paulina and her brother everything they knew about sharing the abundant-life message of their faith. He had adopted the health and wealth lingo and honed his craft after the most prolific of prosperity preachers. From Oral Roberts to Kenneth Copeland, Joyce Myers to Paula White, Unky Benji had followed closely in their footsteps—bringing up his closest nephew and niece in the family trade.

Paulina remembered those early years fondly, working for

Benji at Abundant Life Victory Center in Fairfax, Virginia. The pair would work the aisles collecting envelopes filled with the seeds of faith sown by parishioners expecting to reap a hundredfold blessing from investing in their ministry. She in a puffy powder blue dress, Dexter in a sharp black suit and matching tie. Soon they were traveling across the globe with their uncle as his ministry grew, glimpsing his work firsthand, and its massive fruits fueling their luxurious lifestyle, giving rise to their own ministry interests and opening the door for their later work.

Within half a decade, Unky Benji exported the same ministry model and planted it in Vancouver. Almost like a business franchise, launching the Canadian version of Abundant Life Victory Center in 1987 with a bang and attracting a hungry audience looking for the twin blessings their uncle had given the masses of Northern Virginia: health and wealth. Or more palatably, the abundant life. As with the Fairfax church, the Vancouver one proved to be the right place at the right time for a church offering children of the 60s and 70s who had just emerged from a recession a meaningful crack at the American Dream, Canadian style.

By then, the Bucks name had grown more prominent in the Pentecostal and charismatic circles their family had been frequenting, which led to packed Sunday morning and evening services and a momentum that skyrocketed the Bucks and the Abundant Life Victory Center names into the stratosphere. A decade later, at the turn of the century, Unky Benji founded a ministry school to teach normal people how to do the signs and wonders that Jesus himself performed. He called it The School of Supernatural Ministry. Anyone could pay tuition to learn how to do miracles, speak in tongues, and perform healings.

He taught the classes and included historical material designed to inspire people to emulate the giants of the past. Teachings from the big dogs of Pentecostalism were the foundation of the school. From E. W. Kenyon to Smith Wigglesworth, Oral Roberts to Kenneth Hagin, and even their more recent acolytes from Norman Vincent Peale to Kenneth Copeland—all were required reading. Abundant Life Victory Center never shied away from its doctrinal foundations. And the fruits of its direction proved itself to be a cash cow. Crowds poured into the church, along with the money. That's when Paulina and her brother really began living the dream. One that was threatened a year ago.

Speaking of which...

The twins embraced their uncle in front of the summer home along the second largest of the five Great lakes. It was a six-bedroom, eight-bathroom mansion of red brick that covered just a little less than ten thousand square feet, sporting three fireplaces the size of a person and a dock down the bluff with a garage housing their yacht. A private gate kept out the riffraff, which was mostly the press, bad press seeking ugly stories that twisted their work into something sinister. It also gave them the privacy they needed from some of their more obsessive fans seeking special blessings. A swimming pool, an indoor hot tub, a steam room, a sport court, and more than twenty acres of lakeside land to enjoy was the best part of it all, giving the family their due R&R after serving the Lord.

"It is good to see you, uncle," Dexter said. "But for whatever reason are you here?"

His wide grin faltered some, and his glistening eyes betrayed a secret that whispered something was not right. With him, even.

But then it vanished, the crow's feet at the corners returning to his bronzed, ruddy face. He grabbed Paulina's face with shaking hands and kissed her forehead, then put a shaking hand to Dexter's cheek.

"Come you two," he said in his deep twangy drawl. "We've got work to do."

Unky Benji led them back into the house. Truth be told, Paulina wanted nothing more than to go straight to her bedroom suite and sleep until dawn. Larger than most people's living rooms, it boasted a massive walk-in closet like the one she grew up with, but housing her adult Gucci and Chanel jeans and shirts; a bathroom with a Jacuzzi tub and standup shower, accented by chocolate marble tiles with brown and off-white swirls; and, yes, gold fixtures adorning all faucets and handles and edging the crown molding racing around the ceiling.

Continuing her teenage tradition, a Mercedes-Maybach GLS 600 SUV in a sporty navy blue sat in a six-stall garage anchored at one end of the home, along with Dexter's Aston Martin DB11, candy-apple red. But because they spent most of the time vacationing around the world and staying in expensive hotels, identical copies of each of their cars were housed at estates across the globe. In fact, since their eighth birthday they had spent more time outside America and Canada than inside, having celebrated that birthday in the Holy Land riding camels as part of the celebration at one of Unky Benji's ministry trips.

Every trip from London to Paris, Maui to Morocco, and everywhere in between was filled with privately arranged meetings to pray for and speak a blessing over celebrities, government leaders, and professional athletes from all manner of professional sports—American, European, African, you name it. Wherever they went, Unky Benji's spiritual power lured people of prominence, almost like a Fountain of Youth, the men and women seeking something that could give them a leg up on being more successful than they already were. Rubbing shoulders with the creme de la creme of every society in the world had given them a license to enjoy whatever luxuries Paulina and Dex wanted.

Signs, wonders, miracles, and preaching the abundant life gave them a life their father had only dreamed about. A life that had nearly been in his grasp, yet slipped through his fingers from one false move.

It was the match that had sparked the fire that bloomed into the flame that nearly brought their life to an end.

Nearly.

Because instead of that pathetic one, Paulina and Dexter had been afforded a second chance. Like the phoenix rising from the ashes of their ancestors, they were living the abundant, blessed life.

And they were about to take that life to the next level, as exhausting as it would be to get there.

Soon, they would have their own breakthrough-day.

All because of Unky Benji.

And for his sake...

CHAPTER 16

Silas Grey had seen plenty in his forty years on this third rock from the sun to make a person's head spin.

From his tours in the Middle East after 9/11 and all the carnage and heroism alike, to his experiences in the upper echelons of academia with his research and the politics of university life, to everything that had unfolded the past few years with the Order of Thaddeus and SEPIO—the gunfights and car chases, the glimpses of the Ark of the Covenant and unfolding of conspiracies to thwart a presidential election, even discovering a resurgent Knights Templar and earthly incarnation of Satan.

None of it had prepared him for the supernatural encounter of divine healing that had set the world on fire in the face of a world-wide contagion. What had happened the past few days in Mill Creek Junction certainly took the cake! The rest of the day was spent verifying the truth of the matter.

Both matters.

Silas had ushered Max out of the tent to get the lowdown on what had happened—through the main door, not the backdoor they'd sliced up themselves. Was worried they'd run into the two goons from before, but they were in the clear.

Once in the Escalade, Max told quite the tale Silas could hardly believe. Yet he did. Because it was one that had been a repeat from the last time.

As Max put it, his hearing had completely dried up the past day after it cut out to a tuning-fork ting when they'd last seen him at his bar.

"Just empty space between my ears!" Max had said.

Silas wondered if there was more truth to the matter beyond just a loss of hearing, but he didn't go there. Instead, they talked through what had happened to bring it back.

"Felt like the end result," he had gone on, "of the glory days of 70s rock-and-roll head banging. And thought it was the end of the line for me."

That's when he relayed a similar story that Peter's church secretary had given. Had heard the "holy rollers" were coming back to the Junction for a second day of "holy-roller rollin'" as Max had put it.

"Hemmed and hawed about whether to show my mug, not being the religious type," he'd explained, "But figured why the hell not? Had nothin' to lose after losin' the only thing I'd never, under no circumstances, ever wanted to live without. Some peeps could live without their peepers, others use of their legs. For me it was the ears. Yet there I was, dumb as a post."

Again, Silas was tempted to give some smartass commentary, but held back. Because the next thing Max had said stopped him cold.

He'd explained to one of the black-shirt doorkeepers to the revival tent service that he'd lost his hearing the past day and was lookin' for a miracle. "Fella asked if I'd brought my seed to sow," Max had explained, "and told him I didn't know what smack he was talking about! Dude explained I needed to bring my breakthrough-day best gift if I wanted the Lord to bestow his blessing. Had to be a real good one, too. Seen as how I knew jack squat about these sorts of things, having not darkened a church in years, I beelined it for my bank and withdrew my life savings."

Poor Pastor Peter nearly choked on his tongue at the revelation. Silas couldn't believe what he was hearing, either. Life savings?

That's what Max told the fella when he returned with a stack of Benjamins, which apparently added up to just under ten grand. "Figured it was worth it if I could convince the Almighty to restore my hearing," Max had explained. "Heard about what happened to Cameron and Kat, even Mayor Goodall with his skin condition." Another person Peter knew from town but the group hadn't known was sick, or healed.

The black-shirt had ushered Max to the front, and when the moment of truth came, he bounded up the stairs, dropped his wad of cash in the coffers, took the same prepackaged Eucharistic elements that Torres had, complete with the personal touch of Dexter and Paulina.

"Before I knew it," Max had gone on, "my head was filled with this rushing sound, like the wind at the center of a right wicked twister. And then I could hear! I can hear!"

He'd let out a childlike giggle at the truth of it, eyes bright with emotion and mouth widened into the same giddy grin. If Silas hadn't known any better, it looked like the man had not only experienced healing, but might have even experienced some sort of ecstatic moment in the process—a conversation, even.

Max had said he couldn't make sense of it. All he knew was that for the better part of a day, almost two, he'd been deaf and now he could hear after going through the religious gauntlet of those "holy rollers."

Reminded Silas of the story of the blind man being interrogated by the religious leaders after Jesus had brought back his sight. Couldn't answer all their questions about who Jesus was, whether a sinner or demon possessed, but what he did know was "that though I was blind, now I see."

Same for Max. One minute he was deaf as a head-banging 70s punk-rocker. The next he could hear.

Just like that college kid Peter knew, just like Katrina.

All three healed.

Torres's face had been drawn and eyes downcast, averting Max and disinterested in the conversation. Or perhaps very interested in the conversation, but not what it meant.

For her.

Because as far as they knew, she still had cancer. Which they were trying to confirm that evening.

Peter had a doctor friend from his church who agreed to look over Torres after hours, using medical equipment at Mill Creek General in coordination with her medical scans available through a web portal to evaluate any changes in her condition after the healing service.

The Order was covering the bill, and he and the rest of Torres's SEPIO teammates were waiting in the lobby.

Silas shifted on the cheap plastic bench, bottom aching something fierce and a knot growing in the pit of his stomach from all the crazy. He glanced at his watch and yawned, rubbing his face and wishing he had a cup of coffee. They'd been sitting like that for over two hours now, waiting for word on the result of their theory that Torres's cancer would shrink, disappear even, joining the other ailments that had seemingly vanished during Mill Creek Junction's charismatic healing service.

But no word yet.

And the more he waited, the more Silas felt flat horrible that he had even had the slightest idea of using her as a guinea pig for the SEPIO mission getting to the bottom of what was going on. She'd done her duty like any good soldier, without complaint, but still. And now with the battery of tests the doc was putting her through, and all the hope and expectation that was surely pent up from the reports of other healings—Silas just felt flat horrible.

And he was praying like he'd never prayed before that it had truly worked. That the good Lord above had worked his wonder-working power by pouring out a blessing of healing on one of his all-star teammates.

Closing his eyes, he inhaled a stabilizing breath, the dueling scents of bleach and Lysol flooding his senses. The crappy elevator music added to the misery, assaulting his ears along with the groans and moans and muffled cries of others waiting for news from their loved ones.

Boy, did he hate hospitals. Anything to do with medical stuff, really. Probably because of how much time he'd spent recovering in a makeshift one at Camp Liberty after his best friend was blown to smithereens.

A hand rested on his own and gave it a squeeze.

I. Love. You.

Silas smiled. He squeezed back four times.

I. Love. You. Tooooo!

Then eased his eyes open and glanced at Celeste, his right-hand woman, his partner in crime, his fiancé.

"She'll be alright, love," she said, still holding his hand.

He nodded. "I know. Just feel bad now using her in this way."

"Now, now. Naomi doesn't do anything that Naomi doesn't want to do. Besides, it isn't like there was any risk to her for playing her part in the mission."

"Physically, perhaps. What about emotionally, spiritually?"

She shrugged. "I understand what you are saying, and you really are a sweetheart for thinking of her in that way. But Torres is a strong woman, with her head on tight and heart squared away. As much of a gauntlet as her diagnosis has been for her, emotionally and spiritually as you say, I believe she'll come through the other side of it. Not only physically, because so much can be done now, but spiritually as well. As Paul writes in Romans, '*We know that all things work together for good for those who love God, who are called according to his purpose.*'"

Silas nodded, grunting agreement with one addendum: "Only problem is, we don't know what that *good* is that will be worked through her cancer. Whether for her good with healing or some other."

Celeste nodded, saying nothing and growing silent.

"Speaking of which..."

Silas spotted Torres walking toward them from a pair of swinging hospital doors.

He stood, as did Celeste and Gapinski, then Peter.

Those arms of hers were wrapped around her chest again in a hug; she'd been doing that a lot this trip. Between that and her long face—Silas saw all he needed to see to know it didn't work.

Celeste approached her first. "What's the verdict, mate?"

Torres let her arms fall, her back stiffening and face rising back into place. A show of strength more than a sign of success.

"Tumor's the same as it was a few days ago. Nothing's changed."

"Always something..." Gapinski cursed.

Silas let his held breath out through pursed lips. Ain't that the truth. Not that he was expecting anything different. Because of his cynicism with the whole charismatic carnival and his contrarian nature, he couldn't believe what was happening in Mill Creek was anything close to healing.

But still...Damn. He was holding out a ray of hope for his friend.

He led her and the others back to the collection of plastic couches and chairs. Torres slumped into a pink one, putting her feet up and wrapping her arms around herself again.

"Well, did *anything* come from the holy roller service?"

Gapinski asked. "Something had to have worked. Look what happened to that cat Max!"

Torres shrugged. "Not that the doc could tell. But he said cancer isn't like the cold, where you can pop some zinc tablets and Airborne and expect it to vanish."

"Or a cracker and some grape juice, I suppose," Silas muttered.

"Something like that. Good news is the tumor is stable, so it's not growing. It's just..." She trailed off, settling into her seat with a sigh before finishing: "Just not what I was hoping for."

Hope...

Anger welled up within Silas now. The exact outcome from that blasted healing service preying on the hopes of desperate people looking for a healing touch or a payout was exactly what he warned against.

Now the hopes of one of his own were dashed, her expectations for a miracle from heaven coming down to rid her body of cancer shattered.

And those twins would pay.

Big time.

Silas reached over with a hand on her leg, squeezing it and offering a locked-jaw smile. "You'll kick cancer's ass, Torres. And whatever it takes, we'll be right there with you to support you."

"Yeah, whatever it takes, sister," Gapinski said.

Celeste grabbed her hand and squeezed it, grinning with glistening eyes. "Whatever it takes, mate."

"But with that solidarity," Silas went on, "comes fighting like hell to figure out what in God's name is going on in this town. Not only for your sake, but for Mill Creek's."

He looked to Peter, who sat up straight and nodded, as if to say thanks for the support.

"As far as I can gather," Celeste said, scooting to the edge of her seat, "we have been having a bit of wheel-spinning, haven't we? Poking at the beast without having any luck identifying what it is."

Silas frowned. "Usually at this point we're at least making progress IDing the who, what, where, and why."

Gapinski snorted a laugh. "Or getting our asses handed to us on a silver platter." He leaned back and started opening up another one of those damn chocolate cupcakes.

"Really, dude? You're going to have a midnight snack in front of us during mission planning?"

He froze and stopped, eyes darting to Silas before he slowly started putting it back in his jacket.

"Don't mind him, Matthew," Celeste said. "He was just deprived of sweets as a child. I say have at it if you're hungry."

Gapinski's eyes darted from her to Silas and back, clearly not knowing what to do, caught between the pair.

Silas relented with a sigh, nodding his permission. Gapinski immediately pulled the snack back out and popped the whole thing in his mouth.

"As I was saying...Celeste's right. We're behind the curve with this whole—whatever it is. Faith-healing mystery or whatever. Have been from the start. Admittedly, because I didn't think there was anything here to investigate. No offense, Peter."

The pastor put up a hand. "None taken."

Celeste answered, "So let's have ourselves a think about what we do know, then."

"How about we start with the fact," Gapinski said with full mouth, "that David Copperfield and his twin sister are working the Junction big top bonanza like a Vegas casino show!"

"There we go. Dexter and Paulina Bucks. Nephew and niece to Benjamin Bucks."

Torres said, "They just came out of nowhere, didn't they?"

Celeste nodded. "It appears that way, although I believe they've been working the circuit with their uncle the past few years."

Silas added, "We know they've been franchising the same circuit around the world. From the SEPIO agent reports, they've been to Africa and South America, with something brewing in South East Asia."

"The same places the contagion has spread from," Torres said.

"That's right!"

"Which seems like quite the coinkydink!" Gapinski said.

Celeste nodded. "That is a curious bit. What are the odds a contagion breaks out in the general vicinity of our twins' charismatic revival services?"

"Worse than Vegas odds."

"You're saying they're linked?" Peter asked.

"I'm not sure," said Celeste. "It's a curious bit I've been having a think about since news of the contagion broke, and the Order has been receiving various intel reports from SEPIO agents in the field."

"Something to keep in mind for sure," Silas said, "But what seems to be the unifying theme in all of these stories?"

"The twins?" Torres answered.

"Maybe it's the music?" Peter said. "Some sort of aural trigger embedded in the audio data?"

"That is certainly a unifying element," Celeste said. "But a bit of bargain-bin Kindle contagion thriller, don't you think?"

"Yeah, I don't know," Silas said. "Seems far-fetched to me."

Gapinski laughed. "Even by SEPIO standards!"

Peter turned to him. "More far-fetched than two men gone blind and deaf regaining their sight and hearing?"

Torres added, "Not to mention a woman getting use of her arms and legs back."

Silas frowned, stuffing his hands in his pockets. They had a point. His fingers found the prepackaged Eucharistic elements he'd saved from the service.

Which led to an idea.

He took it out and held it up. Watery purple juice rocked gently inside the tiny plastic cup, with hospital light reflecting off from the aluminum foil seal underneath the thin wafer.

"I wonder..."

"Wonder what, chief?" Gapinski said.

He ignored the man, the memory markers needling his mind with a possibility that seemed entirely improbable.

The Lord's Supper, or the Eucharist as it was called in his childhood Catholic tradition, was the Christian ritual believers celebrated to remember what Jesus Christ had done on the cross. Breaking his body open on those wretched boards of execution, taking upon his very self the punishment for the sins of the world, shedding his blood for the forgiveness of sins and the cancellation of the debt we owed God.

But this—what seemed so central to the charismatic services promising health and wealth...It's like the Bucks twins flipped the script on the sacred rite.

They claimed that ingesting the elements was an ingestion of God's divine power, all in order to restore their own self to health. Almost sounded more Catholic than Protestant, now that Silas thought about it! But in a warped, humanistic way, sapping the spiritual significance of the rite and replacing it with entirely physical benefits—not as a sacramental vehicle for God's grace, but as a vehicle for material gain.

"Love, what do you have?" Celeste said, shaking him from his contemplation.

He sat up straight now, thrusting the prepackaged wafer and juice before the group.

"You hungry, chief?" Gapinski said. "I've got another Choco-Choco if you're—"

"No!" Silas snapped. "The Lord's Supper."

"What about it?" Peter asked, scooting to the edge of his seat now.

"This is what unifies the services."

Celeste gave a knowing hum and sat at the edge of her own seat. "The bread and cup…"

"Wait a second," Torres said. "You think these Stouffer's wannabes are the link between the healings?"

"Why not? I mean, you saw what I did, didn't you? Katrina took the elements, and then was healed. That college kid was up on that stage, and so was that Max guy. Both had presumably taken the same communion cup and wafer—then boom. Healed!"

"Not verified, though," Celeste said.

"But probably. I mean, it was like clockwork," Silas said. "You go up the ramp and there's an usher standing there with a basket of these things." He shook the cup, the juice and wafer rattling inside. "This time they basically required you to pay up before you got your Eucharistic elements."

"Pay-to-play healing?" Celeste asked, face twisted up in disgust.

"Exactly. Which Max said he himself had to do, remember?"

"Dropped his life savings inside," Peter said, shaking his head. "I remember."

"And then after that you got one of these, Torres!" Silas was grinning with satisfaction now, feeling like he was really on to something.

"Not to rain on your brain-storming parade, love," Celeste said, "but the Lord's Supper is a common Christian rite. Why is it surprising that it is central to this one?"

"She's got a point," Peter said.

Silas shook the package of juice and cracker again. "No, there's something about this part of the service that's central to what's been happening here in Mill Creek. I just know it."

Gapinski cleared his throat. "Except you're forgetting one thing, chief."

"Yeah, what's that?"

He glanced at Torres, saying nothing except widening his eyes.

"Except you're forgetting I didn't get healed," she answered for him.

Silas went silent. Couldn't argue with that. Which might have just blown his theory up. Probably did.

"Look," Celeste said, sitting forward. "It appears we need to have a long think about the implications of the charismatic movement and its promises. Perhaps do some digging into the history of it all to have a firmer grasp on its implications for what is happening now, unearthing something that might aid in our mission here in Mill Creek Junction."

Peter suggested, "We could use the library at Grand River Theological Seminary."

"Brilliant!"

"Good idea," Silas said. "But us, not you."

"What are you playing at, Silas?" Celeste asked.

He pointed at her and Torres. "I'm sending you two to Mumbai. The Bucks's next stop on their faith-healing tour."

She almost protested, but then cocked her head in consideration. "I suppose that makes sense." She looked at Torres. "You up for a bit of overseas travel?"

Torres rolled her eyes with a sigh. "Why does everyone keep asking me if I'm alright? I'm not dying! I've got breast cancer."

"Sorry, mate. Meant no offense."

She frowned and nodded. "And I'm sorry for biting your head off. I feel fine. I really do. Would rather be figuring out this latest mess the Church has gotten itself into than holed up in my apartment worrying about my test results. No way you'll keep me from nailing the Bucks, anyway. Not on your life..."

"Then it's settled," Silas said. "I'll lead Peter and Gapinski here through the research side of things, maybe go snooping around the big top up town again. Celeste and Naomi will head to Mumbai to scope the twins out more directly."

"So guys and dolls again, eh?" Torres said.

"Sounds like a musical," Gapinski quipped.

She frowned. "It is, dingbat."

"Oh..."

"While we're at the seminary," Silas said, "perhaps we can see an old friend of mine."

Peter nodded. "Calvin VanDyke. I can see if he's free. I'm sure he'll offer some good insight."

"Sounds good. Everyone understand your orders?"

The group nodded in affirmation.

He stood. "Good. Then let's roll."

CHAPTER 17

It was an easy twenty-minute drive to Grand River Theological Seminary, Gapinski driving with Peter riding shotgun to guide the way with Silas in the back.

Along the way, Peter explained how he had chosen GRTS—more because of divine intervention than anything else.

"After I left a campus ministry position in Washington, DC—"

"DC?" Silas said. "You never mentioned that."

He shrugged. "Didn't see the need to."

"What was the nature of your ministry, Peter?" Gapinski asked.

"I met with guys for prayer and Bible study at Georgetown University."

"Georgetown?" Silas said again with shock. "I did my under-grad work there."

Peter turned around with a smile, marveling at the small world. "No kidding? Small world. And a shame what happened to the Dahlgren Chapel, with those terrorists blowing it up those years back."

"Uh, yeah, real shame..."

Silas and Gapinski exchanged knowing glances. Peter

wondered what that was about. Looked like a real story behind that one.

"Anyway, when that door closed, felt like seminary was the next logical step. Applied to a few places, GRTS and a school out in California, and was accepted to both. Had every intention of moving to the West Coast, but for some reason I couldn't shake this feeling that God was taking me back home. Which was super odd because I'd never been one to make decisions based on some subjective God-told-me-so feeling. Much too rational for that."

"I hear that," Silas said.

Peter went on, "The more I prayed about my future and thought about moving to SoCal, the more I felt this strange pull to study in Grand Rapids."

He glanced out the windshield at the world zipping by along the highway, chuckling at the memory. Couldn't help marveling at all God had done to drag him back home. Never would have chosen it himself, but thankful he'd gotten the providential tug from the Lord's sovereign hand. Especially given all that had happened the past several years...

"It's funny, because I couldn't stomach the idea of coming home to a place I vowed I'd never return."

"Why's that?" Gapinski asked.

Peter shifted. "Mostly because I'd changed so much from the place I'd grown up in. But also because of pride, thinking myself better than my hometown. Better than my parents, even."

"What was it you thought you were better at," Silas said, "if I may ask?"

"Mostly at doing the Christian faith. So there was an arrogance there. But it also stemmed from the fact I felt I no longer fit with that version of childhood faith. Like a fish out of water."

"And what version was that?"

"Could be described as Christian fundamentalism. Independent Fundamental Baptists Churches of America was the denomination of my childhood church."

Gapinski snorted a laugh. "I fight and blast Christians anywhere."

Peter laughed. "So you know what I'm talking about!"

"What are you talking about?" Silas asked.

Turning off the highway, Gapinski explained, "Just a funny alternative meaning to the IFBCA acronym Grandpappy used to use."

"Sounds like quite the bunch," Silas said.

"They were good people," Peter said, "and way less fundamentalist than you might imagine."

"So you were allowed to play cards?" Gapinski quipped.

"Sure. We could even go see movies."

"But no sex before marriage."

Peter smirked. "Of course not! And definitely no dancing."

"No dancing?" Silas asked, face twisted up with confusion. "What kind of nonsense is that about?"

"Don't you know, chief?" Gapinski replied, to which Peter joined him, saying in unison: *"Because sex could lead to dancing!"*

They shared a laugh at their shared Baptist culture.

"Makes me happy I was raised Catholic," Silas said.

"Yeah, well, what I was raised on was fine enough," Peter said. "Had a good foundation in the Bible. Only problem was, it didn't prepare me for what the world outside my four church walls was really interested in asking about faith, life, and everything in between. Which led to me stumbling into this new conversation reimagining the Christian faith, Prosurgent."

"Oh, yeah," Silas said. "I seem to recall hearing rumblings about some of their leaders making waves with books and conferences. Mostly a Protestant evangelical thing, right?"

"That's right. And at the start it seemed like a good thing, reimagining how the Christian faith connected to our postmodern world. I mean, so much had changed from the version

I'd grown up with. And when I had a crisis of faith during my ministry days in DC, I didn't know where to turn. Prosurgent helped me through."

"How so?" Gapinski asked.

Peter took a breath, gearing up for a conversation he hadn't intended. "Well, the version I'd grown up with gave me a good foundation in the Bible and all. Only problem was, that it had answers to none of the questions my friends at Georgetown were asking."

Silas hummed with interest. "Tell us more about that."

"Well, the version of my Christian faith was all about how to get to heaven when you died. And fair enough, it's a pretty important question."

"Except heaven really isn't the point. It's the resurrection of the dead, but go on."

"Spoken like a true Catholic."

He put up a finger. "No, a true Christian rooted in the historic creeds of the Church. As the Nicene Creed says, '*We look forward to the resurrection of the dead, and to life in the world to come.*'"

Peter laughed. "Touché."

"And amen," Silas said with a wink.

"Anyway, the point was that my friends were interested much more in life before death than life after death. Like, what does Jesus' good news and God's good life mean for life right now, in *this* life? For issues of justice and the environment, for marriage and identity."

"For issues of hope and healing..." Silas added, touching closer to home.

"I hear that," Gapinski said. "My own background seemed to be more heavenly minded to be of any earthly good."

"Right? And those questions sent me into a sort of crisis of faith."

"Why was that?"

"Because I didn't have any answers to them! Long story short, that sent me on a journey to really dive deep into what it means to be a Christian, what it means to follow Jesus and believe in what Christians have always believed."

"And what did you learn?" Silas asked, sitting forward now.

"What I learned was that what I needed, what the Church needs along with my friends, my generation, is not to reimagine the Christian faith but to *rediscover* it. To rediscover the once-for-all faith entrusted to the saints."

Silas leaned back, one end of his mouth curling upward. "I don't know, Gapinski. Sounds like we've got a potential SEPIO recruit here. Guy's parroting our mission verbatim."

Peter chuckled. "The pastor's life is more my style than any of those car chases and gunfights you were talking about earlier."

"You get used to it," Gapinski said.

"I don't know about that. But I will say that interest is what led me to call up VanDyke and get you guys to Mill Creek Junction. Because what I saw, what we've all seen, seems to be a far cry from that once-for-all faith. And as someone who has had my own share of health scares and lived to tell about it, it's a topic near and dear."

"You said cancer," Silas said, "isn't that right?"

Peter nodded. "That's right."

"Cancer, at your age?" Gapinski said.

Peter took in a breath, the memory still fresh from a few years ago. "Thyroid cancer. So the good kind, if there is such a thing with the big C. But, yeah, at thirtysomething, definitely not what I expected!"

"I guess not."

"But you had been a campus minister," Silas said. "And was this while you were at seminary, training to be a pastor?"

"That's right. During my second year."

"And yet you'd gotten cancer?" Gapinski asked. "Doesn't seem right."

Peter shrugged. "I'm not sure it's wrong. Fact is, none of us are guaranteed health, or wealth for that matter. Not like those bozos in that big top claim."

"I can understand why this fight is personal, then," Silas said. "It is for us as well."

Peter sighed. "I'm sorry to hear about Torres's cancer."

"Doesn't sound advanced, and radiation should do the trick, but…"

"But it sucks anyway."

Gapinski chuckled. "That's one way of putting it."

"And I think we should say that. Torres should, we all should! In fact, one of my professors from GRTS liked to say that part of what it means to be a Christian is embracing the fact that life sucks before Jesus returns."

Took a beat, but the Escalade got it, ahhing and nodding in acknowledgment of that fact.

"God does heal today," Peter went on, "and I hope he does in your teammate's situation, just as he did in mine, but health isn't guaranteed. And our joy shouldn't be dependent on our circumstances anyway, whether we're healthy or not, whether we're wealthy or not."

He stopped and took a breath, chuckling to himself and shaking his head. "Sorry, don't mean to get my preacherman on." They chuckled along.

Silas said, "Sounds like what your professor was trying to say is that suffering and trials are just a fact of life in this fallen world. Jesus said that in this world we'd face troubles."

"Exactly!" Peter said. "But what else did he say? *Take courage; I have conquered the world!*"

"And even when we are limited by our health and physical ailments," Silas added, "that doesn't have to limit our impact for God and the good of the world. I think of the Apostle Paul himself, who said that it was because of some sort of physical infirmity that was the cause of his first announcing the good news of Jesus to the Philippians."

"That's right. Paul's probably the most famous example of a believer who faced suffering, and he was this super apostle!"

Gapinski nodded. "That's right. What was it he said in his second letter to the Church of Corinth? *A thorn was given me in the flesh, a messenger of Satan to torment me, to keep me from being too elated.*"

"And then he went on," Silas added, "*Three times I appealed to the Lord about this, that it would leave me, but he said to me, 'My grace is sufficient for you, for power is made perfect in weakness.*"

"*So, I will boast all the more gladly of my weaknesses,*" Peter continued quoting from Paul's letter, "*so that the power of Christ may dwell in me. Therefore I am content with weaknesses, insults, hardships, persecutions, and calamities for the sake of Christ; for whenever I am weak, then I am strong.*' The idea was that in Christ Paul was strong, despite his circumstances, despite the health scare he had."

"And even more," Silas said, "he would delight in whatever weakness the world threw at him, so that he could delight all the more in Christ."

Gapinski whistled. "Look at you two! Better watch out, reverend, Silas will give you a run for your money."

Peter laughed. "Fine by me. I'll take your preaching on health and wealth any day over those bozo twins. Sounds like you're way more rooted in what the Bible actually says on the matter."

"Speaking of which..." Gapinski said, turning into a long drive leading into the seminary campus.

The parking lot was filled with cars, the students driving last-century vehicles and faculty and staff riding in this-century style. The building itself was unimpressive: functional cinderblock architecture from the seventies rising two stories. Lots of memories in the place. So much change.

Gapinski parked the Escalade near the entrance, and they got out.

"After you," Silas said, gesturing toward the door.

Peter nodded and headed into his old stomping grounds.

Hoping to the good Lord above there were answers waiting for them inside.

He led the SEPIO agents into the main seminary building on toward the library anchored next to a large pond at the back of the connected buildings.

It was as functional on the inside as it was on the outside— gray cinderblock walls, punctuated by plush couches and table-and-chair setups for group studies that tried to imbue the stale atmosphere with a dose of Starbucks ambiance. Six classrooms lined a single hallway on either side that stretched from the main gathering space to the faculty offices off to the side, each housing long narrow tables and chairs enough for thirty students. Your typical 70s-era utilitarian box that smelled like it too—old wood and the dampness of a basement masked only by the dueling scents of new carpet and coffee.

"Nothing to write home about, that's for sure," Silas said.

"Says the man whose academic experience was on the East Coast!" Gapinski said.

He chuckled. "True. I should probably hold my tongue."

"Where was that?" Peter asked.

"First at Georgetown undergrad then at Harvard for PhD work before working several years at Princeton. So yeah, probably makes me a little biased for the Victorian architecture and rigorous liberal arts academics."

"A little?" Gapinski asked with a grin.

Silas smacked his shoulder; Gapinski yelped and shut his mouth.

"At least the library looks promising," Silas said.

"Smells better too," Gapinski added. "Like it was built this century instead of last generation."

"Now who's snooty about the joint?"

The library was an earlier addition to the building, rising three stories and stretching the length of half a football field. Rows of metal bookshelves dutifully stood like soldiers standing at attention, bearing their knowledge and insight. Taking in a breath, the heavenly tang of ink and earthy pulp sent Peter's head spinning and wishing for a chance to go back to school. Especially now that his town was embroiled in all the crazy!

"Peter Young?" a voice bellowed from behind.

Peter spun around, finding a familiar portly man with a shock of dark brown hair and a face with the warm smile that got him through three years of graduate school.

"Dr. VanDyke," Peter said, extending his hand with a grin. "Long time no see!"

The professor took it. "Calvin is fine, Petey. Don't worry. I don't take it personally."

He chuckled. "Yeah, sorry about that."

"And the venerable Silas Grey," the professor added, turning to Silas. "I see you got my message."

"Not sure venerable is right, Calvin," Silas said, "but I'll take it."

Peter chuckled. "You two know each other well?"

"Not well," Silas said. "We've had a few interactions over my work on the Shroud of Turin. Calvin here was one of a few Protestant academics who took an interest in the Christian relic."

"While most of my esteemed colleagues," VanDyke said, "have written off the purported burial cloth of Jesus with the imprint of a man in death's pose as nothing but a Medieval forgery, my spidey senses have told me otherwise."

"That, and my research, right?"

"And that," the professor said with a smile.

Silas chuckled. "We've caught up at conferences every few years, sharing drinks and laughs and academic war stories. Been a while, so good to see you."

"I take it life at the Order of Thaddeus is treating you well?"

"Can't complain."

Peter scoffed. "I should think you should be doing more than not complaining, with protecting and defending the faith and all."

"Yeah," Gapinski added. "I'd say it's a pretty awesome gig. I mean, you've got us to work with!"

"In that case, I could use a vacation," Silas replied.

"Mill Creek Junction's not exactly Cabo," VanDyke quipped. "And shouldn't you all be flying around with capes and multi-colored tights anyhow, not traipsing through a stuffy library? You know, saving the world from no uncertain doom, and the Church for that matter."

Silas laughed. "We're not that sort of organization. But I do thank you for that message. Seems like a stroke of luck you called when you did, given what's been going on across town and now around the world."

VanDyke shrugged. "No luck about it. It was—predestined."

"Spoken like a true Reformed Protestant," Silas said with a smirk.

"Speaking of Reformed Protestants," Peter said, "I wondered if you had time to share your perspective on what we've been dealing with in Mill Creek."

The professor checked his watch and frowned. "I don't have long. Teaching systematic theology in twenty, but I can chat. Why don't you come back to my office."

CHAPTER 18

Silas followed VanDyke as he led him and Peter and Gapinski back through the commons area to his office.

Passing a table of students working on their Greek vocabulary, and even more studying—or cramming, as was probably the case—a tinge of longing rose within for what he had left behind. What he was forced to leave behind after he was sacked from Princeton, in many ways brought on by the inciting incident called the Order of Thaddeus.

Although, had it not been for Celeste leading a group of SEPIO operatives to save his backside, he would have been dead anyway. So he supposed he should be grateful for the circumstances that led to him wandering through the lobby of a Midwest seminary getting to the bottom of a small-town charismatic plot instead of teaching at an Ivy League school and writing the next journal article on a long-lost Church relic that would put him on the map.

He wondered how his other teammates were doing, and sent up a prayer that the good Lord above would keep them safe—that he would especially bring a healing touch to Torres, doing a mighty miracle work in her body that had nothing to do with the carnival show back in Mill Creek.

Passing several classrooms in session, VanDyke took them down a long vanilla hallway bathed in awful fluorescent lighting to a number of windowed doors peering into book-lined offices. His was at the end, door standing open into a cramped space that just accommodated the visiting trio over-looking a large pond outside and the undergraduate campus. Following him inside, the sights and smells reminded Silas of his days back at Princeton.

As he would expect, each wall but the window was lined floor to ceiling with books, even cresting around the doorway. Had to have been a thousand books stuffed away in that room. Some old ones, too, looking to be from the nineteenth century, and all categorized by a system that arranged sections by topic, alphabetical by author. A professor after Silas's own heart! There were the early Church fathers followed by Medieval scholars, running through to the Reformation and on to the modern era, with names he easily recognized and some he didn't.

The sight of all those books combined with the dueling scents of ink and pulp on top of coffee and a breakfast sand-wich made Silas wish he were back in the classroom. Where he could sit with his books and pore over a latest research project, chomping away on a cinnamon raisin bagel and sipping coffee from his stained, chipped mug bearing the crimson Harvard logo—sometimes bearing something a little stronger of the fermented variety if said research wasn't going too well and he was up against a hard deadline.

Then there were the students and their questions that made him sing songs of delight when it was clear they were really taking the material, and their own religious journey, seriously. Could do without the helicopter parents screaming at him about little Johnny's F for failing to turn in his assignments on time, but the rest—boy, did it pluck a heartstring that made him long for those simpler, safer days when the world wasn't riding on his shoulders.

VanDyke pulled two padded metal chairs from a small wood table shoved in the corner against the towering bookshelves and brought them in front of his desk. Silas gestured for the others to take them while the professor commanded his plush leather chair from behind his desk. He didn't mind standing in the slightest, working and thinking better on his feet.

Leaning back, VanDyke asked, "So the prosperity gospel is the topic of the hour?"

"Appears so," Silas said, crossing his arms and leaning against the wood table.

"Well, what do you want to know?"

"I assume you've heard what's been going on in Mill Creek Junction? The charismatic revival meetings, the healings."

The professor snorted a laugh and shook his head. "I've heard about them, alright. About as believable as any other so-called faith healings through the years from those types."

Peter glanced at Silas before saying, "Yeah, about that..."

Silas cleared his throat and spoke up: "We can pretty much guarantee what's been going on in Mill Creek is legit." He nodded to Peter and added, "Peter and I witnessed two of them firsthand, then a third."

"What?" VanDyke exclaimed, sitting forward. "That's crazy-talk."

"You're telling us. But what we can't understand is what's going on beneath the surface. What we should think about it all, especially what it is the Bucks are trying to pull."

Peter added, "I thought we could drop by and have a chat with my old professor about it all. Maybe give us background information on the movement. Give us something to go on as we sort through the mess, and the miracles."

"You've certainly come to the right place," VanDyke said.

"Plenty in the library on the charismatic movement and prosperity gospel. But I doubt what happened in Mill Creek is a miracle. I don't care who you say was healed."

"Why do you say that?"

"Come on, Petey. Calvin! I'm not your professor anymore."

He chuckled as his cheeks flushed. "Fine, *Calvin*, why do you say what happened at the north end of the Junction wasn't a miracle?"

VanDyke explained, "Well, because in the New Testament we see that miracles, performed either by Jesus or the apostles, were meant to authenticate the gospel of Jesus Christ. That's what characterized them, that was their purpose. Hebrews 2:4 makes that clear, saying that God validated Jesus' testimony about who he was *'by signs and wonders and various miracles,'* as it says. Think about the Samaritan woman, and Jesus' supernatural knowledge about who she was, the things she did. That miracle confirmed to her that he was the longed-for Messiah. Then all Jesus' acts of healing—from the blind to the deaf, the leper to the paralytic, even raising the dead! The Apostle Philip performed exorcisms, healings, and other signs alongside proclaiming the good news about Jesus. And on and on."

"You're saying," Silas said, "true New Testament miracles always pointed to the person of Jesus Christ and his work of salvation."

VanDyke snapped his fingers. "Bingo. So if God's glory isn't magnified and the gospel, the good news about rescue in Jesus, isn't proclaimed—well, then, if whatever is happening at those services in Mill Creek don't clarify and enhance both, then they aren't miracles of God. Nothing but voodoo magic and illusionary tricks."

Silas nodded, following the logic and agreeing. From what he remembered, none of the religious services had anything to do with magnifying and glorifying God. Certainly not proclaiming forgiveness of sins and rescue from death through

Christ's sacrifice on the cross. Basic features one would expect from a sermon of some revival tent meeting if it were truly about proclaiming the gospel.

Instead, the services seemed nothing more than some Christianized Tony Robbins pow-wow with a bit of that voodoo magic VanDyke mentioned thrown in for good measure. Totally human centric with some promise of a healthy, wealthy, professional upwardly mobile middle-class abundant life. And that wasn't even touching on the truly crazy part when the Eucharist was used as some prop for it all, how it was used to channel the illusory tricks of healing.

Although, they couldn't get away from the fact at least one person was healed who they could verify was paralyzed...

"Can I ask a knuckle-headed question?" Gapinski asked.

Silas shook away his introspection. "Sure thing."

"How are we defining miracle?"

VanDyke chuckled. "A little low on the cookie shelf, isn't it?"

Gapinski frowned, his neck reddening. "Maybe..."

His smile faded. "Oh, that wasn't rhetorical? Well, no dumb question, I always say."

"No! I mean, we went over it in the bar, but it's still fuzzy."

"I think Gapinski has a point," Silas said, giving cover to his teammate. "Probably should have a common starting place to move forward."

Leaning back in his chair, VanDyke said, "True miracles transcend the observable laws of nature and are designed, precisely designed, to authenticate the Gospel, the good news of God's crazy love in Jesus' life, death, and resurrection. Anything that fails to align with this gospel agenda is clearly aberrant."

Silas nodded. "I think the idea is, it neither neglects God's direct interaction with the world nor crosses into deism, where God is like the clockmaker who just set the world in motion and bailed."

"Exactly. The Lord continues to take part in our human story—all of our stories, really—guiding and directing our affairs through his providential actions. And I like what Jürgen Moltmann says about miracles, *'Jesus' healings are not supernatural miracles in a natural world. They are the only truly natural thing in a world that is unnatural, demonized and wounded.'*"

Silas hummed. "I like that. Meaning, miracles aren't an interruption to the natural state of things, but a return to that natural order. It's about God restoring things to the way he originally intended things at creation."

"Exactly."

"That makes sense," Gapinski said. "Miracles aren't magic, because they're not about fulfilling our every whim. Like making soda start gushing from my kitchen faucet or a bucket of KFC extra crispy chicken legs show up at my door."

Silas smirked. "You would go there, wouldn't you."

"Annnnd..." he added, throwing him a look to back off, "a miracle pretty much defies natural explanation because it doesn't make sense. Like when someone is cured of cancer."

Gapinski's face fell, and eyes widened at the slip. He took a breath and winced, smiling sheepishly and adding, "Sorry about that. Mentioning the Big C, and all. Given what it means to all of us."

VanDyke furrowed his brow, glancing at the man and clearly noting something but not addressing it. Instead he said, "Really what it boils down to is God's sovereignty."

Silas inhaled a contemplative breath. "Interesting. Why do you say that?"

"Because the idea of God's sovereignty means that he makes eternal decrees over his creation, while also continually and providentially working in and through it on behalf of his creation."

"I don't follow," Peter said.

"What I mean is that even when God is not doing miracles,

providing that bucket of KFC or curing cancer—" VanDyke threw them a wry smile, which no one seemed to appreciate. Clearing his throat, he shifted and continued, "Anyway, God is still guiding the affairs of the world through his powerful word and toward his perfect ends. That's true in the big stuff of the world, like wars and pandemics. It's also true in the little stuff in our own lives, like making sure we've got enough food to eat and healing us when we're sick. Whether it's keeping the sun in place or keeping your job when your employer is sold to some multinational corporation, God's in it all."

"Just not in Mill Creek Junction, though," said Silas, pointing with his thumb toward the door.

"What that sounds like is much more like miracle-manipulation than anything else."

"Miracle-manipulation?" Gapinski questioned.

VanDyke nodded. "Preying on the hopes of desperate people to secure or maintain power, or get rich, or perpetuate some teaching. Nothing new under the sun with that. It has flat existed since the early Church and throughout every corner and pocket of Church history, creeping into modern churches particularly in the 'name-it-and-claim-it' theology of the health-and-wealth prosperity preachers."

"Like Tweedledum and Tweedledee back in the Junction."

"Looks that way."

Peter shifted in his chair. "Doesn't all this talk about God's sovereignty mean we're just sock puppets on his heavenly hands?"

"Petey..." the professor said with a frown. "I thought I taught you better than that!"

"I agree with pastorman, here," Gapinski said. "Doesn't it?"

"No way!" VanDyke exclaimed.

"That was a pretty resounding negation," Silas said.

"It is, because God's sovereignty doesn't mean we don't have responsibility or free will, or discount the fact that bad things happen to good people because the world is bad and broke and other people are bad and broken."

"I suppose that's sort of a divine tension we have to live in, isn't it?"

"And be content to live in. God's sovereignty and human free will should humble us into a greater understanding of who we are and what we're capable of in the world. The Bible reminds us that God is the one who rules and reigns over all things, he is infinitely powerful and is the sustainer of all things. We're not. Not even close! We are finite and dependent beings who have been created with limited freedom to serve and submit to God in all things."

Gapinski huffed and crossed his arms. "Well, then if God rules and reigns and is so powerful, as you say, then why do bad things happen to good people?"

The tension ratcheted up suddenly at his question, and he seemed to realize it. He relaxed some and sighed. "Sorry about that. Didn't mean to bite your head off!"

Silas glanced at his partner, knowing what was behind it. Looked like he was having as hard a time with Torres's diagnosis as she was. Knew they were close. Just not that close.

VanDyke put up a hand. "No worries. But if I may say, all of this has seemed to have hit a nerve."

Silas shifted and nodded. "It has. One of our teammates had some tests recently that came back showing she has cancer."

"Oh, no," the professor said, his face slumping into a rather pastoral countenance. "I didn't realize all of this talk was so personal."

Gapinski sat back and forced a smile. "Well, it is. And I don't know what to do with all of it. What to *believe* about it all. Miracles and their place in our everyday lives. The Christian hope thanks to Jesus' good news, the gospel. All this talk on God's sovereignty, his rule and reign, his providential purpose!"

The room went quiet at his display. Silas slumped back against the table, feeling the weight of how the talk was affecting his teammate, all of them really after Torres had been diagnosed with cancer. But he was also wondering about his questions.

Lord Jesus Christ, Son of God, how do you work in the world, where are your miracles? What is our Christian hope, in this life, and how does your sovereignty work to right the world, to provide for us and protect us?

His mind immediately jumped to that fateful 9/11 day, when those planes slammed into the Twin Towers, then into the Pentagon, snuffing out his father's life in a blazing inferno. Was God sovereign over *that*?

And then it went to his brother, Sebastian, who had been molested by their childhood priest, eventually leading to him not only abandoning the faith but waging war against it. Was *that* part of God's providential purpose in the world?

Then there was his mother, who died giving them birth. Why didn't God intervene to save her?

He shuddered at the thoughts, his heart growing unsettled by the questions and haunted by the memories. His faith even faltering some at it all...

God, where were you—where are you now?

VanDyke continued, "Remember what Paul says in the Book of Ephesians, chapter 1. He reminds us that God *'works out everything in conformity with the purpose of his will.'* Everything, from our finances and families to our health and relationships. And then think about what Job went through."

Gapinski smirked. "Yeah, hell on earth!"

"Colorful, but it works. The man lost his health, his wealth, even his children. And yet, how did he respond to God? With questions, curses, raised fists?"

"No. I guess you could call it submission."

"That's right. Submission to his sovereignty. Here—"

VanDyke reached for a worn black Bible resting on his desk and flipped it open. It was visibly scared by years of use, decades even, the pages marked by faded black underlines and fluorescent highlights. "Here we go. Listen to Job's response in chapter 42 after unimaginable suffering." He read:

> *"I know that you can do all things; no purpose of*
> *yours can be thwarted. You asked, 'Who is this*
> *that obscures my plans without knowledge?'*
> *Surely I spoke of things I did not understand,*
> *things too wonderful for me to know."*

"So at one point, Job did question God because of what he went through. But then he realized there were things that happened in life, things that happened in his own life that he might never fully comprehend. And instead of trying to manipulate God to get him to work his magic to make him healthy or wealthy, he rested in knowing that God was in control, regardless of the outcome. That God was God, ruling and reigning over the world, even over his own painful circumstances."

He closed his Bible and set it back in place. "Truth is, and this can be confusing with all the crazy chaos we've witnessed in recent years, but God's sovereignty still makes sense when bad things happen to good people. May not be easy to make sense of or swallow it as reality, but the Bible shows us time and time again that even when it looks like evil has triumphed, God will ultimately win and his purposes, for us and his glory, are served."

"In other words," Silas said, moving it along, "the Christian belief in God's sovereignty matters a great deal to the Church."

VanDyke said, "And I would go so far to say that it's not even Christian to deny the sovereignty of God, which frankly the prosperity gospel does in spades."

"How so?"

"Think about it. It makes God out to be a puppet and raises us up to be puppet masters who can make God dance to our tune, get him to dole out money and heal us by the things we utter in faith."

"Like some abracadabra incantation."

"That's right. And let me make clear my objection here. It's not that I'm against Christians healing in the name of Jesus or trying to subvert the sovereignty of God by doing so. Nor do I contend God isn't active in the world doing just that, healing bodies and providing for our financial needs."

Gapinski said, "Just not at the whims of greedy, needy Christians."

He furrowed his brow and sat back. "Sort of. But for me, it's more than that. Prosperity theology has no connection to Christian theology. It isn't good news; it is fake news, a fake gospel. Its message has zero connection to the Bible, and what it promises ultimately fails. God never assures his people that they will be healthy and wealthy—in this life, anyway."

"Then what is our hope," Peter shot back, "if the gospel doesn't make any difference now?"

The professor chuckled. "Reminds me of some of our conversations during your years here."

"And like before, it sounds like you're evading the question."

"Oh, I'm not either." VanDyke shifted in his chair, as if buying a few seconds to get his thoughts in order. "The prosperity gospel is no gospel at all because it distorts the real, genuine gospel by making God's good news about getting all this stuff—getting out of debt or getting a job, getting cured of some ailment."

"In other words," Peter said, "it makes the gospel about us, instead of Jesus."

"Now you're getting it! But our problem isn't a bum leg or credit card debt—not to make light of either. Our problem is sin, which Jesus dealt with once and for all on the cross.

Forgiveness of sins, adoption into God's family, the resurrection of the dead and eternal life—*that* is our true hope, both now and later. Physical healing's got nothing on the fact our soul's been resuscitated back to life!"

"Amen to that!" the pastor said.

Silas nodded. "I agree. Amen."

Checking his watch, VanDyke startled. "Uh, oh. I'm late for class."

"Been there," he said with a chuckle. "Sorry for taking all of your time."

The professor stood, gathering some books and papers. "Glad to help."

Leading the group back down the hallway of offices, VanDyke apologized for having to go. Peter walked with the professor to his class, the two catching up briefly.

Silas began walking toward the commons area when he noticed he was alone.

"Silas?" he heard from behind. Faint and pathetic.

Gapinski!

He spun around to find him sprawled on the carpeted floor. Motionless.

CHAPTER 19

"Gapinski!" Silas shouted, running over to his friend and kneeling down at his side.

Guy's limbs were all cattywampus. Legs and arms turned and twisted. Not broken or bent. Just twisted.

He instantly had a flashback to that fateful mission in Iraq, that damn roadside IED blowing a hole in their Hummer's side and sending his best friend cascading onto his lap.

What was left of him, anyway.

This wasn't nearly as bad, but seeing Gapinski lying on the floor like that, combined with the image of his teammate from Iraq flashing before his mind's eye—it spiked his blood pressure and froze him with indecision.

"Silas..." Gapinski said, voice quivery and panicky and searching for someone to make sense of what had just happened.

Him.

Which snapped Silas out of it and back to the mission at hand.

He swallowed hard. "What the heck hap—"

"I can't feel my legs," Gapinski interrupted in a rush. "Or arms. Or anything below my neck, for that matter."

"Are you alright?" Peter said, running up to them with VanDyke in tow. "Heard you down the way."

"I'll call an ambulance," VanDyke said, whipping out his cell phone and pushing back some gawkers who had begun to gather a few office doors down.

"What happened?" Silas said again, heart hammering in his head with the prospective answers to that question.

"I don't know!" Gapinski answered. "I was walking out of the prof's office, and all of a sudden everything went numb. Like when your arm falls asleep, and it's all tingly. Next thing I knew, everything below the neck faded to black."

"Like, you passed out?"

"No! I said below the neck. Head was fine. It was everything below! Couldn't feel nothing. Still can't!"

Silas ran a hand through his hair, not having a clue what to do.

Peter offered, "Maybe we should get your limbs back in place. Maybe that'll help."

He nodded. "Good idea." The two repositioned Gapinski's legs and arms so they were straight and not all twisted. "How's that, anything?"

"A big, fat negatory," Gapinski said, voice betraying clear panic and face shining with a sweaty sheen now.

Silas threw a worried glance at Peter. Whose face had gone white and slack with wide-eyed fear. The pair of them knowing exactly what was going on.

The contagion.

And it had struck SEPIO.

One of Silas's own!

Lord Jesus Christ, Son of God, do something! What should we do, what should I—

Then it hit him.

The leftover prepackaged Eucharistic elements he'd swiped from the carnival!

Fishing it out of his jacket pocket, he popped off the chintzy plastic lid for the cracker.

Which fluttered to the carpet like a feather!

"Sonofa—"

Silas caught himself, remembering where he was. But chuckling just the same at echoing Gapinski's own trademark exasperation.

Thought the damn wafer would crumble into a thousand pieces when it hit the floor, but it held firm. Even then, every one of his Catholic-raised bones wanted to cry out in regret at the sacrilegious faux pas—the memory marker of Christ's Body touching the unclean carpet like that.

But he held it together, crossing himself on instinct.

Picking up the paper-thin wafer, he brought it to Gapinski's mouth. "Here, take this."

He could barely move his head, his eyes doing most of the work. "What's that?"

"The communion wafer. From the Bucks service."

"Now you want to use me as a guinea pig like you did Torres?"

That stung. But Silas let it go. "You saw what this thing did. Healing that college kid and Max. Taking away their blindness and deafness."

"And don't forget Katrina," Peter added.

"Exactly! She was paralyzed. Then after she ate this—" Silas held up the cracker, then the plastic container with juice. "—then drank this, she seemed to regain use of her limbs."

"That's right. She suffered the same sort of sudden onset paralysis, the doctor had called it, as you just did now. So it's worth a shot..."

Gapinski's eyes darted back and forth between the wafer and tiny cup, chest rising and falling with rapid indecision.

"I don't know..." he said, face creased with a mixture of fear and skepticism.

Silas huffed. "Just try it, alright! We've got nothing to lose, soldier!"

Instantly regretted his outburst. But in the heat of the mission, when things went sideways, sometimes bedside manners had to be sent out the window.

His partner's mouth opened to offer a familiar Gapinski retort, but none came. Instead, he extended his tongue with wide, pleading eyes—as if saying this better work!

Silas didn't waste time. He hoped it worked too.

He placed the wafer in his mouth, praying something happened.

"The body of Christ, broken for you," Peter muttered.

He glanced at the pastor, nodding and offering a weak smile. Might as well make it official.

Gapinski swallowed the wafer and opened his mouth for more.

Silas peeled back the foil seal, then lifted the man's head. Carefully, he poured in the juice, those Catholic bones of his not wanting a drop of it to dribble down into the carpet. Cleaning up the memory marker of Christ's Blood was far harder than his Body! It's why priests never allowed lay people to handle the chalice; what happened if it spilled?

On cue, Peter intoned, "The blood of Christ, shed for you."

Silas set Gapinski's head back on the carpet and crossed himself on instinct again.

"Ambulance is on its way," VanDyke said, shuffling up to their side.

Silas thanked him but held out a hand to give them space. Only a few minutes now and they'd know whether that ambulance was necessary.

The minutes ticked by at an agonizing crawl. Silas's chest was heavy with wait, and his head was spinning at the turn.

Not Gapinski, Lord. Not Gapinski...

Resting back on his haunches now, Silas took in a measured

breath. Then he began the counting ritual he'd developed back in Iraq when things got crazy. Centered him, slowed his breathing, released building anxiety.

For those such times.

999, 998, 997, 996...

Gapinski lay still, swallowing some more as if it would help get every morsel of the unleavened cracker and grape juice down to speed up the hoped-for healing.

988, 987, 986, 985...

More seconds, more minutes. Still nothing.

Silas heaved another breath through his nose, the ritual doing bupkis this time. He didn't know how much more he could take!

974, 973, 972—

"Guys..."

Silas startled at Gapinski's voice, shuffling back to his knees and to his side. "Something happening?"

"You could say that!"

Gapinski held up an arm and was wiggling his fingers. Then he pointed to his feet, where he was moving them around as well.

It worked!

Silas glanced at Peter with wide-grinned success, throwing him a thumbs-up for good measure.

Thank you, Lord...

It was really working now, Gapinski easing his large frame into a wincing sit.

"Easy, big fella," Silas said. "Can we get him some water?"

"I've got Dasani in my office," VanDyke said, running off to fetch it.

He thanked the professor, sirens wailing now in the near distance.

"Looks like all the fuss is for nothing," Gapinski said, easing around to his knees to stand.

Before biting it hard on the carpet.

"Whoa there, partner," Silas said, putting a hand on his back. "Stay put till the pros arrive."

"I'm fine..." Gapinski tried to stand again, but faltered. This time to his knees before straightening to his haunches. So that was some progress.

A pair of EMTs came into view, pushing a yellow reinforced gurney topped with a large red medical bag.

Gapinski glanced at them and shook his head. "Always something..."

"What's the problem?" one of the men with a trimmed salt-and-pepper beard asked.

Peter gestured to Gapinski, who was sitting now. "Some sort of sudden onset paralysis."

The man looked at his clean-shaven younger partner, eyes widening briefly before turning his attention to the SEPIO agent. The other one grabbed the bag and fished for a blood pressure monitor.

"Why do you say sudden onset paralysis?" the bearded man asked Peter, shinning a penlight in Gapinski's eyes.

He looked to Silas, who nodded him onward. "Had a parishioner suffer the same thing a few days ago."

"Parishioner?" the younger man asked, strapping on a cuff to Gapinski's arm.

"I'm a pastor. She's my secretary." The two EMTs glanced at one another, causing Peter to chuckle nervously. "It's not like that. Anyway, she had a similar thing happen to her, like Matt here. Everything below the neck had stopped working. Her doctor at Mill Creek General said it was just that, sudden onset paralysis."

The older EMT muttered a curse and shook his head.

"I know, tell me about it," the younger one said, reading the computer hooked up to Gapinski for vitals.

Silas glanced at Peter, who shrugged. He asked, "What do you mean, tell me about it?"

"This is the eighteenth such case the past day."

"*Eighteenth?*" Silas and Peter both exclaimed.

Gapinski snorted a laugh. "And here I thought I was a diamond in the rough..."

"Is that unusual?" Silas asked.

The two EMTs chuckled. The bearded man answered, "You could say that."

The pair kept working on Gapinski, doing—whatever it is EMTs do in these situations. And him playing every bit the part of the difficult patient.

Silas stood and pulled Peter aside, saying lowly, "What are the odds this episode and those others have something to do with the contagion?"

"I'd say a pretty sure bet. But how would he have gotten it?"

Silas's gut clenched with the question. How, indeed? And who else from their team had been infected? Him and Peter, Torres and—

Celeste?

He shook away the question, clenching his jaw and nodding back toward the commons area that led to the library.

"Come on..."

He started off when he heard a complaint from behind: "Guys, don't leave me!"

Silas spun back to Gapinski. "We'll be back. Just follow the doctors' orders and we'll see you soon."

"But...!"

He ignored him, hustling back down the 70s-era brick hallway and toward the new library standing like a beacon of hope in these confusing times.

"What are you thinking, Silas?" Peter asked, trying to keep up at his side.

"I'm thinking there's still more to this charismatic, prosperity gospel healing stuff that'll put these pieces together for us—right inside that vault of knowledge." He pointed at the library just up ahead, a few students giving them sideways glances. "As I told my students back at Princeton, if at first you don't succeed—research, research, and research some more."

"And does that solve all your problems?" Peter asked.

He threw him a sideway smile. "Sometimes. Come on, let's spread out. Grab anything you think could help us land the plane to this dang mission."

He went to turn away when Peter grabbed his arm.

"Hey, I'm sorry about your friend back there. Looks like he'll be alright, thanks to you."

"Not me. Looks like it's thanks to that crazy Lord's Stouffer's meal!"

"Either way, he'll be fine. Things will be fine. We'll figure this out."

Silas nodded. He hoped he was right.

Then the two got to work.

CHAPTER 20

MUMBAI, INDIA.

A rumbly shudder rippled through the cabin of the Falcon 7X private jet, a change in the eddies and vertical air currents coming in off the Indian Ocean mixing with the land.

Paulina knew it was nothing to worry about. But she gripped her armrest anyway, thankful her uncle had sprung for the best in private aviation, instead of going cheap, like one of their colleagues and family friends in the business. Rumor had it one man had bought used jets from Tyler Perry for half of what it cost Unky Benji for their own bird.

Two for half the price of one. What a cheapskate.

She smirked then glanced outside the cabin window, the turbulence calming down to nothing. The quiet hum of the three Pratt & Whitney engines nearly lulled her to sleep as she reclined in the soft, tan leather chair. Add to that the dark-mahogany accents running the length of the cabin along with the minibar stocked with thousand-dollar bottles of champagne and cheaper hundred-dollar bottles of wine and other booze at the rear, and she could get used to this kind of life.

Strike that: She *had* gotten used to it. Going on thirty years now.

At a cool $52.3 million, the luxury jet was the latest in top-of-the-line air travel for the uber-rich. Or flush preachers globetrotting to save souls on a mission from God. Because why fly commercial when God invented private aviation? At least that's what Unky Benji had said. Besides, with all the demon-filled people in those tubes, it wouldn't be right for a man of God to fly commercial.

She smiled. Or a woman of God.

Unky Benji had said that too. And got in hot water with the media about it.

"You can't imagine what it's like!" he had said to a nosey, pagan reporter with one of those scammy, sleazy evening broadcasts. "This dope-filled world and these dope-filled people do all sorts of crazy things. And getting into a long tube with a bunch of demons like that would be deadly!"

Dexter had cringed from the characterization, but Paulina thought it made sense. As Paul wrote in Ephesians, chapter 6, *'our struggle is not against enemies of blood and flesh, but against the rulers, against the authorities, against the cosmic powers of this present darkness, against the spiritual forces of evil in the heavenly places.'* Problem is, those doped-up people carry them along for the ride in their row M middle seat!

Of course her uncle had explained as much to the reporter, but she didn't care. That blonde bimbo twisting his words to make it sound like Unky Benji believed people themselves were demons.

"No, I never said that—and don't you ever say I did!" he'd responded, eyes wide and wild like she'd never seen him before. "Jesus loves people and so do I!" he explained, all smiles. "But people get wrapped up in alcohol and internet porn and bumpin' and grindin' on the dance floor—so do you think that's a good place for a preacher like myself to be contained inside with such forces while preparing to go preach God's word to desperate souls?"

Was as good as any explanation Paulina had heard, which was enough for her. Brother, though—that was a different story.

She took in a tired breath, closing her eyes and savoring the sweet smell of creamy leather while savoring the soft feeling of privilege beneath her fingers. Her long, manicured fingers stroked the supple leather-wrapped armrests, taking another deep breath of filtered, ionized, private-jet air unsullied by a hundred grimy passengers.

Glancing back outside, the world below coming into sharper view now as they neared their destination, she brought a half-drained glass of Dom Pérignon Brute to her mouth, the crystal cold against her lips. Bright fruity bubbles of apricot and lime, laced with toast and vanilla tickled her nose as she tipped it back, the buttery liquid sliding down with welcomed ease. It was the last bit of the second bottle she had uncorked mid-way through their journey to the next leg of their mission. So close now she could feel it! But between the whirlwind of the last several days, on top of the jetlag catching up to her, she needed something to take the edge off.

And two bottles weren't going to do it.

Paulina drained the glass and raised it in the air. An attendant dutifully arrived with the familiar *thop* of a cork sliding out from another bottle of Dom Pérignon. What's another three grand in champagne when you've already let loose six?

As her glass was filled, she caught sight of a cloud floating next to the jet that sent her pulse soaring with delight.

An angel! With the body and head of a human and wings outstretched like a swan. White and lithe and glimmering in the sunlight. She even glimpsed a rainbow off in the distance.

A sign from above!

All would be well.

He would be well. Unky...

The attendant finished, and Paulina went to take a sip, her

head light with the delight of what she'd glimpsed as much as the alcohol, when the plane dipped. Pale liquid sloshed over the sides. She held the glass steady as they hit another wave of turbulence, then took a sip and set it down before the next one rolled them.

She licked the spilled champagne off her hand, her taste buds dancing with more of that apricot, lime, and toasted vanilla concoction. Letting a pleasurable sigh slip, she glanced over at Dexter. He was completely checked out, his head rolling to the side as one final bump of air knocked them around in their descent toward destiny.

Taking another sip, the alcohol working its magic again, she frowned. Brother had always been the sensitive of the twins, a bleeding heart who had felt uneasy about the family business seeking to help the less fortunate, the destitute and desperate.

Not that he didn't mind the Air Jordans and ripped designer jeans and gold chains he wore growing up. Nor did he mind the romp through Burj Al Arab hotel in Dubai with the gold-plated toilets, or the Four Seasons in Paris and London and Madrid, or even the Emiliano they'd recently stayed at in São Paulo! It was all the other "trappings" of their calling he couldn't overlook. The slums and ramshackle apartments, the beggars and naked children running through the streets, the military hired guns keeping back the desperate from touching the tassels of their cloaks.

Wanted to have his cake and eat it too, is what he wanted!

Perhaps the only thing that kept his head in the game was Unky Benji. Dex knew family was everything. The family business even more.

It was bigger than either one of them, Dexter and Paulina, because their uncle was bigger than them. Bigger than the mission itself.

Which was inseparable from the mission.

Speaking of which...

The Falcon 7X banked south after veering out across the Indian Ocean, the brilliance of the sun reflecting off from the azure water below in tiny sun-kissed waves. Mumbai loomed ahead as they dipped for a landing, a portfolio of towering buildings rivaling anything from the West making up the majestic skyline of glass and steel. A return trip after a trial run she hoped would yield dividends that would set them up for life.

Especially Unky...

The second most popular city after the capital Delhi and seventh in the world with 20 million people, it is the commercial, financial, and entertainment capital of India, responsible for its rise in status among developed nations. A thriving white collar workforce and rising middle class have made it the crown jewel among the nation's cities.

The City of Dreams.

Paulina knew better, however, that the glories of capitalism masked a darker world. A desperate world. A hopeless world.

Filled with millions of people who needed to find their breakthrough day. Who needed to tap into the abundant life of God's blessing.

Which the Bucks were ready to deliver.

With the proper seed-sowing faith, of course.

The jet landed with ease, the tires skipping once before whooshing to a stop at the end of the runway on a bed of feathers.

Dex stirred now, bringing his seat upright and rubbing the sleep from his eyes. He raised the silk shade covering his window, the bright sunlight sending his hands to his eyes again.

Paulina giggled, reaching for the one gloved in white. "Good morning, sleepyhead."

"Good morning," he croaked, squeezing her hand in their special code.

I. Love. You.

Her smile widened, and she replied: *I. Love. You. Toooo!*

They shared another pleasurable grin before Dexter dropped her hand and reached out his arms for a stretch. "What time is it? What day is it?"

She glanced at her watch, a pink-gold Rendez-Vous Moon ringed by fifty-four diamonds clinging to her wrist by a red leather band. A gift from Unky Benji when she turned twenty-one.

"Just after one."

"Local time?" he asked, between chugs of Veen Finnish spring water. "Which is where again?"

She frowned, slapping his arm playfully. "Stop. You know good and well we've just landed in Mumbai."

"Yeah, yeah, yeah." Taking another swig of water, he asked, "Think we'll get as good a crowd as that small Michigan town?"

Paulina scoffed. "As Mill Creek Junction? What a puny crowd!"

"Puny? Looked packed to me."

"Five-thousand people is not packed! The top faith healers of our lifetime have drawn crowds in the hundreds of thousands. From Brazil to Bangladesh, Nigeria to Kenya."

"Bangladesh is a country, not a city, nitwit."

She drained her champagne and raised the glass for the attendant to take away. Then promptly slugged her bother in the shoulder; he yelped and apologized.

As someone retrieved the glass, she added, "As I was saying…I'll be disappointed if we don't match those numbers, and more. One of our colleagues in the business even had crowds numbering in the millions at a single healing revival meeting."

"Jeez Louise!" Dex turned to face her now as the jet taxied into a darkened hangar. "You think we could reach that much mon—err, people? With the gospel, I mean?"

Took every ounce of energy not to crack a smile. Paulina

knew her brother well, and could see the dollar signs beginning to attach themselves to those million-numbering crowds. His uncle taught him well.

Like she'd said: Wanted to have his cake and eat it too!

"What do you figure our trip to Mumbai will be?" he asked.

Paulina shrugged. "Who knows? But we very well may eclipse seven figures for the first time."

"Seven figures..." Dexter mumbled, slumping back in his seat and looking out the window.

She knew what he was thinking, so she grabbed his hand again; he turned her way. His face was drawn. Sullen, even. As if he couldn't help but think about the people behind those dollars.

Which she aimed to put front and center.

"Don't think of the dollar signs," Paulina said with a smile. "Think of all the people we'll be helping. The lives changed. The breakthrough days we'll be sparking by calling forth the abundance of God's blessing—right upon all those millions. People with health problems and marriage problems. People needing a job or a car or some other sort of breakthrough!"

He took a beat, but one end of Dexter's mouth curled upward. He nodded, saying, "I suppose you're right."

Paulina's smile widened into a grin. Squeezing his hand, she said, "I know I'm—"

She was interrupted by the stench of jet fuel and smog, combined with unwashed bodies and feces riding in on a hot breath from a just-opened service door leading outside.

Paulina instantly recoiled, as did Dexter.

"Shut the door, you motherless goat!" she shouted to the knucklehead attendant up front, throwing her arm across her face.

The woman just stood near the front aircraft service door.

"Shut the door!" she complained again, swatting at the

woman now instead of cussing up a storm that might end up on WeShare.

"Sister, jeez! What's the problem?" Dexter asked.

Door closed now, Paulina settled back in her seat, head leaned back and eyes closed. "Remember the last time we were here? The smell was awful! I don't want to deal with it until we absolutely must." She opened one eye and drilled it into the offending flight attendant. "Don't open it again until customs arrives. Am I clear?"

The woman averted her gaze, then nodded, scurrying away before arriving with the third bottle of Dom Pérignon and champagne glass.

Paulina considered her gesture. Almost passed, but she grabbed her glass for one final pour. Why not? They were about to make history. Or so she hoped. If what they had planned worked, then they would be set.

And her uncle...

Might as well celebrate early.

Finishing the pour, Paulina dismissed the woman and promptly took a mouthful of the fresh-fruit pale nectar, the bubbles tickling her nose and settling her nerves.

In short order, the door was thrown open and customs came to inspect their papers before authorizing their stay.

Descending the stairs, Paulina held her breath and dashed to an awaiting silver Rolls-Royce Phantom. Thought she would pass out from the stench, but she made it in time to inhale the sweet scent of new leather and polished wood. Dexter followed close behind, and soon they were being whisked through the cramped streets of Mumbai toward their destination, thank the Lord of Hosts!

Paulina marveled at the traffic, wild and erratic and chaotic, cars zipping in and out of non-existent lanes. She hoped they'd make it to the hotel alive with all the chaos! It was slow go, and now she hoped they'd make it in time for the evening's crusade.

Joining in the arterial flow, the car picking up its pace, she looked outside at the world beyond. A world she had once known yet barely remembered thirty years on. A world of struggle and simple pleasures, of eking out mere existence and roaming through life with quiet desperation.

Tall buildings of glass gleaming in the sunshine gave way to short squat ones of stone, and soon a wasteland of urban decay Paulina did not expect. Out of her line of sight but within range, she glimpsed huddled bunches in dirty dull clothes sitting in concrete city gutters and naked children playing in garbage piled high in the near distance. Rail thin with ribs jutting out, despair and desperation their only clothing, she had to admit her stomach churned at the sight.

"How anyone could live..." Dex voiced, trailing off. Swallowing and shaking his head, he added, "It's all beyond me. How the Lord of Hosts himself can allow it."

She let it go, though she understood the sentiment. But she was only focused on one thing. And it wasn't the people of Mumbai.

Dexter couldn't let it go.

"Those are our people, Paulina. Our people!"

Paulina scoffed. "What silliness are you talking about? They're not our people. Our people are—"

"You know what I mean! The ones from childhood. Our friends, our family working those mines in West Virginia. Barely any running water, which was polluted and dirty anyway. Barely a passing education, reduced to slinging coal. Contracting the same black lung disease that dad got. Going mad like—"

"Silence!" Paulina roared. "Do not speak about our family. About father and mother—"

She stopped short, closing her eyes and taking a breath.

Gentle, Paulina, gentle...

She forced a smile and moved closer to Dexter, resting a

hand on his leg. "You're tired, you're jet lagged. Probably have a bit of the nerves, that's why you're so melancholy. Just—"

Dex shrugged her off, leaning against his door and staring out his window again, pulling his leg in closer. Away from her.

"And here we are," he went on, picking at his white glove, "on our way to the Mandarin Oriental Hotel, passing hopeless and helpless people—the very same people coming to us to receive an abundant-life blessing. And all I want to do is tell our driver to pull over, get out, and hold these people. Get them help, real help. Not our..."

Heat flashed up Paulina's neck at the insult. She clenched her jaw, knowing what he was going to say.

She couldn't let it go.

"What, *our* help?"

He didn't answer, holding his gaze outside.

"You sound like those news critics on CNN! The ones who've hated on Unky Benji our entire lives. But these are needy people, Dex! Our needy people, who'll go home blessed with hope, who will be healed."

"Oh, I know they'll be healed alright," Dexter sneered. "If those cotton-pickin' packs-o-communion are packing the same sort of punch they did stateside."

A cold panic spread from Paulina's kidneys, coursing through her body from head to toe. He wasn't supposed to know about those. What they were capable of.

What they meant...

She knew her eyes had gone big and were still open with shock, mouth hanging open with the same dry confusion and tasting of the copper tang of adrenaline.

So she blinked, then shut her mouth, carefully crossing a leg and pushing a stray blond lock behind her ear.

Gentle, Paulina, gentle...

Swallowing, she asked, "How did you know about that?"

Dexter had turned away, the sunlight flashing against those

pools of azure that had captivated her as a child.

"Unky Benji. Who else? And the lie—"

"Stop..."

"I just don't understand why you didn't tell me. Why I was left in the dark." A heavy sigh escaped his parted lips before he added with a mutter, "You always were his favorite..."

There was a sadness to him Paulina had not heard in a long time. Especially directed toward her.

She pulled herself together, explaining, "Things moved quickly and Unky needed someone he could trust to execute the plan." Dexter's eyes narrowed, glistening with emotion. She put up a staying hand. "I only say that to explain. There was so much on the line, so much money. And then...well, things happened to bring us to this point."

He faced her now, and he nodded.

"We're almost there, Dex! I promise. For our sake, and Unky Benji's."

Dexter nodded before turning away. Then he smirked. "Would you look at that..."

He pointed out the window at a green billboard, an elder's kindly face smiling at them and the words *'Pray for India Rally'* in white, along with the venue and dates.

Beneath the billboard lay what he was probably pointing out. An encampment of some sort, with people in rags, some naked children milling about ramshackle huts of discarded cardboard and wood.

"Pray for India, indeed," he said before reclining in his seat, folding his hands across his belly. "Wake me when we arrive."

Paulina wasn't paying him any attention. For sprawled across the face of the massive billboard was a familiar face. One the twins had known since childhood.

Unky Benji Bucks.

The corners of Paulina's eyes pricked with tearful emotion.

If only he could join us...

CHAPTER 21
MILL CREEK JUNCTION.

Silas flipped through research material next to Peter in a tiny room overlooking the campus pond. The pair was seated around a tiny table piled high with books and printed material. It was heaven!

They had spent hours gathering and wading through stacks of books and journal articles trying to find something—anything that would make sense of all the crazy.

It was slow go, which frustrated the heck out of Silas. Wanted to get to it, put this behind them, but all of it was just a rehashing of what Victor Zarruq had shared earlier.

"Here's something," Peter said, holding up a thick book bound in green faded cloth.

Silas looked up from his own thick cloth-wrapped tome. "What's that?"

"An interesting history on this chick, Aimee Semple McPherson."

"Who's that?"

"An early prosperity preacher who built herself up as a holy conduit of God himself. On an overseas trip, she claimed God chose her to change the course of Church history."

"Humble gal, I take it."

"Something like that. She claimed God spoke to her directly. Listen to this…" He read:

But behold, I chosen and ordained thee, that thou shouldst go forth, and clear away the debris and contamination, with which they have covered and obscured the light of My Word. I have chosen thee and called thee by name that thou should speak unto My people. Look not upon the pages that contain the theories of men, but upon the burning, flaming words of My Word as revealed and illuminated by the Holy Spirit which I have given unto you.

Silas smirked. "Spoken like any cult leader. World's been rife with them for centuries. And the Church. All claiming some sort of divine message apart from Scripture."

Peter nodded. "Says here she was quite the showman, too. Or showwoman—whatever the correct term is nowadays."

"Show*person*, perhaps?"

"Regardless, the lady would use set builders to create an almost church-like soundstage on which her awe-inspiring production was set, lining up wheelchairs and crutches all along the stage to make people think that all these people had been healed of their ailments. Anyone who had claimed to be healed was paraded across the stage."

"Boy, does that sound familiar!"

Peter looked up from his book. "The Bucks."

"Sure thing."

"She wasn't the only one of her day. The showmanship of prosperity preaching seems to be a common theme."

"Who else?"

"This lady Kathryn Kuhlman. Similarly packed stadiums

with entertaining music and displays of miraculous healings, giving inspiring messages filled with jokes and tear-jerking anecdotes."

Silas leaned back in his chair. "Sounds like a real feminist entrepreneur."

"She was, putting on a rip-roaring show, making exaggerated claims of healings, while also sprinkling in sermons presenting the gospel with an altar call. But the climax of the event was always the offering."

"Of course. What else?"

"Apparently, people gave hand over fist, too," Peter went on, "the money flowing in like it does in modern prosperity ministries. She taught that if the people gave to God, then he would give them what they wanted. And boy did she spend it, too. Hundreds of thousands of dollars shopping in Beverly Hills."

"California?"

He looked at him with a wry grin. "You know of any other Beverly Hills?"

Silas frowned and blushed with embarrassment. "Suppose not."

"And check this out. Apparently communion was also part of her show."

"The Eucharist?"

"Another way of putting it, but yeah."

"Interesting…"

"But controversy found the woman," Peter went on, "when a one Dr. William Nolen investigated her healings. The doctor studied people who claimed Kuhlman healed them at her Minneapolis revival meeting. Except he couldn't verify a single one. In fact, one woman whom Kuhlman said had been healed of lung cancer actually had Hodgkin's disease, and was unfortunately definitely not healed. Then someone else with cancer in her bones apparently tossed aside her braces and ran across the stage to the cheers and hoots of the crowd—only to have her vertebrae collapse the next day and die four months later!"

Silas leaned forward, disappointment worming his way inside. "So you're saying none of the purported healings were real?"

Peter closed the book and threw it on a pile. "Nope. Most of what I've read hasn't had anything close to verification of actual healings. Just power-of-suggestion mumbo-jumbo and cheap parlor tricks to get people to keep showing up—"

"And handing over the Benjamins."

"Exactly." Peter nodded toward Silas. "Find anything interesting?"

Silas sat forward to the book he was reading. "Mostly a deep dive in the theology behind it all. Beginning with this guy E. W. Kenyon, whose mantra was, 'What I confess, I possess!' Claimed confession always goes ahead of healing. Don't watch symptoms, watch what you say, and be sure that your confession is bold and vigorous."

"Sounds like a transcript from a sermon by those two twins, Dexter and Paulina."

"That's true," Silas said, recalling their exhortation for people to speak into existence their destiny. "But it's worse than that."

"How so?"

"For Kenyon, and for every other prosperity preacher after this grandfather of the movement, Christ's atonement was central to our right as Christians to claim healing and wealth."

Peter scrunched up his face. "His death on the cross for our sins, his shedding of blood for our forgiveness and eternal life gives us the *right* to healing and wealth?"

Silas nodded. "Yeah, gut wrenching twisting of the gospel, I know. According to him, Christ's work on the cross might be complete, but for Kenyon this was only the beginning."

"How so?" Peter said.

"Kenyon adopted the New Thought emphasis on mind, spirit, and universal laws to show that we can look to the cross a guarantee of benefits that are *already* bestowed to the believer—not merely as promises of things to come later."

"Alright, but isn't that what we believe?"

"Not like this."

Silas leaned over the table now, scanning with growing dread. "For Kenyon, Christ's substitutionary atonement, his sacrificial work on the cross paying the penalty in our place, basically subsidized a number of spiritual and legal transactions. He insisted that humans were primarily these spiritual entities like God."

"Sounds like gnostic spacesuit theology. That we're just these drops of spiritual essence trapped in these physical shells."

Silas chuckled. "Spacesuit theology. Nice."

"That one was Doc VanDyke's."

"Sounds about right. And, yeah, you're right about it being gnostic. And apparently Kenyon's gospel hinged on it, as well as his explanation of what happened on the cross. He taught that in humanity's fall from grace, Satan gained legal authority over us, becoming our spiritual father—which resulted in sickness, poverty, and death. Christ offered humanity the light of revelation, teaching and showing us the true abundant life God intended for us. Christ's resurrection reunited our spiritual nature with God's own essence, breaking the power of sin and restoring our legal rights to rule over the earth."

"Again, sounds gnostic."

"Not only that, but that little-god theology of the Church of the Theotites we mentioned before comes into play. Kenyon believed the starting place of our new life was divine union with God, where we were legal shareholders of certain rights and privileges. All of this was taken up a notch with Fred Bosworth."

Peter leaned back in his chair. "Who's he?"

Silas shook his head. "Not important. What is, is that Bosworth looks like he shares Kenyon's own beliefs about our healing being a legal right, secured by Christ through his death, and put into effect through the use of a positive confession. Listen to this..." He read:

Confession puts God to work fulfilling His promise, bringing our words into reality. Our move is to expect what he promises in His Word, even before we see the healing. We know that He always moves when it is His turn. Our confession is our own move: it forces God to act in reaction. Never, ever cry out 'Lord, heal me if it be thy will!' For this is not true confession, but introduces doubt. Remember: A spiritual law that few recognize is that our confession rules us. Thus, we confess that our healing has already been bought and paid for by the blood of Jesus! It is our legal right. So name it and claim it!

"Egads! That's messed up. But that reminds me of something." Peter sat up again and rifled through his pile of research. "Ahh, there it is."

"What is it?"

"A book called *Blessed*, by Kate Bowler. Basically a history of the American prosperity gospel."

Now Silas sat up. "Sounds right on the money! No pun intended."

Peter chuckled. "Suppose it's hard to avoid them, but the part that caught my eye was something on health and the cross."

Flipping to a dog-eared page, which sent a shiver through

Silas at the desecration, the pastor scanned it for the passage, then announced, "Here we go. On page 141 she explains how prosperity preachers insist the atonement promises divine healing. Listen to this..." He read:

Prosperity teachers, though varying widely in interpretation and focus, agreed on three fundamental ideas. First, healing is God's divine intention for humanity. Second, Jesus' work on the cross earned not only redemption from sin but also deliverance from its penalties: namely, poverty, demonic interference, and sickness. Third, God set up the laws of faith so that believers could access the power of the cross. Believers' primary task was to live into the power of the resurrected Christ by applying faith to their circumstances, measuring their lives and bodies for evidence of spiritual power.

"What a load of crock!" Silas exclaimed, shaking his head. "And let me guess, she says it's all rooted in Isaiah 53:5, right?"

"Bingo."

Silas quoted the passage from memory: "*But he was wounded for our transgressions, crushed for our iniquities; upon him was the punishment that made us whole, and by his bruises we are healed.*'"

"The Bucks twins quoted it in their healing services, clearly connecting the cross to our physical healing, not spiritual."

"None of this—from these bozos in the past to the Bucks message in Mill Creek—is even close to vintage Christianity!"

"Pure heresy it is, the prosperity gospel," Peter agreed, tossing the book to the table.

"Which is no gospel at all. It's the very opposite of Jesus' message for us to '*take up your cross and follow me,*' casting aside our own personal, selfish agenda and following him into his life, wherever it may lead."

"You know, I've been listening closely to the Bucks's preaching, and so far there's been nothing whatsoever on repentance and forgiveness of sins in Jesus' name."

"That's because neither is the point of the prosperity gospel! They preach health, wealth, and prosperity. That's it. A message dressed up in biblical language that's entirely deceptive of the truth of what they're selling."

Peter chuckled. "The Bucks's message is so man-centered that Benjamin literally wrote a book on it: *The Power of I Am!*"

"What?" Silas exclaimed.

"Oh, yeah. I've been researching them some and came across it. The book isn't about the power of God, who calls himself 'I Am' in the Bible."

"In Exodus, when Moses wonders who he is."

Peter nodded. "Exactly. But this book ain't about that. It's about people claiming—literally claiming the name of the God revealed in Scripture as themselves! All in order to name and claim earthly stuff."

"It's wicked. Evil."

"Think of the fact that even Satan quoted Scripture to Jesus in the wilderness when he was tempted. Think about the Serpent in the garden—a crafty little bugger who was very good at motivating Eve to claim her own breakthrough day."

"And we all know where that led to!"

"Right?"

Silence settled over the room, the pair considering what they were up against.

"So returning to what we were reading," Peter said, slumping back in his chair. "These prosperity preachers use and abuse the atonement to mean that God guarantees your health and wealth because Jesus shed his blood for people's souls."

"Worse than that, they promise that Jesus' crucifixion *paid* for these earthly riches, not just our eternal life."

"Which is where the Lord's Supper comes in."

"The Eucharist, but that's right. Literally ingesting the memory markers of Christ's death to guarantee health and wealth. Changing the beautiful work of our Savior into some sick, petty transaction to buy earthly goods."

"Except it works..."

Silas scoffed, dragging out the empty plastic cup he had used on Gapinski. He went to respond but couldn't. Because Peter was right. It had. On Peter's assistant, Katrina; on that college kid, Cameron; on Max Blade, the bar owner.

On Gapinski even!

Somehow.

"Somehow..." He held the plastic cup between his thumb and forefinger, spinning it around in contemplation. Made not a lick of sense.

"Here, let me see that," Peter said, motioning with his hand.

Silas set it on the table between them. "Help yourself."

He picked it up, eying it with a squint and spinning it around between his fingers as Silas had.

Silas leaned back, putting his hands behind his head to noodle on something that had bothered him.

"Except," he said, "it didn't work on Torres."

Peter glanced at him with a frown, then nodded. "What's up with that?"

"Clearly there's more than meets the eye here."

"Clearly. What's your guess at this point?" He went back to the cup, picking at the foil seal still clinging to the edge.

Silas shrugged. "Some sort of synthetic chemical, a drug inside the wafer and juice that heals."

"Sounds pretty Michael Crichton, if you ask me."

"You got a better idea? Because no way are these people

being touched by the Holy Spirit! Not when Torres didn't get healed. No way, no how."

"Why do you suppose the Lord's Supper, or whatever this is—why didn't it work for her?"

Staring at the ceiling, Silas shook his head with a sighing huff. "Haven't a cotton-pickin' clue."

The two sat in silence, the HVAC hum filling the tiny space as their only soundtrack.

"Comida?" Peter said, eyeing the foil seal still attached to the plastic cup. "Hmm..."

Silas looked at him. "Yeah, why?"

He shrugged. "They make a bunch of snacks in town. There's a big factory north of the tracks. Didn't know they made these Lord's Stouffer's too."

Silas's eyes went wide. "Snacks?"

"Yeah...why?"

He leaned forward. "Like Choco-Chocos?"

Peter furrowed his brow. "Not sure, why do you—"

"Because Gapinski's been eating those cotton-pickin' things this whole dang trip!"

"Now that you mention it, I guess he has."

Silas stood, organizing the books now to leave. "Why didn't you say so earlier?"

Peter joined him. "Didn't put it together until I saw the label. You think this means something, that there's some sort of connection?"

He took a breath, one end curling upward with hope. Finally, a break!

Maybe...

"Only one way to find out." Silas headed for the door with his books.

Peter hustled to keep up. "How? Where are we going?"

"To the Comida factory, of course."

CHAPTER 22

MUMBAI.

Over a million people...

O Paulina still couldn't believe it as she paced backstage, downing a bottle of that Veen Finnish water Dexter had been nursing the flight over as the band and choir revved up the crowd packed into their revival service. She hadn't eaten much since they had arrived at their hotel, picking through a few pieces of fruit and munching through a dark chocolate bar filled with nibs. 100% cacao, of course. With the way her nerves were playing with her stomach, she hadn't eaten much since either.

First time, too, the way anxiety was coursing through her now. Usually much more collected, much calmer. She had been on stage most of her life. Had grown more than accustomed to the performance-art aspect to the revival services, bringing just the right turn of phrase to offer hope for those seeking a blessing from the Lord Almighty.

But...

None of what she had experienced before had anything on what she was about to face. Attendance estimates had sent her heart sailing into a heady stratosphere of adrenaline-infused dread.

Dread for the expectations. Dread for the optics, with the whole world looking on now. Especially since news had been flying across the world, from the BBC to CNN to Al Jazeera and back that the contagion was raging across the globe. It was a global pandemic now.

With a particular hub centered around Mumbai, on top of those scattered throughout Africa and Brazil and the American Midwest.

Didn't take a genius in epidemiology or sociology or psychology to know how a population of nearly 20 million people would react to news of the cure to that global pandemic seemingly landing on their shores! Lines outside the stadium had formed within hours of news reaching India that the traveling Abundant Life Victory Center would soon touch down, with hundreds of thousands hoping for access to the only thing that seemed to cure the neurological infection stumping scientists and doctors the world over.

The Bucks blessing.

By now, people across the world had heard countless stories of bona fide, verified healings coming from a curious sect of Christianity globetrotting from continent to continent the past week—from the large cities of Nairobi and São Paulo, to the curiously small town of Mill Creek Junction in America. Video footage of the revival services themselves had made their way to the internet, along with testimonies from those cured and even some of their treating physicians—all confirming that something was indeed breaking through the disease that had sent the world reeling back into a wicked recession and threatened to dismantle the social order.

Blind had received their sight. The deaf were hearing again. The lame and paralyzed had stood back to both feet and were jumping for joy!

Doctors were stumped by the news, with verification not meeting the normally strict criteria of medical science but showing promising results with the mysterious neurological contagion that had gripped the globe and sent it back into lockdown mode.

The mainstream media had approached the stories with caution, but still aired several anecdotes alongside the normal panic porn that kept the world gripped by fear. Stories of hope to balance the chaos created by the contagion across the globe. Most of the stories of healing were told and shared on WeShare, however, the social media platform serving as the de facto news source for a global populace snookered the last go around of such global contagion catastrophe.

Which created a ready-made market for what the Bucks were selling.

Healing. New life. A renewed life, free from blindness and deafness, lameness and paralysis.

Just like Jesus, and the abundant life of blessing he originally brought.

Taking another sip of water, she wiped a line of sweat beading at her forehead. It was hot as heck that day, a miasma of humidity after an early downpour threatened to cancel their revival service completely. Praise God it cleared, and the sun was coming out! But in its wake was a wicked heat that hung with a wretched thickness. Made Paulina regret her wardrobe choice: a belted tight-fitting black Gucci wool-blend cady mini dress, gold buttons running down the center. Had to look the part she played, but why she didn't think to wear something silkier was beyond her.

Taking another sip and splashing her face with some of the Finnish water that fetched $25 a bottle, she considered the original bearer of healing, the one who had called on his disciples to do greater miracle than what he did. The Gospel of Luke, chapter 4, came to mind. She closed her eyes, quoting it from memory:

The Spirit of the Lord is upon me,
because he has anointed me
to bring good news to the poor.
He has sent me to proclaim release to the captives
and recovery of sight to the blind,
to let the oppressed go free,
to proclaim the year of the Lord's favor.

Jesus had read that passage in the Book of Isaiah one morning in his hometown synagogue. It was a prophetic passage foretelling the Messiah, the one who would come to finally make things right, finally put the broken, busted world back together again.

Finally put broken, busted people back together again.

The poor who struggled under the weight of debt or hunger or homelessness. Those imprisoned to their appetites and bad choices. The blind and other medically oppressed, spiritually even. This was the abundant life of blessing God had always promised his people!

Jesus said he was the one all of Israel had been waiting for their whole lives—the one the *world* had been waiting for since the dawn of time.

They were still waiting. Waiting for God to work his miracle wonders in this world, in this day and age!

And Paulina signed up to the cause, along with Dexter. But it was her that Unky Benji had brought closer into the family business over the years, showcasing her on stage and handing her the reins over the past year when things became clear his show couldn't go on.

Of which the Mumbai revival service was the fruits of that long year of planning.

Because of the crush of people trying to touch the tassels of Paulina and Dexter's robes, they altered their strategy: instead of one service they had two in order to accommodate all the people seeking healing. Early estimates had placed attendance near a million—which they would handily pass the first go around. And with the second service waiting in the wings...

She ran the numbers again, knowing the average yearly salary for most Indians was just over $2,000. Knowing part of their program called for sowing their seed of faith to receive the abundant-life blessing of the Lord...

Paulina felt faint at the thought, leaning against a crate filled with the cure those people sought.

They very well could cross the billion-dollar mark.

Billion. With a 'B'!

She threw back the rest of her water, face flush from the rising, stifling heat as much as the thought of all that money!

Everything they needed would be in place after that one visit to India. But there was no room for error.

Unky Benji's very life was at stake...

She moved out from the shadows now, looking out over the assembled bodies before her—some groping for air with a walking stick, others bound to wheelchairs, and still more straining to hear. Took her breath away, the crowds arrayed before her and fading out into the outermost parts of the property. Like a sea of ants desperate for provision. More than two dozen sound systems were spaced out throughout the vast area, accompanied by large screens that would project their message.

The choir struck up a familiar song now, a hymn from childhood. "Just as I am." While the band led the way, she pressed a hand against her forehead and leaned against one of the speakers belching a strong bassy undertone out into the sea of people. All crowded and pressed together on that hard gravel ground. She imagined that by the end, estimates would put the total number for all of the services at more than two million people. Maybe three.

At nearly 20 million strong, that meant at least ten percent of Mumbai's population would turn out for the Bucks brand of hope. The prospect was staggering.

And delightful.

Hope...

The word rose within her like an anthem riding on one of the myriad of bubbles from those glasses of champagne she downed on the flight over.

Like those ants all scattered and scurrying about, hope rose within her.

But for a very different reason.

It wasn't for her.

But for Unky Benji.

It was what drove many to follow Jesus back in the day. Hope for sight, hope for their hearing, hope to move around again.

Hope that God was finally showing up to do what he had promised: put the broken, busted world back together again, restoring it to the way he intended it to be at the beginning— before Adam and Eve screwed things up!

Later in the Gospel of Luke, chapter 7, followers of John the Baptizer approached Jesus after news had spread of the healing and hope he brought. John wondered if he might be that very one whom they had been waiting for—the Messiah, come to put the world to rights. The one whom Jesus had read about in the Book of Isaiah, who would bring about the health and wealth and release everyone longs for.

Jesus thought about it, then answered much the way he did at the very start of his ministry. He replied, *'Go and tell John what you have seen and heard: the blind receive their sight, the lame walk, the lepers are cleansed, the deaf hear, the dead are raised, the poor have good news brought to them. And blessed is anyone who takes no offense at me.'*

The blind saw, the deaf heard, the lame and paralyzed walked, the poor had good news brought to them...

One end of Paulina's mouth curled upward.

History was repeating itself; the abundant life of blessing was returning in force.

Mumbai, today is your breakthrough day...

CHAPTER 23

MILL CREEK JUNCTION.

Silas hated stakeouts; always had since his days with the Rangers.

Nothing but long stretches of time doing nothing, which was torture for a man of action like him who wanted to just get to it—resulting in aching backs and barking calves; leading to rumbly stomachs that needed filling and full bladders that needed emptying.

Five hours camped north of Mill Creek Junction had handed him and his comrades all of the above. But the way he figured it, it was par for the course as far as SEPIO missions went. Especially this one. Add the unexpected shoot-out or car chase, resurgent Knights Templar or kamikaze drones exploding overhead, or any number of levels of crazy into the mix and the evening could get really interesting, given SEPIO's track record.

Only time would tell.

But for now, all was quiet on the Western Front, aside from the comings and goings of several commercial freight trucks the past few hours. Came in like clockwork: ran in packs of three every hour on the hour; ran out in packs of the same every half hour on the half hour. Hauling away who knew what variety of junk-food snacks, in addition to those Stouffer's Eucharistic specials.

The sun was cresting toward the horizon now, the sky big and wide in that small-town, Midwest sort of way, but it didn't matter. Low-lying clouds, gray and foreboding and full of rain, threatened to make an already crappy stakeout even crappier. All they needed was a good downpour to put an exclamation point on it all.

Silas and Gapinski, along with Peter who insisted on tagging along, were perched on a berm behind a line of pine trees a quarter mile away from the Comida factory, pistols at their backs and binoculars at their eyes. It was a sprawling compound of several buildings, all interconnected with ventilation spewing out the scents of baked goods doused in enough chocolate and caramel and other confections to give one a coronary just sniffing at the air. Massive cylindrical vats sat anchored to the sides of one building, four of them standing at attention.

Made Silas think that might be ground zero for their little mission.

But first, it was wait time before it was go time. He just hoped the wait was worth it.

After Peter's revelation that the prepackaged Eucharistic elements were manufactured in town, Silas hustled back to Gapinski, who had been released by the EMTs with a clean bill of health. They insisted on carting him off to Mill Creek General Hospital, but he wasn't having any of it. And neither was Silas, who needed his agent to put plans together to infiltrate the factory where those abominations were manufactured. Getting on the horn with Zoe back at HQ, she started the back-end research on the joint while the crew got their gear together. After grabbing a quick bite for the road, they set up shop behind the line of pine trees facing their target.

Waiting for the window to act that would blow this whole mission wide open.

At least, that's what Silas hoped. Because so far they had a whole lot of nothing with a whole heck of a lot of open-ended questions still begging for answers.

A rumbly noise caught his attention. At first he looked at the sky, thinking it was thunder, but realized it was coming from stage right. He glanced at Gapinski with a raised brow.

Who smiled with a sheepish giggle. "Stomach. I swear."

Silas smirked and got back to his binoculars.

"Seriously!"

"That Subway cold-cut combo wasn't enough?" Peter said, stifling a giggle of his own.

"Heck, no!"

"But didn't you get a foot-long?"

"I'm big boned, alright?"

"Alright, keep it down," Silas said, binoculars still trained at the food processing plant.

Peter shifted to his knees between the two SEPIO agents, looking toward the factory himself now. "So what's the plan, anyway?"

Silas adjusted his view. "Wait for an opening."

"To do what?"

"Get inside and have a look around."

"What, like break into it?"

"Pretty sure that's what 'get inside and have a look around' means."

"But isn't that illegal?"

"Yeah, but only if you get caught," Gapinski said behind his own pair of binoculars.

Peter sat back, running a hand through his hair. "I'm not sure I'm down with B&Eing."

The pair of SEPIO agents turned to him as one.

"B&E?" Silas said with a smile.

Gapinski snorted a laugh. "Sounds like you've been watching too many reruns of COPS, fella."

"We're not going to damage or steal anything. Just figure out what the heck the Bucks twins are up to."

Peter furrowed his brow and rubbed his chin, clearly searching for words. Not a look Silas liked at the threshold of a mission.

Turning back to the plant, he said, "If you want to bail, now's the time to do it. We'll understand. But there hasn't been a set of trucks rumbling through in the last forty minutes."

Gapinski added, "And I haven't seen any sign of the night watchman in about as long either."

Peter sat up now. "Night watchman?"

"Yeah, the Rent-a-Cop scoping the perimeter every thirty minutes on the quarter hour, like clockwork."

"How do you know all this?"

"Too many stakeouts to count, dude."

Silas trained his binoculars at the plant's backside again for one more look. "No more trucks, no more guards. Makes me think things have wound down for the night."

"Which means what?" Peter asked.

Satisfied, Silas stuffed the binoculars in his gear bag and withdrew his Beretta. "Which means it's go time."

He slid out the clip and did a once over on it before shoving it back inside. Filled to the brim and ready for action.

Gapinski did the same with his Sig Sauer. Not Silas's choice of weapon, preferring his Army-issued throwback, but it got the job done.

"What, with guns?" Peter said with shock.

"Yeah, what'd you expect?" Gapinski slid his own clip back inside and shoved the weapon at his back. "That we go in with glitter and rose petals?"

Silas hoisted the bag over his shoulder and stepped out from the line of trees, Gapinski following. He turned back to

Peter, saying, "Again, feel free to check out, but we do things SEPIO's way, alright? Your call."

Peter ran a nervous hand through his hair again, but stood and nodded. "Let's do this."

Silas took off down the hill toward a chain-link fence ringing the manufacturing compound, topped by barbed wire. Made for the section of fencing running along the building with those vats he'd spied earlier. Didn't take long before they reached it, thankfully under the cover of darkness. These jokers really should upgrade their lighting. Noticed a few bulbs burned out along the building perimeter.

Silas threw off the bag and opened it to retrieve a set of bolt cutters, which he handed to Gapinski. He got to work cutting a line down the fence while Silas checked his phone for messages.

He smiled. Zoe had come through, providing a blueprint of the facility. Should come in hand while navigating the place.

Gapinski stood and handed back the cutters. "All set."

"This doesn't feel right..." Peter complained, glancing around and heaving nervous breaths.

Silas looked at him. "Never does. But it's all we got at this point. And it beats the alternative."

"Yeah? What's that?"

"Letting those charismatic whack jobs get away with— whatever it is they're getting away with."

Peter frowned, but nodded.

Gapinski was through the fence first, his large frame squeezing through with more noise than Silas cared for. Peter was next, easily slipping through. Throwing the bag over his shoulder, Silas joined them, the three making for the building shrouded in darkness.

When a blinding brightness was cast across the damn property!

Apparently those dark lights weren't burned out after all.

"Always something!" Gapinski cursed, taking off toward the plant with Peter close behind.

Silas pounded after them, expecting an alarm to come blaring up or train of armed guards to come storming out some door hidden in the lawn.

Blessedly, neither came.

They reached the building in no time flat, finding a shadow between the high-powered lamps and slipping inside.

"Jeez Louise, chief," Gapinski said huffing. "You didn't tell us there were Friday-night style lights we had to worry about!"

Silas heaved a breath himself. "Didn't know we had to worry about them!"

"You don't think they saw us, do you?" Peter asked on a shaky breath.

Withdrawing his Sig, Gapinski shrugged. "Who knows? But—"

Squawking hinges stopped him cold.

From behind. Down a ways.

The three spun around and crouched, pressing in against the building and trying to melt into the shadow as much as possible.

Through the glare of the added security lights, Silas could see an open door at the end of the building above a set of stairs.

A short, portly man waddled outside and down the stairs, whistling some tune he didn't recognize. He stopped at the end and leaned against a pipe handrail, the security lights flipping off and plunging the property back into darkness.

Peter audibly sighed with relief. Gapinski grunted with disapproval at their newest partner's reaction.

Silas held his breath—waiting, intuiting, preparing for what might come next.

A small flame flickered to life in the darkness, followed by the familiar burn of a cigarette's end. He suddenly craved a dose of nicotine himself. A cancer stick Celeste would say with a finger wag, his fiancé not caring for an old habit he resurrected last year—which he had pretty well put to rest, thank you very much!

Still, between the lights and the man's appearance, he could use a dose of relief. Instead, he resorted to using the wartime trick he'd developed to calm himself in tight situations, counting backwards from a thousand.

Blessedly, the man's casual demeanor—relaxed, whistling, having a smoke while the lawn flared up with alarm—told Silas there probably wasn't anything to worry about. Probably happened all the time with how far they were out in the country. Rabbits or raccoons wandering onto the property and tripping the security lights.

Gapinski sidled up to him, saying lowly, "I say we take him."

"I agree."

Peter went to protest, but Silas silenced him with a digging hand on his shoulder. The pastorman was starting to get on his nerves. Understood this was so far outside of his league and orbit of comprehension that he didn't know what to do with it all. But once on mission, protests ceased and orders were followed. No question about it.

Especially his mission, with him in charge.

Peter sighed but relaxed, seemingly resigning himself to the plan.

Which Silas put into motion immediately, slowly putting the bag on his back and crouching before padding forward. Thankfully, the way was paved in grass, so their footfalls were muted. He could tell Gapinski was close behind and figured Peter wouldn't wait around alone.

The orange burn flared again, closer to the man's face now. Which meant they didn't have much time before he finished. Either he'd strike up another or return to his post.

Either way, Silas had to time it all just right on his approach. Too early and he risked setting the man off—and anything else he might be lugging around with him. Too late and they'd miss their window of opportunity to take the guy before he ran back inside.

Thirty feet away now, the darkness a mercy on their approach.

The guard's face flared orange one final time before the faint glow went end over end into the grass, a foot coming down.

Which led to a whole host of what-next questions.

Will he light up another and stick around? Or head back inside? And if the latter, will he spin with his back toward Silas, or turn toward him before turning to head back inside?

Variables, variables, variables. Nothing he hadn't handled before, or couldn't handle. But every option had an equal and opposite reaction that could make or break the mission.

Moment of truth.

The guard put his hands in his pockets, like he was reaching back inside for the nicotine goods.

But then he tilted his head back and stared up into the sky, taking a breath, then a moment.

Right before he turned back toward the entrance door.

Not spinning with back toward Silas, but his generous belly swinging toward his position.

Locking eyes with him as he continued padding forward. And freezing, like a deer caught in the glare of a grizzly.

Damn...

Time for Plan Q. Which was usually how it went with SEPIO.

Putting every one of those years of varsity high school football to good use, Silas hauled ass toward the man.

Who brought his hands out of his pockets.

Which instantly snapped Silas into defense mode, fearing he was either reaching for a weapon or already wielding one.

So he did the same, withdrawing his Beretta and pointing it

squarely dead-center mass.

Eliciting a frightened squeak from the guard, who threw his hands up to shield himself as if about to get run over by a freight train!

"On the ground!" Silas commanded, Gapinski coming up behind him now with his own weapon drawn.

"D-D-Don't shoot!" the guard squeaked again, thumping to his knees.

"Nice and easy…"

Which was exactly what it was.

Silas quickly reached the man and shuffled behind him, wrapping a hand around his neck and squeezing.

Man folded like a used bathrobe, slumping into Silas's arms.

Shoving his weapon at his back, he gently set the guard down on the grass against the building.

"What d'ya do that for?" Peter exclaimed.

"Keep your voice down," he commanded, fishing out a set of keys and an ID badge that should come in handy. "And get inside. We don't have time for Monday-night quarterbacking."

Pastorman opened his mouth to protest again but snapped it shut it, then shut up.

Good man.

Standing, Silas pushed past Peter and took the stairs by two to the door Mr. Rent-a-Cop had come from. It was closed, with one of those standard black security panels standing guard to the right. He slapped the ID against it and waited.

Took a beat, but soon the security panel flashed green before a click sounded inside the door.

Silas withdrew his Beretta again and eased open the metal entrance, crossing himself on instinct before plunging into the void.

Praying to the good Lord above the answer to the mystery to all the small-town crazy was waiting inside!

CHAPTER 24

Silas's eyes quickly adjusted to the inside of the factory, which was lighter than the darkened night outside, but not by much. A set of security lights hung in the corners offering the only relief inside the vast space taken up by manufacturing equipment. And quite the equipment it was.

More vats joined by conveyor belts were anchored throughout the dim space. Dormant tracks rose high above, probably three stories, where they roamed through boxy metal monstrosities before continuing on through a wall into another room. Digital panels, lying dormant as well, were arrayed throughout the facility near the conveyor belts and on the side of those metal boxes. Looked like a real 21st-century outfit.

The smell of baked goods and confection was stronger inside now. Reminded him of his grandma's homemade cookies. Grammy's secret was fresh butter and a tablespoon of real vanilla. Silas's was emptying a second bag of chocolate chips into the batter when Grammy wasn't looking!

Padding forward, weapon extended, he continued on past a conveyor belt devoid of any cookies or any of those Choco-Chocos that had made Gapinski sick. And definitely no sign of those prepackaged Eucharistic elements. Production had been shut down for the night, which hopefully would make their job easier.

Because a production shutdown meant no prying eyes. That was the hope, anyway.

But the mantra 'hope for the best, prepare for the worst' had served him pretty well with the Rangers in Iraq, and gallivanting across the world for SEPIO. So he raised his Beretta higher and forged ahead, weaving past more empty conveyor belts as his partners trailed close behind.

The room extended into another vast space filled with the same kind of machinery gleaming polished steel. This time no homemade cookie smell. Baked bread was strong on that side of the compound. But not the yeast kind. More the cracker kind.

Like the Eucharistic wafer kind.

"Smells like crackers," Gapinski said, nose aimed toward the ceiling and gathering in the evidence.

Silas nodded. "That's what I thought. Let's check it out."

He took a step.

When a whacking clang, followed by a tumbling thud echoed their way from another part of the compound.

Sending the three intruders hitting the deck!

"What was that?" Peter whispered on a worried breath.

"Company," Silas growled on his haunches—Beretta ready, willing, and able to give a hidey-ho.

"Always something..." Gapinski echoed, mirroring Silas with his Sig Sauer.

Silas spotted the faint flicker of light sweeping low through another entryway on the other side of the labyrinth of equipment before it glinted of one of the metal conveyor belts.

Heart was beating a wicked beat now, his lungs looking for purchase and head pounding with possibilities. The thrill of the mission was on.

More sounds echoed toward them. This time scrapy and

scrambling, with a few more thuds joining the chorus. But plasticky, not metallic.

Easing to a crouched stand, Silas motioned toward the direction of the sound. Gapinski joined him, and they both started off.

With Peter whispering objections from behind.

Should have left the noob outside after the Rent-a-Cop incident. Couldn't worry about that now. Pastorman would have to sink or swim on his own two feet.

Another slice of dim light spread across the backside of the next room over, this time looking like it was coming from some sort of office, windows clouded by shades or tinting film. Definitely someone inside, and the closer they got he could see a doorknob lying on the floor in pieces and a metal door fully opened.

Looked like someone beat them to the punch!

Gripping his Beretta, Silas padded forward on careful feet.

When a muffled sneeze was thrown up.

From behind!

Silas spun around to find Peter doubled over with his forearm slung across his face.

Dammit!

He threw a wide-eyed look of irritation at Gapinski who shrugged with clenched jaw and an always-something shake of his head.

Sneeze was muffled enough that they might skate by unnoticed.

Might...

But again, back to the Rangers's unofficial mantra: hope for the best, prepare for the worst.

So Silas got to preparing.

Weapon extended and breath held for their descent on the new LZ, he rushed forward with the hope of mitigating any fallout with whatever element of surprise remained.

Room was dark now, that slice of light no longer dancing around like before. Either it was resting for later use, or was put away when their cover was blown to high hell.

It was quiet, too. No more scrapy, scrambling sounds. No more shuffles and whispers of plastic.

Nearly at the open door now—

Where a sudden bright light swung out from the void, blinding Silas momentarily and sending him back on his heels.

"Don't move!" a voice commanded, growly and gravelly behind the brightness shielding the hostile from view.

Couldn't see a dang thing with the way his retinas were flaring up from the sudden change in lumen dynamics.

But he echoed the same command: "Don't move!"

Tried to sound convincing, with his Beretta back out in front, but he wasn't sure it was working.

"Yeah, pal. Not a muscle," Gapinski said, backing him up, but with the same squinting blindness.

"I've got you in my sights, partner," the voice growled again, "and I ain't letting up. Now drop your weapons!"

Silas hesitated, but knew they were sunk.

The mystery man took a shuddering step forward, giving the light a shake for good measure—which offered the flash of a pistol barrel.

"On your knees!" he commanded.

Silas clenched his jaw and narrowed his eyes, throwing a glance over his shoulder to Gapinski who frowned but nodded him to comply. Didn't want to in the slightest, but he did, Peter already on the floor and his SEPIO partner joining him on the cold concrete. He held up his hands and joined them.

Light swung away, and Silas caught a better sighting of that pistol. Heckler & Koch, if he placed it right. Guy was older, but fit, with a bald eight-ball head flanked by ears shaped sort of like a Gremlin, oversized and jutting out. Held one of those plus-size phones flaring up its flashlight toward them in one hand and that damn weapon in the other. Looked like a good aim, and good shot, so Silas didn't dare try anything.

Yet.

Through the open door, a desk lamp cast a dim yellow across a desk filled with stacks of folders and papers. Looked like they'd been rummaged through.

Which begged the question: Who was doing the rummaging?

And why...

"Wait a minute..." a voice rose from behind. Peter's, adding with disbelief: "Johnny Pope?"

Took a beat, but the hostile—or whatever he was—the Johnny character replied, "Pastor Young?" Didn't sound at all happy about the recognition, either.

"Johnny Pope?" Gapinski said with raised hands, looking up at the man. "Sounds like a superhero."

"A Catholic priest, actually," Peter explained.

"*Former* Catholic priest," Johnny corrected. "That was a long time ago."

"My bad. Sorry."

"Your last name's Pope?" Gapinski asked with a smirk. "Isn't that a bit too on the nose?"

"Pope is my stage name. Papadopoulos is my last name."

"Ahh. Got it. Is that Dutch, or what?"

Johnny frowned. "Greek."

"This is all very romantic," Silas said cutting in, "a meet-cute in a food processing plant, and all. Could make for an interesting bargain-bin romance novel, but would you mind sharing how the hell you two know each other?"

"And can we stand?" Gapinski added. "My knees are barking something fierce!"

Johnny motioned with his H&K before stuffing it at his back.

Silas stood, followed by his partner and the pastor. This had better be good.

"What's this about being a priest?" Silas asked.

"Like I said, *ex*-priest," the man said.

Peter explained, "He's a private investigator now, working freelance gigs."

"Which begs the question, Mr. Pope," Silas said, crossing his arms with interrogation.

The mystery man snorted a laugh. "Mr. Pope was my father. Johnny's just fine."

"Alright, then, Johnny. What are you investigating? Why are you creeping around in the dark in some food processing plant, breaking into offices and such?"

"I could ask you the same thing."

"We'll get to that, but seeing you here with these papers and folders all strewn about inside an office with a broken door and its knob lying in pieces on the floor—raises all sorts of questions."

He smirked, nodding toward the shattered knob. "That guy had a run-in with a crowbar."

Silas noticed it lying on a table next to a stack of open folders he'd eyed earlier from the ground. "Come on, man, give it to us. What's your business here?"

Johnny went to answer but snapped his mouth shut, throwing a glance at Peter as if to ask if the coast was clear.

Peter nodded. "It's alright, JP. I imagine we're on the same side on this."

"Really? And what side is that? I don't even know who you are!"

"We'll get to that as well," Silas said, regaining control. This was still his operation. The last thing they needed was for it to get blown by some small-town P.I.

"You can trust them," Peter said. "They're with me."

Johnny eyed Peter and the two SEPIO agents. Then he took

a reluctant breath and answered, "Gideon O'Donnell hired me."

"Who's that?" Silas asked.

"Local attorney," Peter answered.

"To do what?"

Johnny explained, "To provide some investigative background for a product liability lawsuit he's preparing to file against Comida."

"On what grounds?"

"On the grounds they made his clients paralyzed and blind!"

Silas didn't flinch at the revelation, throwing Gapinski a sideways look that was reciprocated.

Sounded like they'd come across the right kind of P.I.

"Who are his clients?" Peter asked.

"Sorry. Can't say. Confidentiality and all."

"I understand that," Silas said, "but does this have anything to do with the carnival that rolled into town the last week?"

Johnny took in a breath, crossing his arms now. "Why, is that why you're here?"

Looked like the P.I. was trying to regain control of his own operation, not wanting to let it get blown by some out-of-towners. Couldn't blame him. Silas would do the same. So he thought it was about time they came clean. Give a little to get a little, as they say.

"That's right," Silas said with a nod. "We're with the Order of Thaddeus. Gapinski and I."

Johnny twisted up his face in confusion. "The Order of whatchamacallit?"

"When the carnival rolled into town a week ago," Peter explained, "I phoned a former professor friend of mine from the seminary I attended. Wanted to get his advice on what I'd seen. See if he knew anyone who could help us out. He connected me with Silas Grey, here, Order Master."

"Order Master? Sounds like some bargain-bin paperback conspiracy thriller."

"We get that a lot," said Gapinski.

"So who are you?"

"The good guys," Silas said.

"In my line of work, that's not always as clear cut as it seems."

Peter jumped in: "They basically defend the Christian faith from attacks, mostly from outside the Church."

"Like the Knights Templar, or something?"

Gapinski snorted a laugh. "No, silly! They ran from us down a darkened street in Rome!"

Silas sighed and shook his head. They didn't have time for this.

He said, "Look, we're here for the same reasons you are. To get answers. We've got good reasons to believe all the random illnesses affecting Mill Creek are connected to the equally crazy healings north of town at the revival service. And all the rabbit trails and loose ends lead here. To Comida."

That seemed to get Johnny's attention. "Really? Go on."

Silas explained what had happened to Gapinski at the seminary, how he had gotten the same sudden onset neurological disorder that had affected others, and how it seemed like the contents of the prepackaged communion cup healed him— just like all the others at the revival service. He explained how the Lord's Supper was a central component to the sort of charismatic Word-of-Faith Christianity on display at the revival services. Yet he was sure however those Eucharistic elements 'healed' was less spiritual and more something else. Which he hoped to determine at the food processing plant.

"Sounds like we're on the same team after all." Johnny stuck out his hand. "So why don't we get to it. We've got a lot of ground to cover if we want to crack the crazy."

Silas shook it. Seemed like a straight shooter who could be

trusted. And given the conspiracy that seemed global in nature, they could use all the help they could get. Especially a former-priest-turned-private-investigator!

"So what have you found so far?" Silas asked.

"Not much. I'd only just gained entrance when you ran across my rummaging."

"What brought you here to begin with?"

Peter asked, "You said something about some product liability lawsuit? What's that about?"

Johnny nodded. "That's right. Gideon's client, well clients, a husband-wife pair, each suffered blindness and paralysis respectively. From what we can gather, it all happened after eating food made by Comida."

"Choco-Chocos," Gapinski said, "wouldn't happen to be on their menu, would they?"

"Not that I'm aware. Mostly TV dinners."

Silas smirked and shook his head. TV dinners. The irony, given those prepackaged Eucharistic meals were apparently made in the same facility.

"We best get to it." Looking to Gapinski, he said, "How about you and Peter have a look around the facility. Look for anything that we could use to link the contagion to the Bucks and the healings. Johnny and I will hang around here and sort through this paperwork mess."

Gapinski nodded. "Will do, chief." Peter looked reluctant, but he nodded as well.

The two left, then Silas and Johnny got to work sorting through a mess of folders and papers in a cramped office that reminded Silas of his Princeton days. Except this joint had no style whatsoever, with scuffed, plain white walls lined by metal filing cabinets instead of wood bookshelves under dormant fluorescent lights. Although the Mr. Coffee in the corner, glass carafe caked black, certainly felt close to home. An ancient PC desktop computer lay asleep on a green metal desk from the same 80s era. Silas figured he could get Zoe in on their fact-finding mission by opening up the device for a look under the hood, but that would take time. Time they didn't have.

Frustration mounted as Silas riffled through his file cabinet, pulling out a folder filled with shipping receipts. Shuffling through, he found nothing but flour and corn syrup and any number of familiar gobbledygook ingredient names stuffed in most modern foods.

"Found something," Johnny finally said, hunched over his own folder.

"What's that?"

"Shipping manifests."

Silas leaned over. "For what?"

"Acetylcholinesterase inhibitor, it reads."

"A classic chemical used in nerve agents, disrupting an enzyme that catalyzes the breakdown of acetylcholine, a neuro-transmitter."

Johnny looked to him with a raised brow.

"Something I picked up while working for the Army Rangers."

"Then maybe you also know what atropine is?"

"Sure. The antidote for nerve agents."

"Well, Comida sure ordered a helluva lot of both. Barrels of this stuff."

He passed the shipping manifest off to Silas. He scanned it with disbelieving eyes.

Helluva lot of barrels is right. Straight from a manufacturer in China. Came in on shipping containers bound originally for a shell corporation posing as a pharmaceutical company before making its way to Comida. Near as he could gather, it came disguised as a component of a muscle relaxing cholinesterase inhibitor. Knowing how inundated port inspectors were with these sorts of shipments, Silas figured it passed easily without scrutiny.

"And look at this." Johnny held up another page and pointed to a scribble on a signature line that rang familiar.

Yet was entirely unexpected.

"Paulina Bucks?" Silas said with disbelief.

"Looks like your charismatic chickadee is running this joint."

"Looks that way…"

Gapinski appeared with Peter through the doorway, grinning from ear to ear.

"Find something?" Silas asked.

"You could say that!" He nodded to Peter. "Show him."

The pastor held up a clear plastic trash bag filled with the familiar chocolate cupcakes. Then another, filled with the similarly familiar unleavened wafers.

Peter explained, "Found these next to conveyor belts way in the back."

"Just sitting there," Johnny said, "like they'd come off the same chute, right next to one another?"

"Exactly. Looks like someone forgot to take out the trash."

The P.I. snorted a laugh and shook his head. "Criminals…"

"What's better," Gapinski said, setting a jug of some clear liquid on the desk, "we found this junk farther back in a line running from vats that made their way into the final product."

Silas eyed it, knowing exactly what it was.

"Sat in something labeled acolyteo—cholester—something or other. Couldn't remember how to pronounce it."

"What about acetylcholinesterase?"

Gapinski's eyes went wide, and he looked to Peter in dumbfounded disbelief.

Peter nodded. "That sounds about right."

"How'd you know?"

Silas answered, "Because we found receipts of the stuff used to inhibit neurological function."

"Like causing people to become paralyzed?" Peter asked. "And blind or deaf, even?"

"Exactly."

"Always something..." Gapinski growled.

Johnny folded the manifests he had found and slid them inside his jacket. "So let me see if I get this right. Through their Comida operation, these Bucks characters are intentionally poisoning people."

"And then offering the only known antidote," Silas finished. "It's the only thing that makes sense!"

"That's messed up," Peter said.

"It's psychotic!" Gapinski growled, pounding a fist into his palm.

"Agreed," Silas said.

"But why?" Peter asked.

Johnny shrugged. "Why do most people do anything with such brazen self-interest?"

"The Benjamins," Gapinski said with a nod.

"Money makes the world go round, my friend."

"And charismatic whack jobs bent on world domination."

"I don't know," Silas said, crossing his arms and widening his stance. "Seems too simple an explanation."

"The simplest usually is," Johnny replied.

"You're talking about Occam's razor," Peter said.

"In my line of work, when a patient comes in with a cough and runny nose, it's safe to assume it's a head cold and not herpes."

"Eww," Gapinski said with a shudder.

"And in our line of work," Silas said, "when the Church is involved and there's a global conspiracy on the scale of the Bucks's operation that's undermining the historic Christian faith—things are far from simple, and there's usually a bigger player at work, or more."

Gapinski nodded knowingly. "Nous. Or that new Theoti outfit."

"Exactly."

Johnny laughed. "Now you all do sound like some bargain-bin paperback conspiracy thriller! Which I don't even want to know about. Either way, we may not know the *why*, but we do know the *how*. Or at least have a pretty good sense of it."

Silas nodded. "Which makes this thing a whole different thing."

"How so?" Peter asked.

"We'd been assuming all the healings at the charismatic revival service were real. At least, I did, after I thought it was a load of nonsense."

"But they were," Gapinski said. "You admitted so yourself. Peter's friends, me for crying out loud!"

Silas shook his head. "No, not real. *Staged.* All of it. They fed people a poison that made them sick, across the world. Only to stage these healing events that offered the only cure. I don't know how this all works out, the technical science and medicine of it all, but that has to be the answer."

"I see what you're saying," Johnny said. "It's like giving someone a cryptic note without the cypher. Could be a billion possibilities to unlocking the code."

"That's the way I see it, yes."

"And those prepackaged Eucharistic elements, the cup of juice with the little cracker slapped on top—they're the key, the cypher the body uses to unlock the cure."

"Exactly!"

"Then the delivery system for the original poisoning comes from this processing plant." Johnny waved an arm toward the equipment outside the office. "From those damn TV dinners my clients ate."

Silas nodded "And the chips and snacks, the Choco-Chocos you ate, Gapinski."

"Always something..." he growled. "And there goes my appetite for junk food for the next decade."

Peter added, "Katrina was munching on a pack of the same snacks the day I saw the carnival the first time. Didn't catch that until now, the memory just surfacing."

"There you go!" Silas said.

"But Torres didn't," Gapinski said. "I offered her one of my Choco-Chocos, but she didn't take one. Probably why she didn't get healed from the service either. Didn't have the poison, or need the antidote."

Silas nodded with a frown. He was right. His partner's disease was far different from the one manufactured by the Bucks. Which would require a whole other healing antidote. The actual healing touch of Christ, not some made-up nonsense cooked by charismatic crooks.

"From what I understand," Johnny said, "Comida is a global conglomerate with facilities across the world, too. Not just localized to Mill Creek and the Midwest, or even the US."

"Let me guess," Silas replied, "they've got their fingers in places like North Africa and Brazil and India. The global hotspots for this blasted contagion that's been circling the world the past week."

"Sounds about right."

The group fell silent, all arguments and reasoning having been spent.

"Only problem is," Gapinski finally voiced, "how do we prove it?"

"Know any pharmaceutical scientists?" Peter asked.

"Or an epidemiologist?" Johnny said.

Silas frowned. "I just hope Celeste and Torres can put the final pieces together..."

"Or the world is screwed," Gapinski said, shaking his head.

That was pretty much the long and short of it.

Silas went to answer when a sound caught his attention—then a glimpse of something.

Through the doorway, in the distance.

A door on rusting hinges, giving way to two men in black. Moving toward their position.

And fast.

CHAPTER 25

No room to think about what came next. Had to act faster.

Silas looked at Johnny and Peter. "We've got two unknowns in black coming up fast."

Johnny immediately withdrew his H&K.

"Put that away! We've got seconds to act, and that's going to do nothing more than scare whoever it is who's coming our way."

"What do you mean to do?"

Silas took a breath, then a beat. "You'll see. You two stay put. Don't do anything stupid."

Nodding to Gapinski, he gestured to the door and left without waiting for a protest from the ex-priest-turned-P.I.

A pair of heads peeking up above the parapet of food processing equipment were fast approaching now as the two SEPIO agents padded around a massive steel vat anchored to the concrete floor.

Silas's mouth filled with the taste of copper as adrenaline coursed through his body, jolting his heart and lungs into motion even as he got into position.

Just a few more beats...

And there they were. Right on cue.

The two hostiles rounded the office entrance where the other pair were waiting.

As bait.

"Who are you?" one of them commanded in a Southern lilt that reminded Silas of the jokers from the tent north of Mill Creek.

"I was about to ask you the same," Johnny said, voice calm, cool, and collected, betraying not a hint of what might come next.

Which Silas figured was now.

Nodding to Gapinski, the two sprang from behind, executing the same play he had with the Rent-a-Cop.

Each taking one of the whack jobs with arms wrapping around their necks.

There was the expected struggle, more than the night guard offered, that's for sure. But it didn't take long before both men were down on the concrete in no time flat.

"Check his neck," Silas ordered as he did the same to his own downed hostile.

Gapinski looked at him knowingly before leaning down for a look.

Pulling off the black hood, Silas yanked down the collar.

Nothing but white skin. Didn't look like the goons from a few days ago, but figured they were part of the same crew.

"What're you looking for?" Johnny asked.

"A telltale sign of an old enemy."

His partner yanked down his hostile's collar. Then looked over at Silas and shook his head.

"What about the wrists?" Silas reached over to his own man as Gapinski did the same.

"What ancient enemy?" Johnny probed, standing over them. "What're you talking about, and what aren't you saying?"

Silas looked at the guy, who clearly wanted answers. Reluctantly, as he searched his guy, he offered, "They're called Nous. An ancient enemy of the Church hell bent on destroying the faith. Terrorists who've been part of recent plots to undermine Christianity and bring about its destruction."

Johnny turned to Peter. "Is this guy for real?"

Gapinski stood. "Clean."

"Same here," Silas said with disappointment. "Dang. I was sure it was Nous."

"Or Theoti, I suppose," Gapinski added.

"Who?" Johnny asked.

"Just another run-of-the-mill terrorist whack job bent on destroying the Church."

"You both sound like that Dan Brown joker."

Ignoring Johnny's skepticism, Silas ran a frustrated hand through his hair. "If it's not Nous, or Theoti, then who the heck are these—"

A ricocheting explosion of gunfire overhead cut him off.

The four hit the concrete.

Just as the *rat-a-tat-tat* of automatic weapons flared up hot and heavy with relentless pursuit.

So Silas snagged the only option available to him, in a reversal of Michelle Obama's advice: When they go high, we go low!

He hit the deck and pinched off three *pop-pop-pop* rounds of this own, then again: *pop-pop-pop*.

Gapinski got the hint and joined the fun, adding his own *pop-pop-pop* to the mix.

Which the hostiles definitely didn't expect.

And resulted in their weapons suddenly discharging a *rat-a-tat-tat* rejoinder, spraying bullets out across the parapet of equipment and up the concrete walls to the ceiling.

Metal struck metal, this way and that—and something high above that wasn't any good.

Gas started hissing something fierce from a set of pipes at

the ceiling, followed by the sparking of more bullets, the hostiles continuing their assault.

Which ignited the hissing gas into a flaming arc that reminded Silas of the flamethrowers the Rangers used to eliminate brush from roadsides so IED bombs couldn't be concealed.

Snapped him into gear right quick, too, because that memory told him everything he needed to know about what came next.

"We better make a run for it," Silas said.

"Don't have to tell me twice!" Gapinski said.

"Where?" Peter hissed on a frightened breath. "How?"

"How?" Johnny said with a smiling snort. "With your twinkle-toes feet, that's how. Come on!"

Without another word, the man took off.

Silas grabbed Peter by the collar and shoved him after Johnny, then pointed at Gapinski. "Go with them and make sure they make it out alive."

"What are you going to do?"

"Make sure we're not followed."

"But—"

"That's an order. Now go!"

Without waiting, Silas darted between two conveyor belts, popping off a pair of *pop-pop* shots to draw the hostiles' fire and attention.

It worked.

Angry *rat-a-tat-tat*s chased him as he slipped into an adjoining room, the fire growing from behind and blazing orange lighting his way even as thick smoke started following his trail.

Triggering a blaring alarm and the sprinklers from above!

He kept running, those blasted sprinklers doing more bad soaking him than good putting out the fire! His Beretta was slippery in his hand now from the soaking, and his clothes clung to him with inhibiting annoyance. Strobe lights warning of doom flickered around him, lighting his way but obscuring his path and creating a fun-house confusion that set his mind spinning.

Coughing through the thickening haze and crouching now, he weaved through a dizzying gauntlet of conveyor belts and pressed onward past more of those silvery boxes gleaming orange and red in the firelight racing along the ceiling.

But he knew the truth of the matter.

He was lost in the maze of equipment.

Silas spun back, head ringing with the blasted siren, the acrid smoke and furnace blazing at the ceiling screwing with his head. But for the humming chug of the fire racing through the factory now and ear-splitting alarm shrieking, there was nothing else to give him bearing on the situation.

No feet slapping the ground in pursuit, no calls from hostiles, no more *rat-a-tat-tat* weapon fire. It was as if he'd descended into the seventh circle of hell, Silas was all—

The barrel of a pistol suddenly shoved into his back.

—alone...

Then an arm spun him around at the shoulder and aimed that weapon for his head. "Don't move, partner."

One of the all-neck goons from the Mill Creek fairgrounds, face sweaty and sooty and looking not at all happy.

"We meet again," Silas growled. "Where's your better half?"

"Mumbai."

"Must be heartbroken," he smirked, lowering his arm and trying to conceal his Beretta.

"You think I was born yesterday?" The man outstretched his other hand. "Give 'er here."

Clenching his jaw with resignation, Silas handed it over. The goon shoved it at his back and gestured with his own weapon. "On your knees."

"Are you kidding me? We're in the middle of a blazing inferno! We need to get the heck—"

He punched off three livid *pop-pop-pop* shots into the ceiling.

"*On your knees!*"

Silas narrowed his eyes, but complied. "Who are you?"

"Security. Who are you? This is the second rodeo, partner. I thought I told you to get lost?"

"Yeah, well, never was one to take orders. Ask my former CO."

The goon smirked. "What are you doing here?"

"Fact finding."

Eyes went big, but only briefly. "And what did you find?"

"Enough to send your bosses to the Hague for crimes against humanity. And you, if you are who you say you are. Heinrich Himmler's excuse that he was just security didn't go over too well back then, so I'd get out while you can."

The man laughed now. "Fat chance. You're about to get char-grilled, partner. So it don't matter what you saw if you're not around to talk."

He leaned forward with a grin. "I'm not the only one fact-finding—*partner.*"

He startled now, the world continuing to swirl black and orange, growing hotter by the second.

"What I can't figure," Silas said, trying to distract the hostile while he thought of something, "is why they wanted to destroy the faith like this."

"Destroy the faith?" he twisted up his face with confusion. "You think that's what's going on here, boy?"

"Sure looks that way."

"They wanted to help the faith! Help people look to what the good Lord offers the world through Jesus' abundant life. Give 'em hope, healing."

"By poisoning them?"

There were those eyes again.

"Oh yeah, *partner*," Silas growled. "We've got the full story. We know all about what's going on here."

The goon shrugged with a grin Silas wanted to smack to kingdom come. "Sometimes people need a dog and pony show in order to believe. Once the contagion is under control, and life gets back to normal, just think of all the people who will be flocking to the Church! Looking to Jesus for the hope that is theirs through his gospel of abundant living."

"But it's false hope, and a false gospel! And mark my words, we're going to expose them as the crooks they are."

Raising his weapon again, the goon growled, "Not on your life partner."

Silas took in a sharp breath, nearly choking on the smoke descending lower now. His eyes narrowed and crossed toward the end of the barrel.

Waiting for the inevitable...

"Hey!" someone shouted from behind the goon.

The man spun around.

Right before his head snapped back and body sprang from its legs, landing in a heaping, unconscious pile at his feet.

"That'll leave a mark," Gapinski said, wincing as he shook his hand.

Silas stood, stepping over the hostile whose face was oozing blood now. He turned over the goon and retrieved his Beretta, then shoved it at his back.

"You disobeyed my order."

Gapinski shrugged. "Heard the shots and came running. Besides, you said make sure they make it out alive. I put you in that 'they' camp."

"I meant the pastor and P.I."

"Are we really going to debate semantics after I just saved your ass from the fires of hell?"

"Good point." Silas slapped his back and nodded. "Thanks."

"Righto, chief, but let's leave the kumbaya for later, this place is about—"

A crash from behind jolted the SEPIO pair from their debate, the roof collapsing from one of the adjoining rooms.

"Less talk, more running!" Silas exclaimed.

"Don't have to tell me twice. Follow me!"

Gapinski led them through the gauntlet of equipment as the world around them continued to burn. The suffocating heat and acrid smoke was soon replaced by a gentle cool breeze and fresh air, the door standing wide open at the end of the long room leading back out to freedom.

Silas picked up the pace double-time, kicking up his legs and working his arms like he was a teenage quarterback again.

Soon they were out into the darkened night, and he was gulping merciful lungfuls of air.

Johnny and Peter were waiting at the fence, the pair motioning for them to kick it into high gear back to the opening Gapinski had cut earlier.

"Thought you were a goner," Johnny said, shoving Peter through the slit in the fence. Gapinski was next, then Silas helped Johnny follow.

"Thanks for the vote of confi—"

BOOOM!!!

A phantasmic show of fire and fury from behind cut him off.

The force of the explosion tossed Silas like a rag doll. A punch to the back that sent him sailing, with head whipped back and arms outstretched as if coming in for an embrace.

Took all of three seconds before he was eating grass and dirt, a fireball from Satan's abyss blooming behind him with a scorching heat.

Which was far better than what those other hostiles were eating, that's for sure.

Thankfully, Gapinski and Peter and Johnny had all made it

out with him. Not that they were faring all that better, the men moaning and wincing from the explosive force, their faces cut and dirt covered.

Silas eased onto his back, then sat upright, face illuminated by the orange-red glow of the burning Comida plant.

The board of directors aren't going to like this one bit...

CHAPTER 26

MUMBAI.

hat the heck am I doing...

W That was the first thing Torres thought when they arrived an hour ago at Chhatrapati Shivaji Maharaj International Airport Mumbai after a rough flight across the Pacific in an Order-issued jet through the night.

Chasing a childhood phantom, that's what.

At least it was for a good cause. Both professional and personal...

She and Celeste hailed a taxi and slogged their way through the smoggy city streets packed with *muy loco* drivers! Far crazier than from her country of birth, Mexico. Not that the *gringos* of her adopted homeland in *El Norte* were much better. But theirs was a special kind of rage that exploded in bursts rather than a general ignoring of traffic lights and merge patterns and rights-of-way across the populace.

India seemed to be a wicked combination of it all, giving Torres a sour stomach worse than she had experienced on the ocean when she worked for her uncle's undersea salvage operation.

The pair zigzagged this way and that, with barely any

visible lane lines. Not that anyone was paying much attention to them anyway! The skyscrapers seemed to add to all the madness, the towering structures of glass and steel funneling the honking and shouting and grumbly last-century cars as they all piled into and through and beyond the downtown city on toward destiny.

Which, judging by the traffic and the reports coming in from Order HQ monitoring WeShare traffic, looked to be heading in the same direction.

The massive fairgrounds on the outskirts of Mumbai for a charismatic healing service peddling the same hope dished out in Mill Creek Junction.

Three hours later, wading through the traffic and fighting with their cabbie to keep his promise to take them to their destiny, they arrived at a sprawling plane of trampled grass and mud, thanks to a deluge of rain. But it didn't matter to the hundreds of thousands who came seeking their breakthrough day.

Took some doing, but Torres and Celeste managed to push and shove their way to the front to get a better eye on things. Sound was a bit blaring given they were in a side area near the cluster of speakers broadcasting another sappy worship song about the abundance of God, if you could call it worship. More like self-congratulatory drivel than anything that could be considered divine veneration.

From their perch, Torres observed several people bunched in several huddles around what looked like volunteers, all wearing bright orange lanyards. Eyes were closed, heads were bowed, arms were raised in penitential expectation while the volunteers shouted what sounded like prayers in the native tongue. Couldn't very well understand what they were saying, but it was clear the only hands-laying and prayer-receiving these people would get was from those volunteers, not the Bucks themselves.

Torres spotted that she-wolf now, perched off to the side, taking in the view. With her designer dress and loads of gold jewelry. Sipping on some fifty-dollar bottle of spring water, probably from some Nordic nation. Getting ready to dish out the goods that her *papá* and *mamá* themselves had fed off from those many years ago.

Of course, Paulina couldn't be bothered with the people down below, she supposed, the twins content to run the service from the stage. So they enlisted hired hands to pray for the sick, just like Benji Bucks—until Papá handed over that envelope of cash, then the big dog got involved! Bet they were scoping for potential testimonies, too, to bring onto the stage in order to give bona fides for the Bucks's work of God.

Staring at the huddled masses of sick and desperate people, Torres couldn't help but get her adrenaline all fired at the sight, the memory resurfacing of her own parents and their own desperation for relief from life's suffering.

Shaking her head, she let a curse slip: *"Qué demonios?"*

"What was that, mate?" Celeste asked.

Without breaking her stare, Torres answered, "What in the world is this? *How* in the world could this be happening? I mean, just look at all of these people! So much desperation, so much thirst for hope! And seeking it from the spigot of demons."

The thoughts ran through her head at the songs blaring from the stage. She couldn't shake the emotion from it all. And not because of the music.

Dios mío...

Torres wondered where God was in all of this, tears streaming down her face now as she took in the view of desperate bodies pressing in toward the stage for a touch of the Bucks's strange blessing.

Caught sight of a child with clouded eyes clinging to his

mother with desperation in front of them. Surely blind. Why, for what reason?

A sea of wheelchairs had virtually encircled them. Others were crying out from behind and to their sides, seemingly in pain. Praying for deliverance, for help, for healing. It was like something out of a horror flick, it was so *loco*!

But this wasn't a movie, and this wasn't staged. At least as far as Torres and Celeste could gather. From the news reports flying around the globe, the contagion was real, and it seemed like Mumbai had been a super-spreading hub of what epidemiologists had determined to be some sort of neurological contagion that was spreading across the world. Though *how* wasn't yet clear.

What was clear is that hope sprang from the Bucks's charismatic healing circus. The mainstream media wasn't widely reporting it, other than a few puff pieces here and there on a Third Great Awakening hitting small-town America back at Mill Creek Junction. WeShare was a totally different story!

Between the testimonial posts and video footage from Mill Creek and elsewhere flying across the site—the world knew where their hope and healing was found.

And it wasn't with their respective governments or hospital systems! The last plague pretty well shot trust in those institutions to hell and back anyway.

So the fact people showed up in droves for the revival spectacle wasn't at all surprising. None of it was staged, the myriad of desperate people seeking healing, seeking hope.

All from the Midas touch of a pair of twins. And by the hundreds of thousands, perhaps even a million!

From their perch near the stage, Torres surveyed the crowd of the most desperate of the desperate arrayed across the grounds behind. Reminded her of the time she and her *padre y madre* visited the elder Bucks, Benjamin, in Mexico when she was a teenager.

The revival service that changed her life forever...

The memory of that fateful trip to Guadalajara still sat in Torres like a sour stone. It was still hard to bear and carry after all these years. Still stirred her, sending her pulse soaring with a white-hot rage and stomach plummeting to the trampled grass with an aching sadness.

It wasn't only that it had led to her parents' death; that was hard enough. It was that they had made the six-hour pilgrimage riding on the hopes of the Bucks grift—Papá searching for a piece of the health-and-wealth pie for both himself and for his bride; Mamá wondering whether she might find the healing all those others had experienced at the hands of the supposed holy man.

Torres had seen the glinting glimmer of expectation in both their eyes as the preacher spoke, their eyes watering with a belief that the abundant-life power of God would visit them that evening, through that man.

What did it leave them? Dead.

And what did it leave her? A bankrupt orphan at sixteen. Had it not been for her tío, who knows how her life would have turned out. Probably turning tricks in some dark alleyway in old city Puerto Vallarta for middle-age Americans from one of the many cruise liners that came to port each winter.

And there she was, at a reprisal of Benjamin Bucks's charismatic revival service by his twin niece and nephew—sandwiched between a set of speakers near the stage and thousands of Indians seeking the same thing her father had sought: the hope of God's abundant-life blessing.

There was also a sad irony to it all: the very disease that drove her Papá into the arms of Benjamin Bucks was what she herself was now bearing in her body. Cancer. Though she hadn't admitted it earlier, part of her hoped the service worked its magic on her back in Mill Creek Junction. That the elements, infused with whatever juju power Dexter and

Paulina claimed was ours by right of Christ's death on the cross, had cured her cancer.

She wiped a tear trickling down her face, then her nose. Both at reliving the memory of her parents' death, but also at the silly hope the heart of the gospel—the bread and cup, bearing the memory markers of Christ's death—would do anything tangible for her in this life.

And yet, what hope does the gospel offer if only for the next?

Torres didn't have an answer to that question. Not then, not now. And it still haunted her…

But enough trips down memory lane. She had been as prone to such trips while on duty with the Israel Defense Force as she was while on duty with SEPIO.

Taking a breath and shaking her head, she told herself now what she'd told herself then: *Concéntrate en el partido, Naomita!*

Focus on the match, little Naomi!

Same now as then. Time to get her head in the game.

Because she had work to do exposing these *idiotas* for what they were.

Blood-sucking, white-washed tombs.

And they weren't gonna get anyone else killed if she could help it.

She startled when a hand rested on her shoulder.

"Oy, sorry about that, mate," Celeste said above the din of music. "Didn't mean to give you a fright."

Torres caught her breath and offered a smile. "No, it's alright."

"Are you alright? You looked a bit teary-eyed. Have been the past week. I'm not one to pry into one's business, and figure it has something to do with your recent diagnosis, but…"

Her smile faded. Looking down at the back of the legs of those in front, she wondered if she should share what had riled her up again. The memory of her parents, and their death.

Wasn't one to share her business with others, to let them in and all. But...

Perhaps she should, given the stakes.

So she did, turning to Celeste to explain it all from the beginning.

CHAPTER 27
PUERTO VALLARTA, MEXICO. 1996.

The door opened on those crummy rusted hinges that Mamá always complained about, right before it slammed shut with force.

I knew who it was before I heard the voice. Sure as an afternoon rain coming off the Pacific Ocean and blowing through Puerto Vallarta. Right on cue.

"Rosa, Naomi! Estoy en casa, mi princesas!"

Didn't even have to peek outside my room to know who it was.

Every day, same time, same greeting, Papá would come home from a full day at the car lot on the north side of town just in time for dinner. With his princesses.

But he sounded different this time. Like he was carrying news he couldn't wait to share. Good news. Sold an extra car that day, or got the promotion he had been begging his boss for over a year now. Maybe he won the lotto! Though everyone in Mexico knew Melate, the most popular lotto in the country, was rigged to favor the government; rarely did it pay out.

So I was definitely curious.

"Boy, do I have a surprise for you two!" he sounded, voice carrying through our two bedroom apartment on the ground floor of the even crummier apartment complex.

Climbing off my bed, I heard mi mamá squealing with delight. I giggled as I opened the door to find Papá twirling her around in a dance they used to do when I was younger. When times were happier, merrier, less problematic.

The problems started when Papá took this job at the dealership. It was the only thing available after a prolonged economic crisis when the economy cratered through a rise in inflation and unemployment. How anyone could afford a car during those times was beyond me, but there he was, working the lot on top of a myriad of other things the dealership had him doing—cleaning, accounting and bookkeeping, even some mechanical work in the shop out back.

But none of it seemed to be enough to keep our family afloat. Part of it was because the outfit he worked for was a shady one, where the pay didn't seem to add up to his work. Even when he sold a car, the promised commission didn't match what he thought he was owed. The excuses sure flowed from his boss and owner, but the money sure didn't. Such was life during those days.

It was made all the worse when Mamá was diagnosed with breast cancer a few months ago. Sent Papá's blood pressure skyrocketing with worry, not only for Mamá's health but how they would pay for the treatments. They argued about it constantly, which only added to mi mama's own anxiety. Told him they just needed to have faith that Jesucristo would provide for their needs—whether curing her cancer or paying for the treatments to make it through.

Papá wasn't having any of it. While he believed in God, and attended Mass every Sunday with his family religiously, he still believed you had to make your own luck. That life was in the creation of your mind and execution of your two hands and feet! So he worked even harder, worked longer hours and an extra day, all to provide the money that would help Mamá get better.

But now, seeing them dancing in our cramped living room, banging into our tiny eating table and couch and almost knocking off a vase—all those troubles seemed to float away.

And I had to know what was going on.

Running down the hallway, smiling and laughing now at the sight, I heard Papá pleading with Mamá.

"But Rosa, I can feel it in my bones!"

They were no longer dancing, no longer twirling around. Things had settled back into their normal, sad rhythm.

Mamá sighed and shook her head. "You always say that, Gabriel."

And it was true. It was one of Papá's constants, saying to Mamá ever since I could remember when I was still a little niñita, convinced his fortunes would turn the corner any day now. They rarely did, but that didn't stop him from continuing with the refrain.

It was most common since taking up the job at the car lot. He would come home after a long, grueling day's work trying to convince men they should upgrade their ride for their marriage and family and prestige in the community. One would bite, another wouldn't, most would offer the well-worn excuse they needed to 'pensarlo' overnight. Sometimes they would return after thinking it over; most would not. So given the odds, you'd think Papá would have changed his tune rejection after rejection, or at least changed keys.

De ninguna manera!

Translation: No way, Jose!

I knew I had inherited his stubbornness. Or perhaps stick-to-itiveness. Either way, I was my father's daughter: No way would I dream of changing tunes or changing keys or whatever when life handed me lemons. I'd hand it back a lemon meringue pie, mixing and matching new ingredients to bend life to my will. Just like Papá.

Which was what he was doing. But what he was suggesting...I didn't understand it, and neither did Mamá.

"You want to go where, Gabriel?" she asked.

"A church service, in a field outside Guadalajara."

"Guadalajara?" I asked, perking up at the sound of the capital city of our Jalisco state. Wasn't sure about no church service, but a trip to the city meant fine food and new clothes. Maybe a pair of

shoes, even a new crop top to fit in with what *mi amigas* had been wearing the past few weeks.

"Your father has some *muy loco* idea to drive six hours—"

"Less than five hours, Rosa..." Papá interrupted. Then promptly shut his mouth when Mamá gave him that look, hands planted on her hips.

"*Cinco horas...*" she said, drilling Papá, "to some tent service put on by a *muy loco gringo!*"

Papá scoffed. "He is not crazy, Rosa! That is blasphemous."

"It is only blasphemous if it is speaking about God."

"Well, he is a man of God, a minister!"

"Who is this minister?" I asked, folding my arms and leaning against a plaster wall shedding paint like dry, dead skin.

"Benji Bucks," Papá answered.

Now Mamá scoffed. "That swindler from El Norte?"

"More blasphemy, Rosa. He is not a swindler!"

"It's not—"

"I don't care what you think! It is not right to disparage a holy man like Benji Bucks. Especially when he has given us the chance to sow our seed of faith in order to reap an abundant harvest of blessing!"

"And what sort of blessing is this that you are speaking of?"

"For one, a promotion to senior manager of the car dealership I've been slaving at and have been trying to get without success the past year."

"*Una promoción?*" Now Mamá scoffed. "That is why you want to drag me and Naomi half way across our state?"

A flash of anger mixed with hurt flashed across Papá's face. I didn't understand where this was coming from, but I sensed it was important to him. And I felt a little bad Mamá was tearing his idea to shreds without any consideration. Knew the feeling!

But he let it go with a shrug. "I figure it is due, that I am owed, and the Lord can deliver through a seed sown into the Bucks ministry."

"What kind of seed are you talking about, Gabriel?" Mamá asked.

He gave a half smile, running a hand through his thick, black hair. "Just a modest gift, Rosa. That is being all."

"Pesos, you mean?"

"Just a modest amount."

"Ai yai yai! You want to give our money to that swindler on top of us attending?"

"He is not a swindler! How many times do I have to tell you? He is a man of God who is a channel of the Lord's abundant life, his blessings of provision—his...healing even."

That seemed to stop things cold. But also seemed to shift things in Papá's favor.

Mamá opened her mouth to say something, then shut it and seemed to relax some until she nodded without a word.

Took a second for it to register, but then Papá's mouth widened into a grin. And he grabbed Mamá and started twirling her around again, dragging me into the dance until we were all laughing and squealing with delight. Before long, we were changing into our Sunday best and heading out into the day to make the evening service.

The five hours did indeed stretch to beyond six, just as Mamá predicted, but she kept her mouth shut. Seemed like the whole state had turned out for the revival service, the traffic was so bad! Add to that the packed parking lot and terribly long lines getting into the massive tent anchored to the lot and we didn't think we would make it in time.

But we did, squeezing our way toward the middle closer to the front at the edge of the standing-room-only crowd just as the preacher took the stage. There he was, Benjamin Bucks himself.

I giggled at the name as it was announced, thinking the name seemed too ironic for a man promising the blessings of God. Might as well have been named Benjamín Pesos, it was so perfect!

He was shorter than I expected him to be, a slight man with

tanned skin and wearing a powder-blue suit. I could see gold jewelry glinting from his fingers under the lights hanging from black scaffolding raised high toward the top of the soaring tent, and he spoke with a drawl that sounded different from the gringos who visited our resort town during the winter. Less refined, more low class.

Yet there he was, a man who spoke with authority, telling stories about God's abundant-life blessing. How he had never been sick a day in his life because of the words of faith he spoke over himself. How, "If I want to believe that God will deliver me a $65 million dollar plane, you can't stop me! The same is true for you!" And apparently the Lord did deliver just that! And three houses, five cars, closets full of clothes, and refrigerators full of food—all because of his faith activating the blessings of God.

I didn't know what to think of it all, but I sure knew what Papá thought of it. His face was alight with delight, with awe, with expectation at what God would do for him. Couldn't get a read on Mamá, but she seemed to be as mesmerized, especially when the preacher continued speaking about the signs and wonders that had flowed from his ministry. Men regaining their sight. Women casting aside their wheelchairs. Even people being cured of cancer.

Mamá's face suddenly brightened at that revelation. A ping of hope coursed through me as well. Perhaps there was something to what this man was saying. That we could activate God's blessing on our life, his healing power, with enough faith. Surely it worked for others. Why would a man of God lie about it, especially in front of thousands of people?

Could it work for us? For Mamá?

"We are samples of Jesus, we are super beings!" Reverend Bucks went on, "Whatever is true of Jesus is true of you. The abundant life he himself has flows to us through his life, his very Spirit living in us and in the world. And the way to activate that flow is to not only speak your faith by affirming the blessings of God are yours by right. But also to show your faith with a seed sown in faith."

Several people nodded in affirmation around me, with several more audible shouts of "Amén!" I wasn't really sure what the man meant, but Papá did. I saw him reach into his jacket and withdraw a large envelope, pulling it to his side out from Mamá's view.

"As the ushers hand out your own personal seed-sowing envelope," Bucks said, "repeat this prayer after me—"

Back and forth it went, the minister and the crowd echoing one another:

> This is my seed. I sow it into God's Kingdom this day.
> I sow because I love God and want to see God's
> abundant life show up in my life. I believe when
> I sow my best seed-gift, it shall be given back
> unto me a hundredfold—a good measure, pressed
> down, shaken together, and running over! I
> thank you in advance, Lord, for abundant-life
> opportunities that will come my way. Thank you
> that heaven's storehouses will open wide to me
> this day because of my seed-sowing obedience.
> Thank you, Lord, for the abundant-life blessing
> that God has poured out upon my life and the
> prosperity you have promised me in your Word.

Finishing, Bucks shouted, "We declare this day that God is obligated to pour out a blessing upon y'all when you sow your seed—a good measure, pressed down, shaken together, and running over!"

"Vamos, Rosa. Vamos!" Papá said, grabbing Mamá's hand and shoving past me, the envelope grasped firmly in his other hand.

There was a brief exchange, Papá explaining that Bucks was going to offer prayers of healing down at the front of the stage. He had heard about it on the radio, and he wanted to be first in line. I could tell Mamá was skeptical, hesitant even. But she went, the two of them for the longest time. Others swarmed the stage with them as several familiar hymns swept the rest of us up into spiritual ecstasy.

An hour later, the two returned. Both had bloodshot eyes, and their cheeks were streaked by tears. I wanted to ask what had happened, but I didn't dare; couldn't tell if the tears were of joy or sorry, happiness or anger.

The music kept playing and others kept singing and praying, but we left. Papá had come for what he wanted; Mamá looked like she'd had enough.

My parents walked arm in arm, so that was promising. I didn't say much of anything, not wanting to disturb the good vibes.

Reaching the car, Mamá turned to Papá and asked, "How much was in that envelope, Gabriel?"

"No es nada..." Papá said dismissively, getting inside the car.

"It did not look like nothing!" Now Mamá got inside, as did I. "It was looking like our entire life savings was in that envelope, it was so thick!"

She was right. It did look thick. One of those large office envelopes people stuffed papers inside.

Papá's eyes got big and he looked away, wringing his hands together so that I thought they would fall right off.

"Gabriel..." Mamá said, voice low and shaking and searching. "Please do not tell me you drained our savings for this."

"Nada mas!" he said, raising a finger with a clenched jaw.

Papá started the car without answering any further, revving the engine as a stand in for his rising irritation. Still saying nothing more, he backed out and stormed out of the parking lot.

The ride home was not a pleasant one. It was dark now, a light rain washing over us and the road.

An hour in, Mamá huffed and finally had the conversation she had wanted to have before.

"What did you put in that offering plate?"

"De qué estás hablando?"

"You know what I am talking about, Gabriel! I saw you speaking with one of the ushers, handing over a big fat envelope before we

were visited by that muy loco Reverend Bucks. Eyes went big and bright right before he placed his hands on me and prayed, so he must have known what you did."

Papá went silent, hands gripping the steering wheel while the rain picked up pace, the whippers the only sounds apart from the droplets smacking the windshield.

"How much, Gabriel?" Mamá asked again, not letting up.

"Bueno. If you must know Rosa. It was our life savings."

"Ahorros de toda la vida?" She gasped and clutched her chest. "How much was that?"

A tighter grip, followed by a further clenching of his jaw until Papá offered through gritted teeth: "Nearly half a million pesos."

"Nearly half a million pesos?!" she screamed, eyes filled with emotion and face red with rage.

"But it was for you, mamacita. And me. For us, for Naomi!"

I gasped myself, slumping into the seat. That was over twenty thousand U.S. dollars.

Twenty thousand dollars...

Probably not enough to get the treatment Mamá needed without some more divine intervention, but surely enough to get it started. Give her enough of a life while the doctors continued exploring options.

The rain was really picking up now, large pellets hitting our metal roof with an echo that sounded like we were caught in a battle between the Sinaloas and Zetas on that darkened street!

But Papá y Mamá kept at it, the pair raging at one another for a good stretch of the highway leading home. Yelling and screaming, crying and pleading. I was stuck in the middle of it all.

And then I saw it. Up ahead through the rain.

A pair of bright white headlights drifting into our lane from the other direction.

Crossing the median and heading straight for—

My heart seized in my chest; my brain froze with indecision.

Until I managed to strike a warning. Something deep in my lizard brain awakened from the ping of adrenaline, kicking my mouth into autopilot. Had to do something, anything while my parents argued with obliviousness.

So I screamed, "Papá look—"

The impact was sudden and total. It was as if my very soul had shuddered through me, the crunching shock from the crash was so jolting, my body flying forward into Papá's seat with a smack before bouncing back.

Which sparked an explosion of stars.

That sent my head blooming with pain.

And my nose erupting in a geyser of blood.

All before I blacked out in a void of nothingness.

By the time I had awakened I was in a hospital room, the dueling scents of bleach and blood clawing at my lungs. Light was filtering in through closed white lace curtains adorning a modest window in a square cinder block room painted over white, faint beeps and pings echoing softly around me.

I felt him before I saw him, a hand grabbing my own that sent a startling shock up my arm and into that lizard brain again—telling me to fight or flee.

But then I saw who it was.

Tío Juan...

I managed a smile, trying to sit up. But then a hollow lightness came over my head before I slumped down into my pillow.

"Sobrina!" Tío said, rushing to my side. "Keep still, Naomi. Just lay still."

I swallowed, my mouth like sandpaper. Gesturing to the water, Tío brought the plastic cup with straw to my mouth. I took a sip, the liquid lukewarm but welcomed. After another, I took in a deep breath, my ribs screaming at me to stop. So I sighed and did.

"What happened?" was all I could manage.

He hesitated. "You don't remember?"

I tried, but shook my head.

A nurse interrupted our conversation and began attending to my wounds, which I would later learn were numerous. Broken nose and collarbone, shards of glass in my face from the shattered window, broken ribs and legs from the impact of Papa's seat plowing into me.

"There was an accident, sobrina. A terrible car accident."

"Un accidente de coche? But..." And then I remembered.

The crazy tent, then the car ride with pounding rain.

The argument, the yelling, the screaming.

The pair of bright white lights. Drifting, veering, coming at us!

I sucked in a panicked breath, taking in the room with equally panicked eyes. I was alone. No other bed, no other visitor.

And no Papá or Mamá!

"Dónde están papá, mamá?"

Tío hesitated, glancing up at the nurse who ignored him, fixing her attention on the stitches on my face.

His non answer sparked something within. A deep cold spreading out from my kidneys, across every ounce of my aching body, from head to foot.

I asked the question again, voice quivering this time: "Where is Papa, where is Mama, Tío?"

His eyes filled with tears I had never seen before, and his lower lip began to quiver.

And that's when I knew.

My parents were dead.

Ironically, it was during that revival service when my faith began to fray. The promise of health and wealth ended instead in my family's death and my poverty, an orphan without any monetary claim after Papá handed over our savings to Benji Bucks.

And I wasn't sure I would ever be able to recover it again. By it, I didn't mean the sown seed; that money was long gone. I meant my faith. In ministers, yes, and perhaps the Church that enables such leaches to work their magic on the desperate, the hopeless.

But faith in God.

After what I witnessed, what happened to mi familia—no way was I ever darkening the door of a church again, much less getting involved in the Church.

No way, no how!

CHAPTER 28

MUMBAI. PRESENT DAY.

Torres wiped another line of tears from both cheeks, drying her hands on her jeans and looking toward the sky for relief. The clouds had parted some now, and a slice of sunshine was finding their patch of earth just right. The light was warm against her face, a kiss from heaven.

Perhaps it was a sign of things to come.

"Oh, Naomi..." Celeste said, wrapping an arm around her shoulders and giving them a squeeze. "I knew you had been adopted by your uncle after some horrendous car crash, but I had no idea the extent of things!"

"No one does. Never felt much like talking about it, to be honest."

"I can imagine. And I can't imagine what that was like. But it also makes sense why you were so insistent on taking part in the mission, even with the recent news of your health, wanting to see it all through, especially the Bucks's demise."

Torres nodded. "*Si...*"

"Suppose it's a marvelous mystery that the Lord Almighty chose to exchange your ashes for beauty—using you for his Church and all the past few years, despite the circumstances that led to the gut-wrenching split in your story."

She nodded again, saying nothing more.

"Here's what I propose," Celeste said, mouth drawn into a thin line of determination.

She turned to her. "Yeah, what's that?"

Celeste nodded toward the stage. "Let's get these lunatics. The whole lot of them! For your mummy and daddy, as much as for yourself."

She smiled. "Deal." Then she glanced over her shoulder, her stomach churning at the sight of all the people arrayed behind them and around from their perch near the stage. "But what about them? What do we do to give them hope—and more importantly, kill their false hope?"

Celeste followed her glance, face falling and head giving a shake. "I'm not sure. But we'll think of something. We always do."

"A buck and a prayer, eh?"

"That's the SEPIO way."

Torres laughed now. "Ain't that the truth!"

The song Torres hadn't paid any attention to ended on a closing chord with a rattling of the cymbals for good measure, whipping the crowd up into an ecstatic frenzy as the band-leader crooned a now familiar refrain: *Breakthrough, break-through, breakthrough-oo-oo.*

The crowd went wild, as if a global rock-band sensation was resurrecting an oldie-but-goodie from their vault. Right before they joined in, shouting:

> *Breakthrough, breakthrough, breakthrough-oo-oo.*
> *Breakthrough, breakthrough, breakthrough-oo-oo.*
> *Breakthrough, breakthrough, breakthrough-oo-oo.*

"I think I'm going to be ill," Celeste said, mouth turned upward with revulsion.

Torres nodded. "I know the feeling..."

The large crowd was dancing and swaying their arms under the parting clouds, lit by powerful pink and blue and yellow beams of light flashing from the stage.

Now the verse:

> *It's your breakthrough-day*
> *God's showing the way.*
> *Health and wealth by right they're yours.*
> *It's your breakthrough-day.*

The band struck up the familiar chorus again before winding down with another rattling of the cymbals and whacking of the drums that rivaled Larry Mullen of U2 sensation.

Then out stepped the main attraction.

Paulina and Dexter Bucks. Hands clasped together at the center before their adoring crowd. They raised them in triumph, their other hands waving before a sea of shouting, clapping, screaming fans.

"Now I really do think I'm going to be ill," Celeste said again.

"It's like they're worshiping them or something. Not the Lord!"

"Suppose that's the truth of it, isn't it? Who appears to be offering the abundant life these people are desperate for—God or the Bucks?"

"Yes, Mumbai!" Paulina said, mouth wide with a white-toothed grin.

Brother Dexter didn't look as enthused though, his lips drawn into a flat line and jaw clenched, the hand with the white glove holding the microphone limply. Probably jet lagged, but it was an interesting contrast.

"Today is y'alls breakthrough day. And look—" the woman

gestured toward the sky, a slice of blue visible now through the gray canopy of clouds. "Looks like the Lord Almighty agrees!"

This brought an expected bout of cheers and amens from the audience.

"Time and time again, the Lord breaks through our addictions and our debt, our broken dreams and broken relationships, our blindness and paralysis—he breaks through it all to shine down upon us his abundant-life blessing. Isn't that right, brother?"

She gestured to Dexter now, who seemed to startle at the hand-off, his eyes flashing wide and chest heaving with a breath before recovering.

But he quickly got into character, grinning from ear to ear and mirroring his sister's own gestures toward the heavens.

"Indeed, sister. This is the breakthrough day Mumbai has been waiting for, because we believe the Lord is set to visit y'all this day. To send his angel armies from heaven itself to wipe away y'alls poverty and raise y'all up to a new level of prosperity!"

Torres snorted a laugh and shook her head. Our poverty? Up to a new level of prosperity? Who was he thinking? There was no *our* and *us* about it! He was globetrotting in a multi-million dollar jet and swimming in Benjamins—probably literally, too, like that cartoon Scrooge McDuck character from her favorite *gringo* childhood television show. And how did they use those millions? To buy designer T-shirts and jeans and shoes, add a sixth home in the Bahamas and another Lamborghini Diablo to their stable of luxury vehicles. No way were the Bucks interested in wiping away poverty. Not in the slightest.

It was all about the Benjamins. Benji Bucks and his heirs' prosperity!

"We are samples of Jesus, we are super beings!" Dexter went on, "Whatever is true of Jesus is true of you."

Torres's breath seized in her chest, her head blooming with the fierce memory of that fateful day back in Guadalajara.

The very same words had been used by Benji Bucks right before that final blow. The one when Papá handed over their family's life savings, leading to the argument that led to the car crash that killed her parents—leaving her penniless and parentless.

"The abundant life he himself has flows to y'all through his life, his very Spirit living in us and in the world. And the way to activate that flow is to not only speak your faith by affirming the blessings of God are yours by right. But also to show your faith with a seed sown in faith."

Her head was swirling now, even as the people nodded in affirmation around her, with several more audible shouts of *"Amen!"*

Again, the same seed-sowing invitation. Man even sounded like Benjamin, that Southern drawl as grating to her Mexican-born ears as the first time she heard it at sixteen. Thought she would lose it then and there, a rage rising inside and every one of her nerves tingling with activation.

Until a hand gently grabbed her arm.

"You alright, mate?" Celeste asked lowly. "You look like you've seen a ghost..."

Torres took a stabilizing breath and swallowed. Then nodded. "*Si, estoy bién.*"

Celeste nodded back, Paulina continuing now where her brother left off.

"Give, and it shall be given unto you, Jesus declared! A good measure, pressed down, and shaken together, and running over. For with the same measure of abundance that you give, the same measure of abundance shall be given to you again. God said it, we believe, by right it's ours!"

That stirred up the crowd again, a wave of expectant cheers and amens filling the vast field of faithful.

"What a load of crock!" Celeste said. "The passage in Luke isn't even speaking about giving, but judging other people. A complete twisting of Scripture, that is."

"Suppose that's the way it's always been, isn't it?" Torres said. "I seem to recall the Serpent in the Garden of Eden doing the very same thing, getting Eve to take the bite of the forbidden fruit by changing the meaning of the Lord's command."

Celeste hummed with a smile. "Insightful, mate. That's true. Just goes to show what we're up against."

"It is in our act of giving that we show forth our faith," Paulina went on. "And it is our faith that activates the blessings of God. And we expect an abundance of blessing activation this day to take care of not only y'alls financial needs, but y'alls physical ones as well. The contagion that has been ravaging the world is about to come to an end. Right here in y'alls backyard. Today!"

With that smile gleaming across her face again, Paulina looked at her brother, as if handing it off to him to land the plane.

Dexter hesitated, taking a breath before taking a step back. Then he glanced at Paulina, as if telling her to land the plane herself.

"Do you see what I'm seeing?" Celeste asked, leaning in.

"I think so. Trouble in paradise, perhaps?"

"I'd say."

"What do you think it means?"

"Not sure. Maybe nothing. Maybe something."

"That's some epic MI6 analysis right there."

Celeste frowned. "Thanks for the vote of confidence, mate. Only time will tell what it might mean, I suppose."

The awkward exchange extended into an awkward silence. But only for a few beats before Paulina took back the reins.

"Because this day—this breakthrough day—I declare that

nervirus is dead! It is destroyed, I declare, with all the faith of our collective conscience arrayed before me this day."

Then she did something unexpected. She stepped to the edge of the stage, leaned forward, and blew a raspberry out into the air above. The bright stage lights even caught an explosion of spittle as the breath exploded from her mouth.

Celeste laughed at the dramatic gesture, then covered her mouth when a family in front turned with a glare.

"Didn't see that one coming," Torres said, stifling a giggle herself.

"I blow the wind of God on you *nervirus*," Paulina said, face dead serious if she left any doubt about her intentions. "With all the authority of a child of God, I declare that you are destroyed forever and you will never be back!"

The world around them erupted in a raucous celebration, arms raised and voices shouting amens. There were even eruptions of ecstatic utterances in tongues Torres hadn't heard before.

"Mumbai has gone mad!" Celeste marveled.

"I suppose if you've been hardest hit by the contagion, and some woman of God declared it destroyed, that you might recover from it when you didn't think you had a chance—I suppose you'd go a little *loco* too."

"I suppose."

Paulina continued, "We want to send this contagion packing and unleash the abundant-life blessings of God upon this land—but we need to exhibit the proper amount of faith. After all, it is faith that moves mountains, as Jesus said."

She turned toward her brother Dexter now, making a slight gesture with her hand and nodding for him to jump in.

He seemed to startle, as if being awakened and recalling his line in the script after being prompted by the director of the play.

Which Paulina certainly seemed to be!

"Remember what Scripture says," Dexter said with less enthusiasm than normal, sidling up to his sister with an outstretched arm. "What you sow, you shall reap. So we want you, to, uh, consider sowing a generous seed into this movement of God this day in order to weep—umm, not weep, sorry. In order to *reap* an abundant-life harvest of God's, well, his blessings upon y'alls life."

That was it. Then he stepped to the side, his head sinking and eyes casting downward.

Torres couldn't help but note how much his voice seemed timid, strained even. And was there a hesitation, a reluctance in the way he stumbled and groped for words? Odd...

"That's right, brother," Paulina said, jumping back to take control, not missing a beat. "Ushers will begin wandering through the aisles—"

And they did, men dressed in suits coming from all directions taking their places.

"—when they come your way, reach out in faith for your own opportunity to personally sow a seed in the Lord's work in Mumbai. We know he wants to do a mighty-miracle wonder in this great land. But recall what happened in Nazareth, his very own hometown, when Jesus made a visit. *'He did not do many deeds of power there, because of their unbelief'* we read in Matthew 13. So take advantage of your very own seed-sowing opportunity this day—if not for yourself, then for your community!"

"How utterly manipulative..." Torres growled, the pain of that childhood memory rising to the surface again.

"Agreed. Wretched," Celeste said.

Envelopes were being handed out like candy now, and people took them with eagerness. Paulina said, "Now repeat this prayer after me—"

Back and forth it went, the woman and the crowd echoing one another:

> *This is my seed. I sow it into God's Kingdom this day.*
> *I sow because I love God and want to see God's*
> *abundant life show up in my life. I believe when*
> *I sow my best seed-gift, it shall be given back*
> *unto me a hundredfold—a good measure, pressed*
> *down, shaken together, and running over! I*
> *thank you in advance, Lord, for abundant-life*
> *opportunities that will come my way. Thank you*
> *that heaven's storehouses will open wide to me*
> *this day because of my seed-sowing obedience.*
> *Thank you, Lord, for the abundant-life blessing*
> *that God has poured out upon my life and the*
> *prosperity you have promised me in your Word.*

Torres held her breath through it all, recalling the same prayer from the service her and her parents had attended. Apparently the Bucks script hadn't changed a beat in twenty-five years!

Finishing, Paulina shouted, "We declare this day that God is obligated to pour out a blessing upon y'all when you sow your seed—a good measure, pressed down, shaken together, and running over!"

Obligated?!

Torres nearly choked on the word. "What the heck?" she said aloud, but was drowned out by the cheering and clapping of agreement around her.

The woman raised her hands now, high above her head with fingers spread and eyes closed. "Now Mumbai, after having sown your seed and showing forth your faith, I want you to declare with me the reality that *nervirus* is dead and gone. That the Lord, because of the cross of Christ, is obligated to activate in response to our collective faith and destroy this disease that challenges his very divine authority—declare with one voice after me: The almighty God!"

Several voices repeated the phrase with gusto: *The almighty God!*

"The El-Shaddai!" Paulina continued.

The El-Shaddai people recited, more this time.

"The God who is more than almighty!"

Again, still louder: *The God who is more than almighty!*

"He's more than enough to meet our needs!"

He's more than enough to meet our needs!

"He is the miracle-working God!" Paulina continued, arms still raised upward, eyes closed now as if in some ecstatic trance.

He is the miracle-working God! the gathered echoed as one.

"The nutter has popped her lid!" Celeste said.

Torres snorted a laugh. "I'd say!"

"We declare today!" the woman went on.

Joined by: *We declare today!*

"We speak in faith to this atmosphere!"

We speak in faith to this atmosphere!

"From India to the United States!"

From India to the United States!

"To the state of Maharashtra to the state of Michigan!"

To the state of Maharashtra to the state of Michigan!

"From Mumbai to Mill Creek Junction!"

From Mumbai to Mill Creek Junction!

"And anywhere else in the world controlled by the dark forces at work!"

And anywhere else in the world controlled by the dark forces at work!

Without taking a breath, Paulina continued plowing onward, whether she was working from a script or speaking extemporaneously, it wasn't clear.

What was, was that Celeste was right: *Esta mujer estaba loca en su cabeza!*

Super crazy in her head, indeed...

"Almighty wind!" Paulina went on.

As did the crowd who was acting as a single conduit of prayer: "Almighty wind!"

"Blow this contagion away!"

Blow this contagion away!

"Heat!"

Heat!

"Burn *nervirus* from our midst!"

Burn nervirus from our midst!

"She's gone stark-raving mad, she has!" Celeste said.

"What the heck does she think is going to happen?" Torres said. "Like seriously, that *nervirus* is going to just go away at her command, or what?"

"Appears that way."

"In the name of Jesus Christ, we declare it!" Paulina commanded.

In the name of Jesus Christ, we declare it!

"Apparently so..." Torres said, her head swimming with disbelief at it all.

Celeste gestured around them. "And this is the impression, these hundreds of thousands of onlookers are getting of Christianity. That we can just command God at our every whim."

"What's worse is the impression they're getting of *Jesucristo*!"

"How so?"

"Because when *nervirus* doesn't just disappear, then it's his fault, isn't it? Or I suppose those gathered together—that their faith wasn't strong enough to activate the powers of God."

"It's all so sickening..."

"And unending."

Torres was right. Paulina wasn't through. Not by a long shot.

"Satan, bow your knee to our declaration!" she went on.

As did the audience: *Satan, bow your knee to our declaration!*

"You fall on your face before the sons and daughters of God!"

You fall on your face before the sons and daughters of God!

Suddenly, Paulina lunged for the stage again, extending her body and throwing her arms back. Thought she was about to fly right out at the SEPIO pair in some sort of body-surfing maneuver Torres hadn't seen since college!

Instead, she lobbed another one of those crazy raspberries, her lungs heaving a breath until it sailed from pursed lips, the lights above catching spittle in their glint.

Then she declared, "We blow the wind of the Holy Spirit on you with all divine authority!"

The audience echoed: *We blow the wind of the Holy Spirit on you with all divine authority!*

Amazingly, those around the pair of SEPIO women also echoed her raspberry! All heaving a breath and pursing their lips and sending some sort of holy breath gusting out into the world—but for what reason it wasn't clear, and didn't at all make sense!

What was Paulina doing, manifesting the Holy Spirit with some sort of talismanic show of magic?

It was all so *muy loco* Torres couldn't decide whether to bust out laughing or shrink back with cringe. A sickened rage also began to rise, because it reminded her of the Mesoamerican shamanism she had studied in graduate school while earning advanced degrees in anthropology. It was like Paulina Bucks was summoning the same animistic spirits that those ritualists did in pre-Colombian times, burning leaves and spreading entrails and drinking herbal concoctions that sent them into ecstatic states—all trying to conjure and cajole the spirits to do their bidding.

That's all this was. A modern version of those pagan rituals. Only brought into the Christian service trying to bend God to Paulina's will.

"You are destroyed forever from these people!" She went on.

And the people echoed: *You are destroyed forever from these people!*

"Hear our declaration, God Almighty, and may it be so!"

Hear our declaration, God Almighty, and may it be so!

"The Lord says it is done. The Lord says it is done," Paulina repeated, her body moving forward, then back as she continued the refrain. "The Lord says it is done. The Lord says it is done." More swaying from front to back. "For I hear victory, victory, victory, victory in the corridors of heaven. In the corridors of heaven!"

A cheer rose from the crowd, massive and crescendoing and expectant. It drowned out Paulina now, who was shouting on repeat: "Victory, victory, victory, victory!"

"The repetition of words and phrases," Celeste explained as it continued, "is key for Word of Faith types like the Bucks."

"How so?"

"Because they believe our words activate God's power to work a miracle on our behalf, expressing faith and binding God."

Torres shook her head. Sounded just like those Mesoamerican shamans she studied.

Especially now that those around them were dragged into the utterances, swaying back and forth as they repeated after Paulina those same creepy words: *The Lord says it is done. The Lord says it is done. For I hear victory, victory, victory, victory in the corridors of heaven.*

But now Paulina launched the service in a totally new direction.

"For angels are being released right now," she crowed, hands lifted toward the heavens and voice shrieking. "For angels are being dispatched right now."

Suddenly, she launched into a bout of ecstatic utterances: "*Hamanda-acha-atta-starrracha-atta-bacca-bacca-honda-honda-*

rrratta-atta-santa-anda-batta-ossa-macha-ratta-honda-santa-ritta-richa."

Then she returned to her—message? Torres had no idea what to call it, it was so wackadoodle!

"For angels have been dispatched from Africa right now, Africa right now. From Africa right now, they're coming here and all across the world. They're coming here in the name of the Almighty. From South America here they come! They're coming here and there and everywhere!"

"What the hell is she going on about?" Celeste said, face twisted up with the same confusion Torres had.

"An ironic question, given she seems to be driving the Devil away!"

"From Africa and South America," Paulina continued. "From all across the world. Angelic forces upon angelic reinforcement. Angelic reinforcement upon angelic reinforcement to send *nervirus* packing and the abundant-life blessing of God spreading across Mumbai!"

That got the audience revved up again, the cheers and shouts of victory swelling to new heights.

"Amen!" she finally said, people screaming the same while many around broke out in tear-filled ecstatic dances. The crowd swelled toward the stage now, as if trying to touch the woman who was bringing the hope they so desperately sought.

But something was missing.

Make that someone.

"Wait a minute..." Torres said, craning her head around toward the stage for a better look as the pandemonium continued.

"What's the matter?" Celeste asked.

Torres walked several paces toward the stage, ignoring her and trying to push through the swelling crowd.

Celeste pressed after her, catching up as she reached the

side, giving them a perfect glimpse of both the front and back-side of the area.

"Oy, mate," she said, grabbing Torres's arm. "Where's the fire?"

"It's Dexter Bucks," Torres said breathlessly, still searching the stage but knowing the truth of it.

"What about him?"

"He's missing."

"What are you going on about?"

She turned to her, eyes wide. "He's gone."

Celeste craned over her shoulders, looking around as well now. "But where to?"

"I don't know, but I think we should find out where."

"And *why*."

Torres nodded, then took off toward backstage.

CHAPTER 29

"Fake it till you make it, *Naomita*. Fake it till you make it..."

It was all Torres could do to keep it together, beelining it for black canvas walls that rose into a tent anchoring the stage's backside and cordoning it off from the main area. She raced alongside it seeking an opening.

For what reason, she wasn't quite sure. Call it a hunch. A gut feeling about the other half to the Bucks show. She had noticed it back in Mill Creek Junction, when the twins laid their hands on her and her hopes were riding high that they might actually do something with her cancer. Of course, they hadn't, but the fervency of Paulina was intoxicating, much more than her brother Dexter.

He seemed more like a reluctant participant. Or at least someone who had been playing a part for so long that they didn't know what else to do, but their heart wasn't in it anymore. Like a band that was a decade past its prime, but kept at the concert circuit or played Vegas because the money was good and what else were they going to do. But at the height of their newfound fame, offering healing and a remedy during a worldwide contagion, he was MIA.

Which was *muy extraño*.

Very strange, indeed...

She heard a voice rise from behind: "Naomi! Oy, wait up, mate."

But she kept plowing forward, trying to find a way backstage.

Rounding a bend, she caught two attendants guarding an opening into the backside. She smiled at her find.

Lo encontré!

Taking a stabilizing breath, Torres approached one of the goons.

Who promptly put up a hand. "Sorry, credentialed staff only."

So she gave them what they wanted, whipping out her Order credentials that carried the seal of the Vatican in a shimmering gilt that told those bozos all they needed to know.

They each squinted at the upraised badge, then looked at Torres.

She smiled and nodded at the men before easing past them through the parted curtain.

The pair folded like a bad poker hand, letting her slip past. The Vatican's seal tended to do that to people.

With Celeste apparently hot on her heels. "I'm with her," she said, flashing the same credentials as the pair made it into the bowels of the backstage.

Fake it till you make it is right!

Now to find the scoundrel Dexter Bucks and get some answers from that *gringo idiota!*

Torres picked up her pace through a surprisingly large space, her eyes trying to adjust to the darkness.

Until Celeste caught up and grabbed her arm. "Slow down, mate!"

"*Lo siento...*" Torres turned toward her partner, taking in the place as her eyes adjusted—which wasn't much.

Darkened and cramped, with tables at the end of the stage, computers and sound equipment piled on top. The same pinewood cases they'd glimpsed back in Mill Creek Junction—no doubt filled with those crazy Eucharistic elements that had turned everyone's stomach. A few people sat at the equipment, and others milled about with coffee cups in hand chatting it up.

But no Dexter Bucks. That she could see at least.

"Torres…" Celeste said lowly, sounding exasperated, annoyed even. "Please tell me there's a good reason why we just infiltrated the backstage of the Bucks's charismatic revival."

"It's Dexter," Torres said, glancing around again and seeing no sign of the man.

"What about him?"

"He's gone. *Desaparecidos!*"

"What do you mean he's missing?"

Torres went to respond when she startled. "You know Spanish?"

"Enough to get me into trouble. Now what is it you're going on about?"

"I noticed it back in Mill Creek. *El muchacho* was completely out of it, not at all engaged like his sister."

"Well, they did just land after embarking on a globetrotting healing tour from Africa to South America."

Torres shook her head. "No, it was more than that. Like he was going through the motions. And now he's nowhere after their most important stop."

Celeste glanced around now herself, face furrowing with confusion.

"But that could mean anything," she finally said. "He could be having a struggle with the sniffles or some sort of stomach ailment."

"Maybe. But did you catch the way the twins interacted?"

"I suppose it did seem like there was a bit of a thing between them."

"Definitely tension."

"Then what are you saying? What are you proposing?"

Torres went to answer when a slice of brightness interrupted her response.

Down the way and at the edge of the backstage.

Illuminating the face of *El Muchacho* Bucks!

She grabbed Celeste's arm. "Look! He's lea—"

"Hey!" someone shouted. Twangy and Southern and vaguely familiar. "You two, stop right there."

The women spun around in the direction of the raised voice.

Finding one of the all-neck goons from Mill Creek sauntering toward them, joined by a newcomer!

Torres frowned. "Guess those Vatican creds carry *nada* street cred in these parts."

They neared, then stumbled with a start, the goons glancing at one another. "Wait a minute," Thing One said, face twisting up with irritated recognition. "I know you…"

"Best if we exit stage anywhere, mate," Celeste said, backing up.

"Dexter looked like he had it right." Torres spun back around and took off toward the slicing light that had faded back to darkness.

The two goons sent up a halting command.

The two SEPIO agents promptly ignored it.

Finding the exit, Torres pushed through. Instantly blinded by the brilliant sunshine. She threw up her hands at her eyes to shield them as they adjusted.

Catching sight of Dexter climbing into a very expensive-looking import. Aston Martin, if she placed it right.

Without waiting for Celeste, Torres took off toward the man, Dexter easing the car out of its spot and pulling away.

A number of other cars sat parked. Part of the entourage she figured.

Which meant they might, just *might*, be armed and ready with keys stashed away for quick entouraging!

Dear God, please, please, please...

She pounded across the flattened grass and tried the handle to the driver's side door of a black Mercedes.

Locked tight.

Celeste seemed to pick up on her plan, jumping to the next and trying the same.

Nothing.

She hopped to another Mercedes as the goons called out from the exit.

"Come on, come on, come on..."

Again, *nada!*

She cursed in her native tongue, heart sinking at the inevitable conclusion that their only lead was zooming away.

With no way for them to pursue.

Moving to the last in line, she got the same sad result—when a horn blared from the end of the line.

Spinning toward the sound, her frown turned upside down.

Celeste jangled a pair of keys at the side of a black Mercedes sedan and shouted for her to hop in.

Just as Goon One ran after her with a look that could kill. Though she was pretty sure he wouldn't, just maybe get her and Celeste thrown in an Indian jail.

But she wasn't going to take any chances!

Squeezing between two silver BMWs, she rounded one front end just as the goon came up to the car's backside.

"Come back here!" he shouted as Celeste roared the car to life down at the end.

Torres snorted a laugh. "Yeah, right..."

She tore down past the bumpers of one, two, three cars toward Celeste, her passenger's side door opening just in time for her to slide in.

"Punch it!"

And Goon One did, whacking the trunk with his fist as Celeste sped away.

"Not you! Celeste!"

"That was a close one, mate," Celeste said, rumbling across the grass and gaining speed toward the Aston Martin that looked like a cherry-red toy car at this point.

"We're losing him..."

"I'm on it. But I do hope your plan pans out. Because grand theft auto isn't something I care to have on my rap sheet anytime soon."

"We still might get a grand theft auto rap even if it does pan out! But nice job, *amiga*."

Torres offered Celeste her hand with a grin. Her partner slapped it as they spied their target slipping out from the lot and onto a very busy Indian street. She pushed the Mercedes until it popped out to join the flow.

Horns honking and hands raising in one-finger salutes.

"Yeah, bugger off..." Celeste scolded, pushing the German engineering now. "Do you see him?"

Torres craned forward, trying to glimpse the red target through the river of vehicles streaming by. Her heart spiked at the truth of the matter.

No. She didn't. In the snarled mess of traffic, everything ran together.

They'd lost Dexter!

"I don't see him," she said in a panic, leaning right then left in search.

"I don't either."

"Drive after him!"

"What do you think I'm—"

Celeste slammed on the brakes and blared the horn as a rusted pickup shedding white paint like leprosy veered into her lane.

She veered into the other then floored it, sailing past the

buzzard before weaving into another lane to continue the pursuit.

"Jeez Louise, sister! Nice *coche* chops!"

"Thanks, but these blokes are giving me a run for my pounds, that's for sure!"

"You're doing great."

"Silas taught me a thing or two the past few years."

"While on mission?"

"No, driving in DC!"

Torres chuckled, then sucked in a startled breath.

Espera, lo veo!

"Sorry, mate. Didn't make it that far into Rosetta Stone—"

"I see him, the *coche rojo*. Go there!" Torres instructed, pointing to an opening in the next lane that would get them closer to their target.

Celeste skated into the other lane, nearly clipping a silver Honda hatchback.

"Now punch it!"

"The backseat is back there, mate," Celeste complained, hiking her thumb toward the rear.

"*Lo siento...*" Torres leaned back and let her teammate do her thing. Which she did, quite well she had to admit.

Cars were zooming by and cutting them off, and the blur of businesses and high-rises from entering the city was maddening. But Celeste held steady. Bobbing and weaving through the tangled web of cars, she caught up just as Dexter hung a right onto a thoroughfare that looked like it was taking them far away from the city again.

Two car-lengths behind, the SEPIO pair followed Dexter through four lanes of traffic. He never slowed, never sped. Never even changed lanes. Just a steady pace where the buildings became smaller, and every sign of anything close to modern urbanism became fewer. Sad looking two-levels of brick and wood eventually became the standard, with even the more modern vehicles fading into rust buckets two to three decades old. Gas stations, restaurants, grocery stores replaced corporate behemoths. High-rise apartments faded to ramshackle piles of bricks with clothes lines strung out between units weighed down by thin garments of faded greens and reds and blues.

Had to have been driving almost an hour now, Mumbai proper far behind in their rearview mirror.

"Where do you think he's going?" Torres asked.

Celeste shook her head. "Haven't the slightest clue. Not sure the bloke knows himself."

"Except..."

"I see it. Hold on."

Dexter suddenly veered to the left lane, making for an off-ramp. Celeste followed, careful not to trail him with obvious intent but making sure they weren't left behind.

Down below a steep off-ramp, they came to a stop sign, the charismatic preacher gliding through and turning right. Celeste followed his lead, the road leading to a very different world from Mumbai.

Darkness seemed to shroud them, even though the rest of the world above was mostly sunny, with animal clouds dancing to a far different tune sung down below. A sad one filled with broken glass bottles and plastic cups, wet and crumpled newspapers, and used diapers and needles littering the sides of the road.

The highway rumbled overhead high above, and the decrepit buildings they glimpsed above were pressing in against them. It was as if the rest of Mumbai glided along in oblivion, or intentional ignorance from their ivory roadway above, while an entirely different part of the country ran on down below.

The road they were on led past an encampment of sorts, an entire shantytown of tents and ramshackle huts, with thin, shirtless children scampering about, and women in dirty, faded dresses wandering about carrying metal buckets or balancing wicker baskets on their heads. No men seemed to be around; perhaps they were working, or trying to find provisions of some sort for their family.

Torres sank lower in her seat. Not because she didn't want to risk being seen, but out of a deep sadness at what she was glimpsing. A reminder of the corners of her childhood hometown her modest middle-class upbringing had narrowly avoided, but still looking all-too familiar.

And yet, there in a dark corner of Mumbai, she was also coming face to face with the same kind of despair that had driven her parents to seek out the Bucks's hope.

An elder man with a bandaged stump for a leg limped by on crutches. Two children, each missing an arm, scampered around a hut made of cardboard in the distance. Still others were lying on mats with vacant expressions.

What was this place? It was all so confusing.

She was even more confused why Dexter had driven in these parts.

And was now parking on the side of the road!

"Look, there," Torres said, gesturing to the brake lights beaming red across from the hellish scene.

"On it." Celeste eased the car in front of the face of an abandoned building that had slumped in a terrible palsy, its roof caved in and bricks scattered about a narrow walkway butting up against the road. It angled away slightly from Dexter's car, so hopefully it was enough to remain undetected.

The pair of luxury vehicles remained that way for a while. Two sedans sticking out like sore thumbs, parked auspiciously on the outskirts of modern civilization.

"What do you suppose he's doing?" Torres whispered, fearful raising her voice would raise an alarm.

Celeste answered, "Better question: Why do you suppose he's doing—whatever it is he's doing?"

She went to respond when the shrill of a mobile phone rang through the cabin.

Startling the pair whose every nerve had been frayed from the pursuit.

Celeste clutched her chest, sighing at the name on the face of her device. "It's Silas. Probably giving us a ring to check in with our progress."

She answered the call, putting the phone on speaker.

"Celeste, it's Silas here, on speaker with Gapinski and Peter."

"Here with Naomi on speaker. How are things?"

"We've been having it out over here," he said, sounding like he'd aged a decade.

"What happened?" Celeste asked.

"Long story. But the short version is we know what's going on."

He told them everything they had discovered in Mill Creek Junction. Beginning with the sudden onset paralysis that Gapinski had experienced, followed by Silas's quick thinking to use the leftover communion package, bringing instant relief and a cure, leading to a connection between them and a food processing plant in Mill Creek. He skipped all the middle parts —which Torres took as the good parts that'd aged Silas a decade—and got to their discovery.

A connection between those Choco-Chocos Gapinski had been stuffing his face with and the prepackaged communion cups.

"Blimey..." Celeste said, staring open-mouthed at Torres.

She felt the same disbelief. "You really think those twins are crazy enough to poison the entire world only to wield the only antidote?"

Silas answered, "Yes, we do."

"But how on earth could they scale something like that?" Celeste asked.

"Good question," Torres said. "It would take factories around the world to pull something like that off."

Another voice came on the speaker now, unfamiliar. "As in an entire food packaging and distribution network on every inhabited continent, you mean?"

She threw Celeste a confused look. "Well, yeah. But who the heck are you?"

"A new friend," Silas simply said. "Comida is the manufacturer of the prepackaged Eucharistic elements the Bucks have been shelling out on top of those Choco-Chocos Gapinski was eating, among many other foods. And they have exactly that kind of scale to pull this off, with plants and distribution agreements with almost every retailer you could imagine."

"I'll give you one guess who owns Comida," Gapinski piped up.

"*The Bucks,*" Celeste and Torres said in unison.

"Binga-ringo."

Silas said, "So, yeah, they could pull it off."

"So let me see if I have the long and short of it," Celeste said, shifting in her seat. "The Bucks created some sort of neural contagion embedded inside the food produced by an outfit that also manufactures the communion cups with juice and wafer, which also serves as the serum for the contagion."

"That's right."

"So, what," Torres said, "these whack jobs profited off poisoning, like, a billion people?"

"No, the way we figure it, the food is simply a loss-leader for the real money-making venture."

"The revival carnivals promising health and wealth..." Celeste said with marvel.

Torres pounded a fist on her leg. "Sonofa—"

"Naomi..."

"Sorry. But this is seriously messed up!"

"Tell me about it," Silas said. "The only question is, how to expose it all and bring the Bucks down in the process."

"We might be able to help on that front," Celeste said.

"How so?"

"We've followed Dexter Bucks to a dodgy part of Mumbai. Appears the bloke may not be as solidly on board with the Bucks conspiracy."

"Really, how do you figure?"

"Call it a hunch. The man left mid-way through the service here, and we followed him to some shantytown."

"Whatever you do, there's one more thing you should know. Something our new friend from Mill Creek found."

"What's that?"

Silas told her, explaining a document some former priest found in a stash in an office before it blew to hell and back.

The women looked at one another with understanding.

There it was. The motive. Now it all made sense.

"Uh, oh..." Torres pointed out the window. "Speaking of which."

Dexter had gotten out and was crossing the street!

"Oy, Silas, we've got to go!" Celeste said.

"Everything alright?"

"We'll let you know in a bit. Cheers!"

Ending the call, the two slipped out into the afternoon cresting toward evening.

Hustling after the man, Torres prayed God would give them answers.

And a way to end this mess.

CHAPTER 30

Torres shielded her nose as the SEPIO pair ran after Dexter. Stench was overwhelming, the heat of the day and post-rain humidity having bloomed the mixture of smog and human waste and river pollutants into a toxic stew that hung over the area like a miasma of death. Seemed exponentially greater here, where the collection of Mumbai's sickest and poorest and dirtiest congregated.

Yet there was Dexter Bucks, strolling into the heart of the village of ramshackle huts of cardboard and sheet tents, wearing thousand-dollar designer jeans and a hundred-dollar T-shirt, and similarly priced shoes and chains. The people didn't seem to notice, mothers and children and older men carrying on with their life, as if invisible to and from the world.

A wind whipped through the encampment, and several faded white sheets drying on a line flapped and fluttered, Dexter disappearing through them.

Torres hustled toward the line, spreading the large billowing blankets aside in pursuit.

Except there wasn't anyone to pursue.

Dexter was missing!

"Come on," Celeste said, pushing farther into the encampment, the impoverished people eyeing them suspiciously.

The pair searched around the shacks of cardboard and sheet tents, but came up empty. Torres felt uneasy now, the pair farther under the underpass. The growing darkness was disconcerting, the cloying stench disgusting.

"I don't get it," she said, arm brought to her face again.

When a voice boomed from behind: "Who are you and what do you want?"

The SEPIO pair spun around to find Dexter Bucks, feet spread apart and hands flexing into fists, face set hard with narrow eyes and a clenching jaw.

Torres asked, "How did you know we were following you?"

"When you're in my line of work, you expect to be followed by the leeches of the media. But you don't look like any paparazzi I've ever seen."

She didn't know whether to be offended or take that as a compliment. She took a step forward, hoping to get to the bottom of it all.

"Stay where you are!"

"It's alright," Celeste said, putting out a calming hand. "We're just here to talk."

"I don't have any money on me, if that's what you're after. Although my watch is worth a considerable sum. A Patek Philippe. Here, take it."

He quickly unlatched the band and took it off, holding it out with a jiggle for them to oblige.

Torres snorted a laugh. "No offense, but I wouldn't take your blood money if you were tossing it from a helicopter! And that watch is no Rolex."

Celeste threw her a look, telling her all she needed to know.

Zip it!

So she did, letting Celeste do all the talking.

"We're not here to take your money, Dexter," she said.

Which seemed to put him on guard even more.

"Dexter? How do you know my name?" he asked. "Who are you?"

"I'm Celeste Bourne, and we, Naomi Torres and myself, are with an ecclesiastical organization called the Order of Thaddeus."

"Order? Like with the Vatican or something?"

"Or something. We are tasked with contending for the once-for-all faith entrusted to God's holy people, the Church."

"Jude 3..." Dexter said, recognition flitting in his eyes.

"Precisely. We've been following your work, beginning in Mill Creek Junction, after an acquaintance became concerned at the show you were putting on in his hometown."

This revelation loosened him, his scowl softening some and shoulders slumping. He put his watch back on his wrist and nodded. "Go on."

Celeste took a breath and glanced at her partner. Torres nodded her onward, ready to get to it.

And she did, explaining all they had witnessed firsthand after being summoned to Mill Creek by a local pastor, as well as what Silas and Gapinski had found at the factory. She laid it all out, Dexter's face falling and going ashen. Looked like he might retch from the revelation. Torres hoped he did.

"So you see, Dexter," Celeste finished, "we've got you and your sister nailed on a global conspiracy to infect the masses and profit off their healing. All the evidence of the chemicals you stuffed into the food and those Lord's Supper accoutrements from your Comida factories around the world."

He went to respond, but snapped his mouth shut, face draining of all color now. He went silent, and they let him stand that way for the longest time.

Until he spoke up: "From our gilded cages," Dexter said, voice strained and low and quiet, "we've looked down on the crowds of sick and diseased people, the poor and debt-ridden, those desperate for a touch, a word even that will bring some measure of hope and actual relief for their circumstances. Whether they've got cancer or are suffocating under a mountain of debt."

Torres narrowed her eyes and shook her head, not understanding what *loco* nonsense the guy was spouting off.

"We're supposed to heal these poor souls!" he shouted, raising his hands. "But of course, it never happened like we thought it would. Like Unky Benji promised it would. Eventually, I saw it all for what it was. A sham. One charade after another filled with fake stories and power-of-suggestion mumbo jumbo to string people along with enough hope that they'll give us their money till their bank accounts were bled dry."

Torres had to do everything in her power not to lunge for the man. Her papa was one of those whose account had been bled dry—right before they bled dead!

Dexter went on, "Of course, early on I wondered why they weren't being healed. These people we ministered to, who were supposed to grow up healthy and wealthy. Their lives were supposed to be brimming over with joy-filled abundance. Nope. It was all a big fat lie. Still is."

He glanced around the encampment, a wetness to his eyes glistening in what little light seeped down into the underbelly of Mumbai.

"All I ever wanted to do was help people live their best life now. Our people, *my* people! Not make them sick. But Paulina... she just couldn't stop herself."

Celeste glanced at Torres, furrowing her brow. She didn't know what he was talking about, either. But it seemed Dexter might have been as conned as Mill Creek Junction and the rest of the world.

Torres felt for the guy. Sort of. But she had a few words for the younger Bucks.

"You know John 10:10 is raised up as a name-it-and-claim-it

promise," she said. "*'I have come that they may have life, and have it to the full,'* Jesus said. But this is twisted to mean that God desires for you to have Lamborghinis and ocean-view mansions and job promotions with six-figure salaries."

Dexter nodded, taking a deep breath and sighing.

"This is not even close to the abundant life offered by Christianity! Nothing close. The abundant life of the true good news of the Christian faith is not a comfortable life for a mere seventy years. No, it's eternity with Christ your Savior in a recreated world!"

"I know, alright!" he yelled.

Torres pressed, "To think that I am in any way the master of my own destiny and the ruler of my own world is ludicrous! Frankly, it's something the prideful side of humanity wants to carry but is far too heavy a load."

"I know, I know. What do you want from me! I've already told you it wasn't my idea, but Paulina's. And I feel sick."

"What I want," Celeste said, stepping back into the ring. "Is for you to explain why. We know how, and you claim it wasn't to destroy the faith. For some reason, I believe you. What we don't understand is the purpose."

Torres nodded. "Yeah, *idiota*. As far as we can tell, it was nothing more than a massive get-rich-quick scheme. To fill your coffers and peace out with a life of luxury."

Dexter fell silent, shifting on his feet. Torres and Celeste pretty well knew the why, based on what the fella Johnny Pope had discovered in some Mill Creek factory. But they wanted him to say it, to confirm it.

And he did, taking a deep breath before speaking.

"Unky Benji is dying."

"What do you mean?" Torres said, face drilling him with inquiry and making him spell out every word.

"I mean, he is sick, with a rare genetic disorder. Something to do with his heart, but I'm not entirely sure. What I do know is that he doesn't have long. Not unless we can buy a cure. Which numbers into the millions of dollars to buy the best science has to offer, with research and therapy."

"And you and your sister," Celeste said, "dreamed up a scheme to get those millions."

"To milk those millions," Torres said, "from the desperate, more like it!"

Dexter shook his head. "Not my idea. Unky Benji and Paulina. He was desperate for a cure, and so was she. I was too, but I resigned myself to the fact our uncle was sick and dying. Not Paulina. She couldn't handle losing him. Not after all he had done for us after losing our parents."

"Losing your parents?" asked Celeste.

He took a breath, lower lip quivering, as if reliving a memory. "Father, Unky Benji's brother, believed he too should have been endowed with the powers to bring health and wealth to the world. From our home in West Virginia, he saw the success his brother had—"

"And wanted in on it," said Torres.

Dexter nodded. "Except he had nothing more than a high school education and was a coal miner, for heaven's sake! He also got sick with black lung disease, and Mother—well, she had mental problems that pretty well sealed the deal. Between Father's health problems and Mother's schizophrenia, those were sure-fire signs that the abundant-life blessing of God was surely not on him!"

"How did they die, then?"

He shrugged. "One night, Father torched our house. Took a bottle of pills while the rest of us were sleeping. Couldn't handle what his life had amounted to, we figured, and wanted to take us all down with him. We would have died along with them, but Paulina saw the fire and got us out before it all collapsed. We were the only survivors, and Unky Benji took us in, giving us a second-chance life."

Torres asked, "Is that how you got those burns on your hand, why you keep it covered?"

Dexter glanced down at his naked hand, white glove removed. Massaging it, he nodded, saying nothing more.

"Given all your uncle has done for you," Celeste said, "I can understand why Paulina would go to such lengths to help him. To ensure he himself regained the health he offered others."

"She was very attached to him—*is* very attached," Dexter corrected. "Anyway, apparently the idea was to make the world sick enough to need our services, so that they would come flocking like they used to in Unky Benji's glory days. Then we'd make enough money to find a cure and save his life. But..." He paused, taking a stabilizing breath. "But it got away from us, from Paulina."

Torres smirked. "I'd say."

"The entire world is on lockdown now," Celeste said, "and reeling from a contagion that has caused real harm to people!"

"What do you want me to do about it? What's done is done. I'm sick about it, I really am! Besides, she's got the whole plan worked out. It's going off without a hitch. And I've been side-lined from the get go, not knowing the extent of it." He ran a frustrated hand through his hair, eyes brimming with a surprising rise in emotion. "She forged ahead at the request of Unky Benji himself, who thought I was too soft. Wouldn't get on board with it all. I suppose he was right..."

"But you can help, don't you see?" Torres said, stepping toward him.

"What do you propose?"

She glanced at Celeste, an idea percolating within. Her partner flashed her a smile and nodded her onward.

So she went for it, explaining the plan that would bring this whole thing to an end.

And expose the Bucks for the crooks they were.

CHAPTER 31

"Where is my cotton-pickin' brother?"

Paulina paced the backstage, waiting to greet the crowds in Mumbai for the second faith-healing service. The high-noon sun was pivoting toward the horizon now, but Dexter was nowhere to be found. Going on twenty-four hours now. And no one knew where he was.

Not least of all her.

The piece of work had stormed off the stage yesterday midway through the first service, right before it got good! After his half-hearted performance, he slipped out the back as the actual healing part to the service started, hundreds of thousands of Indians flooding the stage to receive their abundant-life blessing. The blind, the deaf, the paralyzed and wheelchair bound had dutifully lined up to receive their healing touch from the Bucks twins that had gone viral across WeShare—emptying their supply of the Lord's Supper.

All of it had worked like clockwork, the throngs practically shoveling their life savings at Paulina and her volunteers to get their hands on the bread-cup elements. The packages that held the cure for the blindness, and deafness, and paralysis that had hit Mumbai particularly hard. Which made sense, given they were one of the original testing sites for the brilliant plan to become the premier Christian healers of the world, a destination for the destitute, offering hope to the hopeless. After all, if one could put a pandemic to rest, what couldn't they do?

The festivities had gone without a hitch, hundreds of thousands getting healed of *nervirus*—as expected. Reports of the blind seeing, the deaf hearing, and the paralyzed casting aside their wheelchairs spread across WeShare like wildfire. They were going to be rich. More importantly, with all that money Unky Benji would get the cure he needed. He would live!

And Dexter wasn't around for any of it.

He'd been acting funny all morning after he'd spouted off during their drive from the airport to the hotel. He didn't stop at the hotel, going about how they were taking advantage of the desperate, giving them false hope.

Freakin' bleeding heart! After all, they had been through together, after all they had accomplished. Not only giving hope to the hopeless, and putting their future ministry on a surer footing. But more importantly for their uncle.

Receipts were still coming in, but already it was obvious they had taken their largest haul ever—even surpassing Unky Benji in his ministry endeavors.

Cresting the million-dollar threshold by a mile!

Between that and today, she and her brother were set to haul in a multi seven-figure payload, maybe even eight— enabling them to pay for the research and experimental gene therapy cure that would keep Unky Benji alive.

But Dexter was nowhere to be found! He hadn't come home last night and wasn't answering his phone. No one on her staff had seen neither hide nor hair of the man. The band was winding down for their appearance, and they were expected soon. She couldn't do it alone; she'd never done anything without her brother, her twin, her soulmate!

What was she going to do?

Paulina threw back a swig of champagne she had been nursing from all morning waiting for her brother to show. She resumed her pacing, whipping out her phone and readying herself to send a text pleading for Dex to answer.

When she heard a familiar voice rise from behind.

Her heart leapt, breath catching in her throat, head filling with adrenaline delight at the turn.

Spinning toward the newcomer, her eyes pricked with emotion and throat clenched with the same. Nearly dropped the glass at the sight of her brother standing there, wearing his trademark skinny jeans and V-neck, decked out in gold chains and that chunky watch Unky Benji had gifted him at twenty-one.

"Dex..."

A part of Paulina wanted to walk over and slap his face with what he'd put her through, an anger rising within her at his antics! But she didn't, she couldn't. She held it together, downing the rest of her champagne, setting her glass down on a table, and sauntered over.

"Nice of you to show up, Dex."

"Sissy!" he ran over and threw his arms around her. "I am so sorry for being so MIA."

She returned the embrace, but noted how different it felt. He was guarded, body separate from hers. There was a stiffness to it, a reluctance even, as if he were putting on a front, a show. It didn't make sense.

Paulina's head swirled with what she was sensing as he explained where he had been.

"I had to take a walk and clear my head."

She pulled away, folding her arms. "That was some walk! And how could you abandon me like that, letting me run the show all alone?"

"I know," he moaned, twisting his face up with what came across as regret. "I was a jerk for leaving you in the ditch like that. But I suppose after the past two weeks, and with the emotion of Unky Benji's illness, I needed a breather."

She held his gaze, face flat and unemotional, not giving an inch of sympathy or forgiveness. He would have to work hard for both…

"Go on," she nodded.

He took a breath. "Walking the streets of Mumbai, I came to realize you were right. We are giving people hope. And isn't that the best gift to give?"

She loosened some, Dex looking like he'd returned to his senses. "When did you return? I checked in on you last night and you were still out. I was worried sick!"

Dexter frowned, looking like he was moving in for another embrace. But Paulina took a step back. Wasn't going to happen.

"It was after midnight some time."

"I waited up till two!"

"Must have been after that."

"But I didn't hear you come in, and you know how light a sleeper I am. Doesn't make—"

"I don't know, alright!" he interrupted with frustration.

He took a breath and apologized; Paulina let it go.

"Then where were you this morning? Searched for you before the show."

Dexter ran a hand through his hair, averting his eyes. "Left early again. More soul searching."

Paulina went to respond when a cheer was thrown up, and the bandleader gave a boisterous *'Hallelujah!'* followed by: *'Are you ready for your breakthrough day?'*

More cheering, another *'Hallelujah!'*, this time from the united crowd, right before the familiar chorus broke out that was their cue.

There was something about his answers that was off, and concerning. But Paulina couldn't worry about that now. Time to make magic again.

"I suppose that's our cue," Dexter said softly, face downcast and shoulders slumped.

Paulina extended a hand. "Suppose it is."

He smiled at the gesture and took it with his white-gloved hand. She squeezed it thrice, the Morse Code of their relationship.

I. Love. You.

He responded in kind, squeezing it four times.

They grinned at each other. He was back.

Dexter said, "Best get to it."

"For Unky Benji," said Paulina.

Then they walked out to get into place.

Showtime...

———

Torres rolled her eyes and sighed. There was that *muy loco* chorus again.

> *Breakthrough, breakthrough, breakthrough-oo-oo.*
> *Breakthrough, breakthrough, breakthrough-oo-oo.*
> *Breakthrough, breakthrough, breakthrough-oo-oo.*

If the cancer didn't kill her, that chorus sure might. And yet...

She glanced behind her at the hundreds of thousands of people singing and dancing to the tune, all hoping and praying it would be their very own breakthrough day. Where the heavens parted and God's abundant-life blessing broke through into their lives, making them healthy, wealthy, and wise.

It was a day very much like the one she and her parents had shown up to. Bright and sunny and full of hope and expectation. Papa expecting a new promotion and healing for his bride; Mama mostly going along to humor and support her husband, but secretly expecting at least some answer to prayer for the longings of her own heart.

And look where it got them...

Sometimes it took everything in Torres not to just give up on faith—on God, when it seemed like her prayers went unanswered, and the fallenness of the world seemed to overwhelm her without any sign of God's miracle-powers; on the Church, when *muy loco idiota pastores* took advantage of the hopes and fears of desperate people like her parents, like herself, in order to build their platform and pad their bank accounts.

There was a grunting heave-ho behind her as Gapinski set down a large wicker basket on the ground near the stage. Silas and Celeste were hustling back to their position at stage left after having dropped off their own package.

"Everything all set?" Torres asked Gapinski.

Heaving a breath, he wiped his brow and grumbled, "Could have used a helping hand, sister, but yeah, we're set."

"We dropped off our package at our end," Silas said, coming up with Celeste, Peter Young having stayed back in Mill Creek.

Torres nodded, her stomach a bundle of nerves. It was a daring move, one that might have far-ranging consequences. But so be it. She knew it was what was needed to bring the whole house of Bucks cards to the ground. Knew it was necessary to make them atone for what they had done across the world.

What Bucks senior had done to her parents, even.

The song ended and out strode the twins, their designer outfits and perfect hair and waving hands throwing up a cheer from the crowd.

Showtime...

"I suppose this is it," Gapinski said.

"Suppose so," Torres said, playing with the orange lanyard complements of Dexter. The other SEPIO agents wore the same around their necks, marking them out as Bucks volunteers and giving them full access to the grounds.

And enabling them to execute what came next.

"You sure about this?" Celeste asked, comment more directed toward Silas than Torres, who had come up with the idea.

He took a breath, glancing at the large basket Gapinski had dragged over and back at the one they'd dropped off. Thought he might pull the plug on the whole shebang, then and there.

But he didn't.

Silas said, "It's the only way to go." Then he nodded toward the stage and added, "Besides, no going back now."

"Good afternoon, Mumbai!" shouted Paulina with gleaming teeth, her one hand gripping a handheld mic and the other working the crowd.

Dexter was beside her doing the same, playing the part Torres prayed he was still up to playing.

"What do y'all want?" he called out. "What do y'all want, I ask? Call out your deepest desires to the Lord this day. For today is your breakthrough day!"

A few voices began rising, scattered throughout the vast grounds. But then more followed, with shouts of a house and a job, healing from blindness and cancer, the voices collecting into a magnificent roar rippling throughout the field.

Torres's stomach lurched at the adulations. They had no idea...

"Amen," Dexter said, nodding and pointing out into the crowd. "Amen. Well, I'm here to tell y'all this day that by right, those desires of your heart are y'alls because of the cross! And we apprehend those cross-shaped blessings by celebrating their memory markers."

"That's right, brother!" Paulina said, taking over. "Every malignant power aligned against y'all is broken by the cross. For by his stripes—"

She turned the microphone toward the crowd, who dutifully shouted back: *'we are healed!!'*

Gapinski snorted a laugh. "Fat chance of that today."

Torres ribbed him to shut up; he yelped and apologized.

"That is right, Mumbai!" she shouted, a hand raised and eyes closed. "Every enemy that is aligned against y'all, let the Lord strike the ground for y'alls children with victory!"

She stepped toward the stage, face twisting up and body leaning toward the audience with the same ecstatic posture she posed last go around.

"I hear a sound of abundance of rain," she began. "I hear a sound of victory."

"Blimey, she's at it again," Celeste complained.

"I hear a sound of shouting and singing, I hear a sound of victory. I hear a sound of an abundance of rain, I hear a sound of victory!"

"Sounds like MC Hammer on crack," Gapinski said, "with a dose of the Spice Girls added into the mix."

Torres threw him a glance, but he pretty well put his finger on it!

Suddenly, there were those utterances they'd heard before: *"Hamanda-acha-atta-starrracha-bacca-honda-rrratta-atta-santa-anda-batta-ossa-macha-ratta-honda-santa-richa."*

Now joined by a whole host of others who had been trained in the finer art of speaking in tongues!

"For I hear the sound of victory," Paulina went on, "I hear the sound of victory!"

"That's right," Dexter said, stepping next to his sister to take over. "We break and divide every demonic confederacy against y'alls bodies, against Mumbai and across the world. Against this contagion that y'all have declared through the cross of Jesus!"

The Bucks and the praise team struck up another song, something called "Shout unto God" that gloried in Satan's defeat and announced Christ's victory over death, imploring the Christian to *"lift our voice in victory over every infirmity!"*

This went on for several minutes, Torres tuning it out and waiting for what they came for.

The climactic resolution to this whole sorry saga.

As the song closed, Dexter paced the stage. The blond man looked out at the crowd, his mouth curling with satisfaction. He gripped the mic with one hand and wiped his forehead with the other, saying, "I was going to close right now, but is anyone having back pain?"

Dozens of hands went up. Which wasn't a surprise in the slightest. Who didn't have back pain in this modern world hunched over in front of a computer all day and craning toward their phones?

"What about blindness and deafness?" he went on.

Even more hands raised, and then more yet when he asked about paralysis.

Again, not a surprise in the slightest, given Mumbai was a super-spreading epicenter of the contagion he and his sister had unleashed on the world. Which Dexter was now readying to remedy.

Or so they all thought...

A familiar gilded table was brought out and placed at the center of the stage, the gleaming gold draped by a pure white linen runner with a loaf of bread and jewel-encrusted goblet of wine sitting on top.

"As has been the case in all our services," Dexter said, holding up the loaf now, "we raise up these elements of the cross, the Body and Blood of Christ, to—" the man faltered, seemingly unable to do what he was being called to do. He cleared his throat and continued, "to, well, pave the way for y'alls healing."

He set down the loaf, saying nothing more.

Dios mío...

"What's wrong?" Silas said.

"Cold feet?" Celeste asked.

Torres shrugged, saying lowly, "Stay the course, Dexter..."

"I just hope he doesn't derail the plan," Silas said, face hard and skeptical now.

She nodded, noticing Paulina's face had faltered, a crease flashing across her forehead and mouth frowning before grinning widely and taking over.

"That's right, brother," she said, grabbing the goblet. "Celebrating this Christian rite brings healing power out of the spirit realm and into this one. Y'all have access to the same power of Jesus Christ himself, who healed the lame and leper, the blind and deaf—y'all can participate in y'alls healing!"

Grabbing the loaf, she walked to the edge of the stage, her favorite perch before her audience. Dexter stayed behind, watching from afar.

She went on, "The whole purpose of celebrating the Lord's Supper is to bring healing to your body. It is one of the largest kept secrets of the Kingdom of God, that these elements—the literal blood and body of Christ have been gifted to us to combat the destruction of our bodies by disease and decay!"

A cheer rose from the crowd, clearly agreeing with her and ready to receive the healing touch she promised.

"It is the will of the Lord Almighty—not only that, but the absolute *right* by the cross of Christ that y'all be healed one-hundred percent of the time! Jesus paid too great a price for y'all to continue to wallow in sickness and disease."

Another bout of *amens* and *hallelujahs*! The crowd pressed closer toward the stage now, chomping at the bit for the memory markers that would bring their healing.

"Your right is to have blessed bodies, blessed families, blessed bank accounts—your blessed life now! Beginning with the end to this dreaded contagion that has plagued Mumbai and the rest of the world—" Paulina turned to Dexter now, face faltering again. "He took our infirmities, he bore our sickness. By his stripes we are healed. Isn't that right, brother?"

It was as if she had woken him from a dream, the man snapping back into the moment. He took a halting step, as if willing himself back into the ring. But he got back in, and got to it, sealing the deal.

"Jesus is your personal savior," Dexter said, at Paulina's side again, "who physically experienced and conquered every ache and pain, every blind eye and deaf ear, every lost limb and treacherous tumor! Which means Jesus' pain and victory over these devilish elements of the world are y'alls! So embrace it this day. For today is your breakthrough day!"

Paulina was gleaming again, raising the elements before the crowd. Dexter had regained her confidence.

"So come!" she shouted. "Come as you are to receive your healing, to step into your breakthrough day! At the stage on either side are baskets full of the elements remembering Christ's death. So sow your best seed-gift to the Lord, then eat and drink from the Lord's Table—for by it you will be healed!"

Torres sucked in a stabilizing breath, feeling like she was going to pass out.

Silas leaned over. "Here we go..."

She nodded. It was showtime as much as go time.

For the second time.

Only *Jesucristo* knew what came next...

CHAPTER 32

Paulina had come up for air from a gauntlet of intercessory prayer and apostolic hand-laying, speaking Spirit-filled words over people and activating the abundant-life blessings of the Lord unleashed by the cross.

That's when she knew there was a problem.

The first wave of desperate people looking for a cure to their blindness and deafness and paralysis had come across the stage the past hour. Just as before, they had flocked to the side stairways leading up to the stage, dropping off envelopes filled with their seed-gifts—some thin, many thick, no doubt with both US dollars and rupees that would have to be converted, but still a hopeful sign. Volunteers handed out the prepackaged communion elements, laced with the antidote that would trigger the cypher to decode the virus and unlock the cure to the handful of neurological disorders that had plagued the people of Mumbai the past few weeks.

Except nothing was happening; it wasn't working.

The blind weren't being restored to sight. The deaf weren't getting their hearing back. The limbs of the paralyzed weren't reactivating.

It just flat wasn't working, wasn't *healing*!

Which meant the Bucks weren't healing, neither her nor her brother...

A far bigger deal for the future of their ministry.

Of *her* ministry.

And her Unky Benji's...

Yet they continued to flock, the Indian men and women, even children flooding the stage to sow their seed and receive their abundant-life blessing.

At first, Paulina thought it was simply a delayed response, or perhaps those who'd ingested the original serum causing their neurological disorder simply hadn't reached the stage yet. Their antidote would only work on the infected, not the everyday diseases that afflicted the masses.

But the longer the afternoon stretched on, and the more people left the stage without a sudden miraculous healing from the Lord, a worm of worry began winding itself through Paulina, spreading a cold dread across her body and blooming in her head with dizzying fear.

Finally she broke away from the huddled masses waiting to touch her cloak. "I don't understand..." she muttered on her way to pull Dexter aside. "Why isn't it working?"

Pushing through a bunched line just coming on the stage, the men and women rushing to pop their cracker and throw back their juice, she reached her brother and gently pulled him away from the middle of an intercessory prayer session.

She led him toward the back of the stage, the twins disappearing behind the drum cage as a man with long hair rapped contemplatively on the snare and a guitar strummed on.

"What's the matter?" he asked, licking his lips and picking at his white glove.

Paulina frowned, nodding out toward the stage. "That!"

His eyes darted, but he didn't look. Just folded his arms and shifted to a back leg, playing with that glove again while biting his lower lip now.

As if he knew what she was getting at without saying it.

As if there was something he wasn't saying...

"Dex!" Paulina shouted, the man snapping his head up with a start.

"What?"

She scoffed. "What? That's all you have to say? We've been at this almost an hour, and no one is getting better. No one's recovering!"

"I know, I see it!"

Paulina didn't understand. What did he mean, he saw it? What was his deal?

"Well, what do you make of it?" she snapped, losing patience. "What the heck is going on?"

He went to say something, but didn't. As if he were about to answer her question, explaining it even, but deciding against it. Just stood there, hanging his head again and playing with that damn glove.

Now that worm of worry was blooming into full-on panic. Because not only were they not producing the results the huddled masses on the stage expected—what they themselves expected. It seemed like Dex was holding something back.

That he knew why...

She took a step toward him. "Dex...what's going on? What aren't you telling me?"

He bit his lower lip hard now, teeth marks showing pale against his crimson skin.

Then he took a breath and slowly looked Paulina in the face. "Paulina...there's something I need to tell you."

Her stomach sank, her heart nearly stopped. Dex rarely called her by her first name. It was Sissy or Pauli. Never Paulina.

Heat raced up her neck and bloomed in her head, her clenched jaw sending a ratcheting tremor of rage through her.

"What have you done, baby brother?"

———

Torres saw the argument unfolding from the stage-left stairs, a pair of volunteers having taken over the distribution of the elements at their end while SEPIO waited for it all to unfold.

And unfold it did, the huddled masses of expectant sick all leaving disappointed. Not a single one healed from their blindness, deafness, and paralysis.

Which meant it was true, they were right. The Lord's Supper contained the antidote to the global contagion, triggering the healing the Bucks promised had come from the Lord. In reality, it simply undid what they themselves had given to people.

Same false hope spoon-fed to *Papá y Mamá*, just a different vehicle.

"Somebody sure doesn't look too happy," Silas said, nodding toward backstage.

Celeste nodded. "No, she certainly does not."

Dexter had helped SEPIO secure a batch of the prepackaged Lord's Supper elements without the antidote, leaving all those affected by the contagion unhealed. Completely blowing up their operation. Torres guessed he was spilling the beans. And Paulina was becoming unhinged.

Paulina shoved her brother in the chest, the man stumbling backward but keeping upright.

Gapinski laughed, bringing a fist to his mouth. "That sister packs a punch!"

"Perhaps it's time to come clean," Torres said. "After all, Dexter shouldn't be the only one holding the bag on this one."

"I don't know. After all he's done, I'd say we let the bro get smacked around some more."

"Naomi's right," Silas said. "Time to bring this to an end."

"Finally!"

He nodded, leading the SEPIO crew up the stairs.

Squeezing past a packed group of men and women, blind by the look of it, and much to their protests, the agents hustled up on stage and hanged a sharp right down long, heavy black curtains suspended up above, rounding piles of sound equipment and making for the pair in a heated argument now.

"Do you realize what this will cost Unky Benji!" Paulina screamed, slamming her hands against Dexter's chest again. "His life, that's what!"

"And you can thank us for that," Silas said, coming up quick behind Paulina, startling her with a jolt.

She spun around, eyes going wide and face twisting up with confusion. "You're not supposed to be back here. Who the heck are y'all?"

"Just your resident party crashes," Gapinski said, "here to spoil your fun."

Silas threw him a frown and went to answer when Torres stepped up to the plate instead. "We're the reason your little grift has run its course, not Dexter."

She turned to him. "What are they talking about?"

"It's not important who we are," Silas answered. "What's important is that we know all about what you've done. Spreading the neural contagion through the products of your Comida holding corporation. Using it to manufacture the antidote key you hid away in the prepackaged Lord's Supper elements."

A surprised gasp seeped from her parted lips, her jaw moving up and down searching for words. None came.

"It's over *muchacha*," Torres said, taking a step toward the woman with narrowed eyes. "Including the way you've polluted people's minds as much as their bodies with your lies and deception, their very souls even by peddling a false gospel that makes Jesus' good news out to be a play for the middle-class American dream."

"But it is!" Paulina shouted. "Jesus offers us abundant life—"

"For eternity!" Silas said. "Nothing in Scripture says our faith or our confession rubs God's genie bottle to guarantee some abundant life of health and wealth. That's what you've gotten wrong all these weeks, the lie your Unky Benji has told—"

Paulina lunged for Silas now, smacking him in the chest. "You leave my uncle out of this!"

Torres jumped in front of him before she could go for round two—less to defend the chief and more to confront the woman who represented the threat who had brought her family to ruin.

"Back up, *idiota*! Your lying days have come to an end."

The woman threw her hands on top of her head, as if it were spinning from the turn. It probably was!

"But it's not a lie!" she shouted. "We offer people the hope they can change their circumstances, to trigger God's blessings and—"

"Only God is sovereign, and he chooses whom he blesses! We're not, we don't. You people take God's sovereignty and throw it out the window, insisting we can control God. Which is just so arrogant, the idea that we humans can make God tap to our tune, that we can heal and get rich at our command."

Rage arose in Torres. The pent-up anger lying dormant from decades ago that awakened when this whole mission started began boiling over now.

"That's right," Silas said, leaning in. "And we're going to let them all know what you've done, exposing you and your uncle as the frauds you are."

He turned to leave when Torres grabbed his arm.

"Let me do it," she said. "Let me expose them, tell the world what's what."

Silas hesitated, glancing at Celeste for confirmation.

"She can handle it," she said. "It's the right thing to do."

Sure was. The best thing to do, given her experience with the Bucks and her own experience with the fruits of the fallen world.

Silas flashed her a smile and nodded.

"No—" Paulina lunged for Torres, but was restrained by Silas and Celeste.

Dexter walked up to Torres, handing her a mic. "Take this. You'll need it."

"Shut her down!" his sister screamed at a pair of stagehands working the sound equipment.

"No!" Dexter shouted back, the poor pair caught between dueling siblings. "Don't you dare touch those controls!"

They backed off, disappearing into the darkened backstage void.

"Dex..." Paulina moaned, sobbing now even as she still struggled between Silas and Celeste's grip. "Please, stop them!"

"You better get to it," Silas said to Torres. "We may not be able to hold her off, with the way she's fighting!"

And she was, gnashing her teeth and bucking wildly to get out from under their grip. Looked possessed is what she looked!

"Yeah, go get 'em, She-Ra Turner!" Gapinski said.

Torres took a breath and nodded, spinning toward the stage and dashing out to destiny.

Didn't know what she was doing, not in the slightest. Had always been afraid of public speaking. Yet there she was, pushing through a line of people out toward the edge of the stage to put to rest the ridiculous notion people could muscle their way to prosperity by putting God on puppet strings.

Paulina was screaming from behind, the woman clearly seeing the house of cards collapse around her. She was hysterical, launching into those weird tongues she'd heard twice now.

But Torres pushed it out of her mind, stepping out in front

as people continued swirling around her with desperation, prayers and tongues and songs being thrown up in petition for the health and wealth they so desperately wanted.

Drawing the mic to her mouth, Torres cleared her throat. "Can I have your attention?"

A bout of feedback screeched from the speakers anchored at both sides, blaring across the field. Thought the mic would give out, and the climax to her mission cut short, but the feed held.

She offered a nervous giggle. "Sorry about that. Anyway, my name is Naomi, and I have an announcement."

Torres took a breath, letting the air hang as people turned their attention toward her, confused murmurs settling into a silent intrigue.

Then she went for it: "It's all been a lie. The Bucks are a sham."

A blood-curdling *"Nooooooo!!"* was thrown up behind. Torres looked back to find the woman clawing her way out of Silas and Celeste's grip, clearly unhinged and nearly succeeding in her escape.

Pressing on, Torres explained, "In fact, they've been poisoning you for weeks with the junk food they make through their Comida food company." More startled voices raced through the audience, a panicked head of steam building now. "That's right. The Bucks created the *nervirus* contagion and put it inside our food! They also created the only antidote, which they stuffed inside the Lord's Supper—the cracker and juice they've handed out each service. For a price."

The thought of the desperate lie her parents believed seized Torres, emotion rising up her throat and to her eyes.

"So I am sorry, but your blindness, deafness, paralysis—it was all a hoax. A deadly one, selling an equally deadly hope."

Utter confusion now enveloped the stage and the field of

bodies out front. So Torres launched into an explanation of all that SEPIO had discovered the past week.

Voices rose in a torrent of indecision and doubt, the gathered mass of the desperate unsure whether to believe this foreigner or not—perhaps their faith in God's healing hope crumbling in the face of the deadly lie.

"I'm living proof it was all a sham, because I have cancer and the Bucks didn't heal me. I took the same communion elements, and they didn't work. All of this is no surprise, because the entire operation was a long con meant to bilk you out of your money in order to rake in the millions to keep their uncle from dying."

This seemed to give the audience pause, the desperate quieting some and giving her their attention.

"That's right. The king of prosperity has a degenerative disease. Which goes to show how much his teachings were ridiculous! The prosperity gospel teaches that God is like some sort of cosmic, magic genie who will grant our wishes and every one of our fanciful, selfish whims. Yet Benji couldn't make it happen, even for himself!"

Another murmur ricocheted across the crowd, the people thrown into bewilderment at the turn.

"What's worse," Torres continued, "is that they promise Jesus' death wasn't merely about providing eternal blessing, but that it guarantees earthly riches. All you need is faith to tap into what Christ has paid for on the cross. Perhaps this is the most demonic lie of all, taking the matchless, precious work of Jesus on the cross for our sins and eternal salvation, and turning it into a mere down payment for the fleeting things of this life—a car, a white picket fence, a sack of *pesos*."

People were leaving now, but Torres wasn't through. She needed to get through to them and share what her own father had missed.

"The Bucks teach that God wants you to be healthy, so just

believe that health into existence. God wants you wealthy, so just speak your money into your bank account. They say God wants you to have a comfortable, easy life, and what you confess controls how that life unfolds. Perhaps the most despicable claim is that God sent Jesus to die for your abundant life, so it's already yours. That Jesus paid for your literal monetary debt so you can be debt free. That's not Jesus' good news!"

Some people stayed and listened, others continued to stream out, not wanting to hear what she was saying. She didn't know what to do.

Turning behind, she caught Silas nodding her onward, as well as Celeste and Gapinski, her SEPIO teammates encouraging her to keep going even as Paulina was on the floor sobbing hysterically now.

Taking a breath, and taking courage from her friends, Torres turned back to the audience.

"We can't earn salvation by praying enough or working hard enough, by giving away enough money to make God bow to our wishes like some magic genie! Christian faith isn't about paying some user fee for Jesus' crazy love. It's turning away from our sins and turning to Christ, believing he is the Son of God and we are in desperate need of his rescue—that we are helpless to do what only he could provide."

She was losing them. Only one more shot to offer the real hope of Jesus.

"Let's be real: Sometimes life bites the big one. It sucks. And it's OK to say that! This world isn't the way it's supposed to be. People get sick and die. People starve and lose their jobs. We've all got unfulfilled desires, our lives seem so meaningless. In this life we'll have troubles, heartaches—which God cares about and fixes according to his plan! But our true hope is that Jesus has conquered it all through his death and resurrection. While we may suffer or not make bank, we know that Jesus understands our pain and his gift of new life will last for eternity."

There wasn't anything more to say. What's done was done, and she'd have to trust the Holy Spirit to do the rest.

Turning back, she rejoined her SEPIO teammates.

Just as Paulina broke free!

Socked Silas real good in the gut, then took a swipe at Celeste, catching her in the face before scurrying away. Gapinski tried to grab her, but she slipped away.

Torres ran after her, coming up to Silas, but he grabbed her.

"It's alright," Silas said, hand on her arm. "Let her go."

"But we need to stop her!" Torres pleaded, breaking free before Celeste put up a staying hand.

"Silas is right, mate. Paulina's done for anyway."

"She won't get far," Gapinski said. "After all, there's about to be an INTERPOL warrant out to arrest her ass."

Torres wasn't happy, not in the slightest. But she figured they were right. What was the use when she knew the Bucks's empire was toast, and the authorities would surely make her pay.

The SEPIO agents watched her disappear through a back door, the same one Torres and Celeste had gone through to chase after Dexter, bringing this whole sorry saga to a close.

"So none of what we've witnessed," Celeste said, "had anything to do with a vast, global conspiracy to undermine the Christian faith and destroy the Church?"

"Not this time, at least," Silas said. "And I must say, I'm somewhat relieved the usual suspects were far from this one."

"Not least of which was your brother, Sebastian, I am sure."

He nodded, saying nothing but everyone knew the truth of it. For now he wasn't involved, neither Nous nor that *muy loco* Theoti upstart sect.

Torres added, "Just some scheme to rake in the millions."

"All about the Benjamins," Gapinski agreed.

"For Benjamin Bucks."

"You couldn't script a better made-for-streaming movie!"

Silas nodded. "Ain't that the truth."

Gapinski said, "Hey, you don't suppose we could sell the streaming rights, do you? We'd make bank!"

"*Gapinski!*" SEPIO moaned as one.

"Just sayin'!"

"What do we do about them?" Torres nodded toward the field now clearing of the disappointed men and women who had come for the Lord's healing touch.

Dexter came up to join the group, face gaunt and ashen. "We'll fully cooperate with the World Health Organization to distribute the antidote to those who came today for healing, but didn't get it. Everyone who had gotten sick because of the Comida virus will have access to the antidote."

Silas stepped toward him, putting out his hand. "Thanks for your help, we couldn't have pulled this off without you."

Dexter eyed the gesture and received it, face brightening some but also glistening with emotion at the eyes. "I just cannot believe Paulina went to such lengths."

"When it comes to family," Celeste offered, "what wouldn't most of us do to help a dying loved one?"

Gapinski snorted a laugh. "Not sure unleashing a contagion on the world and sparking another global pandemic rises to most people's to-do lists for our dying relatives!"

"Fair enough, but I'm sure many of us would go pretty far to get them the help they need."

Torres thought about her father, how Papá had brought Mapá to the Bucks circus way back when. How he gave up their life savings to get the help she needed, however much he was grasping at the straws of hope. Look what he had done for his bride, and how it had ended.

She was just thankful she could play a role in getting justice for her parents—for the false hope Benji Bucks had peddled.

And stoping anyone else from getting hurt by that false gospel. That deadly hope.

CHAPTER 33

Silas navigated the hospital corridors with all the grace and dexterity of a fish flopping around on a dock. Hated hospitals; always had. Probably brought on by his trauma in Iraq recovering in an Army field hospital after his buddy was blown to bits.

But there he was, carrying a beautiful bouquet of pink gerbera daisies and blooming white lilies, on his way to meet his crew who had already arrived to sit with their teammate as she stared down the chemotherapy barrel.

Place smelled like antiseptic wipes and Pine-Sol, joined by the metallic tang of stainless steel and probably blood. But he didn't want to think about that one. His mind was set on one thing, and one thing only: hustling to the room at the end of the hallway on the fourth floor of the oncology ward to support Torres. A few days ago, she underwent surgery to remove the tumor, and now was receiving adjuvant chemotherapy to try to kill any remaining cancer cells that might have been left behind or had spread but couldn't be seen otherwise.

Pushing through a wood door, he arrived at the chemotherapy infusion suite to find rows of dark gray chairs occupied by men and women with tubes coming out from them. Some still had hair; others didn't. Some wore their hairless crown proudly, without embarrassment, almost as a badge of honor; others tried covering up their misery and humiliation with bandanas of various shades and patterns.

The place was surprisingly bright, a bank of windows to the right behind the chairs overlooking a garden full of flowering trees and other greenery, even a bubbling waterfall, all adding a degree of cheer to the gloom. It also helped that the walls were painted a sprightly sky blue with some sort of white silhouette flowery, viny decorations across the walls. Looked more like a day spa than a chemotherapy suite. Which Silas gathered was sort of the point.

Each suite was separated by a curtain for privacy, with the oversized recliners looking out at the gardens. Stepping in farther, he glanced around the spacious room of sixteen suites searching for his teammates.

A belly laugh followed by a familiar chide with an English lilt drew him to the back corner. Gapinski and Celeste.

Silas hustled back and parted a curtain to find Torres sitting in one of the gray recliners. Tubes were snaking out from under her shirt, with the two other SEPIO agents flanking her on either side. Peter Young was standing off behind her, having flown in after surgery to pay a visit. His breath was taken away by a sight he did not expect.

Torres was bald. Head shaved close to the scalp. At least he assumed it had been shaved, since she had only just begun chemotherapy.

"Like my new hairdo, chief?" Torres asked with a smile, cupping her hands behind her ears, as if supporting non-existent curls.

Silas smiled back and approached. "As beautiful as ever, Naomi."

"I said she looked like my memaw," Gapinski offered, "after

she tried some mail-order hair dye that made her hair fall out. Warned her teeth would be next if she wasn't careful."

"To which," Celeste said, "I promptly told him to mind his manners."

Torres added, "And I told him he was the one who was gonna lose his teeth if he wasn't careful!"

Gapinski took a step back. "And I know you could make good on that promise, too. Regardless of whether you just had surgery and chemo!"

"Damn straight."

The group laughed, and Silas appreciated the banter. Good to know Torres was in good spirits after all she'd been through.

"Are those gerbera daisies?" Torres asked, shifting in her chair.

Silas handed the flowers over. "Thought you could use some color, considering."

"*Gracias*, Silas." Torres took them and smiled, bringing them to her face. "*Muy hermosas flores.*"

"Yes, very beautiful, love," Celeste said with a wink.

He nodded and crossed his arms, not knowing what to say. He went with, "I heard surgery went well."

Torres nodded. "It did. My doctor said they were sure they got all the cancer, that it hadn't spread." She held up one of the tubes filled with yellow liquid and added, "This is for insurance."

"Right. Well, I'm just glad you caught it in time and we've got all this science to get you back in the game."

"You and me both."

"A bummer you had to go through it to begin with, though," Gapinski said. "The whole, why do bad things happen to good people conundrum."

"I'm not sure God has anything to do with it," Celeste said. "Or rather, God shouldn't get the blame. We live in a fallen world, unfortunately. It's broken, we're broken. But thankfully God holds our future."

"Amen to that," Peter said. "And not to get my preach on, or anything, but isn't that what this whole crazy mission was about the past week?"

"How so?"

"If I may," Silas interjected, to which Peter nodded him to continue. "I've been thinking about this the last week, and what was missing from all those revival meetings we went to, what the Bucks didn't say."

"And what was that?" Gapinski asked.

"The good news of God's sovereignty."

"The good news of God's sovereignty?" Torres asked, shifting again in her chair and wincing this time. "What do you mean by that?"

"God's sovereignty means he's all-powerful, that he's still in control when life goes off the rails."

"Like when a global contagion rears its ugly head?" Gapinski asked.

Silas nodded. "Exactly. Yes, our time on earth right now will be chaotic. There will be pain and agony and it will seem like it runs rampant, without any direction from the Lord. Some of us will get cancer."

Torres nodded, as did Peter, who apparently had his own run in with the disease.

"Some of us have lost loved ones, parents and grandparents." Like Silas had, and Gapinski. "The thing is, our lives are just a blip compared with eternity, and the eternality of God and his sovereign plan."

"Which means if you put it in perspective to our ultimate destiny," Peter added, "the infinite number of years we will spend on the new earth that provides all the healing, riches, and glory we could ever want makes whatever sickness or poverty we might endure now seem like a pittance—especially when we consider our life spent with Jesus."

"Exactly."

"That's the point I wanted to make earlier," Peter went on, "About what we learned a week ago. No matter what we face in this life, God controls it all. Like you said, Silas. There is no reason we cannot trust in his promises for a restored, brand-spanking new future that is far better than what we have now. After all, we know the end of the story."

"What story?" Gapinski asked.

"*The* story! Our human one."

"Oh…"

"Revelation 21 reminds us that Jesus will one day *'wipe every tear from their eyes. Death will be no more; mourning and crying and pain will be no more, for the first things have passed away.'*"

"Which means no more cancer or contagions." Silas said.

Peter nodded. "Don't know about you, but I can't wait for that day. Until then, we wait, in faith."

"Amen to that."

"Spoken like a true pastor," Celeste said. "Mill Creek Junction is fortunate to have you."

"Here, here!" Gapinski said.

Peter chuckled, his cheeks flushing as he ran a hand through his hair. "I don't know about that."

"*Si*, pastor," Torres said. "I agree. *Gracias.*"

He smiled and nodded.

"As do I," Silas said. "And you make a damn-fine SEPIO agent, too."

"Double here, here!" Gapinski said, Celeste and Torres amening in agreement.

Now Peter laughed. "Now I definitely don't know about that!"

Silas said, "Thanks to you, we stopped a bunch of charismatic lunatics from destroying the world and undermining the faith!" He extended his hand, adding, "You're welcome to submit your application to the Order anytime you'd like."

Peter shook it. "I'll pray about that, but I'm pretty sure the Holy Spirit's plan for my life doesn't involve anymore shootouts and exploding factories."

"We'll see about that!"

Silas's leg buzzed with attention, his mobile device calling on him to answer. He pulled it out and read its face.

Victor Zarruq.

He went to put it to voicemail, but something told him he should take it. Not often the man called him. When he did, it was usually important.

Holding up the phone, Silas said he had a phone call and left to take it.

"Hello, Victor. "

"Master Grey, sorry to interrupt, but do you have a moment?"

A shot of adrenaline pinged his gut, spreading a cold dread throughout his body. The archbishop's voice was soft, cautious even, as if he were taking careful steps down a path that led to nowhere good.

"Uh, sure. I was with Naomi at the oncology ward, along with Gapinski and Celeste."

Victor sighed and *tsk*ed himself. "That is right. I had forgotten you all were standing beside her today for her post-operative treatments. I trust all is well with Naomi after surgery."

"Seems to be. And she seemed in high spirits. If there's anyone who can beat cancer's ass, it's Torres."

He chuckled, his voice coming more from his belly this time, which was nice to hear. "Truer words were never spoken. But I would hate to interrupt your time together, so we can have a chat later."

Now the soft, cautious tone returned. Zarruq was being coy,

not getting to it. Which had always irritated Silas. If you have something to say, be direct. Don't beat around the bush.

Pushing through the door into the hallway, he said, "Let's talk now. If it's alright with you, that is. Sounds like something's come up."

There was a pause, then another beat before a soft sigh. "As you wish, Silas."

No Master Grey this time, which was unusual. It must be bad!

"What's happened, Victor?"

"The Order board of directors met today."

Silas leaned against a sanitized-white hallway wall, the dueling scents of rubbing alcohol and steel turning his stomach now. "Alright...Anything I should worry about?"

"Not worry, per se."

Another pause, another beat, another sigh.

Come on, Victor. Get to it!

Victor muttered, "I suppose I should stop pussyfooting around and get on with it. And it pains me to say it, but the board voted to put you on temporary leave."

"What?" Silas stood straight now, that cold adrenaline dread sweeping through him like a winter wind.

"Now, it is only temporary, and pending an investigation into your recent...how shall I put it. *Troubles.*"

"What troubles? What the heck are you talking about. This doesn't make any sense!"

Silas closed his eyes and took a breath, running a hand through his hair. Last thing he needed was to lay into his only ally.

"Sorry, chief. Didn't mean to bite your head off."

"No worries, Silas. And know that I tried everything I could to stave off such maneuvers. But as I mentioned several days ago, before your most recent misadventure, there have been concerns about the manner in which SEPIO has been defending the faith recently. What with the massive explosion in Mill Creek Junction at the food processing plant—"

"That wasn't my fault, or SEPIO's!" Silas exclaimed, his voice echoing back to him through the long corridor. Clenching his jaw, he whispered, "Hostiles nicked the gas lines with their weapon fire aimed at taking us out, then the place caught fire. Probably on purpose, too, to hide the evidence! Gapinski and I could have been killed, not to mention our pastor partner and his P.I. friend."

"Be that as it may, there is also the matter of Mumbai."

"What about it?" he growled with more bite than he intended.

"People were permanently injured, Silas..." That soft, cautious voice returned, now with a bit of an irritated edge.

It was true. The subterfuge, switching out the Eucharistic elements, had certainly worked, exposing Paulina Bucks and her uncle as the frauds they were. But it had the unintended consequence of delaying the antidote embedded in those memory markers from reaching those who needed it—those who had ingested the cipher poison who needed the key to unlock their disease, and heal them.

Silas felt bad about it. Sick, really, wondering whether the ends justified the means given how many people's lives were permanently impacted. Celeste had made the original call after Torres had explained her plan, with his full support after the fact—literally, him and Gapinski and Peter rounding up prepackaged Eucharistic cups from Comida factories around Mumbai. Dexter had warned of the risks, but he didn't listen. Thought it was the right move at the time to stop the Bucks from doing further damage—to the world and the Church. And it was. The contagion was stopped dead in its tracks.

Apparently the top brass up the chain of command thought otherwise.

"So where does this leave me?" Silas asked, ripping the bandaid off himself.

"Suspended, as I said, still with full pay and benefits. But only temporarily, until there is an investigation."

"Investigation..." Which meant questions and second-guessing by those who were the least qualified to judge his actions.

"That is correct. I am truly sorry about this, Silas. Really, I am."

Victor said he would be in touch as things unfolded, then they ended the phone call.

Silas stood in the hallway gripping his phone. Didn't know what to do with what had just happened. With the shift that had just happened in his story.

Another life shift on the other side of a phone call like the one countless people in that oncology ward had received—the C word catapulting them into another dimension.

Much like Torres herself.

This wasn't that, but it was still devastating.

Felt like Princeton all over again. Hell, felt like Georgetown again, with the bomb that exploded in that chapel that shifted his life into the Order of Thaddeus and SEPIO in the first place!

What was he going to do...

The Lord only knew.

Like everything in life—everything in *his* life—his future was in Jesus' sovereign hands. To have and to hold. To fix or let fall apart. God controls it all.

The words Peter had given Torres for her own life shift sprang back to memory: *No matter what we face in this life, God controls it all. There is no reason we cannot trust in his promises for a restored, brand-spanking new future that is far better than what we have now.*

Ain't that the truth.

Another truth rose to the surface now. God's truth about

life, and his involvement with it: *'Do not worry about anything, but in everything by prayer and supplication with thanksgiving let your requests be made known to God. And the peace of God, which surpasses all understanding, will guard your hearts and your minds in Christ Jesus.'*

The Book of Philippians, chapter 4.

Then another, from the Book of James, chapter 1: *'My brothers and sisters, whenever you face trials of any kind, consider it nothing but joy, because you know that the testing of your faith produces endurance; and let endurance have its full effect, so that you may be mature and complete, lacking in nothing.'*

Silas took in a measured breath, smiling at the dose of inspiration from above and pit in his stomach loosening some. Then that peace Paul spoke of descended upon him and a joy even rose within at the chance for his faith to grow.

One of Gapinski's laughs filtered out through the door into the hallway, followed by yet another one of Celeste's chides, with Torres giving it to him in equal measure.

Silas smiled at the sound. The sound of friends, of family.

And he knew that whatever happened, he wouldn't be facing it alone.

With SEPIO at his side—with Jesus Christ himself fighting for him, standing with him, how could he go wrong?

AUTHOR'S NOTE
THE HISTORY BEHIND THE STORY...

For much of my professional writing life, both in fiction and non, I have been a passionate proponent of the vintage Christian faith—usually contrasting it with more liberal, progressive efforts at reimagining the faith, instead of rediscovering what Christians have always believed.

However, there is a similar danger to orthodox Christianity that is posed by a flavor of Christianity coming from more conservative circles: charismatic Christianity and Pentecostalism, the most extreme and concerning manifestation of that in the prosperity gospel. Admittedly, I hadn't paid much attention to it in my academic studies and while serving in pastoral ministry. In the last year, I have been more clued into this danger—and the deadly hope it offers.

So I wanted to explore a story that uncovered those dangers and false hope. What better way than in the context of a contagion that upends life! Both in the global sense, but in the very personal ways we've all experienced various "contagions" that affect our health and finances, ways that have touched close to my own home.

Before we get to the history behind the story, you'll see

some crossover between my other series: Peter Daniel Young was the first protagonist I ever wrote about, starring in *A Reimagined Faith*. And Mill Creek Junction is a fictional small town I created where I've written several short stories about real people living life and exploring faith. I thought it would be fun to bring them all together—and slam them with a conspiracy that turned out to be very different than the Order of Thaddeus imagined.

Now to the book's research and deeper themes. As with all of my books, I like to add a note at the end with what went into the story. I definitely aim to craft an entertainment-first tale, but I also like to add a bit of insight and inspiration for faith. So, if you care to learn more about the foundation of this episode in the Order of Thaddeus, here is some of what I discovered that made its way into SEPIO's latest adventure.

The Prosperity Gospel's Deadly Hope

With every story I tell, a lot goes into research. Several books were helpful in unpacking the history and nature of the prosperity gospel, which I drew inspiration from in several chapters making commentary on the movement (3, 6, 7, 8, 10, 12, 14, 18, 21, 28, 32): *Blessed*, by Kate Bowler; *God, Greed, and the (Prosperity) Gospel*, by Costi Hinn; *Defining Deception*, by Costi Hinn and Anthony Wood; and *Health, Wealth, and Happiness*, by David Jones and Russell Woodbridge.

Like my other stories about an aspect of the Christian faith, I tried to honestly explain the nature, history, and dangers of the prosperity gospel. All of the descriptions of the lavish Bucks lifestyle reflect the obscene wealth of prosperity preachers—from the mansions to the hotels to the multi-million dollar jets! Such misguided focus on making money off the gospel does far more to undermine and threaten the Christian faith and people's own faiths than any sort of vast conspiracy—which is why Nous and Theoti weren't behind this story.

In Victor Zarruq's words, "all prosperity gospel roads are paved with bars of gold—leading one straight into the bosom of the Devil himself." Why is it deadly hope? An excellent book that illuminates both the behind-the-scenes history of the prosperity gospel and its dangers is Costi Hinn's, nephew of Benny Hinn. He offers several reasons why it is deadly hope:

1. **The prosperity gospel distorts the biblical gospel.** "The prosperity gospel distorts the biblical gospel by making the Good News all about you and all about stuff...The abundant life is not a comfortable seventy years, courtesy of the prosperity gospel and leading to infinite suffering in hell if you don't follow the biblical Christ as your Savior."

2. **The prosperity gospel insults God's nature.** "In stark contrast to this truth, the prosperity gospel teaches that God can, like a cosmic magic genie, grant our wishes. The prosperity gospel teaches a version of the nature of God that is so skewed it scarcely communicates one iota of who he is."

3. **The prosperity gospel confuses atonement.** "They use and abuse the atonement to mean that God guarantees your healing because of the atonement for your soul. Worse, they promise that Jesus' death on the cross didn't provide just eternal life; it provides earthly riches."

4. **The prosperity gospel demeans Jesus Christ.** "The prosperity gospel makes human satisfaction to be material and Jesus to be the cherry on top. If it makes Jesus a central focus, it's that he is the main avenue to getting what you want. This version of Jesus is a shell of who he really is. The prosperity

gospel promises people the abundant life that Jesus offers only to deliver a gospel with no Jesus at all."

5. **The prosperity gospel twists Scripture.** "It takes passages that are plain in meaning based on what they literally say in Scripture and makes them to mean something completely different. Like an evil imposter taking a heartfelt letter from a king to his royal subjects and twisting it for self-serving purposes it was never intended to be used for, prosperity preachers take the Bible and twist it into a tool for abuse."

6. **The prosperity gospel is motivated by love for money.** "The prosperity gospel is obsessed with money and material gain. To argue that is to argue that gravity does not exist. It's a fact that we need to keep in mind when we're tempted to buy in to the lies. Nothing good comes from the love of money."

7. **The prosperity gospel produces false converts.** "The prosperity gospel fills pulpits with imposters and the pews with people who either want to be fooled or are being deceived."

8. **The prosperity gospel overcomplicates faith.** "Faith isn't giving money to get his love. Faith isn't paying a fee for his saving grace. Faith isn't going broke to get healed. Faith isn't traveling to a special service to get his anointing. Faith is repenting of your sins and turning to him, believing that he is the Son of God...Christian faith is believing in Jesus Christ for eternal life and experiencing the joy, freedom, and blessing of knowing Christ for free!"

9. **The prosperity gospel ruin's Christianity's witness.** "The prosperity gospel couldn't be worse for our Christian witness. Men and women who preach the prosperity gospel on Sunday are laughing all the

way to the bank on Monday. The world looks on as it makes a mockery of Jesus, the pastoral leaders of the church, and the Bible as the foundation we stand on for teaching."

10. **The prosperity gospel abuses vulnerable people.** "What these desperate, vulnerable people need is a pastor who will love them, protect them, and give them real hope."[1]

God's Gospel Hope

What is the hope of the gospel? That was the driving question at the heart of this story. Is it, as the Bucks twins suggest, a life free from trouble—where our bank accounts are brimming with dollars and pounds, our bodies are free from disease and injury, our jobs meet our every professional expectation, and our house is three stories high with a two-stall garage and a white-picket fence? Not in the slightest.

What is that hope, the hope of the gospel? Silas gets it right in his little sermon in the final chapter:

"Yes, our time on earth right now will be chaotic. There will be pain and agony and it will seem like it runs rampant, without any direction from the Lord. Some of us will get cancer...Some of us have lost loved ones, parents and grandparents. The thing is, our lives are just a blip compared with eternity, and the eternality of God and his sovereign plan."

Peter offers an important addition as well:

"Which means if you put it in perspective to our ultimate destiny, the infinite number of years we will spend on the new earth that provides all the healing, riches, and glory we could ever want makes whatever sickness or poverty we might endure now seem like a pittance—especially when we consider our life spent with Jesus...No matter what we face in this life, God controls it all. Like you said, Silas. There is no reason we cannot trust in his promises for a restored, brand-spanking new future that is far better than what we have now. After all, we know the end of the story."

As he alludes, the Book of Revelation 21:3-4 promises our broken, busted world will be put back together again someday by God himself: *'He will dwell with them; they will be his peoples, and God himself will be with them; he will wipe every tear from their eyes. Death will be no more; mourning and crying and pain will be no more, for the first things have passed away.'*

In the meantime, we don't mourn like those without hope. Instead, we cling to the promise that one day Jesus will return with the true gift of abundant-life blessing twisted by prosperity preachers as a middle-class American life. One Calvin VanDyke explains to Peter:

"...our problem isn't a bum leg or credit card debt—not to make light of either. Our problem is sin, which Jesus dealt with once and for all on the cross. Forgiveness of sins, adoption into God's family, the resurrection of the dead and eternal life—*that* is our true hope, both now and later. Physical healing's got nothing on the fact our soul's been resuscitated back to life!"

God's Healing Touch

If the promised abundant life is really eternal life, something we're waiting for down the road, does that mean God doesn't bless us now, with healing or provision? Certainly not! Jesus makes it clear in Matthew 6 that God clothes us and gives us food—he provides for our financial needs!

Then what about healing? Does God heal today, in the same miraculous ways the Bucks promised? This one is a personal one for me, since Peter Daniel Young's story mirrors my own with thyroid cancer, diagnosed when I was thirty-three. The good kind of cancer (if there is such a thing!), but the Big C nonetheless. Miraculously, between my biopsy and surgery to remove it, the tumor had apparently died. The doctor believed the biopsy needle disrupted the blood supply, which he had never seen before.

Now, I am well aware my cancer story isn't even close to other people's cancer stories. Not only in kind and severity but also in outcome. As a young pastor, I presided over a funeral of a man about my age who died of a more severe cancer after a sixteen-month battle, leaving behind a wife and twin boys. So I know cancer and other illness end very differently than my own.

But the fact remains, my tumor died! Was that a miracle? I like the discussion between Calvin VanDyke and Silas Grey about the biblical definition in chapter 18, and what Jürgen Moltmann says about miracles, "Jesus' healings are not supernatural miracles in a natural world. They are the only truly natural thing in a world that is unnatural, demonized and wounded."[2]

As Silas said, miracles aren't an interruption to the natural state of things, but a return to that natural order. It's about God restoring things to the way he originally intended things at creation. Cancer isn't what he intended, or any number of other evil things in this world. God uses both the miraculous and mundane ways to restore the created order to the way he intended things to be, as we see with Torres's healing and also with my own—we both had surgery and post-op treatment.

But as Gapinski wisely remarked, "Miracles aren't magic, because they're not about fulfilling our every whim. Like making soda start gushing from my kitchen faucet or a bucket of KFC extra crispy chicken legs show up at my door." A little tongue in cheek there, but that's the danger of the prosperity gospel: it puts God on puppet strings to answer our every whim. True New Testament miracles always point to the person of Jesus Christ and his work of salvation.

Which means if God's glory isn't magnified and the gospel, the good news about rescue in Jesus, isn't proclaimed—if whatever happens at charismatic services like Mill Creek Junction doesn't clarify and enhance both, then they aren't miracles of God. "Nothing but voodoo magic and illusionary tricks," as VanDyke explained.

God's Sovereign Plans

All of this gets to one of the other themes of the book: God's sovereignty, that he makes eternal decrees over his creation, while also continually and providentially working in and through it on behalf of his creation.

I'm writing this in 2021, and the pandemic is still raging in parts of the world. Let's be honest: it sometimes feels like God is absent and the world is spinning out of control. However, the divine attribute of God's sovereignty reminds us that he is still guiding the affairs of the world through his powerful word and toward his perfect ends.

That's true in the big stuff of the world, like wars and

pandemics. It's also true in the little stuff of our own lives, like making sure we've got enough food to eat and healing us when we're sick. Whether it's keeping the sun in place or keeping your job when your employer is sold to some multinational corporation, God's in it all. It may not feel like it, but Job's words are instructive: *"I know that you can do all things; no purpose of yours can be thwarted. You asked, 'Who is this that obscures my plans without knowledge?' Surely I spoke of things I did not understand, things too wonderful for me to know"* (Job 42:2-3).

Fact is, we're not going to fully understand God's plans for the world; I certainly can't understand how a pandemic fits into them! But the hope of the gospel is that God is still here, he is not silent, and he is in control of it all—guiding his creation toward a perfect end and using evil to achieve those ultimate good purposes. We may not understand it—and we won't on this side of eternity—but we can trust this to be true, that *'all things work together for good for those who love God, who are called according to his purpose'* (Romans 8:28).

This is vital to true Christianity, and denying it is un-Christian. Which is the problem with the prosperity gospel. "The prosperity gospel certainly denies the sovereignty of God to the extent that it demeans God to the position of a puppet and elevates man to the position of a puppet master who makes confessional demands by faith. It does this by considering faith as a force and God as the one who must respond to our faith."[3]

This point was driven home in chapter 28, where Paulina plays the part of mystic shaman offering up ecstatic utterances and commanding God to bow to her commands to rid the world of *nervirus*. Remarkably, Kenneth Copeland and Paula White, two prominent prosperity preachers, performed a similar staged ritual trying to bend God to their wills. Borrowing their language and behavior, I fictionalized it to tell this part of the story.

My goal with my fiction is to tell an entertaining story that thrills, with a dose of inspiration and insight into faith. I think somewhere between a 90-5-5 and 80-10-10 balance is about right, where the 90 and 80 percent split largely favors entertaining my readers, and insight and inspiration makes up the rest. I'm happy the feedback I've gotten is that I mostly get this right, not being too preachy and giving readers an escapist read.

I admit this book may have been preaching a bit more than usual this time around! But given the stakes, and recent events (from the pandemic to economic and social collapse) resulting in questions about our Christian hope, perhaps I could be given a bit of grace this go around.

The issue of this version of Christianity is an important one. As Torres's childhood story illustrates, the prosperity gospel is feeding off of the hopes of needy people—people desperate for financial provision and miraculous healing. In the end, it may not be a vast conspiracy like many SEPIO missions, where cultic entities are behind the scenes but rather is much more about unbridled greed. However, the gospel and faith is just as threatened.

Research is an important part of my process for creating compelling stories that entertain, inform, and inspire. Here are a few resources I used to research the history behind the prosperity gospel:

- Bowler, Kate. *Blessed: A History of the American Prosperity Gospel*. New York: Oxford University Press, 2013. www.bouma.us/hope1
- Hinn, Costi W. *God, Greed, and the (Prosperity) Gospel*. Grand Rapids: Zondervan, 2019. www.bouma.us/hope2
- Hinn, Costi W. and Wood, Anthony G. *Defining Deception: Freeing the Church from the Mystical*

Miracle. El Cajon, CA: Southern California
Seminary Press, 2018. www.bouma.us/hope3

- Jones, David W. and Woodbridge, Russell S. *Health,
  Wealth, and Happiness: How the Prosperity Gospel
  Overshadows the Gospel of Christ.* Grand Rapids:
  Kregel Publications, 2017. www.bouma.us/hope4

NOTES

Author's Note

1. Costi Hinn, *God, Greed, and the (Prosperity) Gospel*, 170-178.
2. Jürgen Moltmann, *The Way of Jesus*, 98.
3. Hinn, *God, Greed, and the (Prosperity) Gospel*, 96.

ENJOY DEADLY HOPE?

A big thanks for joining Silas Grey and the rest of SEPIO on their adventure saving the Church! **Here's what's next:**

If you're ready for another adventure, you can get a full-length novel in the series for free! All you have to do is join the insider's group to be notified of specials and new releases by going to this link: www.jabouma.com/free

Want to dive deeper into Peter Daniel Young's backstory of faith, start with *A Reimagined Faith (Book 1)*, then jump into *A Rediscovered Faith (Book 2)* to start the anticipated 4-book series of faith, life, and everything in between.

You might also like my apocalyptic sci-fi thriller series, *Ichthus Chronicles.* Set 100 years in the future, the last remnant of Christianity is threatened from forces inside and outside the Church, written in the vein of the *Left Behind* series. Start the adventure today: www.jabouma.com/books/apostasy-rising-1

If you enjoyed the fictional small town of Mill Creek Junction, devour more stories at: www.millcreekjunction.com.

If you loved the book and have a moment to spare, **a short review is much appreciated.** Nothing fancy, just your honest take. Spreading the word is probably the #1 way you can help independent authors like me and help others enjoy the story.

GET YOUR FREE THRILLER

Building a relationship with my readers is one of my all-time favorite joys of writing! Once in a while I like to send out a newsletter with giveaways, free stories, pre-release content, updates on new books, and other bits on my stories.

Join my insider's group for updates, giveaways, and your free novel—a full-length action-adventure story in my *Order of Thaddeus* thriller series. Just tell me where to send it.

Follow this link to subscribe:
www.jabouma.com/free

ALSO BY J. A. BOUMA

Nobody should have to read bad religious fiction—whether it's cheesy plots with pat answers or misrepresentations of the Christian faith and the Bible. So J. A. Bouma tells compelling, propulsive stories that thrill as much as inspire, offering a dose of insight along the way.

Order of Thaddeus Action-Adventure Thriller Series

Holy Shroud • Book 1

The Thirteenth Apostle • Book 2

Hidden Covenant • Book 3

American God • Book 4

Grail of Power • Book 5

Templars Rising • Book 6

Rite of Darkness • Book 7

Gospel Zero • Book 8

The Emperor's Code • Book 9

Deadly Hope • Book 10

Fallen Ones • Book 11

The Eden Legacy • Book 12

Silas Grey Collection 1 (Books 1-3)

Silas Grey Collection 2 (Books 4-6)

Silas Grey Collection 3 (Books 7-9)

Backstories: Short Story Collection 1

Martyrs Bones: Short Story Collection 2

Group X Cases **Supernatural Suspense Series**

Not of This World • Book 1

The Darkest Valley • Book 2

Against These Powers • Book 3

Luck Be the Ladies • Novelette

End Times Chronicles **Sci-Fi Apocalyptic Series**

Apostasy Rising / Season 1, Episode 1

Apostasy Rising / Season 1, Episode 2

Apostasy Rising / Season 1, Episode 3

Apostasy Rising / Season 1, Episode 4

Apostasy Rising / Full Season 1 (Episodes 1 to 4)

Apocalypse Rising / Season 2, Episode 1

Apocalypse Rising / Season 2, Episode 2

Apocalypse Rising / Season 2, Episode 3

Apocalypse Rising / Season 2, Episode 4

Apocalypse Rising / Full Season 2 (Episodes 1 to 4)

Faith Reimagined **Spiritual Coming-of-Age Series**

A Reimagined Faith • Book 1

A Rediscovered Faith • Book 2

Mill Creek Junction **Short Story Series**

The New Normal • Collection 1

My Name's Johnny Pope • Collection 2

Joy to the Junction! • Collection 3

The Ties that Bind Us • Collection 4

A Matter of Justice • Collection 5

Get all the latest short stories at: www.millcreekjunction.com

Find all of my latest book releases at: www.jabouma.com

ABOUT THE AUTHOR

J. A. Bouma believes nobody should have to read bad religious fiction—whether it's cheesy plots with pat answers or misrepresentations of the Christian faith and the Bible. So he tells compelling, propulsive stories that thrill as much as inspire, while offering a dose of insight along the way.

As a former congressional staffer and pastor, and award-nominated bestselling author of over forty religious fiction and nonfiction books, he blends a love for ideas and adventure, exploration and discovery, thrill and thought. With graduate degrees in Christian thought and the Bible, and armed with a voracious appetite for most mainstream genres, he tells stories you'll read with abandon and recommend with pride—exploring the tension of faith and doubt, spirituality and culture, belief and practice, and the gritty drama that is our collective pilgrim story.

When not putting fingers to keyboard, he loves vintage jazz vinyl, a glass of Malbec, and an epic read—preferably together. He lives in Grand Rapids with his wife, two kiddos, and rambunctious boxer-pug-terrier.

www.jabouma.com • jeremy@jabouma.com

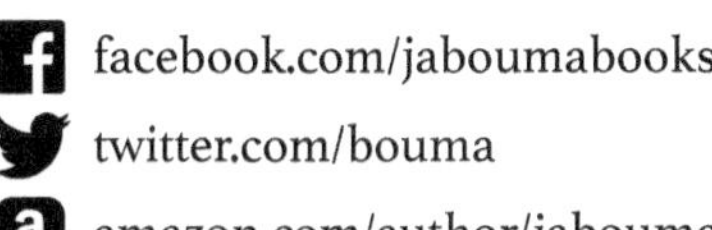

facebook.com/jaboumabooks

twitter.com/bouma

amazon.com/author/jabouma